For the Birds

BY CRISSI LANGWELL

For TS and JV

A strange passion is moving in my head.
My heart has become a bird
which searches in the sky.
Every part of me goes in different directions.
Is it really so
that the one I love is everywhere?

Rumi

Chapter One

I never expected to see him again. But there I was, watching as some tall, leggy blonde stumbled against him, grabbing his shoulders as he held her up and smiled too close—intimate close. The kind of close that included inside jokes and all-night conversations, coffee in bed after morning lovemaking, and slow dancing in the kitchen while waiting for the pizza to bake. The kind of close where you could look at the other and just know when he was ready to leave, or he needed to be rescued, or you'd spend every day of your life falling in love with him all over again.

The kind of close I thought we had and then mourned for almost a year after he left. I thought I had moved past this shit. Seeing him smile as he helped steady her was just as surprising as seeing him at all.

Then he turned my way. The crowded banquet hall. The lights. The music. All of it disappeared and I saw only him. And I panicked.

That was the exact moment I knew I wasn't over Sonny.

"Blake," I hissed, turning to find my date. He was talking with two women who were much too young for him. I would have been jealous, except we'd stopped our casual fling months ago and discovered we made much better friends than lovers. Plus, he made a great date…when he wasn't hitting on the guests. I rolled my eyes as he ran his hand through his sun-bleached surfer hair, the way he'd done dozens of times when we first met. His mating dance, apparently. Next he'd…yup, there it was. A smile tugged at my lips as he removed his jacket as if this room was too hot. Even in his white dress shirt, his muscle definition was unmistakable. So much so that one of the girls clutched his bicep as she laughed, part of her own ritual. I glanced back toward Sonny, then quickly looked away. My face burned as I realized he was watching my every move.

"Blake," I repeated, this time gentler as I sidled up to him, sliding my hand along his arm as the girl removed hers. He looked down at my hand, then at my face, his blue eyes shooting daggers even with his charming half-grin.

"Ladies, this is Cricket, a very good friend of mine, and the event planner for this swanky soiree." He leaned close to my ear. "This better be worth the interruption," he hissed.

"Have their parents signed waivers?" I shot back.

"They're interns," he whispered. "They have to be legal." He pulled away as his hooded eyes crinkled with his lopsided grin. "Cricket, this is Summer and Haley."

"Charmed," I said, pulling him away, feeling Sonny's eyes following us.

"Did anyone ever tell you what a cock block you are?" Blake asked when we were out of earshot. I turned toward him, wrapping my arms around his neck. His hands naturally fell at my waist, resting at the curve of my back. His pinky finger unexpectedly brushed my exposed skin, and I twitched, much to his amusement. At this, I laughed, harder than necessary, my head tilted back as if he'd said something hilarious. When I glanced in Sonny's direction, I almost shrank under his fiery glare. His leggy friend was no longer there, and he stood facing me, facing us, his hands in his pockets, his chestnut curls falling across his forehead. Even from across the room, his eyes appeared darker than usual.

"Oh, I see," Blake murmured, looking toward Sonny. With a single finger, he turned my head so I was facing him. "Who is he?"

"Sonny."

Blake gave a slow nod. He glanced at Sonny again, a millisecond look, then back at me with a sly grin.

"That's the guy? That's why you could never commit to me?"

"Blake." I winced, embarrassed as I pulled away. I wasn't one to play games, so why was I doing it now? "Sorry," I said, just as he pulled me back against him.

"Don't be sorry," he murmured, his face close to mine. "Let's make him jealous." And then he crushed his mouth on mine, his hold keeping me in place as I pushed against his chest, his tongue touching my lips, asking for entrance, which I never granted. When he finally released me, I caught my breath, resisting the urge to smack him. I peered back in Sonny's direction, but he was gone.

"Over there," Blake said, nodding toward the exits. I looked just in time to see Sonny's retreating back before the doors closed behind him.

"Damn it." I stepped away from Blake and sank into a chair at the edge of the banquet room. I'd planned every detail of this event, but now everything felt too loud, the decorations too gaudy. I buried my head in my folded arms on the table in front of me as Blake scooted into the same oversized chair. He rubbed my back as I breathed, wondering what the hell I was doing.

"That was the Scottish guy, right?"

"Yes," I mumbled into my arms.

"The one who moved away and took your dog with him?"

"His dog," I corrected, face still covered.

"You mourned that dog as much as you mourned Scotty."

"Sonny," I corrected him, lifting my head. "And how would you know?"

He draped his arm across my shoulder. "Sweetheart, I was your rebound, and you came to me in pieces. That was clue number one. But clue number two was after you'd had a glass of wine. Once that glass was empty, you couldn't stop blabbering about that dog. How sweet he was. How he laid his head in your lap. How his ears flopped when he ran. And mostly about how he loved you best."

"He did love me best," I sighed, fiddling with the saltshaker on the table, spilling it slowly so that a small white mountain grew on the black surface. "But he wasn't my dog, so it doesn't matter." I brushed the salt away, then gave Blake a sideways glance. "I didn't know I told you much of anything about Sonny or his dog. That must have been annoying for you."

"Nah, it wasn't like we were serious or anything."

"So why didn't you ever ask me about any of it?"

"You mean when you were sober?"

I nodded.

"Because if you'd wanted to talk about it with me, you would have brought it up yourself."

I smiled at him, squeezing his hand.

"You're a good friend."

"The best," he agreed, and I squeezed harder until he winced.

"Ms. Stone?"

I released Blake's hand and stood, my face reddening at our casual position since I was kind of on the job. Kind of, because I was told to enjoy myself, but also because I knew to never let my guard down. This was especially true as Stuart Jackson, president and CEO of Jackson Technologies, approached our table, beaming at me with his hand outstretched. For weeks, I'd been the picture of professionalism, skipping my casual attire—Blake liked to call it my hippie wear—for pencil skirts or pressed slacks, all while Mr. Jackson and I planned this party to the tiniest detail. And now he'd caught me, all dressed up, draped next to Blake like I was several drinks in. I hadn't even had a drop.

"I've told you, Mr. Jackson. It's Cricket," I said as I accepted his handshake. "Congratulations on your award. Fastest Growing Tech Company in the North Bay—that's quite the accomplishment."

"Thank you, Cricket. And it's Stuart to you." He turned, and I noticed an older man standing behind him, smiling politely at me, wearing a designer suit that appeared just as expensive as Mr. Jackson's. "This is Charles Finnigan, an old friend of mine."

"Mr. Finnigan, of course," I said, reaching around Mr. Jackson to shake his hand. "Finnigan Estates supplied the wine for tonight's event. I'm particularly fond of your Cabernet Sauvignon."

"Then, I hope you'll accept a case of it. I'll get your information from Stu."

"Oh, I couldn't."

"I insist. Consider it a bribe. I'd like to hire you for my next event, especially after Stuart has been singing your praises for weeks." He looked around, gesturing at the party continuing behind him. The dance floor was now packed with people dancing, no sign of stopping despite the late hour. Choreographed laser lights sliced through the room, shining jewel-toned beams that moved in time with the music. A dessert table on the side was covered in every kind of cake and pastry imaginable, guarded by six ice sculptures in the shape of different sea creatures, a nod to Mr. Jackson's love for the ocean. At the exit, guests were handed gift bags with organic soaps, a small bottle of wine, a mini box of chocolates, and a few other trinkets, all donated by local vendors hoping to catch the attention of some of the more elite guests at this event. I smiled as I saw two women at the door going through their bags before leaving, exclaiming over the gifts inside. My gaze drifted, lingering on the door Sonny had exited, wondering if he'd come back. Did I want him to come back? What would I say?

"Didn't I tell you Cricket was a damn artist?" Stuart said, bringing my attention back to him. I laughed, shaking my head.

"Hardly. I just know the right people, and they put it together. They're the real talent."

"Don't sell yourself short." Blake sidled up to me and touched my arm. "You're the one with the vision. I mean, look at how smoothly everything has gone. You haven't had to address any issues at all tonight."

I blushed under the compliments but smiled graciously in response. I was proud of my work, but the praise felt excessive, especially since so much of this came easily to me. I'd never been one to stand in the spotlight, so taking care of the details from behind the scenes was a natural fit. It allowed me to be a part of the fun, but also to slip out once I was no longer needed.

"She's really something," Stuart said to Blake. "You're a lucky man."

I shook my head. "Oh, he's not—"

"I feel lucky every day," Blake cut in, slipping his arm around my waist. My ears felt inflamed; they were probably as red as my hair. This whole charade felt ridiculous. Why continue it? I hated lying, particularly to someone as important as Stuart Jackson, and even more so to Charles Finnigan since it sounded like we'd be working together soon. Blake squeezed my side, and I looked at him. His eyes focused on mine as if he could hear my inner argument over the lie. Sighing, I smiled and let it go, turning back to Mr. Jackson.

"Thank you again for trusting me with your celebration." I glanced around the room once again. "Everything is going well, right? Should I—"

"Relax," he said. "Everything is perfect. Tonight, you're my guest. Enjoy. Get another glass of wine. Take your man for a spin on the dance floor."

"Actually," I said, peering at Blake, feeling the ache in my feet and the tiredness behind my eyes, "I was considering calling it a night, if you don't mind. That is, unless you need me?"

"I'm afraid I have an early morning," Blake added, which was true. When he'd agreed to this date, I'd promised we'd leave by eleven, figuring the party would be winding down. Judging by the high level of activity still happening on the dance floor, it looked like it was going to be a long night.

"It's a shame you have to leave," Mr. Jackson said. "But I understand."

I rummaged through my tiny purse, trying to find the stack of business cards I always brought with me to events. I'd designed the cards myself, with my company's name, Bees Knees Events, in large letters against a burnt sienna background, and a small bee flying near a honeycomb pattern. The back was a sunshine yellow with my contact information and a bright sunflower along the edge. I loved the happy summer feel of these cards, and they were normally hard to miss. I huffed when I came up short, figuring I'd left them on my bed. I shot Mr. Finnigan an apologetic look.

"I'm sorry, I don't have my card on me. But if you have your phone I can shoot you my information, if you'd like."

"Don't worry," Mr. Finnigan said. "I'll get it from Stu when he tells me where to send your wine. Have a wonderful night, and we'll be in touch."

Both men shook our hands, Stuart pausing when he bid Blake goodbye.

"She's a gem," he said, and his smile reminded me of the way my father used to look at me. "You take care of her."

"Every day," Blake said, bringing me closer to him.

Once the men were out of earshot, I hip-checked Blake, then shot him a mocking glare.

"Every day? That ship never even made it to port."

"Hey, a man can dream, right?" He ducked when I moved to smack him. "I'm kidding! But dude, if you keep getting in the way of me getting laid, I might have to paddle up coochie creek." He raised his eyebrows a few times, glancing over me like I was a meal.

"Ew, no!" I moved out of reach, laughing as he pretended to grab for me. "But why would you tell them that? I was trying to make Sonny jealous, not everyone."

I hid the electric shock that went through me as I said Sonny's name. It brought back every emotion I felt when I saw him standing across the room.

"I know. I saw Sonny talking with Mr. Finnigan earlier. If you really want Sonny to think you're with me, I have to cover the bases. What if they're more than acquaintances? They probably aren't, but it doesn't hurt."

I listened to what he was saying, the shame settling over me like a wet towel. "Oh god, I'm such an idiot. Who does that? Pretends to be in a relationship? I mean, how juvenile can I be?"

"It was a little scandalous," Blake agreed. I shot him a glare.

"You're not exactly innocent," I said. "I just flirted. You practically mauled my mouth." I groaned again, realizing just how bad this looked to Sonny. "I panicked," I admitted. "I saw him with someone else and I didn't want him to see me alone. I mean, he obviously moved on with some gorgeous woman, and here I am dumpy, lonely, and, if I'm being honest, hardly over him."

"First off, you're not dumpy. You're kind of hot."

I rolled my eyes, but the smile returned to my mouth.

"Second, I think this is the healthiest thing you could have done. You aren't over him, but he's moved on. Don't *you* want to move on?"

"Kind of." *No. Maybe.*

"Don't you want to show him that your door is closed, too, or do you want him to think you're still lusting over him."

"I'm not lusting over him." *Lie.*

Blake peered in my face, his eyes narrowing as he studied my expression. "Right," he said with a laugh. "Look, you'll probably never see him again after this night. So stop worrying about it, okay?"

"You're right."

We headed toward the exits, cutting through the swarm of people on the dance floor. Blake led the way, my hand in his so I wouldn't get lost. I couldn't help glancing at every table we passed. As if I could find a remedy. As if Sonny would be there. All I saw were people paired into couples, conversing over salt and pepper shakers as flashing lights tattooed their faces.

We reached the coat check, and the woman behind the counter handed me my coat and purse. I took one final look behind me. I wanted to leave, but I couldn't shake the feeling that I wasn't quite done here. Blake opened the front door, and a blast of icy air rushed at my sweaty skin. I shivered, hugging my coat around me. Blake was already halfway across the parking lot when I finally followed. His headlights flashed as he unlocked the car, and he was in the driver's seat by the time I opened the passenger door.

"Can you wait a moment?" I asked. "I forgot something inside. I'll be right back."

This is so stupid, I thought as I turned and trotted back to the banquet hall. I buttoned my jacket as I ran, my heart rate increasing over what I was about to do. *This is the last time*, I promised myself.

The attendant on duty nodded me in, and I waved my thanks as I rushed through the door. Looking around, I scanned every person in the room before heading back to the spot where I'd last seen Sonny. I took deep breaths as I approached. Even though he wasn't here, I felt him everywhere. My stomach did a slow roll as I dwelled on my actions tonight, and the anger in his eyes afterward. He looked like he wanted to punch Blake, to take me back, and it unnerved me. But then again, he'd moved on. Maybe he thought I was stupid and saw tired, lonely old me under the facade of a slinky dress.

I shook my head. Blake was going to wonder where I was if I took too long. Standing in the exact spot Sonny had been when I saw him, I looked to the table at my right, my pinky finger brushing the saltshaker. Glancing over my shoulder, I wrapped my hand around the shaker, then moved it in so I could snag its peppery twin. No one was looking. My heart caught, just like it always did at this moment, and I liked it. With a slight movement, I lifted them into my jacket pocket, feeling the weight hang against my chest.

"Feeling wild, eh?"

I whipped around, my hands falling against Sonny's hard, familiar chest. He caught me at the waist, his mouth twisted into his usual sexy smirk. "Hey Cricket," he said, his Scottish accent piercing me, melting me, stealing the breath from my lungs.

"H-hey, Sonny," I breathed, feeling the floor under my feet as I silently prayed not to fall. And then I did the only thing I could think to do.

I ran.

Chapter Two

The shakers felt like a hundred pounds in my pocket, ninety-nine of those pounds attributed to Sonny. As Blake drove, I pressed my hand against them to keep the shakers from clinking together. The last thing I needed was for him to ask about them. I was mortified enough, thanks to Sonny.

Once Blake dropped me off and I was safe in my apartment, I pulled out the shakers and studied their long necks that tapered into metal caps. I paused before my hallway closet, still staring at the shakers. It was ridiculous how I kept doing this. Some people collected rocks to commemorate moments. Other people recorded them with photos or a journal entry. I collected table spices like a weirdo. I felt silly, recalling Sonny's voice in my ear.

Feeling wild?

Was he mocking me? Maybe. But not to be mean. That wasn't his nature. Or maybe it was, since I hadn't seen him in over a year. What if he hated me now? Thought me plain and boring? What if asking if I felt wild was his way of telling me I would never get more exciting than this?

Oh my god. What if I never got more exciting than this?

I opened the closet, facing almost two-hundred pairs of salt and pepper shakers lining the shelves. It began as something for kicks but grew into a full-blown obsession. Some of them looked similar to the ones in my hands, long and skinny with a rounded tip. Others were short and fat, like the kind you find in a diner. A few mini shakers sat in front, holding maybe three servings of salt. One pair was made of thick marble, the salt a swirled pink and the matching pepper in black. There were plastic shakers, metal ones, cobalt blue glass ones. There were even a few grinders I'd brazenly stolen.

All the shakers were different, except for one thing— they each had a story. I could tell you the moment I took each one, what was going through my head at the time, the way I felt before they were in my hand, and the relief I felt after. Like the ones I stole at a high school acquaintance's wedding, the only single person in a sea of couples as she recited her vows. Or the ones I stole at the airport after Meadow was whisked off to her first travel blog assignment in France. Or the ones I took from a small kitchen at the funeral home where we said goodbye to my parents. Or the small, unassuming glass shakers that sat off to the side, the ones I stole when Sonny let me know he was taking the job in Wisconsin.

I knew it wouldn't work the moment he told me, even as I agreed to give long distance a try. He was aware of my shaker fascination, how it blanketed my insecurities like a drug. But he didn't know about the ones from the café that I'd slipped into my pocket when he broke the news he was leaving. If he'd known, he'd also have known how I really felt. Maybe he wouldn't have left.

Or maybe he still would have, and that would have been worse. So I kept those shakers secret.

I set the long-necked shakers next to the ones from that night, allowing them to touch in their space on the shelf. Taking a deep breath, I surveyed the rows of shakers for a moment, accepting that this was my life—a spinster who got deep thrills over insane habits—and then closed the closet door.

The hallway to my bedroom was lined with family photos, all the ones my parents had hung over the years. Even though I'd seen them a million times before, I paused now to look over the pictures, stopping at the one of my sister and me in kindergarten. We were holding hands while wearing matching dresses, our same long red hair in braids. I remembered that day with vivid detail because it was the first time we were separated. As twins, we did everything together. But on our first day of school, Meadow had been placed in Miss June's class, while I was in Miss Olson's. Miss June brought her dog to class and played guitar during lessons. Miss Olson thought it was fun to practice sight words. Meadow would come home with vibrant finger paintings, her hands colored red and purple. Miss Olson scolded me for coloring outside the lines. The only thing that made that year any fun was lunchtime, when Meadow would find me and we'd stay glued together until the recess bell rang.

Looking at our family photos, our bond was unmistakable. There was one photo of my dad pushing us on the swings at a park in Sonoma, both of us wearing Mickey Mouse shirts and wide grins on our faces. There was another when my parents were younger than I was now, each of them holding a copper-haired baby on their hip. Photos from our short-lived days playing soccer, the night we went to prom, the day of our high school graduation.

At one time, the house had been rowdy and full of a good kind of chaos. Now, the hall was filled with echoes from the life we once had. I took a deep breath as I studied the final photo, the one I hung on the wall next to the framed images my mom strategically placed. It was the photo Sonny took of my sister and me after the funeral, our heads bowed together, our hands against the tree my parents had planted in our yard the day they moved in.

This was the home we grew up in. Then, after the car accident that took our parents, it became ours. And now, I was the only one here. Once Meadow's adventure blog took off, she gave up any sense of permanent roots and opted for traveling the world on the dime of her many sponsors. While she jumped from hotel to Airbnb, I stayed home and absorbed all the responsibilities of homeownership.

I was happy being a hometown girl, though, and taking over my family home was a natural fit. The house looked much like it did as I grew up, with the same yellow painted walls and matted gold carpet (now aged a dingy brown), my father's plaid armchair in the corner of the living room by the window, and large picture windows framed by heavy curtains in burgundy. It was dated, for sure, but I loved the memories attached to everything around me. Just like the shakers, I could pull stories from everything in the house, from the way my mother looked at me over our antique dining table to the way my father sipped coffee in the wrought iron rocking chair that faced the garden. Keeping it the way they made it was like keeping them here with me. That, and this had always been my safe space, the place where I could be unapologetically me. I didn't need a mask here. I didn't need to fake a smile. I didn't need to be bigger or better or more successful. In these walls, acceptance was our religion, and love was the way we practiced it. I couldn't imagine living anywhere else.

I padded to my bedroom at the end of the hall, the one across the way from my parents' old room. Their bedroom was mostly used for storage now, though their bed with its canopy made of intertwined branches still took center stage against the far wall. I only went in there to dust or search for some odd trinket, but mostly I left it alone. It was the only room with its own bathroom, and it had the best light. I could think of dozens of great uses for that room, but I just couldn't bring myself to take it over. It felt too personal, too soon. I mean, I'd said goodbye to them. I was living in the home they created. Their presence was everywhere in this house. But their room? It was too sacred. I just wasn't ready, and I wasn't sure I'd ever be.

It was fine, though. My room was the same one I'd had my whole childhood. This was the only room I changed drastically, and I made good use of the small space. I'd modeled it after some ideas I found on Pinterest, giving it an airy feel with sheer white curtains that billowed when I let in the breeze. Lining every surface were leafy green plants, from the fat-leafed monstera to the flirty fiddle leaf plant. Above my bed was a beautiful chandelier I'd scored at an estate sale. It was a pain to keep dust-free, but it made me feel a tiny bit princessy. All the colors in the room were muted and soft, including the downy grey blanket my mother had crocheted for me a year before she died. This lay over the top of my reading chair, and I wrapped myself in it almost every night.

I flopped on the bed, kicking my dress shoes off and rubbing my aching feet as I dumped the contents of my clutch purse onto my dresser. After I removed my earrings, I did my usual Instagram check so I could see what Meadow was up to. But when I unlocked the phone, a message was waiting for me. Not just any message…a message from Sonny.

Shit. Shit. Shit.

I took a deep breath, rotated my head to stretch my neck, and prepared myself to hear his deep, rolling voice so close to my ear. My heart pounded as I pressed the play button, and I let my breath out. But when I raised it to my ear, it wouldn't play. Frustrated, I put it on speaker, but instead of speaker, I pressed the trash button.

Shit! I opened my deleted messages, regretting all the messages that still filled that box. I'd never been good at getting rid of anything, my old voicemail messages included. I found Sonny's message, but then I hesitated. Could I handle this? Did I really want to hear what he had to say? Something told me it would only lead to more mixed feelings. Nothing he said would fix what happened. And yet, if I never heard it, I'd wonder what he said forever.

"Fine," I whispered, then pressed the play icon. Instead, my shaking fingers hit the side of the screen, deleting every single old message I had.

Forever.

Sonny's message included.

Shit. Shit!

I froze, staring at my phone as if I could somehow bring the message back if I were just patient enough. I knew that wouldn't work, though. The only way I could get it back was if I called him up to ask about it. *Nope, that wasn't going to happen.* Maybe text him? *No, not a chance.* The message was gone, I'd probably never see him again, and I was just going to have to work out how to get past this while he lived happily ever after with that leggy blonde.

I'd manage. I'd done it before. But damn, that man still looked so good. And that voice... I was ruined.

I did a quick scroll through Instagram, looking to see if Sonny had created an account in the past week or so. Nope, nothing. He'd never jumped on the social media bandwagon, which had helped him fully disappear when he left my life for good. I supposed that was good since I also wouldn't have to see his relationship on display.

I plugged my phone into the charger, then dragged myself to the shower, shedding my black evening gown on the way before I washed the night down the drain.

Once I was clean and ready for bed, I slid between the sheets and rolled over to go to sleep.

Except, I couldn't. Sonny's voice echoed in my ears, my eyes flying open every time I thought I heard my name. The light from the full moon flowed through the windows, casting leafy shadows on the opposite wall and bathing my room in its milky glow. I touched the pillow next to mine and traced the hollow where his head was supposed to be.

"I miss you," I dared to whisper in the quiet. I imagined him looking back at me, catching my hand in his and bringing it to his lips. The way he used to do. The way he'd stop me in my tracks, stop me mid-sentence, stop my brain from functioning as the touch went from my fingertips to my toes.

"Then never say goodbye," he said in my head, his rumbling voice vibrating through me as if he were here, speaking the words aloud.

I closed my eyes, finally drifting to sleep.

Chapter Three

The sun was just rising over the ridge, casting its gauzy gold rays over the raised beds in the front yard when I went outside to water the vegetable garden. I sipped from the oversized coffee mug in my hand, but my mind was on the phone in my pocket. I'd checked it numerous times already, weighing the pros and cons of calling Sonny back. Pro: I'd get to hear his sexy voice again, feel it rumble all the way down to my toes. Con: I'd have to hear his sexy voice again, feel it rumble all the way down to my toes.

Meeting Sonny was an accident that never should have happened. It was my senior year of college, just after midterms, when I'd decided to blow off some steam at Brew, a local coffee and beer pub in Santa Rosa that had an underground vibe to it—much more my scene than the sorority and frat parties going on closer to campus. I wasn't the only one, though. The place was packed, probably because of Log Flume, a band of geeky guys from Eau Claire, Wisconsin who were playing a bunch of small venues on a cross country van tour.

Apparently, they had a cult following in Sonoma County.

Had I known this, I would have chosen a different place to go. But the band sounded good, and, as usual, I felt invisible in the crowded room. Somehow that gave me comfort—except for when it came to finding a place to sit. The only table left was in the very front, right next to the band, which should have been clue number one that it was taken. I sat there with my coffee and grilled cheese at a huge table meant for more than just me. My mission to be invisible failed. Everyone else was packed around tiny bistro tables or standing with their beers, and I was taking up this giant table for twelve like some kind of celebrity.

I soon found out the table was reserved for the band, which I would have known if I'd paid attention to the giant RESERVED sign in the middle of the table. You know, clue number two. The Brew manager was nice enough about it, but insistent that I move since the band was taking their break soon. I looked around at the crowded pub, then at my plate, the grilled cheese oozing out of the bread. I started to pack things up so I could leave.

"She's with me," a deep voice said behind me, his strong Scottish accent reverberating through me like a note on a guitar string. I looked up at the man who now had his hand on the back of my chair. "Stay," he said as he sat down next to me. "It's a big table and there's room for you here. I'm Sonny."

"Cricket," I said, expecting the usual questions about my unusual name. But it never came. Instead, we spent the time talking as if we really did come there together. He lived nearby and was friends with the fiddler. In his free time, he worked for the band as their unofficial marketing manager. He was also the reason why they had fans on the West Coast, so far from their Wisconsin home. By the time the night was over, we'd swapped phone numbers, promising to meet up sometime in the future.

I'd figured that was the end of things, but he'd texted me that night, asking me out to breakfast.

"Brew makes the best avocado toast in the county," his message said, which I already knew from so many of my early morning study sessions.

"So do I," I'd texted back.

The next morning, I was sitting next to a near-stranger on the front porch swing, enjoying a slice of avocado toast with pickled onions on top while we looked out at my mother's garden.

The rest, as they say, is history. Four years of it...until he messed everything up.

I looked at my phone again, then decided I didn't need to invite this kind of torture into my life. If he called again, I'd pick up. If not, oh well. In the meantime, I'd do my best to forget him.

No, in the meantime I'd focus on more important matters, like watering my mother's garden. Despite the early hour, the bees were already at work on the lavender bushes, and I couldn't help but marvel at their tiny little bodies buzzing around the purple blossoms.

"You're doing a wonderful job," I crooned as I watered the base of the billowing plants to avoid soaking the fuzzy bees. I heard my mother's voice come through me. She talked to the bees, the birds, and the plants the same way she'd talk to a child, asking them about their day and offering encouragement. When I was young, I swore they answered her.

Ours was the only house on the block with a vegetable garden out front. Our neighbors all had traditional lawns, kept meticulous because of our neighborhood's self-formed Community Cares Association, the CCA. The reasoning behind this committee was to keep the neighborhood abreast of different issues and concerns, maintaining a safe and well-kept community. But really, it was just a group of busybodies with too much time on their hands. Their neon-green notices could be found taped to trash cans that stayed out past garbage day, or on cars that allowed too much space between their tire and the curb, or on any house that kept their Christmas lights up beyond New Year's.

Or when anyone's yard was below a certain standard, thus bringing down the neighborhood's property values.

Our yard didn't always look like this. Once we'd had a luxurious green lawn that Meadow and I would tumble around on whenever the sun was out. My dad mowed the lawn every weekend, and the smell of grass was as intoxicating as my mother's baked cookies. But then one tiny yellow flower showed up, followed by soft globes of feathery spores. Meadow and I would blow the dandelion seeds at each other, giggling as some landed in our hair, the rest carried away by the wind.

Then more yellow flowers showed up until the bright green lawn was covered in vibrant sunshiney blossoms. My dad would mow the lawn, but it only spread the dandelions more. Finally, my mother made him stop.

"The bees, George," she'd said, pointing at the honeybees that were constantly dancing all over the flowers. Citing an article she'd read about the dangers honeybees faced in a world of weed killer and climate change, my mother insisted we let the yard go wild. "Once the bees are gone, we're next." And so, our mission became to save the bees, blowing even more dandelion seeds across our feral, jungle-like lawn, and celebrating the blossom-drunk honeybees stumbling between vibrant blooms.

My mother recycled the first notice left by the CCA, alerting her to the violation our lawn was committing. The second notice, she ripped up into tiny pieces and added the blinding green flecks to our compost. The third one, she picked a small bouquet of dandelions, placed it in a mason jar, then tied the notice around the lip of the jar with a ribbon. Then she left it next to our mailbox for the whole neighborhood to see.

"Molly, perhaps there's another solution," my father urged, holding the notice for an emergency neighborhood meeting that would convene at the home of Patty Jenkins, unofficial president of the CCA.

"Darling, I don't think you understand how important this is. It's a matter of life and death."

My parents never argued, but when they came close, they used pet names like weapons.

"Sweetheart, I understand completely," my father insisted, "which is why I have an idea."

Dad hatched the plan for a vegetable garden out front, and my mother tilted her head, mulling over all the bee-friendly plants she could think of to take the place of the illegal dandelions.

Before the date of the meeting, my parents had torn out their front lawn, dandelions and all, built raised beds, spread the compost, and planted their own personal

Eden. The CCA meeting was canceled with no explanation, though once the garden took off, we sure saw a lot of Patty Jenkins as her daily stroll seemed to include the sidewalk in front of our home. My mother would sit on the porch swing, sipping iced tea while she swayed back and forth, offering a wave until Patty hurried away. The garden stayed wild, but in a contained kind of way, with squash vines snaking their leaves around the tomatoes and marigolds, strawberries caressing the fragrant earth, cosmos lifting their pink faces to the sun…and lots and lots of honeybees.

I kept the front yard garden my mother started years ago, adding rows of beaming sunflowers, towering cornstalks taller than my head, and blossoming trees that had cost me a fortune, but now bore fruit like ruby red cherries, slightly sour apples, and juicy succulent peaches that always dripped from my chin to my shirt. Like my mother, I whispered my own secrets to the plants, cradled the tiny vegetables on the vine while I measured their growth, and thanked the bees for letting me spend time in their unruly home. Watering the garden was like walking on holy ground. It was where green things grew, and where I grew, as well. It didn't matter what was going on in the world, in my mother's garden everything was fresh and new, sacred and safe, and full of magic.

My phone vibrated my backside, and I fumbled with the hose as I grabbed it, half hoping to see Sonny's name.

Who was I fooling? I fully hoped it was Sonny. It wasn't though.

"Hey Meadow," I said, turning the water back on.

"Hey yourself, Cricket," she said. "How's Petaluma doing?"

"Barely waking up. It isn't even seven yet."

"I'll never get used to the time difference," she said with a laugh.

"You have to stay in one place to get used to something," I pointed out. This time, Meadow was talking from Sweden, where she was supposed to be for the next three weeks. Last week it was Brazil. Next up was wherever the next lifestyle company sent her, all in exchange for promotion on her blog and Instagram account, Wandering Meadow. At last count, Meadow had 250K Instagram followers, and I have no idea how many on her blog. What I did know was that she got to travel the world, and I got to see it through her eyes while safely staying home.

For identical twins, we sure were different.

"So, don't get mad," she said. "But I have a package heading your way, and it's supposed to arrive today."

"Is it another plant of the month club subscription?" I asked. "Because I won't be mad about that." Meadow, my minimalist twin, was constantly sending me things, some from her sponsors and some that she'd used as props for Instagram and then had no use for. I didn't have use for most of these things, either, but I had the hardest time throwing things away, or even telling her no. However, the plants had been one of the highlights. Since Meadow didn't have a place to stay, she had no use for monthly plants. That, and she had somewhat of a black thumb.

"No, and the subscription runs out next month. Sorry."

"Bummer. My house is beautiful thanks to that. So, what is it this time? Please tell me it's not another expired collection of hot sauces from around the world."

"No, but I think you're going to love it. I'll just let it be a surprise."

"Fine, be that way."

"Let me know what it gets there, okay? At least, shoot me a text. I'm going to some hot party in Uppsala, and I probably won't hear your call."

Another difference. Meadow could make friends everywhere, and she was usually immersed in the nightlife. Whatever party she was going to tonight would be posted throughout the week on social media. As for me, no one would be interested in my ideal night: curled up on the couch with a good book while diffusing eucalyptus and lavender. Sometimes popcorn was involved. None of this went on my Instagram, of course. My most recent post was last month when the tomatoes were at full harvest, and of my fifty-seven followers, I think only my sister liked it.

"How was last night's event?" Meadow asked. I sucked in a sharp breath, which she must have heard. "That good, huh?"

"The event was fine," I said. "I took Blake with me so I wouldn't have to go alone."

"Did he stare at your rack all night?"

"Nah. I mean, he glanced a couple of times, but only because I looked pretty hot."

"Of course you did," she said. "You look like me."

"Anyways." I gave a short laugh. "Sonny was there."

This time, she gave the sharp inhale.

"Are you okay?" she asked.

I turned the water off, the plants fully drenched. Then I moved to the porch swing, the chains creaking as I rested on the wooden bench.

"I think so. I don't know." I picked at a loose thread on my sweater, tucking it back into place as I thought of the look on Sonny's face while he watched me with Blake. "He was there with someone, and I panicked, so I made Blake pretend he was with me, and now I feel totally stupid. To make it worse, Sonny called last night and left a message and I accidentally deleted it without hearing what he said."

"Wait, what? You deleted it? You can't retrieve it?"

"I tried!" I released my hold on the ground so that the swing pitched forward, and then back in a gentle movement. "But I accidentally deleted it again."

"Who does that?" she asked. I huffed loudly through my nose, even though I'd been asking myself the same thing.

"Me, apparently."

"Maybe call him back?"

"No!"

"Okay," she said, laughing. "But you're going to wonder what he said for the rest of your life."

"No, I won't." The swing was slowing, and I pawed at the ground again to keep it moving. "I'll get over him like I did the last time."

"Right," Meadow said. "Like the last time. And when did you get over him, exactly?"

"Shut up." I stopped the swing and then hugged my knees to my chest. "Look, I can't call him. I know that would be the totally reasonable and mature thing to do, but I've already missed that train. I mean, I faked a relationship right in front of him."

Meadow was silent for a moment, and I could practically hear the gears turning in her coppery head.

"So," I continued. "You're not even going to give me a clue about what's arriving today, are you?"

"Are you changing the subject?"

"Absolutely."

She laughed. "You're just going to have to wait. Hey, I need to go. My date is here to take me to dinner."

"Date? Seriously? Didn't you just arrive in Sweden two days ago?"

"Yeah, but this is a friend of a friend."

"They all are," I said, laughing. "Seriously, be careful. There are a lot of weirdos out there."

"I'm always careful," she said.

I tooled around in the garden a little longer after we hung up. My mind kept doing mental gymnastics around whether to call Sonny or not. I kept landing on a big fat NO, but not before going through the reasons why maybe I could, and then what I'd actually say to him.

Hey Sonny, some party, huh?

It's been a while. Last time I saw you, you were choosing Wisconsin over me.

Oh, that guy? He's just a good friend.

How's your new friend? You know, the leggy one.

I couldn't call him. Truth be told, anything sensible I had to say would dissolve the moment I heard his smoky voice. Not that I had anything sensible to say anyway.

Once the garden was free of weeds and my wooden bowl full of that morning's harvest of cherry tomatoes and string beans, I stowed my gardening tools and wound up the hose, then headed inside for a second cup of coffee and a shower. At the same time, Sonny used to make fun of me for this morning ritual until I'd surprised him during one of his showers with a fresh cup of black coffee. That morning he took a longer than usual shower.

"It's almost as good as drinking a lager while bathing," he'd said when he finally exited the bathroom, his naked skin glistening from shower water as he held his drained coffee cup. "I think I get the hype." From that point on, he took his second cup in the shower. Just like me. Sonny's presence was infused into this ritual, despite being my habit first.

I couldn't shake him. I saw him everywhere and in everything. Even though I'd survived my whole life without him before I'd known him. Here it was, a year after we broke up, and he still affected me.

The faint sound of the doorbell reached the bathroom as I lathered shampoo into my hair. I turned the water off to make sure I heard it correctly, and my heart lurched as someone pounded on the door.

Sonny.

It was completely implausible, of course. I mean, why would he just show up at my front door after so long? But then, why would he show up at a party I had coordinated, or leave me a voicemail that I deleted?

I pushed aside the shower curtain and wrapped my soapy hair in a towel, then another towel around my body. It wasn't until I was running down the stairs that I realized I maybe should have put something different on.

A robe. My sweats. Anything that was less revealing than a two-by-four piece of Terry cloth wrapped around my nudity. Still, I didn't let it stop me from flinging open the front door.

Had I given this some thought, I'd have waited long enough to peer through the peephole to see who was there. And had I given myself time to process all of this, I'd have found it interesting that Sonny was the first thought that came to mind when someone rang my doorbell, and my reaction was to rush from the shower so I wouldn't miss him. But it wasn't Sonny on the other side. It was a bewildered delivery guy who gave my near-naked body a once-over before thrusting an electronic clipboard at me.

"Sign here," he squeaked out.

Meadow's delivery. I stared at the wooden crate by the delivery guy's feet, then nearly jumped out of my towel when a loud *squawk* erupted from inside.

"What is that?" I asked. He shrugged, now trying to look everywhere but at me.

"Seems like a bird," he said. "There's another package on the truck, if you'll, uh, wait here." He didn't wait for my reply before racing back to an unmarked truck idling in front of the house. Still holding the clipboard, I bent down carefully and peeked in one of the air holes. The bird squawked again, and I caught a look at its eye peering back at me. The delivery guy was now coming back with a large cardboard box, and I shook my head as he came closer.

"No," I said. "Take it back."

"What?" He set the box down at the bottom of the steps. "I can't do that, ma'am." I cringed at the *ma'am*. I was twenty-seven, nowhere near a *ma'am*. "Can you please sign?" I was ready to keep arguing, but the uncomfortable look on his face made me pause. The guy, a kid really, looked barely out of high school, and there I was, sopping wet, barely dressed, holding his clipboard hostage. Sighing, I gave in and signed the screen.

"Name?" he asked, one foot already pointed in the direction of his truck as he took back the slightly damp electronic pad.

"Cricket Stone," I said. The name was barely out of my mouth when he raced to his truck, leaving me alone with two large packages, one of them holding a giant bird.

Chapter Four

"What am I going to do with you?" I muttered. The bird squawked in response. I knelt to lift the crate, feeling the towel slip just enough that I realized this job required slightly more clothes than I had on. "I'll be right back," I told the bird, closing the door and heading upstairs to find something to wear. The suds in my hair crackled next to my ear as I pawed through my dresser. I tugged a pair of yoga pants over my shower-damp skin, then slipped a tank top over the twisted towel on my head.

The packages were still there on the step, and I was almost disappointed no one had stolen them yet. I had to get a dolly to bring the bird in, and I ignored its loud complaints as I set the crate in the middle of the living room floor. I accidentally inserted my finger in one of the air holes and yelped as the bird nipped at my finger. It didn't break the skin, but it was enough to leave a mark.

"You nasty creature," I hissed, rubbing my wound as I went to retrieve the other box. I opened that one first, relieved and dismayed at the same time to see another box, a picture of a birdcage on the outside, *Some Assembly*

Required printed on the outside. At least I had a place for this animal Meadow had sprung on me, but the cage made it more permanent.

I was no good with pets. Actually, that's a lie. I was good with Buoy. But in the end, he was Sonny's pet, not mine. Other than Buoy, I didn't really have any experience with taking care of my own animal. As nature-loving as my parents were, they were not the type to get animals. My mom reasoned that animals were meant to be wild, and a pet was against the natural order. The reasoning stuck with me, though I think the biggest reason I never wanted my own pet was because I had no interest in putting something's life in my hands.

And now I was stuck with this bird. I called Meadow's cellphone, letting it ring until I got her voicemail.

"You got me a bird?" I shrieked a little louder than I'd planned. The bird squawked as if joining my panic party. "What the hell am I supposed to do with a bird? How did you even get this thing?" I breathed out, trying to think of something else to say that wasn't another question. "Call me when you get this. I don't care what time it is over here, just call me."

I hung up, then glared at the box. The towel on my head was slipping out of its wrap, and I took it off, my hair falling across my shoulders in dried soap clumps. I flung the towel across the room, missing the bird box by inches. Not that I wanted to hit it. It wasn't the bird's fault it was here. But if I were to actually choose to domesticate an animal, a large and obnoxious bird was the last animal on my list.

The bird couldn't stay in the crate forever, but the cage was still in its box, unassembled. I glanced at both boxes, feeling inadequate, especially as the bird was now loudly flapping its wings inside its cramped space. What first? Build the cage? Let the bird out? Go buy it food? I finally settled on the cage first, because I didn't want the bird flying everywhere. Meanwhile, the bird had increased its squawking, and I knew I needed to build this cage quick if I wanted any peace, whatsoever. Was peace even allowed in my vocabulary anymore, now that I was a bird owner?

I opened the cage box and slid the contents out on the rug, then stared helplessly at several iron sides, a tray and base, and a bunch of screws, nuts, and other tiny things that were supposedly going to be sufficient enough to keep a giant bird from escaping. There were instructions, and they showed the kinds of tools I'd need, so I got my dad's toolbox from the garage and then sat cross-legged on the floor while I organized the cage pieces. That's as far as I got before I realized I was in over my head. That, and the damn bird's squawking was making me want to tear out my shampoo-coated hair.

I picked up my cellphone again and called the only person I could count on in an emergency.

"Are you busy?" I asked Taye. She'd been my assistant for only six months, but the girl was a genius. She'd just graduated from Sonoma State University, my alma mater, when she reached out to me for an internship, hoping to get some hospitality experience under her belt while she worked on her MBA. It only took one week before I realized she was so much more than an intern, and we worked out a plan that would allow her to continue with her studies while also handling all the organization and coordination aspects of event planning. My business had just started picking up to a pace I couldn't keep up on my own, so the timing was perfect. Now I couldn't imagine my business, or even my life, without her.

"Nah, girl, I was going to call you anyway to go over tomorrow's schedule. What you need?"

"Something that's definitely not in your job description," I said. Then I explained the bird situation and the cage that sat in pieces in my living room.

A half-hour later, she walked in my front door carrying a grocery sack of vegetables and dragging a bag of pellets.

"You look like hell," she said, taking in my mid-wash hair. As usual, she looked like she walked off the pages of a fashion magazine for boho skater chicks. Her pants hung loose on her slender frame while she wore a tight tank top and an open hoodie over that. She usually had on chucks and long socks, but this time she wore cute strappy sandals, her toes painted a fluorescent blue. Her dreaded hair hung to her waist when she wore it loose, but today she had her hair in a large bun, a few knotted strands hanging down and brushing her neck. Her mahogany brown skin amplified the light grey of her eyes. If Taye didn't want to go into a business profession, she'd have a solid chance at modeling.

The bird, who'd been quiet for the last five minutes, heard Taye's voice and began squawking again.

"Uh, Cricket? What kind of bird is it, exactly?" Taye set the bags down, peering at the crate behind me.

"I don't know. A big one. I think it's a parrot or something, but I'm too afraid to look in case it escapes."

Taye quickly closed the doors, shutting the living room off from the rest of the house. This had always been an odd feature about this room, but now it seemed refreshingly convenient. As Taye approached the crate, I huddled wide-eyed against the couch, trying to make myself small. Carefully, she pried the top of the crate off with a crowbar from the toolbox and then peered in. I yelped when a large blue bird leaped from the crate, landing on the edge only to knock it and itself to the ground. It hopped, unscathed, and then pulled at a piece of the shag carpet. From beak to tail end, the bird had to be at least two feet long, though the tail was as long as its body. Offsetting the cerulean blue of its back and wings, the bird's underside was a vibrant yellow, though part of its feathers was missing from its chest in large bald patches. It flapped its wings, screeching, and my eyes widened as I took in its wingspan.

"Holy hell, that's a huge bird," I muttered, then patted the floor to draw its attention away from the strand of rug it loosened. "Hey, knock it off."

"It's a blue and yellow macaw," Taye said, looking at her phone screen. She held the phone toward me, and I took it, seeing the identical bird on the screen. I scrolled down, skimming the notes on it. Pellets, good. Vegetables, also good. Cage. Oh, no.

"The cage isn't going to work," I said, looking down at the tiny pieces just as the macaw noticed them too. Then it was a race to get all the nuts and screws back in the box before the curious creature swallowed any of them. It squawked at me when I managed to clean them all up, then fluttered into the air and landed on my shoulder.

"Shit! Is it going to attack me? Will it poop on me?"

"Girl, for being Miss Mother Nature, you sure are freaking out right now," Taye said.

"I'm glad you think this is funny. I've never had a bird in my house before, or one about to eat my face."

"It won't eat your face," Taye said. She crouched near me and offered the bird her arm. The parrot's talons dug into her sleeve when it transferred over to her. I rubbed at the angry red scratches on my bare shoulder.

"How do you know so much about macaws?"

"My brother has African Grey Parrots. They're not as big as this guy, but they have a lot of the same characteristics. And if you treat them right, they're the most lovable things ever. Aren't you, Mack Bird?"

"Great! Invite him over. See if he wants a new bird."

"Derek moved to Venezuela three years ago, so that won't work. But it's almost noon there, I could text him." Her fingers were already flying over the screen, the macaw tugging at one of her dreads while she did. As much as I didn't want a bird, I had to admit this one was beautiful. Taye looked like pirate royalty or even an island princess with this gorgeous jewel-toned bird draped over her shoulder.

"Why do you think it has bald patches?" I asked her. "Do you think it's some kind of disease?"

"It's most likely stress." She finished typing, then placed her hand under the bird's feet. It obediently moved to her hand, and she lifted it at eye level, studying the featherless areas. As if to answer the question, the bird began grooming this area, to which Taye gently nudged its beak away. "Yeah, it's stripping the area raw.

We don't know the bird's history, but even just a change of scenery like this can affect its mental state."

I was about to ask if it was permanent, but Taye's phone rang.

"Hey, big bro! How's Venezuela? How's the little guy?" She paused, listening. "Aw, I can't believe he's already two. I'm going to have to make a trip out there soon. Give Julian kisses from his Auntie Taye, okay?" She set the bird down on the back of the couch, and then paced near the window while she asked him questions about the bird. I half tuned in, but was also too engrossed in what the bird was doing—if it was going to tear up my couch or poop on it, if it would fly at me without Taye's gentle touch, how I was going to handle this once she left.

Nope, she was never leaving. Taye lived here now. I wasn't letting her leave.

"All right, Chica, I have some information for you," she said, slipping her phone in her pocket. "First off, you're right about the cage. A bird like this really can't be in one this small. The best kind of enclosure is one large enough for it to spread its wings and fly, especially since this one doesn't appear to have its wings clipped."

"People do that?" My stomach did a slow roll, just thinking about someone taking away a bird's ability to fly.

"Some people do because they believe it keeps them safer. You know, to keep them from flying away, or crashing into walls," she said. "But not everyone does this. Obviously not this parrot's previous owner, thankfully. Right, little guy?" She perched on the edge of the couch, stroking the bird's back until it climbed on her leg. The more I watched its interaction with Taye, the less tense I felt about it. The bird did seem friendly enough. Maybe it wouldn't take my face off.

"So, what kind of enclosure are we talking about?" I asked.

"Derek has an outside aviary where his parrots live, though he also has his house set up for times when he brings them indoors. The weather here is mild enough that we could build something like that outside. There's that huge space at the side of the house that would be perfect."

"Okay," I said slowly. "But what do we do in the meantime?"

"He says to set up a room, preferably a room you'll be in often, with large branches and toys. One you don't mind getting a little trashed."

"I don't want any room to get trashed," I said, but I looked around the living room. I didn't know what I was going to do about the shag carpet. But with the large windows, plus the French doors that closed it off from the rest of the house, this seemed like the best choice. I just had to clear out the furniture.

"Here's the deal," Taye said, eyeing my dried soap tangles. "You go do something with your hair while I bird-sit. Then we'll figure out the next part of our plan."

Apparently, the next part of the plan included a reality check. My hair now completely washed, even dried, I sat with Taye at the kitchen table in front of my laptop, pricing out solutions for my new cageless bird while it screeched behind the closed living room. If it—I still didn't know if it was a boy or a girl—were a parakeet or a cockatiel, there wouldn't be an issue. A small cage would suffice, and I'd be on to the next thing. If I didn't care about the macaw's need for wingspread, it also wouldn't matter. But seeing the bare spots on that poor bird's chest and the proud way it flapped its large wings, I knew it needed a large area to move and feel happy.

Regarding enclosures, we were talking thousands of dollars—money I didn't have. When my parents died, they'd left the house to Meadow and me, along with a mortgage they'd been borrowing against for years. Thankfully business was good—good enough that I could afford an assistant like Taye and still make the house payment with Meadow's help. However, there wasn't a surplus large enough to just drop a couple thousand at the bird store.

"What was Meadow thinking, sending me this damn bird?" I muttered, scrolling through a few more enclosures until I finally just closed the laptop. "A cage isn't happening," I said to Taye. "Maybe we could build something?"

"Do you know anything about building?" she asked. I thought back to the cage in a box, and how, even with instructions, I was at a loss.

"Not a clue," I admitted. "So now what?"

"I guess we take everything out of the living room the bird will destroy—"

"That's everything," I interrupted. She shrugged in agreement.

"We could probably bring some branches inside to give it somewhat of a home. Maybe the living room can become a rainforest room, or like a jungle. You may not even need an enclosure."

"We'll see," I said, though I was doubtful. The bird was now quiet, and I felt my insides tighten just wondering what it was destroying. But as much as I wanted to check on it, I also wanted to forget about it for the moment. "So, you wanted to go over this week's schedule?"

"Oh, yes," she said. She re-opened my computer and navigated to my calendar, which I saw had a few new events on it.

"Charles Finnigan already called?" I asked, looking at the meeting set up for Monday at noon.

"Actually his marketing director did," Taye said. "He set up the meeting at The Bird House in Santa Rosa. Have you heard of it?"

I nodded, smirking at the ironic name of the restaurant. I'd only been there a few times, thanks to the pricey menu, but considered it one of my favorite restaurants. The food came a la carte as small plates, and it was tempting to order one of everything since each dish was so delicious. "Did he give any hints at preferences, or tell you what the party was for?"

"Mr. Finnigan and his wife are celebrating their fiftieth wedding anniversary," she said. I nodded, smiling as I took notes on a pad of paper. I loved doing anniversary parties. I may have struck out in love, but it was thrilling to plan an event around someone else's love story. "He didn't say much about preferences," Taye continued. "He did say that Mr. Finnigan would be there at this preliminary meeting to discuss some things, but was leaving most of the planning to the two of you."

"That makes sense," I said. "What's his name?"

Taye peered closer at her notes.

"Edison McIntyre."

My heart stopped. *Sonny.*

"Oh, shit," I said, then smothered my mouth to keep from saying anything else. Once again, last night's chance encounter played through my mind, including the stupid charade with Blake.

"Someone you know?" Taye asked. She had no clue who Sonny was, as she'd started working for me after we'd broken up.

"No one special," I said quickly. "I mean, we went out for a while, but the relationship ran its course."

She looked at me for a moment, scrutinizing me under her infamous Taye stare. She wasn't buying it.

"He's the one who had the dog, wasn't he?"

How the hell... "It was nothing," I lied, my stomach tying in knots just thinking about Sonny.

"Mm-hm." Her raised eyebrow confirmed she didn't believe me. "At any rate, Edison said that Mr. Finnigan is leaving in a week for a special three-week cruise with his wife to start the celebration, and plans to return just before the event, which is..." Taye maneuvered through the calendar before landing on a date next month. "...October thirteenth, a Friday."

"Friday the thirteenth in October. Does he want black cats and witch's hats, too?" The joke was lame, and I knew it. But I was still recovering from the knowledge that I'd be planning an anniversary party with the guy who ruined me for love.

I only half-listened as Taye went over the rest of the week. I nodded at the appropriate times, but my mind was occupied by the disaster I was walking into, starting with tomorrow's lunch.

What the hell was I getting into? I contemplated quitting, but it went against my policy—take any and every job I get, and never embarrass a client. If I quit, I'd break both of those rules as this was Stuart Jackson's good friend. I had to take the job and work with Sonny. And somehow, I'd have to leave my heart out of it.

Chapter Five

The parking lot at The Bird House was already packed by the time I squeezed my mom's old Honda Civic into the last spot near the end. The car was on its last leg and should have been replaced three years ago when I inherited it, but there was never any money. Besides, the thing still ran, even if it took a little longer to start in the mornings and I had to crank the windows down by hand.

I was early, so I took the opportunity to check my phone again. Meadow still hadn't returned my call, which wasn't unlike her, but frustrated me just the same. I really needed an answer about that damn bird. It slept well enough the first night, but yesterday afternoon it managed to tear a hole in the couch cushion. It was the last piece of furniture I had to move out of the room, and I figured one more day wouldn't hurt. Obviously, I was wrong.

I was also wrong about this spot, as the car hogs on both sides didn't give me much room to get out. I opened my door a crack and realized there was no way I could fit through. Just when I thought it was hopeless, the lights flashed on the car parked on the passenger side. I pretended not to notice the frustrated look the driver shot at me after they'd squeezed into their car, and I fiddled with my broken radio until they'd pulled out of their spot. Then I slid over the center console, falling into the passenger seat just as another car pulled in. Luckily, there was enough room this time, and I opened my door before the other driver could. I looked up, tripping over my feet in my hurry, to see Charles Finnigan patiently waiting for me to move out of the way…and Sonny sitting next to him in the passenger seat, an amused look on his face.

Shit.

"It's fine. This is fine," I muttered, trying to look casual as I leaned awkwardly across the passenger seat to lock the driver's side door, and then the passenger side before closing it and moving aside. As much as I wanted to evaporate into the warm afternoon air, I waited at the back of my rusted white car for Mr. Finnigan and Sonny to join me. Clutching my purse in front of me, I pretended the last few minutes never happened as I stood with my strappy flat sandals together while my maxi dress moved in the breeze.

I'd taken an embarrassingly long time getting ready that morning, unsure what one wears when preparing to do business with one's ex-boyfriend. I'd started with a *can't be bothered* look, putting on a knit dress I often gardened in because of the large, bright strawberries splashed across the material. Thanks to a matching strawberry apron I found on Etsy, it never got stained, so it was fine to wear in public. Still, just because I wanted to show Sonny I didn't care, it didn't mean I needed to show up to a nice business lunch looking like a casual piece of gigantic fruit. So I went the opposite direction, putting on a grey pencil skirt with a blazer, just like the formal business outfits I wore when meeting Stuart Jackson at his high-rise office in San Francisco. With my hair in a French twist, I looked in the mirror and saw someone who was trying too hard to be someone I wasn't. The hair came down, the skirt came off, and I was left staring at my closet. That's when I decided to stop trying to make an impression and just go as me. The gold mustard maxi dress was one of my favorites, with a Roman style to its ropy gathered straps, the high banded waist that complimented my figure even on my fluffiest days, and the way the skirt flowed to my ankles. I felt like sunshine, or, if I was being bold, like a sun goddess in this dress. And yet, this sun-worshiping dress was also completely appropriate for a business lunch in the heart of Wine Country.

Of course, I imagined a sun goddess was much more graceful than I was, and I only hoped my wide smile would make up for my passenger side exit from my jalopy. To his credit, Charles Finnigan seemed to disregard my awkward display as he exited his shiny black Lexus, coming toward me with arms open wide.

"You, my dear, are a breath of fresh air," he said as he hugged me instead of the customary handshake. He pulled away and then gestured to Sonny. My stomach did a slow roll, taking in Sonny's sideways smirk, the shadow of his neatly unshaven face, the private joke in his eyes, and how he towered over both of us. I caught a hint of his scent on the passing breeze, a familiar blend of woodsy juniper and eucalyptus which brought back memories of curling up on the couch together, my face against his chest as I breathed him in.

I didn't know how I should act. Did Mr. Finnigan know about us? Sonny answered that for me when he extended his hand.

"Edison McIntyre," he said in his thick accent, my heart leaping as he clasped my hand in his. The amused squint of his eyes didn't help, our secret history flowing between us, unbeknownst to Mr. Finnigan. "Charles has told me all about you," Sonny continued. "I look forward to us working together."

"Likewise," I said, sliding my hand from his and creating distance with a sidestep. Sonny stuffed his hands in his pockets and rocked on his heels, just like he used to do when I amused him, usually when I was irritated about something he did. Back when I loved him, just his sly grin was enough to quell my frustration. This time, I had to look away, conflicted by the warm sensation that spread over my body, mingling with my annoyance. The confused feelings continued as Mr. Finnigan led the way to the restaurant and Sonny remained at my side as if we had come here together.

"You look nice," he whispered. I glared at him in response. He held his hands up, as if signaling defeat, but the expression on his face continued to show how humorous he found all of this. I quickened my steps until I was walking alongside Mr. Finnigan.

"So, my assistant told me how you and your wife are celebrating fifty years of marriage," I said, grinning widely even as I tried to ignore the feel of Sonny's gaze on the back of my head.

"Sometimes it feels like a year, others it's like a hundred," he said with a laugh. "My Lilith puts up with a lot being married to me. That woman deserves a party and so much more."

"I've seen the way she looks at you, Chuck," Sonny cut in. "That woman still thinks you hung the moon and stars for some reason." He reached forward and opened the door before either of us had a chance, motioning his arm in an *after you* gesture. "Ladies first," he murmured to me. If Mr. Finnigan wasn't waiting for me to make a move, I would have taken this as my cue to turn back around and walk away. *Ladies first.* Sonny McIntyre stopped putting me anywhere close to first when he made the decision that ultimately ended us. I moved past without even looking at him, then waited by the hostess station for Mr. Finnigan to give our name.

The Bird House was one of those types of restaurants that felt fancy while also offering a warm, relaxed vibe. Located in a rehabbed farmhouse on Santa Rosa's main throughway, the inside of the restaurant had been designed with a French Country style in mind to embrace its Farm to Table approach. The result was a combination of elegant chandeliers and rustic birdcages hanging from exposed wood beams, vintage hickory floors the color of warm caramel, several different dining rooms with eggshell white walls and coordinating wallpaper with dusty blue block prints, thick-framed windows, a narrow staircase leading to yet another dining room, and an old-fashioned bar at the center of it all, complete with mahogany wood and mirrored shelves. I took my time drinking in my surroundings, unsure when I'd be back again.

The server led us through the main dining room and up a staircase to the porch balcony that overlooked the restaurant's gardens. Large shade sails sheltered the balcony seating from the late summer sun, keeping the outdoor space cool in the unseasonably warm weather. Our table was next to the railing, and I waved off Sonny with a tight smile when he tried to pull my chair out for me, as if this were a goddamn date. My cheeks burned, and I looked quickly at Mr. Finnigan to see if he noticed. Thankfully, he was gazing out at the garden.

"What a view, isn't it?" He took the seat across from me and opened the wine list. He nodded with appreciation as he read. "Should I get a bottle of something?" he asked, looking at me. "Any preferences? I remember you're a fan of Cabernet Sauvignon. Any of these catch your eye?"

I glanced over the wine list, even though I hardly knew enough about wine to make an educated choice on labels. I usually chose according to price, and it was hard to go wrong at a restaurant like this. I did know that I wanted something a little lighter than red wine, though, and noticed a Finnigan Estates brut rosé on the list.

"Since summer is almost over, would a sparkling wine be okay? I see one of yours here. Unless you'd like something different, Mr. Finnigan."

"Please dear, I've never been one for formalities. I prefer Charles or Chuck. And you like Cricket, right?" I smiled, nodding in agreement. "And Edison here seems to like Sonny, even though that hardly sounds like a Scottish name. But to each his own, I suppose."

"You can blame my father for that one," Sonny said with a deep laugh that went straight to my toes. I breathed out slowly, my fingertips tracing the curved design of the cherry wood salt grinder on the table. I didn't even realize I was doing it until I felt Sonny's eyes on me, bringing me back to two nights ago. *Feeling wild?* I quickly put my hands in my lap, knocking the grinder over in the process. My fingers grazed his as we reached for the grinder at the same time, and I drew back as if burned while he turned it upright.

If I was going to work with Sonny, I needed to get hold of myself. I couldn't let him affect me this way.

Charles, seemingly unaware of my wildly beating heart, looked down at the wine list, then nodded in appreciation at the wine I'd mentioned. "The Camille Brut Rosé," he said. "One of my favorites, and dedicated to my love, Lilith Camille. A fitting choice for an occasion like this."

We took a moment to go over the menu, and when the server came back to take our order, we opted to share the bay shrimp wontons, a dozen oysters on the half shell, the heirloom Caprese salad, slow-smoked pork belly, and the roasted Brussels sprouts in a butter sauce. After the server poured us each a glass of Camille, Charles made us pause to note the first sign of a high-quality sparkling wine, which was in the tiny chains of bubbles called *rosaries*.

"It's the bubbles that aerate a sparkling wine, which is why you don't need to swirl it like you would a still wine," he explained. Sonny cleared his throat, and Charles playfully narrowed his eyes at Sonny before winking at me. "Sorry, I could turn this whole meal into a wine lesson. Let's toast, shall we?" He raised his glass, and Sonny and I followed suit.

"To love," Sonny said, but he said it looking at me. My cheeks grew hot as we clinked glasses, and I knew my fair skin was a deep shade of rosé as I dissected what he meant, coming up with numerous possibilities beyond the Finnigans. *To the love we had before Sonny threw it away. To the love he has with his new woman. To the love he thought I had with Blake. To...* I sipped the wine slowly, waiting for my face to cool. Charles wasn't kidding about quality. The bubbles sparked my tongue, and while I wasn't a wine connoisseur, it was hard to miss the notes of melon and honey as the wine slipped down my throat.

"That is divine," I breathed, then took another small sip. "I could drink that every day."

"I'll have my marketing director send you a case," Charles said. "Sonny, send Cricket a case of the Camille."

"With the Cab? Consider it done," Sonny agreed.

"That's not necessary," I started, glancing at Sonny, and then at the expectant look on Charles' face. "Thank you, that's very kind." I paused, twisting my napkin in my lap. "So, the party," I finally said in the most awkward way of changing the subject.

"Yes, the party. What would you like to go over first?"

I pulled out my tablet and started peppering Charles with questions. It was why we were here, but it served as a great distraction from the fact that my ex-boyfriend was sitting across from me, looking better than ever. I tried to ignore him as I made notes about the budget ("no expenses spared," Charles said, to which I warned him that was a dangerous thing to say to me), preferences over his favorite vendors, and details about Lilith and himself, including special moments during their courtship and marriage. Once we got to business, it was easy to escape the amateur I'd turned into around Sonny and revert into a professional event planner. By the time our food came, I knew that Charles and Lilith both loved earthy autumn colors like golden amber and fiery burnt orange, preferred seafood over heavier beef dishes, never had children, currently had seven corgis, and that if it weren't for Lilith's bossiness, they probably wouldn't be married.

"I thought she was going to slug the girl I was going steady with," Charles said with a laugh. "You'd never know it, looking at her. She's a tiny little thing, but she can be quite scary when she's fired up. She'd decided I was the man for her, and she walked up to Beatrice Miller and told her to never come near me again before letting me know we were an item. I should have been put off, but honestly, I was smitten. We've been together ever since."

Sonny stayed silent while I continued gathering details from Charles. Once I had my coordinator hat on, it was easy to ignore him and do my job. As I told Charles about some of my ideas, my gaze wandered in Sonny's direction, curious as to why he wasn't saying anything. I regretted it as soon as I did. His face held a look of admiration that was more confusing than anything.

"The, uh…" I forgot what I was saying as I averted my eyes, scrolling through my tablet while I tried to collect my thoughts.

"The mood lighting," Sonny supplied. I nodded in his direction but didn't look at him this time.

"Right. We have to pick the venue first. But once we do, I have a friend who does some amazing things with light. She can make a stuffy room look like a garden party."

The food was just as enjoyable as the wine, of which I was already on my second glass. The tension eventually left my shoulders and I couldn't help smiling more than before. I even laughed at some of Sonny's jokes, genuinely finding them funny as I admired how damn good he looked in his button-up shirt that revealed just enough of his chest to leave me fantasizing about the rest.

"If you'll excuse me, I need to go pay the water bill," Charles said, setting his napkin down next to his empty plate.

I watched him leave, thinking it strange for him to leave the table to go pay the bill.

"It's his way of saying he has to go to the bathroom," Sonny said in a hushed tone, leaning in. I lost my look of confusion, replacing it with a glare.

"I knew what he meant," I snapped.

His proximity was making the air feel tighter, his juniper scent enveloping me despite the empty dishes between us. Damn, he smelled good. I leaned back, reaching for my water while I cooled my senses.

"So, what happened to Wisconsin?" I finally asked. "I thought you were managing your friend's band."

"I was," he said. "It stopped being a good fit. They're getting too big, and I couldn't give them what they wanted. I guess some things don't work out, right?"

I looked away, his words hitting a tender spot. "How long have you been back in town?"

"Only a few weeks," he said. I did the math, the timeline raising so many questions.

"You seem rather established in your job to have been here only a few weeks," I pointed out. "I mean, Charles, who you call Chuck, is trusting you to help plan this huge celebration."

"I've had the job for several months," he explained. "I've been working remotely until I could tie up loose ends in Wisconsin and make the move back here."

"Why didn't you tell me?" I asked. "You could have called." All the good feelings were starting to evaporate, replaced by a deep heaviness I'd become all too familiar with. This was a mistake.

I wished I'd never taken this job.

"I did call," he said, and I remembered the voicemail message I'd accidentally deleted.

"I mean, back when you knew you were coming home," I said, though I was dying to ask what he'd said. But that meant revealing my bonehead move…or that I cared. "You could have let me know."

"I didn't think you wanted me to call," he said. He ran his hands through his hair, closing his eyes briefly, and I fought the urge to reach across the table and take his hands in mine, as I would have done when we loved each other. "I saw you when I first got the job. You were with someone else, and you looked happy. I didn't want to bother you."

"He's just a friend."

"Come on, Cricket," he said. "You're more than friends. I saw you with him again on Friday night. I never made you smile like that."

"You weren't looking hard enough. I loved—"

"Look who I found!" Charles' voice called from across the balcony, stopping our conversation in its tracks. My insides froze when I saw that woman, the same leggy blonde from the other night, grinning wide, her eyes on Sonny as they approached our table. Up close, she was even more beautiful than I remembered. Worse, she was wearing a pencil skirt with a blazer, similar to the one I passed up, and she looked sexy as hell. I suddenly felt like I was wearing my grandmother's muumuu.

The leggy blonde reached us and leaned down to give Sonny a quick peck on the cheek before turning to me and holding out her hand.

"Cricket! Charles raved about you so much at this morning's sales meeting, we had a hard time keeping on track. That was some party you put together Friday night. You're quite talented, isn't she, Sonny?"

"It was noth… Thank you," I said, deciding midstream to not make myself feel any lower by offering modesty. She had the guy. The least I deserved was praise. I took in her high cheekbones, enhanced by perfect contouring under her deep blue eyes. It made me think of the way Mr. Finnigan's wife chased off that other girl to stake her claim on the man she wanted.

No. I did not want Sonny.

"And that man you were with!" Justine continued. "A couple of our interns were gushing over him this morning. Good thing he has you to keep him out of trouble, am I right?"

I smiled weakly. She was being so familiar with me, as if we were already the best of friends. Meanwhile, I couldn't stop noticing how she touched everyone around her while she talked. First Charles. Then me. Then Sonny, where her hand lingered for what seemed an eternity.

"This is Justine," Sonny said when she paused long enough for him to cut in.

"Oh, sorry! I was moving too fast. I do that sometimes. I've had three espressos so far today, and I'm afraid I'm a little wired. Charles, I'll probably have this year's harvest sold out by the time you get back to the office."

"That's my girl," Charles said with a laugh. "Justine is the head of our sales department, and the one responsible for bringing Sonny to our team."

"Oh stop," she said, her damn hand going back to Sonny's shoulder. "I just let him know about the job opening. He took care of the rest." She smiled at Sonny, who beamed back at her before turning to me. Something on my face must have revealed what I was feeling, because his smile faded and he cleared his throat.

"I need to be going," Justine said, oblivious to the shift between us. She hugged Charles, then squeezed Sonny's shoulder, beaming down at him. "I'll see you soon." She kept her hand on Sonny's shoulder as she reached over and took my hand again. So much touching. I kept my hand limp in hers. "This is the busiest time of the year. I'm just glad Charles took all our advice to go away and let us handle everything. And this party! You're going to be brilliant, Cricket. Oops, there I go again. I better leave so I won't talk your ear off!"

She left, taking my energy with her. I felt completely drained. I wasn't sure if it was Justine, this meeting, or the sparkling wine, but there was nowhere I wanted to be more than in bed, under the covers with a book so I could pretend the rest of the world didn't exist. Was this a precursor to how things were going to go?

To make it worse, the servers had already cleared the table, including the salt and pepper grinders. It wasn't like I wanted them as a keepsake to this weird and awful meeting with Sonny. They were too big and bulky to snag, anyway.

No. I *wanted* them. My head hurt, I felt stuffed after that huge meal, and my ego was flat as a pancake after being around beautiful, sunshiney Justine. I wondered if they lived together. Did she make him a home-cooked meal every morning? Or maybe they were too wrapped up in each other to worry about breakfast. With Justine around, he probably never thought of me at all. Hell, he'd been the one to leave. He probably wouldn't think of me, with or without her.

I kept a smile plastered on my face as we left the restaurant, though the mahogany salt and pepper grinders on every table we passed called out to me like sirens at sea.

"Now that we've met, I feel even better about leaving this party in both of your hands," Charles said when we reached our cars. I still felt something tugging at me inside, pulling me toward the restaurant, and I hugged my arms around my body as if it would keep me stationary. "I'm not taking any calls, but I'm available by email if you need me," he continued.

"We won't need you," Sonny promised, then looked at me. "We have everything under control. Just go and have a wonderful time."

"I will," Charles conceded. "I can't thank you enough."

"No, thank *you*," I said. "For everything. We'll make sure you come home to the celebration of your dreams."

Charles clasped his hand in mine, thanking me again before saying goodbye. He was already entering his car when I turned to Sonny, my eyes looking everywhere but in his.

"I guess I'll see you," I said. "You can just contact my assistant to set up our next meeting. I believe you have your information, right?"

"Wait," Sonny said, rummaging through his shirt pocket before producing a cardholder. "Do you have a pen?"

I dug deep into my hippie bag, searching by feel until I grasped a pen. His fingers brushed mine as I handed it to him, and I inhaled quickly at the jolt of electricity that flowed from his fingers to mine.

Did he notice? His expression gave nothing away. He scribbled something on the back of his business card, and I glanced at the restaurant to keep from watching him. I kept thinking of the shakers. If I stayed in my car long enough, could I make it back inside The Bird House after Sonny and Charles left? Could I snag a pair on my way to the bathroom?

I felt a tug at my shoulder, and I turned as Sonny dropped something in my bag that felt a lot heavier than a business card. I started to look, but he stopped me with a hand on my arm.

"Wait until we leave," he said. He left his hand there for a moment, and I looked into his eyes. My breath caught at the sudden jolt inside me.

He's not yours anymore.

"Goodbye, Cricket," he said.

This wasn't a forever goodbye, but it reminded me of the time when it *was* and I jerked my arm away. *Silly girl,* I scolded myself.

"Goodbye," I said aloud, then forced myself to turn without watching him walk away. The car hog was gone, so at least I didn't have to embarrass myself by climbing through the passenger side again. I unlocked my door and got in, waving as Charles pulled back, both of them waving back at me. The salt and pepper grinders were calling to me, and I was ready to head back to the restaurant. But first, whatever he slipped in my bag. I slid my hand in, my fingertips touching the familiar slope of one object, and then the identical wooden surface of its twin.

"Damn you, Sonny," I swore as I pulled the grinders out of my bag. None of my salt and pepper shakers was this fancy; these were probably worth $50 apiece. But it wasn't about their retail value; it was about the way I felt when I took them. And holding these grinders in my hands, I felt like shit. Not only had Sonny rejected me when he chose Wisconsin over me, but he didn't tell me he was back. He moved on with some other woman who was way more beautiful than me. Then, to top it all off, he let me know how stupid this whole shaker stealing thing was by doing it for me. I *knew* it was stupid. But he knew this giant secret about me and why I did it and was probably laughing at me behind my back.

I reached back in my bag and found the business card. Sonny's familiar writing met me, somewhere between a doctor's calligraphy and a shopping list. He had never been one for penmanship, but over the years I'd learn to decipher it. This one, I had to read three times.

I didn't mean to leave such a long voicemail, but I meant what I said.

Damn.

Chapter Six

My head hurt when I pulled into my driveway, and it had nothing to do with the champagne from lunch. I'd spent the whole ride home gripping the steering wheel, jaw clenched, hard exhales through my nose as I silently cursed Sonny's name. But underneath it all was that familiar feeling of hurt, mixed with a healthy dose of longing.

Sonny looked good. Too good. And Justine showing up at the end of lunch was like a knife twist in the gut. I couldn't get her face out of my head, or the way her hand practically mauled Sonny's bicep right in front of me, or how she smiled at me as if we were friends. The more I thought about it, the more I was sure she knew about my past with Sonny. She probably showed up on purpose, just to lay her claim.

As if I wanted him back.

As soon as I opened the door, all I could hear was that damn bird squawking. I almost forgot it was there, and it did nothing for my aching head.

"I'm coming!" I yelled above its squawks, opening the door to the bird room (formerly the living room). The macaw was flapping its wings at the window, banging against it while squawking as if trying to escape. I'd finished clearing the room that morning, including the couch it had started to tear, so there wasn't much left to destroy. Or so I thought. A portion of the doorframe had been chipped away, and a corner of the room was covered in poop. The newspaper I'd spread was in shreds across the floor.

"Well, thank you for keeping your toilet contained to one side of the living room," I said as I gathered the newspaper into a pile, and then took a damp cloth to the droppings. The bird squawked at me in response. It fluttered near me, and I instinctively threw my arms up to protect myself. It kept its distance but paced the room with its eye trained on me as if it were as scared of me as I was of it. It seemed more feathers were missing from its chest, and I felt terrible despite my resolve not to care about this bird.

I'd texted Meadow before my lunch with Sonny, but hours later the text was still unread. She was probably traveling, but I was stuck with this bird and would have liked a little more information. Something…anything would be nice.

I checked her Instagram for clues to what she was up to, but it hadn't been updated since two days ago. My mouth went dry. Meadow may not have been great about communication by phone or text, but her Instagram was her Holy Grail. She updated her feed at least once a day, if not more. Maybe it really was a travel day.

In the meantime, something had to be done about this bird. I'd read online that macaws craved attention, and I'd kept it cooped up all day long, so I decided to set up camp in the bird room so I could bond with the obnoxious macaw.

This consisted of me reading a book, and the bird trying to eat the pages.

"Get out of here. Shoo," I said, then felt dumb because I was pushing the bird away when we were supposed to be getting to know each other. "Do you need something to do?" I felt around in my bag for something that might resemble a toy, and my hands landed on the grinders.

I hadn't forgotten about them. Quite the opposite. It was like they were calling to me, taunting me from the bag. As soon as my fingers brushed over the smooth wood of one of the grinders, a jolt of shame rushed through me, followed by a fiery thread of anger.

My hands grasped both grinders at once and I pulled them out. All my jealous thoughts about Justine evaporated and Sonny's lopsided grin took her place. I released an involuntary sigh. Running my fingers along the curved edge of the salt grinder, I recalled the delicious way Sonny smelled when he stood close to me, and how I felt the warmth of his hand near my back as we left the restaurant, even though he wasn't touching me.

And then, I flashed back to the way he smiled at Justine. He made his choice when he left me the first time, and I wasn't it.

"I'm not doing this again," I told the grinders, as if they'd deliver the message for me. For a moment, I considered quitting the Finnigan event. The thought of working this closely with Sonny was akin to torture. Every day I would have to face the reality that I wasn't enough for him, and that he'd moved on so easily while I was still picking up fragments of my broken heart.

But I couldn't quit. If I did, he'd win all over again. He'd already upended my whole world by making me fall in love with him, making me comfortable in everything we had, and then abandoning me as if I meant nothing. I couldn't let him take work from me, too. If anyone was to quit, it would be him, because that's what he was good at. I vowed to stick this out, no matter how much our past relationship haunted me.

I laid the salt and pepper grinders on the ground, my fingers shaking with hesitation, then rolled the vessels across the carpet. The bird stopped pulling at the bottom of my yoga pants and chased after the grinders, pecking

at one so that it rolled again. The parrot was bound to leave chip marks on them. In a way, it felt like I was letting the bird peck away at Sonny. Part of me felt bad. But a larger part felt vindicated. I couldn't help smiling as the macaw attacked a grinder and sent it skittering across the room.

The bird occupied, I went back to my book. That didn't last long, though. My phone pinged and I looked at the text that came through.

Blake: *Want to do shots and watch an action movie?*

Action movies, *blech*. Blake was obsessed with any movie that involved explosions, a secret government plot, and no less than three car chases. Bonus if he got to see tits, too. Every time we hung out, he tried to push his bro movies on me, and every time, I swatted down his efforts.

Me: *If you mean* Moulin Rouge, *yes.*

I grinned, knowing he had no idea how much singing was in the movie.

Blake: *That's the one where Nicole Kidman shows her boobs, right? I'm in.*

Me: *She doesn't show her boobs. We're still watching the movie.*

I waited for a few beats, wondering if this would be the time he fought me on it.

Blake: *Fine, make me dinner. I'm on my way over.*

Grinning, I stood and slid my phone into my pocket. I was still stuffed from lunch and would probably skip dinner, but I left the bird (who offered piercing protests as I shut the door behind me) to check the freezer. There were several chicken enchiladas from Trader Joe's and a pint of Ben & Jerry's Chunky Monkey ice cream. Dinner, done.

Hanging out with Blake on a random weekday night was nothing new, but tonight it would be a welcome distraction. He was exactly the kind of friend I needed on a day like this.

While I waited for him, I lay down in the bird room and closed my eyes, hoping to quiet my mind, all while the bird did its best to deconstruct the salt grinder. I heard the click of the front door when Blake let himself in, and moments later he walked into the living room, pausing at the threshold.

"Uh, Cricket? What is that?" Blake asked, closing the living room door and thunking a bottle of tequila the size of Mexico beside me.

"It's a bird. What is *that*? How many of us are you expecting here?"

"Just you and me, and it's all I had. I was going to pour some in a smaller jar, but I was too lazy. I'm taking it with me when I leave. How did you get a bird?"

"Good question," I said, then explained the special delivery. "I'm still trying to decide whether I keep the thing or not. I guess I'm waiting for Meadow to give me the scoop on why I have it in the first place before I figure out the next steps. It doesn't even have a name."

"It doesn't?" Blake shook his head. "Okay, *that's* what the next step needs to be."

"No, Blake. That's how you get attached to animals. Remember those cows at the fair? They didn't have names because those cute little 4-H kids were putting them up for auction."

"Are you planning to eat the bird?"

"No," I said, rolling my eyes. "But if I end up giving the bird away, I don't want to feel close to it."

"Or, you're just afraid you'll like it so much, you won't want to give it away at all."

"Exactly," I said. He gave me a pointed look, and I sighed deeply. "Fine, we can name the stupid bird."

"Great! I'm thinking it looks like a Vin Diesel."

"No," I said. "Besides, we don't know if it's a boy or a girl. It should be a gender-neutral name."

"Okay," he said slowly, looking up at the ceiling as part of his thinking process. "How about Jenna Jamison?"

"The porn star?" I asked.

"She doesn't do porn anymore. Last I checked, anyway."

"No porn star names," I said. "And no boy or girl names. Think harder."

"I'm too hungry to think," he whined. He uncorked the tequila and poured himself a shot, then one for me.

"If you're hungry, there are enchiladas in the freezer," I said as he tossed back his shot. "Tequila isn't a meal."

"No, it's a palate cleanser," he said, getting to his feet. "Do you want anything?"

"No, help yourself to whatever."

I knocked back my own shot when he left, then mulled over every name I could think of…none of which were gender neutral. I finally gave up, pulling out my phone so I could Google baby names. Right there under the letter "A" was the name Avery. Like *avian*, or *aviary*, which was the kind of enclosure I needed but couldn't afford. The meaning of the name Avery was *elf*, but to me, Avery sounded like the perfect bird name.

"Its name is Avery," I said when Blake came back into the room, shoveling half the enchilada in his mouth with one bite.

"I ike ih," he said, his mouth full. He swallowed hard. "Sorry, I like it." He sat on the floor and leaned against the wall next to me, watching the bird while he ate. Avery pecked the salt grinder again, but then noticed the new person in the room. It abandoned the grinder and came over to Blake, who held his plate out of reach as the bird hopped on his lap.

"This has chicken, Avery bird. You don't want it."

"It's probably hungry; I haven't given it dinner yet." Both of us stood, and the bird followed us to the door. "Shoo," I said, nudging it aside and then quickly slipping out, Blake close behind. Avery complained loudly when I shut the door, and I heard it pecking against the door.

"Is it not allowed outside the room?" Blake asked.

"Well, it's already destroyed part of that room. I don't want it to wreck the rest of the house."

I chopped up some broccoli, red bell pepper, and apple, placing them over the pellets. When I returned to the bird room, Avery flew to my shoulder as soon as it spotted the food. I flinched but remained calm to avoid spilling the food. I set it on the floor and the bird left me for the bowl, taking out a piece of broccoli and picking at it until tiny florets covered its beak. It seemed happy enough, and this time I left the room without issue.

"Find a place to sit," I said to Blake, gesturing to the multiple couches crowding the family room as I fiddled with the TV wiring. In moving everything from the living room, I'd only gotten as far as setting the TV on top of my father's old desk in the corner. Now I had to figure out where all the wires went.

"Here, let me," Blake said. He shoved the rest of his enchilada in his mouth, then relieved me of my technician duties. Within moments, he was scrolling through Netflix for *Moulin Rouge.* The bird must have finished its dinner because it was now pecking at the door in between screeching. The opening number started, and Avery only screeched louder, effectively drowning out the singing on screen.

"Are you sure we can't just let him out?" Blake yelled over the noise.

I looked around the room at all the furniture I'd just saved from the bird's destruction. But this was no way to live. Every time the bird screeched, it was like metal on metal, the sound grinding through me. I gritted my teeth, ready to explode.

"It's just furniture, I suppose." I got up, hesitating at the door before finally opening it. Avery hopped forward, peering up at me when it reached my ankles. I moved back to the couch, and the bird hopped after me.

"I think he likes you," Blake said, laughing. "He must not know you don't like him."

"Or her," I corrected. "And I like it fine, I just don't know what to do with it, or how to keep my stuff safe besides shutting the damn bird in the room."

I sat beside Blake, and Avery fluttered to the back of the couch, settling between us. Blake had paused the movie, and he turned to stroke the bird's long feathers. Avery nuzzled into it, turning to give Blake a better angle.

"Looks like someone likes to be loved," he said. "Here, you do it."

I shook my head, watching the two of them instead. I kept waiting for the bird to bite Blake, but it only seemed to be enjoying the attention. My hand shook as I lifted it, and I drew back when the bird noticed my approach.

"Keep going," Blake said, taking his hand away so I could try. I held my breath as I touched the back of the bird. It made a clicking noise in its throat as it moved closer to me, and it took everything in me to not flinch. I petted it gently, noting how soft its feathers were, and how it seemed to relax under my hand. I relaxed, too, applying more pressure as if this were as normal as petting a cat. I felt a tinge of warmth grow inside me, a tug at my heartstrings as I studied the bird and its exotic beauty.

"Crap," I said, glancing at Blake. "I think I'm going to fall in love with this damn thing."

Avery eventually found its home on my shoulder, and this time I didn't push the bird away. It fell asleep as we watched the rest of the movie, and when it was over, neither of us moved so we wouldn't disturb it.

"I finally talked to that girl at the gym," Blake said in a hushed voice. I covered my mouth, eyes wide, trying not to laugh too hard. For all the ways Blake was cocky around women, he'd been hung up on how to approach this girl for weeks. I'd never known him to be this shy about a girl.

"So, how'd it go? Is she having your babies yet?"

"Not yet," he said, shooting me a mock glare. "But I learned her name is Sadie and she just moved here a few months ago. She's a hairstylist at The Lion's Mane and taking classes at the community college. She went to beauty school, but now she wants to be an astronomer."

"Dang, you guys must have talked forever to learn all that."

"Yeah," he said, then sighed, a faraway look crossing his face. "I think I'm going to ask her out. Maybe I'll take her to that place you were always talking about. What's it called again?"

"Ricardo's," I said, immediately brought back to my first date with Sonny. Before he took me, I'd never eaten there, despite having lived in Petaluma all my life. He'd only lived in town a short while, but he swore they made the best fish tacos he'd ever had. That was saying a lot, since the only other way he ate fish was something called Fish Supper, which was basically a Scottish form of fish and chips. But Ricardo's fish tacos, he said, were unforgettable. And they were. And so was he. I started falling for him over that meal, though the two margaritas helped diminish my inhibitions. And throughout our relationship, Ricardo's became ours.

"Wait, you can't," I said, realization slamming into me like a Scottish gale. "If you go there, Sonny will see you." I told him about today's business lunch, and how surprised I'd been to learn I'd be working with him.

"Remember I told you he was talking to that wine guy? I knew something was up," Blake said. "So, we're keeping this…" He gestured to both of us, "…going, huh?"

"Do I have a choice? Don't answer that," I said when he opened his mouth. "I know I have a choice, but if he finds out now, he's going to think I'm so stupid. Plus, it will wreck my credibility with Mr. Finnigan. I have to keep this going." I sighed, stroking the tail feathers of my sleeping bird. Avery moved under my hand but kept his eyes closed. Or hers. He seemed more like a boy bird, whatever that meant.

As for this situation, I knew I'd dug myself into the deepest hole. The moment I saw Sonny with that other woman, I should have just turned and left. That would have been the smartest thing to do. Sure, I would have missed out on this huge job with Mr. Finnigan, but I also wouldn't have to work with Sonny. It could have been the last time I saw him.

"His girlfriend showed up today at the restaurant," I said, turning to Blake. "She's even more beautiful up close. She's the one who got Sonny the job with Mr. Finnigan, and she seemed just as friendly with him at the restaurant as she was the other night."

"Like how?"

I thought about it for a moment. They didn't kiss or anything, but their boss was right there. The way they looked at each other, though…how her hand lingered on his arm, the unspoken words that seemed to flow between them…

"Have you ever been with someone where you didn't need to say anything to have a conversation?"

"Can't say that I have," Blake said.

Sonny and I did, though. Most nights we stayed up late just sharing ideas and dreams with each other. But then there were the times when silence wrapped around us, and all he'd have to do was look at me and a whole novel of thoughts seemed to flow from his mind to mine. And then he'd smile, and I'd know I wasn't crazy.

"They had a comfortable cadence between them," I said. "You know how new relationships tend to be hot and exciting, where you can't get enough of each other? This was like they'd just gotten beyond that and were now at the part where they could be themselves. At least, that's what I gathered."

"And you got all that from having lunch with her?" He raised an eyebrow as he waited for my answer, and I rolled my eyes.

"I didn't have lunch with her," I said. "She stopped by our table for a few minutes."

"Now I really have questions."

"You weren't there," I said. "You didn't see. She'd leave her hand on Sonny's shoulder longer than necessary, and he was the last one she looked at when she left. I'm telling you, she loves him, and he loves her back. And if I'm going to work with him, I have to pretend you and I have that same kind of relationship. If he sees you with some other woman, it will ruin everything."

"Fine," he laughed. "If I can get the nerve up to even ask Sadie out, I'll take her somewhere out of town."

"You're really into her," I said, getting up carefully with Avery resting on my arm. I took him into the bird room and perched him on the branch near the window. "I've never seen you like this," I continued as I closed the door behind me.

"I've never felt like this," he said. "It's all so weird and new, and I barely know her. But there's something about her that's special. Different." He caught himself, taking my hand. "Not that we weren't special, or anything."

I took my hand away, laughing. "Blake, come on. You were my rebound, and I was your opportunity. You don't need to pretend it was any deeper than that."

"You had to admit we had fun," he said, winking at me. I smacked his arm.

"I think we make better friends."

Chapter Seven

I was in the garden when Sonny's white Ford truck pulled into the driveway. It felt like ages since I'd seen it, even longer since I'd sat inside the cab, and now his truck was in front of me like old times. I had to catch my breath as the past broadsided me, along with a flood of feelings I'd been swimming against since Sonny returned. Then I looked down at the hose in my hands and the ratty clothes I was wearing.

Taye and I had been in meetings all morning with vendors. Needing a break, I'd changed into my oldest pair of jeans, a tank top, and a blue plaid flannel shirt, and spent the last hour pulling weeds and picking ripe tomatoes and squash. My mascara was probably washed away by sweat, and my hair was falling out of a top knot. If he'd shown up an hour ago, I would have looked halfway cute. Now, I looked like I'd been rolling around in the mud. Of course he showed up now. And why? We weren't supposed to meet until Wednesday, and I'd assumed it would be at his office.

"I'm not ready for this," I muttered to the bees, setting down the hose and trying my best to smooth my hair.

Sonny gave a silent wave as he stepped out of the cab. I didn't know how to act. Cold? Indifferent? Politely cold and indifferent? Before I could figure it out, Buoy jumped out of the truck, a blur of reddish blonde fur as he raced in my direction. I dropped to my knees as the golden retriever reached me. He jumped around, his tail wagging against all my tomatoes as he soaked up my love.

"Hey boy! I missed you!" I buried my face in his fur, overwhelmed by an unexpected wave of emotion as he settled down and leaned into me, panting heavily with his tail still thumping. I heard Sonny's footsteps, but I couldn't look at him, completely embarrassed at how I was crying over a dog. Okay, it wasn't just the dog. But Buoy's sun-warmed fur was the missing ingredient to every emotion I'd experienced since Sonny showed up again. Besides, no one does therapy like a dog.

"He missed you, too," Sonny said.

Why did his voice affect me so much? His accent rolled through me, and my ears burned as my tears increased. I desperately needed to sniff, but I didn't want Sonny to know how emotional I was being. About a dog. About him. So I focused on petting Buoy until I finally felt in control of myself.

As I discreetly swiped at my eyes, Sonny patted Buoy's head as if he didn't notice, but I knew his tells. The way he avoided my face, looked everywhere but at me while I pulled myself together. He definitely noticed. I didn't want to give him any kind of credit, but I knew he was letting me have my moment. I was the kind of person who teared up at dog food commercials. If someone showed me sympathy, forget it. Sometimes it was necessary. Sometimes I needed that sympathy so I could feel my emotions honestly. But right now, being around Sonny, the last thing I wanted was to collapse into a vulnerable pile of mush.

Did he know he had this effect on me? Did I want him to? I wasn't sure about either. At least he knew to ignore the tears, even if we both were pretending it was about the dog.

"Why are you here?" I asked once my nose was properly wiped on the sleeve of my flannel. He nodded toward the truck.

"The wine," he said. "It seemed silly to have it delivered when I could just bring it over." He peered around me toward the house. "Unless this is a bad time." He looked uncomfortable, glancing at Taye's bright orange Jeep parked next to the Honda. I bit my lip, realizing he thought the poppy-colored car belonged to Blake.

"It's fine," I said, waving my hand without correcting his assumption. "We were just finishing up some things in the house and I took a break to tend to the garden."

"It looks nice," he said. "I think there are more plants than the last time I was here. I mean…" He trailed off, leaving me with the memory of him getting the last of his things before he left for Wisconsin, leaving California for what was supposed to be forever.

"I added another row of planter boxes and cleared out the side yard for more lavender and sunflowers." Why was I telling him all this? It wasn't like he cared.

"Are you still donating to Have a Heart?" he asked. And just like that, I couldn't hide the smile. He remembered.

Have a Heart was a nonprofit that benefited low-income single mothers, raising money through donated produce they sold at the Farmers Market at a booth manned by volunteers and clients. It was a program close to my mother's heart, having been raised by a single mother in a time when women's rights were limited. My grandmother managed to raise three kids without a man when she couldn't even have a credit card in her name. When my mom planted the front yard garden, she reserved most of the produce for this program, dedicating her efforts to the memory of her mother's resilience and strength.

Now I continued the tradition. Supporting Have a Heart made the garden meaningful, but it also kept my mother close. It made me even more proud to be part of this lineage of strong women.

Sonny and I stood there for a moment, words escaping us as we alternated petting Buoy, who was happily soaking up the attention. My hand accidentally brushed Sonny's a few times, sending electric shocks through my fingers and straight to my heart. The awkward silence grew between us, seeming louder than the bees happily humming as they flirted with the lavender blossoms. There was a time I knew everything he was thinking just by catching his eye. Now, I couldn't read him. I mustered the courage to take a peek at him. I thought I saw something familiar reflected in his eyes, but I couldn't trust it. My emotions were too strong to have any idea what he was feeling.

"Thanks for bringing the wine," I said, relieving the mounting pressure of silence.

"Right. Let me grab it."

Buoy and I watched Sonny walk away, and I felt a little ego boost when the dog chose to stay by me instead of running after him. It was the little things. And then there was Sonny lifting a heavy case of wine in his arms. Even under his t-shirt I could see the bulge in his muscles, and holy hell. I swallowed hard, looking away as I tried to catch my shallow breath. Three weeks of this. Could I handle it?

"Where should I put these?" he asked, passing by me on his way to the front door.

"On the porch is fine," I said, not ready to reveal it was Taye inside instead of Blake, but mostly because Avery was loose under Taye's watchful eye.

The bird had been doing better ever since I opened up the rest of the house to him. As long as we watched him, he didn't destroy anything. It had only been a few days, but I was already feeling settled with the bird. Still, I couldn't wait to save enough money to put an enclosure together for him. Any income left over from the Finnigan event could cover it, or at least come close.

Sonny set the case on the porch, then trotted back to the truck for another. At the same time, Taye opened the door a crack.

"Hey, I need to leave for class. Should I leave the bird out?"

"No, I—" I didn't have a chance to finish the thought. Buoy noticed the open door and bolted up the steps, pushing his way in before either of us could stop him. "The bird!" Taye and I raced after him, my heart thumping as I heard Avery screeching while Buoy barked. I'd only seen Buoy around other dogs, so I had no idea how he'd react to a bird. He was a good dog, but what of his instincts?

Both dog and bird were now in the bird room. Avery clung to a large branch leaning against the wall, and Buoy crouched down on his front paws, his butt wagging wildly in the air as he yipped at the bird. The bird flew across the room, and Buoy yelped, jumping up as if to try and catch it. If I weren't so freaked out for the bird's safety I'd find humor in Buoy's grin, or how his tail wildly swept the air. I managed to grab the dog's collar, relieved that he didn't pull against it, as Taye tried to coax the bird to calm down. Buoy's tail never let up, wagging as he whined softly.

"What's going on?" Sonny called, running into the room. He took one look at the bird in the corner, and then took Buoy so I could help Taye with Avery. I managed to get Avery on my arm, but the bird flapped with fervent wings as I held him far from my face.

"When did you get a bird?" Sonny asked, backing out of the room while Buoy tried to stay in. He tugged the dog out, then closed the door, trapping us in the room with the squawking bird.

"Saturday," I yelled over the bird's noise. "You know how Meadow is always sending me strange gifts from her Instagram sponsors? This time, it was a macaw."

He stared at the bird as Taye retrieved Avery from the floor. The bird thankfully quieted down as Taye smoothed his feathers, clicking her tongue at him.

"You're going to have to learn how to do this, you know," Taye said, then shifted her eyes toward Sonny in a pointed way, as if asking, *is that him?*

"I was getting to it," I huffed, ignoring her unspoken question. "Sonny, this is Taye, my assistant. Taye, this is Sonny, er, Edison McIntyre, my... uh... Mr. Finnigan's Marketing Director. He was just dropping off some wine."

Taye's eyebrow raised as she looked from me to him, and then back at me. "Mm-hm," she said, her mouth twisting into a secret smile. *Shut up*, I mouthed to her, and she broke into a full grin. "Wonderful to meet you, Sonny. It's so nice that you make house calls."

"Weren't you saying you have class?" I asked, giving her the same pointed look she'd just thrown my way.

"Crap." Taye dropped the smile and raced to the door. Buoy was on the other side, and she nudged him with her knee as she made her escape. "I'll call you later," she said as she closed the door, and I knew it would have nothing to do with work and everything to do with Sonny.

And then Sonny and I were alone. With Avery, that is.

"So, a bird, huh?" Sonny said slowly, then came in close to get a better look. Avery had calmed down but turned his head to keep Sonny in his view. "You gave it the living room? You must really like it."

"I didn't have much choice," I said. "Meadow sprung this on me without warning, and the cage she sent with him was more for a parakeet than a macaw. A cage big enough for a bird like this costs more than I can afford, and I don't know how to build one, so for now he gets the living room."

Sonny took in the broken doorframe, the wooden branches scratching the walls, and then, to my embarrassment, the salt and pepper grinders, lying among leftover lettuce and carrots with beak marks carved into the wood. These he picked up, brushing them off before setting them on the ledge of the windowsill. Avery flew from my arm, crashing into the window before falling to the ground. Unbothered, he got to his feet and retrieved the grinders, knocking them on the floor before pecking at them.

"Bird toys, eh?" Sonny gave me a lopsided grin, the kind that usually made me melt. Not this time, though. This time, I *knew* he was mocking me.

"Just stop." I glared at him, then turned for the door. Buoy was waiting on the other side, his mouth in a grin as he panted. I moved him aside with my knee on my way out, Sonny behind me as he closed the door. His casually close presence only made it worse. I whirled around, my hands in fists at my side while I felt ready to erupt. "You have no right," I hissed at him. "I told you about the stupid shakers when I thought I meant something to you. You don't get to talk about them, ever. I wish I'd never told you anything." I swiped at the hot tears filling my eyes, hating that my natural impulse was to cry whenever I felt a strong emotion. I wasn't sad. I was furious!

"They're not stupid," he said, touching my arm. I jerked out of his reach, and he stuffed his hands in his pockets as if proving he'd keep his distance. All it did was add fuel to my confused feelings, even under my anger. "And you always meant something to me," he continued. "You still do."

"Right. That's why you left for Wisconsin without me."

"I asked you to come!"

"You knew I couldn't leave!"

Sonny ran his hand through his hair, leaving his dark curls in an array on top of his head. His eyes were like coal under his frustration. "Couldn't?" he asked. "Or *wouldn't?*"

I opened my mouth, but it was like my reasons withered in the air. How could I make him understand? I'd tried before, but I could never put words to it. How could he expect me to leave this home, the only one I'd ever known, and travel all the way to Eau Claire? I'd considered it when he first broached the subject. Just the thought of being without him felt almost like suffocating. But then, I thought about what it would be like to leave my mother's garden, my father's armchair, their tree branch bed, and all the smells and sounds I associated with home that made this place my safety net. That car crash had already taken my parents. I couldn't lose our home, too.

I thought Sonny would let the job go when I told him I was staying. I thought he'd understand all the things I couldn't form into words, that he would look at me and know why I couldn't leave and choose me instead. In the end, Wisconsin won.

"You knew what would happen if you left," I said, turning away so he couldn't see the tears that were now free-falling down my cheeks. "You knew we couldn't survive the distance."

"I didn't know, Cricket, or I never would have left."

"You never *should* have left! You asked me to give up everything for you, yet you weren't willing to do the same for me!" I sniffed loudly, and Buoy pressed himself against my leg as if to comfort me. I was still angry, but something about the dog's worried stance made me laugh, even as I was crying. I wiped my nose on my sleeve and finally turned around, no longer caring that I probably looked like a hot mess. I'd never been a pretty crier. "Well, it's too late now. What's done is done, and we've obviously moved on."

"Obviously," he said. There was resentment to his tone, enough that I looked quickly at him. He shook his head, waving his hand as if waving the words away. "Look, I *didnae* come here to make you cry. This was supposed to be a happy trip. I even brought Buoy to help me out here, and then he had to go mess everything up. I'm sorry he stressed out your bird."

"Avery," I said, sniffing. He broke into a grin, and I could read how funny he thought it was that I had named this weird pet Meadow had given me. I offered a weak laugh—a peace treaty. "And that bird is more resilient than you think. Truth is, he probably loved the attention. He's a little lonely, and I'm trying to work on how we both can be happy in the same home."

"I could help you," Sonny said, then nodded at the couches that surrounded us. "You need your house back, and I *ken*, I mean, I *know* how to use a hammer. I could build an inside enclosure in there so you can use your living room again."

"It's okay," I said, then gestured towards the window. "What he really needs is an outside aviary for days like this. He seems to love watching the birds outside, and he'd probably be happier out there."

"I can do that, too."

I sighed, ready to give my excuses.

"Let me do it," he continued, stopping me before I could speak. "I want to help. I know how special this home is to you, and I know it bothers you to have to rearrange the whole house around this bird. It won't take long, and I'll probably be done by the time we celebrate Charlie's anniversary."

I stroked Buoy's head, wanting so badly to say yes, just to have him nearby. Of course, that was also why I needed to say no. This was a terrible idea. It would only end in heartache. If I agreed, I was setting myself up for disaster.

"Okay," I said.

That evening, long after Sonny had left with Buoy, I sat at the dining room table with a glass of Camille Brut Rosé. Avery kept me company, nipping at the mahogany salt and pepper grinders I'd set in the center of the table. He still believed they were toys, and I didn't correct him. I swirled the glass of sparkling wine, watching the string of bubbles float like a pearl necklace to the surface before taking a sip. It tasted as smooth and refreshing as it had at The Bird House.

I took another sip, then startled at the pair of headlights making their way up the drive. It wasn't late, but the only people who came by were Taye or Blake and they always texted first. Maybe it was Sonny? As the lights got closer, I could tell it wasn't a truck, but a sedan.

The car stopped at the top of the driveway. I stood at the window, watching as a figure stepped out of the backseat, followed by a suitcase. It was dark, and the person's shape was nothing but a silhouette, but I'd know her anywhere.

I abandoned my glass of champagne on the counter and ran from the house, skipping steps to the pathway before throwing myself at her.

"Meadow," I breathed. She shrank, then wrapped an arm loosely around my back. We held each other for several moments as I inhaled the familiar and strange scents that surrounded my traveling sister. When I could finally bring myself to let go, I held her at arm's length and grinned. My smile faded when I got a good look at her. Even in the shadows, I could see the unmistakable cuts and bruises that lined her face. I stepped back and noticed her arm wrapped in some sort of brace, her leg in a cast. Her crutches lay on the ground beside her.

"It looks worse than it is," she said.

Chapter Eight

"What the hell happened to you?" I asked once we were inside. Meadow helped herself to a glass of the brut rosé, sipping as if she were on holiday and not sitting in our family home, looking like she'd lost a fight.

"It's nothing. I had a bad accident. Did you know how good Sweden's healthcare system is?"

"Bad accident?" I peered at her face, at the yellowing ring around her eye. "Like falling into someone's fist? Come on, Meadow, I'm not stupid. Was it a guy? Oh jeez, it was a guy, wasn't it? Was it that guy you went to the party with?"

"August?" she asked. "Nah, he's one of the good guys." She took another sip of wine, then tapped on the table. Avery came running and nuzzled under her hand. I'd never seen the bird so responsive.

"If he's one of the good guys, then who's the bad guy?"

She sighed, then finished off the rest of her wine and set the glass on the counter behind her. "It's nothing, okay? I had a bad accident and got a little scraped up.

I'm exhausted, and it's been a long day. Can we talk about it in the morning?"

I gritted my teeth, wanting to press her further. I didn't believe her for a second. But underneath her bruises, she really did look drained. I agreed with a reluctant nod. I put Avery to bed in the bird room, then grabbed Meadow's bags and led her down the hall to our parents' room. I hated to disturb the room, but there was no place else for her to go without preparation. Her old bedroom was now my office, and the couch was surrounded by so many obstacles she'd never get through on crutches.

While Meadow freshened up in the bathroom, I did a quick dust job of the canopy of branches over the bed, then changed the sheets. By the time she came out, I had the bed turned down and the room was bathed in the soft glow of our mother's antique lamp on the side dresser. I closed the heavy curtains to the sliding door that led to the back garden as she got in bed and turned on her side.

"Goodnight," I whispered, walking softly to the door.

"Wait. Can you stay a moment?" She popped her head up, pulling the covers aside next to her.

I hesitated, glancing around the room, my parents all around us. My dad's golf bag leaned against the tall dresser that still held all his clothes. A fainting couch was positioned next to their closet, which had been used more for holding my mother's craft projects than for actual sitting. A few unfinished projects still covered the floral fabric. A stack of books lay in a pile on my father's side table, including one with a bookmark in it. *Numbered*, by some author I'd never heard of. Whenever I came in this room to dust, I always paused at that book, wistful at how he'd never know the ending.

And then there was my father's side of the bed, which Meadow patted, waiting for me to get in. Tentatively, I slipped between the sheets, inhaling my parents' earthy scent that still existed under the fresh smell of laundry detergent. I laid my head where my father used to lay his, and amid my hesitation, the comfort enveloped me like a hug.

Meadow turned over, an awkward maneuver as she positioned her casted arm between us. Her leg brace lay against my mother's dresser, and I made special pains to avoid her injured limbs as I moved to give her more room. She took my hand, and I brought my other one into the fold. It was just like when we were young, when she used to slip out of her bed and into mine, our hands together while we whispered secrets into the night.

"Do you remember when Dad built this bed?" she whispered now. I squeezed her good hand, thinking back so many years ago when they brought the outside world into our home. We were just kids, and the tree bed seemed like something out of a fairytale. My dad was always tinkering on projects in the shed, but I'd never paid much attention until he carried the bundled branches into the house, putting the bed together in the bedroom. When he was done, the four of us lay on the bed and looked up. I felt like a forest fairy as my eyes traveled over the entwined limbs, the feathers and charms he'd woven between the branches, and a small doorless birdcage hanging from the canopy.

"It was like he grew a tree right here in the bedroom," I said. The bed shook with her laugh.

"No bed has ever been good enough after this one," Meadow said. "For as long as I live, I'll never have a bed as wonderful as the tree bed."

I'd only meant to stay until Meadow fell asleep, but when I opened my eyes again, the first rays of morning were shining through the gap between the curtains. Meadow was still sleeping, and when I peeked at the clock on her side of the bed, I saw it was just before seven—later than I usually woke up.

I slid out of bed slowly, taking care to not rustle the covers. It had been a long time since I'd shared a bed with anyone, so I was impressed I actually slept the whole night through. The canopy branches shuddered as my weight left the mattress, and I held my breath, letting it out only when Meadow stayed still.

Avery was squawking up a storm as I stepped into the hallway, so loud I was amazed we didn't hear him from the room. Like clockwork, and I was late.

"All right, all right," I murmured as I padded down the hall. I opened the door to the bird room slowly, and Avery hopped forward. Leaning down, I picked him up and placed him on my shoulder. "You're so persistent," I crooned, stroking his head as he nuzzled against my cheek. I knew I still had a lot to learn about his quirks and preferences, but I was no longer nervous around him. His signals were getting easier to understand, like how he'd stare something down when he was uneasy, or the way he flapped his wings to make himself seem bigger. Even when Buoy chased after him yesterday, I had a sense he was more intrigued by the dog than scared.

While the coffee brewed, I cut some bell pepper, carrots, and apple, then offered Avery a piece. He brushed my face with excited wings, and I laughed as I helped him to the ground. His bowl of veggies and pellets came next, and he busied himself picking out the apple chunks first. One more thing I learned about him—apples were his favorite so far.

The coffee was halfway done, and I poured what my dad always referred to as *first fruits*, giving myself the strongest cup of coffee from the pot before cooling it with milk and a healthy teaspoon of sugar. Then, still groggy,

I scrolled through my phone, catching up on email, my appointments for the day, and what was happening on social media. Meadow's feed was still stuck on a few days ago, and some of her commenters were getting curious.

"No new posts? I hope everything is okay. Check me out at…"

"When are you coming back?"

"Nothing new. Boring. Unfollowing."

"Waiting for new photos and adventures."

"Amazing content! We'd love to collab. DM us for the scoop."

What had happened to her? Now that I'd seen her condition, her Instagram hiatus made more sense. But what was she hiding? We never kept secrets from each other, even thousands of miles apart. Even things that felt hard to discuss. But this? Obviously something traumatic had happened.

My hands tightened around my coffee cup as I thought of the guy she'd mentioned. *August.* The last time I'd talked with her, she was just about to go out with him. And then she'd gone silent. Even though she swore it wasn't him, that he was "one of the good guys," I couldn't be sure.

A text came through and I glanced down, my stomach flip-flopping when I saw Sonny's name.

Sonny: *Are you ready for the best tacos in the world?*

Was he talking about today? I hadn't yet checked my schedule, and clicked my calendar just as another thought hit me—what if this text wasn't meant for me? What if it was meant for Justine?

But there it was, an appointment at 12:30 with Sonny. I started to click on it just as another text came in.

Taye: *Sonny just blew up my phone until I answered. That boy is relentless. Can you tell him to wait until normal daylight hours before he starts scheduling his dates with you?*

Me: *Business lunch, not date. We have details to discuss about the Finnigan event.*

Taye: *Right. You're on for 12:30 at Ricardo's. Get the bottomless margarita. Wear the hot black dress, the one that leaves little to the imagination.*

Me: *Business lunch, Taye. Not date.*

Taye: *Whatever.*

My phone rang, and Sonny's face filled my screen. I still hadn't deleted his photos from my phone, and I was both glad and irritated that I hadn't as I stared at his heartbreaking grin and brooding eyes.

Get a hold of yourself, Cricket.

"I heard you've been harassing my assistant," I said instead of hello. He laughed, and the rumble of it made me take a deep breath.

"I only texted her a couple of times. She wasn't answering," he said, and I could hear his smile through the phone.

"It's before work hours. Not everyone is an early riser like you." Avery squawked at my feet, and I laughed. "And Avery," I added in. Phone to my ear, I picked up the food he'd scattered around the kitchen.

"And you," he said, and I had a hard time thinking of what to say to that. We were both early risers. It was one of the many things we had in common. There were mornings we were both awake before the sun, though we stayed in bed with our coffee cups, the newspaper in pieces between us. Some mornings we swept the newspaper to the floor, got back under the covers, and...

"Best tacos, huh? That's the real reason you moved back to California, isn't it?" My cheeks burned, trying to forget the benefit of our early mornings while simultaneously wanting to linger on the memory a little longer.

"You got me," he said. "I left Wisconsin because they don't have tacos."

"Not Ricardo's tacos," I pointed out, to which he laughed again. I realized I was bordering on flirtation, and I cleared my throat. "We're on for 12:30," I said. "I'll meet you there."

"*Cannae* wait."

And then he hung up while I was still pondering the way he said it, his delicious Scottish version of *I can't wait.* It was almost like an invitation, like when he used to call me in the middle of the day just to hear my voice, and to plan out our evening. *Cannae wait,* he'd always say, even though we spent every evening together. He never lived with me, but he might as well have. He had a key, and used it often, sometimes while I was working, sometimes after he'd already left, sometimes just to surprise me awake again with adventurous kisses in mysterious places.

I shook myself out of the daydream, then carried Avery's bowl back into the bird room. He followed me in, and there were no complaints as I closed the door, leaving him secure on the other side. I grabbed a second cup of coffee and headed outside to water the garden before the bees woke up.

Meadow hobbled onto the front porch just as I was finishing. Her coppery bedhead hair hung around her face, and despite the yellowed bruising around her eye, she still looked beautiful. Her skin had more color than mine, probably from last week's jaunt in Brazil. Even though it was autumn, she had posted tons of photos of her lying at the beach wearing one of her skimpy bikinis while drinking a *caipirinha* with lime and mint or a passionfruit *batida* garnished with pineapple. Now she clutched her coffee cup, her crutches beside her as she sipped. Her face took on a look of distaste.

"Problem?" I asked.

"Not strong enough," she said. "I'm probably going to need a few more cups before this kicks in."

I guiltily thought of my *first fruits*, but didn't mention it.

"Did you get any sleep on the plane?" I asked.

"Hardly," she groaned. "This kid kept kicking my seat, and I didn't have enough legroom to wear the brace, so my leg ached the whole time. Plus, this guy next to me thought the armrest was only for him."

After I rolled the hose, I fetched her emptied cup and went inside to pour her a new one. Already jittery, I poured myself a glass of water. Then I joined her on the porch, handing her the coffee while I sat beside her.

"The garden looks beautiful," she said, a faraway look on her face as she took it all in.

I looked out on the yard, seeing what she was seeing—the raised garden beds with leafy green tomato plants spilling over the edge, the sunflowers with their faces turned toward the sunrise, the lavender splaying out in purple sprays, and a few sleepy bees gathering their first dustings of pollen.

"Wait till the fall and winter vegetables get going," I said. I eyed the Brussels sprout plants in the corner next to the traveling leaves of the pumpkins that grew larger by the day.

"You remind me of Mom." She tilted her head sideways, looking at me. "She would have loved this so much. It's hard to not think of both of them here. How do you keep from dwelling on them?"

"I don't," I admitted. "I think of them all the time. They're everywhere. But I like it that way. I feel like Mom is right here with me in the garden every time I come out to water, and Dad is sitting in the backyard pointing out the stars at night while rocking in his chair."

"But doesn't it make you miss them more?"

Yeah, it did. But I didn't mind it. It was like this hole inside me that had become a comfortable part of my being. It was still empty, but I was used to it.

"Sometimes," I said. "But I'd miss them even if I weren't here."

"I couldn't do it," she said, turning back to the garden. "The constant reminder. The fact that one day they were here, carrying on like it was just a normal day. The next, they're gone."

I turned to brush aside the coming tears. As much as I thought of our parents, I actively avoided thinking of the way they died. But now I couldn't push away the memory of the Highway Patrol officer at the doorstep telling us about my father's burning car crushed against a tree, the skid marks on the asphalt, and the deer carcass on the side of the road. For months after their death, I woke up with fevered starts, my body drenched in sweat, my racing mind in that car with my parents as we all burned to death.

Still, I couldn't leave this house. Just like Meadow couldn't stay in it. All of it worked out how it was supposed to.

Except for Sonny, I guess.

"I'm meeting Sonny at Ricardo's," I said, anxious to change the subject. This did the trick, because she whipped her eyes from the garden to me, her mouth open in shock before breaking into a grin.

"Girl, you waited until now to tell me?"

"We're working together on that event, remember? Besides, I just found out about the lunch this morning." Realizing I hadn't talked to her since the last time I met up with Sonny, I filled her in on the initial meeting at The Bird House with Mr. Finnigan and him, including the moment Justine showed up. I left out the part about the salt and pepper grinders. Did I say Meadow and I shared everything? That was one thing she still didn't know about me.

"So, you think it's serious?" she asked.

"Yeah, I could just tell."

"Did he kiss her or anything?"

"No," I said, rolling my eyes. "Their boss was right there. Not to mention, me, his ex-girlfriend. She has to know about me." I frowned. "Maybe." Now that I thought about it, she hadn't seemed to recognize my tie to Sonny. If she didn't know who I was to Sonny, then he hadn't talked about me, which meant only one thing—he wasn't as in love with me as I'd been in love with him. Could I have imagined everything? The thought alone made my breath feel shallow and thin.

"I'm freaking out," I admitted, slouching on the porch step. "He's obviously over me, but everything he does is affecting me. And now we're going to Ricardo's."

"You two loved that place. Wasn't it one of those *our thing* kind of places? Like, Ricardo's was your restaurant, flannel was your outfit of choice—"

"I guess he wore a lot of flannel, too," I interrupted.

"If you guys got married, you'd probably wear coordinating flannel outfits and walk down the aisle to Pearl Jam."

I pretended to smack her but drew back when she flinched. She laughed it off, nudging me with her shoulder, but I felt the hair stand up on the back of my neck at her reaction.

"Your song was..." She paused, looking up as she tried to remember. I could tell she was trying to distract me.

"Pearl Jam's 'Black'," I finished for her, but it was an effort to not let my questions spill out with the answer.

"Gah, I love that song," she said. "Whenever I hear that song, I think of you. Of him, too. But of you, mostly."

"Which is fitting, since the song is about a breakup."

She nudged me, but then rested her head on her good arm draped over her uninjured knee, appearing deep in thought. "You really don't think Sonny is here for you?" she asked.

"Not at all," I said. "He's here because his girlfriend, who isn't me, happens to live and work here, and she got him a job. He couldn't stay in California for me, but for her, he moved back."

"Ouch," she said.

"Seriously." I got up, then helped her stand to her feet. "How about I make you a pancake breakfast just like Mom used to make, and then you can help me decide on what to wear for a very serious, not flirtatious lunch meeting with my ex-boyfriend at a restaurant that's no longer our place."

"I'm thinking low-cut and tight-fitting."

"You and Taye, both."

Chapter Nine

I tried my best to squeeze information out of Meadow over pancakes, but she wouldn't budge.

"So, you had quite the adventure," I said, nodding at Meadow's cast.

"You could say that," was her answer. And then she dug into her pancakes as if that was all I needed to know. Except it wasn't.

"Are you going to tell me what happened?" I asked. I waited for her to finish her bite, but she seemed in no hurry. When she realized I wasn't going to give up, she put her fork down.

"Everything is fine," she said. Her tone was firm, and she looked me in the eyes with intense focus. I wasn't going to get anything else out of her.

"Are you at least safe?" I asked, and her expression lightened, followed by a smile.

"I am now," she said.

I left it at that. She was home, and as long as she stayed, I didn't have to worry about her. I'd save my worrying for when she was ready to leave. Knowing

Meadow, that didn't give me a lot of time, and I wanted to enjoy this small eclipse in our separate lives before she orbited out of my life again.

For now, I had other things to focus on. Like how I let my sister talk me into wearing her clothes—high-waisted white pants that made my pancake ass pop like peaches (her words, not mine), a low-cut top with frill that rested between my breasts, and six-inch heels that placed me at almost eye-level with Sonny. I looked professionally hot, I'd give her that. But as I waited near Ricardo's, I wondered what kind of message I was sending to my ex. That I wanted him? Or was it to give him a taste of what he'd never have again?

Meadow swore it was the latter, but I couldn't help wondering if he'd smell the hint of desperation—especially since I was completely overdressed for fish tacos and, maybe, a margarita. I tugged at the top, then shrugged it back up when I saw how much cleavage I was showing.

"Damn it, Meadow," I muttered, wishing I'd kept on the modest tunic and cropped pants I'd originally planned for this lunch meeting.

Sonny rounded the corner and then halted when he saw me standing in front of the restaurant. He looked me up and down, then met my eyes with something reminiscent of the way he used to look at me. I was glad I listened to my sister.

"I haven't been here since the last time we went," I admitted when he joined me.

"Good," he said, holding the door open for me. "I mean, same. Hopefully they haven't changed a thing."

They hadn't. As soon as we walked in, memories flooded my senses alongside the loud Latin music and aromatic smell of tacos. Our usual table was by the window, and I did my best to ignore the couple already sitting there. I couldn't keep from thinking of the times we'd sat there, holding greasy hands over half-finished plates while laughing. Always laughing.

Where did it go wrong?

I diverted my attention to the art covering the walls as we moved between tables in the crowded restaurant. My favorite mural was the Mariachi singer serenading the slightly bored woman in a peasant blouse. I used to joke to Sonny that was me while he sang in the shower. Except I loved when he sang in the shower, how his deep baritone voice echoed off the tiles, warming every single part of my body. Every. Single. Part.

We reached our table, and this time when Sonny pulled the chair out for me, I let him. I sat down, spreading my napkin on my lap immediately. White pants were a magnet for spills, and my clumsy nature made the odds even greater.

"I'll have a michelada," he said as the waiter laid our menus in front of us. "Do you still like the blue margaritas?" he asked me.

I really did. It was my favorite, and only partially because of the electric turquoise color. I knew the smartest thing I could do was have water. I needed to keep my wits about me. And yet, I'd helped finish off a bottle of champagne at our last lunch, and didn't make a fool of myself. Maybe a drink would help me relax.

"Yes," I said, then turned to the waiter. "I'll take one of those on the rocks." We also ordered our usual fish tacos, along with a side of enchilada sauce to dip my tortilla chips in. My mouth was already watering in anticipation.

"Before we start, we need to lay down the ground rules," I said to Sonny once the waiter was gone. He raised an eyebrow at me.

"Ground rules?"

"Yes, ground rules. As long as I'm working with you, I'm not your ex-girlfriend, but the owner of a business your company has hired. That means no mention of our history, and I expect you to treat me just like you'd treat any other professional. Like Charles. That means no more holding the door open for me, pulling out my chair, or showing any kind of affection."

I hated saying that last part. So much of Sonny's charm was in the way he treated me, from the small hand at my back to the gentle way he kissed my forehead. But we weren't lovers anymore, not even friends. And if he so much as brushed his lips against any part of my body, I'd lose control.

"Charles and I hug after every meeting. Is that allowed?" His eyes danced with humor, and I glared at him, biting back my smile.

"If you hug the waiter when it's time to go, I'll consider it."

He laughed, and I noted the playful glint in his eyes. Damn, I was in so much trouble.

The waiter set the margarita in front of me, and I sipped to hide the feelings he was stirring, humming in approval as the refreshing taste of orange and lime filled my mouth.

"Let me try a sip," Sonny said. "I forgot what those taste like." He started to reach for it, but I moved it out of his reach.

"Would you sip off Charles' drink?"

"We share drinks all the time." He laughed, then held his hands up. "Okay, point taken. I'll just drink my super delicious michelada, and you enjoy drinking your girly blue drink all by yourself."

"Oh, I will." I took another sip, and when he faked to grab it again, I jerked it closer to me. Straight off the table. All over my napkin in my lap, which of course meant...

"My pants!" I lifted the napkin and sure enough, my sister's white pants were now stained bright blue right at my crotch and thighs, like a damn target. I glared at Sonny as the waiter rushed to our table, working at the margarita on the floor. He handed me more napkins to work on my lap, but the damage was done.

"Shit, Cricket. I'm sorry." He looked sincerely remorseful, and I could already tell the pants were going to stick to me like glue when it was time to walk out of there. Suddenly, the whole thing seemed so silly. I tried to smother my smile, but the giggles broke through. Then I was laughing. Sonny's face filled with relief, and he laughed with me, signaling to the waiter to bring me another drink.

"No," I insisted. "I obviously can't hold my liquor." And I dissolved into laughter again. Despite my refusal, the waiter still brought me another margarita, which I sipped carefully.

With all the drama aside, Sonny and I got down to business. I showed him a list of my favorite vendors, and we compared it to the list of preferences Charles had left with Sonny. Taye had already placed a hold on several venues for October 13, and I was pleased to see that Merdell Gallery, a restaurant and event space in San Francisco, was on Charles' list of preferred locations. By the time the check came, we not only had the venue location narrowed down to our three favorite picks, but had also chosen a caterer, staging company, and a few other vendors who had impressed me at some of my past events. I knew the Finnigans would love them, and Sonny trusted every company I suggested. When we were done, I took a photo of the list and shot it over to Taye so she could start making calls, and then grabbed the check before Sonny could pull out his wallet.

"It's on me," I said. I narrowed my eyes as he got ready to protest. "Remember? Professional business owner here. I'll pay."

"Enough with your *blether*," he said, and I hid a smile at his Scottish term for *nonsense*. "I'll pay. Rather, Charles will pay. This is company business, and he insisted on paying for any of our meetings. So if we need to discuss this further, say over drinks tomorrow night, Charles will pay the tab."

"Right," I said, though I released my hold on the check and let Sonny take it. "We're not going out tomorrow night because it's too short notice, and I have plans." My plans included sitting at home with my sister and obnoxious bird, but he didn't need to know that. "Besides," I continued, "I'd think Justine would have an issue with that."

"Why would she care?"

"Your girlfriend wouldn't mind if we went out Friday night to discuss business over drinks?"

He'd taken a sip of his second michelada and almost choked. Coughing, he held up a hand as a way to excuse his fit, then sipped from his water.

"No, Cricket. I think she'd be happy if we went out. And how about you? Your fellow looks to be the possessive type. At least, he's a bit handsy. He'd probably have a fit if you went out with me tomorrow night. I'm surprised you're here now, to be honest."

"I can do what I want, when I want," I said, my ears burning in anger. Or maybe it was the margarita. I'd reached the bottom of my glass, and I could feel the warmth of it flowing through my body.

"Then let's go out tomorrow night, Charles' treat, and tie up any loose ends over dinner and cocktails at Stormy's in San Francisco. We could even check out Merdell Gallery. What do you say? Can I pick you up at six?"

"No," I said. "I mean, not tomorrow. Meadow flew in unexpectedly last night and I want to stay close by for a while. I haven't seen a lot of her lately."

"That's great! How is she?"

"She's…good. Same old Meadow, always onto the next thing. But right now she's taking a breather before her next adventure."

I purposely left out the condition she came to me in, though I desperately wanted to confide in him about it. He'd always been my confidante, aside from Meadow. A year past our breakup, it still felt strange to keep this from him.

"So tomorrow's out," he continued. "How about next Friday?"

I rolled my eyes, though I was secretly thrilled that he was persisting. *It's just business, nothing else*, I reminded myself.

"Fine," I said, then removed my napkin from my lap to stand, forgetting about the huge blue stain across my crotch until it was on full display for the whole restaurant. My cheeks burned, but Sonny moved quickly, whipping off the flannel shirt he wore over his t-shirt, and handed it to me.

"Thanks," I said, tying it backwards around my waist like an apron. It was still ridiculous, but better than walking around with a blue bullseye. I turned to lead the way out of the restaurant, and with Meadow's stupid six-inch heels, my ankle gave out. I would have fallen if Sonny hadn't grabbed me. He wrapped his arms around me, his solid form a foundation I could lean on. And I did for a moment, righting my foot and breathing in time with him. Once I was steady, he loosened his hold, but still kept an arm around me.

"Are you okay?" he whispered. I nodded, unable to speak. But now that I was standing, I could feel how the margarita had done its work. My head felt light, and I wasn't sure if driving was a good idea.

"I'm fine," I said, turning to face him. He let go of me finally, and my body felt cold where his hand had been. "I think I might take a walk through the bookstore next door before I head home, though."

I could tell he saw right through me as soon as the words came out of my mouth. He knew my low tolerance for alcohol, especially when it came to blue margaritas. Damn that Curaçao liquor.

"How about we Uber to my house," he suggested. He laughed when I shot him a glare. "No, I don't mean… It's just, I still have a pair of your pajama pants. They're at my house. You can change into those if you'd like to come back to look at the bookstore. Or you can stay for a cup of coffee. I'll take you back to your car when you're ready."

"Where do you live?" I asked.

"Not far from here. Close enough that I walked." He glanced at my shoes. "But I don't mind springing for an Uber."

"Or, I can," I said, my phone already in hand, the Uber app open.

"Still a *bonnie thrawn hen,* I see."

"If you're calling me stubborn, then yes, I am." I skipped the part where he called me beautiful. He grinned, and this time I noticed his cheeks getting a little rosier.

"You still understand."

I couldn't stop listening.

"I think we're breaking the ground rules," I said, then turned to leave.

"Wait, one more thing."

I turned as Sonny left me in the middle of the restaurant to talk to the bartender. I took the moment to eye the salt and pepper shakers on the table. *Did I?* I checked my feelings, my heart. Then I stepped away from the table for the door, leaving the shakers on the table. I looked back just in time to see the waiter approach Sonny near the bar, and I snorted as Sonny threw his arms around him. The poor guy stood there with his arms at his side, engulfed by Sonny's large frame. Eventually he lifted his arms and patted Sonny on the back. Sonny finally released him, then jogged back to me through the maze of tables.

"We can never come back here again," he hissed, then pulled me to the exit. When he opened the door and held it open for me, I let him. After all, he earned it.

When Sonny said he lived a few blocks away, he meant it literally. We could have walked there in five minutes. It still cost me $8.

Sonny's house was adorable, to say the least. It was a sage green craftsman-style bungalow with white trim and a large front porch, perfect for sipping sweet tea while spying on neighbors. He led me through the front door, and Buoy barreled into me as soon as I crossed the threshold. As I stroked the excited dog's golden hair, I inhaled the rich scent of original hardwood floors in the house. All the older homes in Petaluma smelled like this—at least the ones I'd been inside. But Sonny's was layered with a musky hint of juniper that seemed to follow him around. It was intoxicating.

"I put them over here," he said, unaware of my need to inhale.

"What? Oh, the pants." I shook my head of the distraction, following him to the armoire in the living room, Buoy at my heels. While Sonny's back was to me, I glanced at every visible space, searching for signs of *her*. Judging by the unpacked boxes against the wall, he was still settling in, which explained why I came up empty on anything feminine. It also reassured me that he lived alone. I hoped.

"Buoy, leave her alone," Sonny laughed, shooing Buoy aside until he sat on the couch. "Here," he said, handing me the pair of pink and purple flannel pants. I hadn't even realized they were missing, but now that I had them in my hands, I remembered wearing them around his house all the time.

"I can't believe you still have them."

He shrugged, but I noted a hint of pink rising in his cheeks.

"The bathroom is through my room," he said, nodding his head toward the open doorway. I took off his flannel shirt from around my waist, grimacing at my blue crotch.

"Thanks for letting me borrow this," I said. "And for not throwing away my pants."

On my way to the bathroom, I had a hard time not looking at his bed. His whole room smelled like him, bringing me back to times when my head was buried in his chest, our bodies tangled with each other. Now he had Justine. While it bothered me before, I felt ill at the sight of his neat comforter over flannel sheets, two sets of pillows on top, and how she was the one to sleep here with him, not me.

In the bathroom, I took off my heels and tight pants, then slipped on the flannel pajamas. After feeling constricted all afternoon, it was like slipping into a cup of tea. I should have worn one of my usual flowing dresses, or even jeans and a flannel. I'd have been way more comfortable, and the blue stain wouldn't have mattered. It would take a miracle and a lot of bleach to get this stain out of the pants.

Before leaving the bathroom, I eased open his medicine cabinet. My eyes darted across the shelves, taking inventory—one comb, one razor, one manly-scented shaving cream. But next to it all was a glass with two toothbrushes. I recalled how I'd taken over his whole cabinet without even living with him, even keeping spare products there. The fact that she only had a toothbrush here was considerate, even if it annoyed the hell out of me. The more I stared at it, the angrier I became. I knew I had no right to be angry with her, and that only pissed me off more. For a moment, I mulled over how it might feel to do something terrible like throw her toothbrush away, or even dip it in the toilet.

"Get a grip, Cricket," I muttered, physically shaking my head to free me of these childish thoughts. I closed the cabinet door, but my hand brushed against the toothbrushes and they spilled into the sink. I held my breath, listening for Sonny in the other room. I breathed out as I heard his low voice murmuring, and the clack of Buoy's nails, both far enough away to assume I was safe.

I picked up the toothbrushes and put them back in the glass, then moved to place them back on the shelf. That's when I noticed the small saltshaker in the way. I opened the door wider and saw the matching pepper shaker. They were the super tiny kind, like the novelty shakers usually at weddings or other happy events. I always liked these ones best because they were so personal. They were only meant for single-use, and there was something delicate about holding the tiny shaker over a plate of food, how something so tiny could add so much flavor. Plus, they're just cute.

But why did Sonny have them in his medicine cabinet? I couldn't help feeling like they meant something. I was probably reading too much into it, though. Just because I had a closet full of shakers at home attached to all kinds of negative feelings didn't mean these shakers meant something. Why wouldn't someone keep salt and pepper in their bathroom?

Emergency shakers. That's probably what they were. For those times when you just needed a little seasoning… Yeah, I had no idea why they were in there. I placed the toothbrushes in front of them and closed the door.

Sonny was scanning the movie channels when I walked back into the living room. Buoy sat next to him, his head resting on Sonny's lap. He looked up as I entered the room, but then settled back down, the excitement of a visitor already passed. I set my clothes and shoes next to my purse on the floor, then joined them on the couch, sitting on the opposite end. Buoy wagged his tail, arranging his body against my leg.

"Pick a movie," Sonny said, leaning over to hand me the remote. "I'll make some coffee." He stood, and Buoy lifted his head, appearing ready to get up. "Stay," Sonny said, and Buoy groaned in his throat before turning on the couch so that he faced me, his head on my knee.

"A movie feels like a long-time commitment," I called after Sonny as he went into the kitchen. I stroked Buoy's ears as I noted a brief twinge, wondering if Justine kept any special creamer in the refrigerator, or maybe had a cup only she drank out of. The jealousy was a burning ember as I shifted through the movie choices. I paused at *About Time*, the movie about the time traveler. Sonny and I had gone to see it when it came out in the movie theaters, and being the sap that I was, I openly cried at the end. He didn't make fun of me then, or when I cried the next six times I made him watch it with me.

"Oh wow, I haven't seen that movie since…" Sonny trailed off as he sat back on the couch, placing my coffee on a coaster. He smiled at me, and I knew what he was going to say. "Since we watched it," he finished.

I started to switch to another choice, but he stopped me with a hand on my wrist. I looked down at his hand, and he moved it away. My skin still felt warm from his touch.

"Let's watch it," he said. "I *ken* you love it."

I reluctantly agreed, grateful for the dog that separated the two of us. My palms felt sweaty being here, and I was battling a strange combination of nervousness and excitement. All this time, all our history, and we were just sitting on the couch watching a movie. As if we hadn't shared the biggest love story I'd ever experienced. As if he'd never shattered my heart. As if this whole past year never happened. I was sitting there keeping my sweaty hands from shaking by petting his sleeping dog, and he was just sipping coffee, his eyes on the screen as the opening credits began. As if this were no big deal.

"You know, this is really breaking the ground rules." I felt silly as I said it, especially when he rolled his head in my direction, looking at me like I'd uttered something adorably annoying.

"Not the rules, again," he groaned.

"I'm serious!"

"And so am I. Why do we have to have ground rules? Why can't we just work together, and be friends outside of work? Is that really not allowed?"

"It's allowed," I said. "But it's…" I stopped myself. *It's confusing.* But what if I was the only one who was confused? Did I want to admit that to him? "It's just strange," I said weakly. "I'm your ex, and when we're close to each other, we're used to certain…things." I gave him a pointed look, and he nodded slowly. "I just don't want us to mix signals," I finished.

"We're just watching a movie," he said. It had already started, but both of us were now facing each other on the couch, the movie forgotten.

"I know. But we used to watch movies, and, you know…" I felt my cheeks heat up at what I was insinuating. The heat increased as steamy memories flashed at me like a strobe light.

"No, what?"

I opened my mouth, unsure what to say, but then caught the teasing glint in his eye. I gave him a mock glare in return.

"We don't have to be strangers," he said. "In fact, I'd like if we could be friends. Can't we at least have that?" His face looked hopeful, but then I caught the dark shadow that crossed his expression. "Is this because of that guy you're seeing?"

"No," I said quickly. "I mean, he trusts me. It's not that. I just don't…" What did I say? That being this close to him all the time was making me forget why we broke up, making it hard to remember he had a girlfriend, making it difficult to guard my heart? "I just don't want Justine to get the wrong impression."

"She won't," he promised, following it up with a smile and a small shake of his head. As if I were being completely ridiculous. And I was. I knew I was.

"I should probably go," I said, starting to shift under Buoy's head. He groaned, keeping his eyes closed. "I can walk back to my car; you don't have to drive me."

"You just got here," he pointed out. "Besides, what are you going to do, wear those heels with pajama pants?" He nodded at my coffee. "At least drink your coffee. It's pretty good."

I relented, grasping the cup in my hands as I took a cautious sip, then nodded appreciatively at the warm temperature. He'd cooled it with the perfect amount of cream and sugar, just the way I liked it. He remembered. I smiled my thanks, and he nodded back. His coffee was black, as always, and he took long sips like it wasn't scalding his mouth. That was the difference between us. He was never afraid of being burned, while I was more careful. About coffee, I mean.

"So, is this weekend a good time to start building?" Sonny asked.

"Building? Oh, the aviary. I can't believe I forgot." When I'd left the house earlier, Meadow had been sitting on the couch while Avery picked at strands of her hair. They looked so content together, it was like he was her bird and not mine—which made sense, I guess. I still had no idea where the bird came from or why Meadow thought I needed it. Maybe she'd fill me in. Maybe she'd tell me all of the secrets she was keeping, starting with why she was here and no longer in Sweden.

"Meadow and I are just hanging around the house," I said to Sonny. "You can drop by anytime." Then I remembered the condition Meadow was in. Crap!

"It will be like old times," he said, and I glanced at him to see what he meant by it. He just sipped his coffee, as if *old times* meant something completely different than my version of old times. "I'll stop by tomorrow to take measurements and figure out what I need," he continued.

He was going to see her some time; I couldn't keep her hidden away. And why would I? It wasn't like Meadow had done anything wrong…most likely. Maybe she'd even admit what happened if he came over. Knowing Sonny, he might even talk some sense into her.

"I'll Venmo you money for materials," I said. Sonny waved his hand to stop me.

"Chuck has a bunch of stuff at his property, including some fencing panels that might be perfect. He may have everything I need to build it."

"But if he doesn't, you'll let me pay you?"

He rolled his eyes. "Aye, Cricket."

"I'm serious. I don't need your charity."

He breathed out a laugh, shaking his head as I narrowed my eyes.

"Fine," he eventually said. "But let me see what Chuck has first."

Sonny drove me back to my car as soon as our coffee was done. The margarita had worn off, but being this close to him, I had to talk down my beating heart. There was no dog to separate us, and his arm rested near mine on the center console when he wasn't shifting. Occasionally our arms touched, sending chills across my skin. I was addicted to the feeling, and I kept my arm where it was.

"I'll stop by around one tomorrow, if that works for you," he said as his truck idled next to my car. He started to take off his seatbelt, presumably to open my door for me. I beat him to the punch by opening the door on my own. The corner of his mouth upturned, and he stayed in his seat as I slid out of mine.

"Thank you for the coffee, and the ride back to my car."

"Anytime," he said.

It felt weird to let him go without some sort of contact. A squeeze of the hand. An embrace. A kiss. I settled on a smile, then closed the door, taking a deep breath as soon as I was out of his air space.

Sonny's truck stayed by mine as I got in my car. I knew he'd stay, as if I could be mugged in the few moments between his car and mine. I started the car and waved—the signal that my car was fine, I was fine, and he could leave. Which he did. I stayed in my spot, watching his taillights as he reached the end of the street, then turned left. It felt like I'd held my breath the whole time, and I let it out as soon as he was out of view. I looked in the rearview mirror, checking for invisible crumbs, but really checking how I looked after spending the afternoon with my ex-boyfriend. *I look like a starstruck teenager*, I thought, noting the grin that wouldn't leave my face. "That man is going to be the end of you, Cricket," I whispered to my reflection.

Chapter Ten

"Can you see any bruising?" Meadow turned her face to me, and I peered close. There was a slight shadow under her eye, but the rest of her face had transformed into something Instagram-worthy. Her contouring and added highlights made her cheeks more pronounced. The burnt Sienna eyeshadow complemented her blue eyes, making them pop. She had pale pink gloss on her lips, but they definitely appeared plumper than mine.

I turned and looked at both of our reflections in the mirror. Even with her makeup-covered bruises, she looked like a model. Her vibrant red hair framed her face in mermaid waves. With my messy top knot and pale, freckled face, I looked like I was twelve. Especially next to her. I reached for Meadow's mascara and applied a little to my blonde eyelashes.

"You can't even tell," I said, as I recapped the mascara. "But it's not like Sonny won't notice your cast or leg brace." He'd texted ten minutes ago that he was on his way, and I'd already changed three times. I finally settled on a pair of jeans and a flowing boho tunic in a turquoise print. I usually loved this shirt, but today, everything seemed wrong. I put on some lip gloss, then checked the mirror. I was going for the *couldn't be bothered* look. But the makeup looked too obvious. Sighing, I wiped my lips free of gloss, then grabbed a washcloth for my face. "When are you going to tell me what really happened?" I asked.

"I did," she said as she took the washcloth out of my hands. "Leave the mascara on, then put on that tinted Chapstick. Add a tiny bit of concealer under your eyes but blend it with a sponge. Finish it with that tinted powder I have. You'll still look *au naturale*, but with flawless skin."

I shot her a grateful look, then did as she said. "What, that you fell? I don't buy it."

"You weren't there," she said. "And you know how clumsy I am."

"Uh, hardly. I'm the clumsy one, remember? Did you see those white pants I ruined? If you were really clumsy, you wouldn't wear those six-inch stilettos you're always balancing in."

"Not now, I'm not," she said, nodding at her leg brace. On her feet were a brand-new pair of Tom Ford low-top tennis shoes, which probably cost the equivalent of a month's worth of groceries. But for Meadow, they were free, thanks to her sponsored promotions in her Instagram stories. I had a few pairs of my own expensive shoes, paid for by Meadow's sponsors. They were beautiful, all of them—and none of them anything I'd ever wear. I knew I should sell them, or even donate them, but I had a hard time getting rid of anything, especially gifts. So, they remained unworn in my closet.

I heard the knock at the door, and then Avery's loud whistle from the bird room. I must have looked panicked when I turned to Meadow because she put her hand on my shoulder and looked me straight in the eyes.

"Breathe," she said. "He's just a man with a sexy voice, a cute ass, and a panty-dropping smile. You got this."

I gave her a mock glare, recognizing the exact words I'd used the night I met Sonny when she asked me to describe him.

"Thanks for the pep talk," I said, swatting her on the arm. I couldn't smother my grin as I walked down the hall to the front door. *I got this*, I repeated to myself, reaching for the doorknob. But when I opened the door, I inhaled sharply. Sonny smiled down at me, and I wasn't just caught by the crease in the side of his cheek or the intoxicating cedar scent of his cologne. Those were enough to render me speechless, but really, it was the warmth in his eyes, the invitation I used to see daily, the one that melted me every time before I stepped into his arms and accepted his full body hug while he buried his face in my neck.

He combed a hand through his hair. As his grin deepened, I realized I was staring and quickly broke eye contact. I was obviously reading too much into whatever he was doing. Hell, he was just looking at me. Who did I think I was? He was interested in his girlfriend, not me.

"Hey. Thanks for coming by," I said.

"Hey yourself. I left Buoy in the truck, just in case the bird was out," Sonny said. Behind him, Buoy's whole body wagged in the cab. His golden head hung out the window wearing his usual grin.

"Hopefully this won't take long. But thank you. I don't want Avery more stressed out. I think I saw some new feather growth in his bare patches, and I'm hoping he'll stop over-plucking them."

I tried not to breathe him in as he brushed by me on the way into the house. *Damn, he smells good. Did he smell this good when we went to Ricardo's? How did I miss it?*

When we closed ourselves in the bird room, Avery settled on my shoulder while Sonny measured the space. It almost felt natural to have the bird resting on me, and I kept peeking up at him to see if he was comfortable. He preened a wing, then repositioned himself on my shoulder. It was like we'd done this before, and I couldn't help the swell I felt in my heart at the fact that he chose to sit on my shoulder—that he chose *me*.

Dang, if I wasn't falling in love with this stupid bird.

"I can install a wall-length enclosure in here so you don't have to keep the room closed up anymore," Sonny said, and I looked where he indicated the cage would go. He explained the jungle-like environment he'd create in the enclosure, including a misting system to keep the bird cool in the warmer months, plus heat lamps for the winter.

"I'll install durable linoleum to protect the, uh…" He looked at the golden-brown shag carpeting, matted from years of heavy traffic. "…the carpet," he finished.

"That would be good," I said, ignoring the judgment in his voice. In the past, he'd questioned me a few times on why I didn't update anything. I always chalked it up to money, which was true. But even more, it felt wrong. My parents created a home out of this house, shag carpet and all. Updating anything felt like erasing them from the house. Even the aviary felt like an intrusion on the flow of the home. But the more I was getting to know this bird, the more I wanted him comfortable. This was the bird's home now, too. I could keep my shag carpeting and wood panel walls, my father's rocking chair and my mother's flourishing garden. Avery could have a jungle next to the window, giving him the best light in the house.

I left Avery in the room and joined Sonny outside. I secretly studied him as he mocked up some sketches of our side yard. The sleeves to his flannel shirt were rolled up just under his elbows, revealing strong, tan forearms that used to wrap around my waist when he kissed me. He turned, and I felt guilty as my eyes lingered on his backside, noting the way his thighs perfectly filled out his jeans. Not to mention his ass.

Stop it, I chided myself, quickly looking at my cuticles as he turned back around.

"I have metal poles and bags of concrete in the truck bed," he said. "The ground here is fairly level. I could get started on this today."

"I didn't expect you to start until tomorrow," I said. "Are you sure?"

"It's no problem," he said. "I have a few free hours. Honestly, the outside enclosure will be a lot easier than inside, and I'd like to knock out most of the work now so I can take my time inside."

"If it's really no problem, I'd love that," I said. "Let me make sure Meadow has Avery covered so we can let Buoy out of the truck."

"He'll be fine," Meadow said, hobbling down the front steps to be with us, Avery on her shoulder. "He lived with a dog before and didn't seem to mind beyond general teasing. He'll get used to Buoy."

Avery squawked and flapped his wings, but didn't leave Meadow, even outside. I was surprised, and Sonny seemed shocked, too, but for different reasons.

"What the hell happened to you?" he asked.

"I fell," she said, then gave me a warning look. It only solidified my doubts, but I didn't argue the lie.

"Looks like a pretty hefty fall," Sonny said, also shooting me a look. I shrugged. I wanted to tell him I didn't believe her either, but my allegiance was with my sister. Besides, she'd never tell me anything if I ganged up on her with my ex.

Sonny's jaw pulsed as he took in my sister's injuries. The makeup helped, but now that we were in the sunlight, the discoloration of her bruises was more apparent. And then there was her arm and leg. I knew exactly how Sonny felt, seeing her broken arm and bundled-up leg for the first time. He'd always been protective of both of us—at least, he was when we were together. I saw the creases in his forehead, the way he clenched his hands, and I knew he felt something in between fury and helplessness, knowing someone had done this to her.

"Well, if you ever fall again, call me and I'll take care of it," he said, his narrowed blue eyes appearing stormy.

"Right," she said. "Like all the times I could have called you this past year."

I glared at Meadow. She feigned an angelic smile.

"I'm teasing," she continued, waving her good hand as if erasing what she just said. "It's good to have you here again, Sonny."

"For professional reasons," I added, then felt like a complete idiot, especially as I saw her eyes sweep over him, then grin at me. *He's just a man...*

"It's good to be back," Sonny said, still looking at me. I swallowed hard, wishing his words didn't inject so much damn hope in me.

Sonny had done his research on enclosures, and he described his vision for Avery's new outdoor home. The plan was to start by laying the concrete foundation and then add metal poles for the frame.

"I'll leave a few gaps where we can plant trees and foliage," he said. "That way the enclosure will be as natural as possible."

I let Buoy out of the truck while Sonny unloaded the bed. The dog raced around me and went straight for Meadow, who stood her ground despite the barreling dog.

"Buoy!" I shouted, running after him.

"He's fine. He just needs to get his curiosity out," she said. Still, I tensed as I waited for Buoy to jump on Meadow and injure her more. He didn't. He gave tiny hops, but never jumped, whining as he locked eyes with the bird. Avery flapped his wings, but stayed with Meadow, squawking at the dog. I realized the bird wasn't afraid, but taunting him. Or maybe he was just talking to him. I held my breath as Meadow balanced on her crutch, then coaxed the bird to her arm. Slowly, she lowered Avery toward Buoy, who backed up despite his earlier bravado.

"That's a good dog," she cooed. "That's a good bird."

In the end, the whole meeting was uneventful. Avery kept his wings out like colorful flags, flapping them at the dog to make himself bigger. Buoy eventually lost interest and ran after Sonny.

"What if Buoy attacked the bird?" I asked. Meadow turned to Avery, who nuzzled her chin. She kissed the bird's beak, then put it back on her shoulder. She hobbled a few steps closer to me.

"I wasn't sure if he would or not," she admitted. "But that's what wings are for, right? If Avery were in danger, he'd just fly into the trees."

"That's a pretty big gamble." I frowned, studying the bird as he preened his feathers.

"Not really," she said. "Let's just say, I've seen Kauan with an aggressive dog before, and this bird can hold its own."

"Cow on?" I asked. "Is that his name?"

"Kauan," she corrected, enunciating it so that it sounded like *co-won*. "It used to be his name, but Avery is better."

I was silent for a moment. It bothered me that she had all these experiences she wouldn't share with me. She obviously had a history with this bird, but she was keeping it as secret as her injuries. These little slips of information, like revealing the bird's real name, only made it clearer that there was so much I didn't know.

"Why can't you tell…" I started, but the look on her face let me know I'd get nowhere with another demand for information. "Can you at least tell me about the bird?"

"What do you want to know?"

"Where he's from is a good start," I said. "How old is he? Why does he keep plucking his feathers? Who had him before me? Why do I have him now?"

"Is that all?" she asked, laughing.

"It's a start," I repeated. "And I don't think they're unreasonable questions."

"I don't know how old he is or anything about the bare patches," she said. "But he was well-loved by his previous owner."

"And that person was…"

"A friend in Brazil," she answered. "Who died." She looked away, and I caught the mist in her eyes. I reached out and touched her shoulder.

"Hey, I'm sorry," I said. "Did it have anything to do with, you know…" I gestured to her injuries. She shook her head quickly, and I peered closer to study her as if I could read her thoughts.

"Stop it," she said, nudging me away. "I inherited the bird before all this."

"Before you fell?" I asked. She gave a light laugh.

"Yeah. Before I fell."

She stroked the bird's back, and I could practically see her mind turning as she settled into quiet contemplation. Then, with a quick smile in my direction, she turned and hobbled back to the house. Avery stayed with her, his large feet clutching her shoulder. I could tell there was a strong bond between the two of them. I only wished I knew more.

I didn't know as much about Meadow as I used to. I understood this truth even more now, but it still hurt my heart. She was my person, my best friend, my "womb mate," as she often called me. We'd spent our childhood finishing each other's sentences and reading each other's minds. But now? I had no idea what was going on behind her blue eyes.

Sonny worked quickly. When I looked in his direction, he'd already framed the area where the slab would go with a couple of two-by-fours. He was now busy shoveling out the center to make it even. I realized I'd talked with Meadow for so long because I was avoiding him. His flannel was tossed to the side of the yard and his tan skin glistened under the late morning sun. *Lord, have mercy.* He still had those rippled abs lining his stomach, though softer than they were a year ago. It made me want to touch them more, to feel the contrast between his solid muscles and the places that had some give, to press my fingers against his salty skin and reacquaint myself with the curves of his body. I tried not to stare, tried not to think of how much his shining skin reminded me of mornings when he'd stepped out of the shower and dried himself off on me.

No, I'm not going there. I shook myself from the memory and decided the best place to be was anywhere but here, watching him work. Then again, it wasn't like he was hired help. Could I really leave him while he busted his ass for a bird that wasn't even his?

"Hey, got anything to drink?" Sonny asked, and I realized I was still staring at his chest. I averted my eyes, pretending I was looking at Buoy the whole time, who had given up on both of us and was passed out in the shade.

"Yeah," I said, looking back at him, keeping my focus on his eyes and not his naked, sweaty chest that I could almost smell, that I could almost touch.

Stop it.

"Iced tea? Water? Something stronger?" I asked, wondering if I even had any beer in the fridge. The last time I bought beer was for him. Blake didn't drink beer when he was over, both of us preferring shots to hops.

"Maybe we can have blue margaritas when we're done here," he teased, and I rolled my eyes to hide all the ways that simple sentence triggered me. For him, it was just a humored nod to how tipsy I got yesterday. But it reminded me of sitting in his house wearing pajama bottoms, fighting my attraction to him while searching for signs of his girlfriend.

"Iced tea, it is," I answered for him, turning toward the house before he could read my mind.

In the kitchen, I poured a glass for each of us from the tea I'd sun brewed earlier that morning. Then I took a moment to pull myself together. What the hell was wrong with me? He was just a man, regardless of how good he looked with or without a shirt. With a deep breath, I carried both glasses outside, careful about where I looked as I approached him. I kept my eyes trained on the framed area as I handed him the glass, acting like it was no big deal he was half-naked in front of me. Seriously. His chest was no big deal. I definitely did not want to run my hands over it and press my body against him.

Stop it!

He took the glass from me and downed it in three huge gulps before handing the glass back.

"Want more?" I asked. He looked at me, his eyes washing over my body, weakening my defenses.

"Tempting," he said, and I inhaled sharply at the double meaning. Or was it? We locked eyes for a moment, and the air around us felt thinner. "Maybe in a little bit," he continued, offering me a half-smile before going back to digging. I took a sip from my iced tea, trying to cool my hormones.

"Can I help?" I eventually asked. He nodded at a shovel leaning against one of the trees, and I retrieved it.

"You look nice," he said as I applied the shovel to the dirt.

"Uh, thanks?"

"I mean, did you want to change before you start doing heavy labor?" he asked, glancing at my shirt.

"This old thing?" I joked. "Seriously, it's just an old shirt. I'm fine. Besides, I hardly think shoveling dirt is enough to ruin an outfit." I glanced at his sweaty body and looked away again.

"If you say so. This is almost done, anyway."

As I applied my shovel to the earth, I was reminded how hard the ground was. In my mother's garden, the plants and constant watering kept the soil loose and fresh. But here, the dry Petaluma adobe was like digging through concrete. I used the hose to soften the dirt, then Sonny did the same on the section he was working on. Twenty minutes in, and my super cute bohemian top clung to me in unattractive ways with splatters of mud across the hem. I had no choice but to strip it off and work in my tank top. I felt Sonny's eyes on me, and despite my hair sticking to my neck and my minimal makeup running down my face, it was nice to know I wasn't the only distracted one here. Okay, more than nice.

He came near me and touched the back of my neck. Despite the heat, my body erupted into goosebumps.

"You're getting overheated," he murmured, his hand still at my neck. I stayed still, unsure of the right thing to do. Moving away would be the right thing. But with his hand now caressing my sweaty skin, I couldn't move even if I wanted to. I looked up at him, and I recognized the hooded look in his eyes. My breath came in shallow waves as I tilted my mouth toward his, lowered my eyelids, and—

"Yoohoo!"

Sonny and I both looked in the direction of the high-pitched call, and I quietly groaned at the elderly woman making her way up my driveway.

"It's my neighbor, Patty Jenkins," I murmured out the side of my tight smile. What if she hadn't shown up? Would Sonny have kissed me? Did I want him to kiss me? I moved out from underneath his hand, and my neck suddenly felt cold without his touch.

"Dang, that old bat is still alive?" He raised an eyebrow at me. "I would have thought her sphincter caved in on the stick up her ass."

I laughed, swatting him on his bare arm, immediately regretting it as the palm of my hand brushed against his

151

hardened bicep. I lingered, afraid to look at him as my finger lightly traced the line of his muscle.

"Am I interrupting anything?"

I jerked my hand away, then noted how Patty Jenkins eyed my tank top and sweaty skin as if we'd been rolling around in the dirt all day. In contrast, she was wearing a flowered smock, as usual, buttoned all the way to the collar of the shirt she wore underneath. My mom used to tell me Patty Jenkins was raised in a convent, though I think she was just joking. Looking at my neighbor now, with her tight mouth and narrow eyes, I could easily see her as the cliché nun, wearing a habit while wielding a punishing ruler.

"Hi Mrs. Jenkins, it's nice to see you," I said, wishing she would disappear.

"I wish I could say the same, my dear." She waved a hand as if erasing the words. "I mean, it's lovely to see you. I just wish it were on better terms. I have been overlooking your tilted mailbox for a while now, considering the great loss you and your sister have endured. How are you, by the way? I've been meaning to ask."

"We're fine, Mrs. Jenkins." I folded my arms in front of me, waiting for her to get to the point.

"That's wonderful. At any rate, I see your boyfriend here—"

"He's not my boyfriend," I cut in.

"Right. I guess your special friend, or whatever you kids call it these days." She shook her head, and I suddenly understood why the old bat hadn't ever married. "What I mean is that your carpenter friend here seems mighty handy with his tools, and—"

"Mrs. Jenkins, I can fix my own mailbox. Don't worry." The last thing I needed was for Sonny to feel obligated to help me any further. Already, I could feel him chuckling behind me. As irritated as I was with Patty Jenkins, I was having a hard time fighting the laughter bubbling up over his amusement.

"Oh, that would be wonderful," she exclaimed, clapping her hands. "It is a part of the CCA rules that everyone's home maintains a neat and tidy front. I know your yard is, how should I say it, challenging. Your mother, bless her heart, was fighting a losing battle with those weeds. I am sorry to see she laid the burden on you."

My amusement completely evaporated at her mention of my mother and the insult about the garden. I wanted to wipe the stupid, sympathetic smile off Patty Jenkins' face.

"Did you have anything else?" I asked through clenched teeth. "I'm sure you've very busy—"

Oh, very busy," Patty Jenkins agreed. "It's not easy being the president of the CCA for forty years and counting. But someone has to do the hard work, don't they? Speaking of hard work, the real reason I came here wasn't about the mailbox. It's actually about the apparent construction you have going on here. I'm sure you read the CCA rules on noise, but I don't want to assume anything. Are you aware of our noise ordinance?"

I honestly had no idea what any of the rules were, since they seemed to be changing all the time, and since the CCA could not officially enforce any rules. Even still, the penalty of breaking any of these random rules was to have Patty Jenkins breathing down my neck. My mother had weathered the storm of Patty Jenkins with wit and good humor. I was not as good-natured as my mother.

"I promise we'll keep it down," I said, placing my hand on her shoulder and gently nudging her back the way she came. She didn't get the hint. She patted my hand and then held it in hers. I looked back at Sonny and mouthed the word *help*, ignoring the way his eyes danced with silent laughter.

"We'll keep to a low roar," Sonny said, to which Patty Jenkins dropped my hand and clasped her own to her chest.

"Aye, from the Highlands, my lord," she drawled in a mock Scottish accent. "I have watched every episode of *Outlander*. But who needs a TV when they have the real thing in front of them?"

"Aye, milady," Sonny said, winking at me before his face got serious. "A nod's as guid as a wink tae a blind horse."

"Brilliant," Patty Jenkins said, clapping her hands again. "What does it mean?"

"It's something my da used to say when someone wasn't making their point."

I smothered my smile behind my hand as Patty continued to grin, the meaning completely escaping her.

"We will keep things down," Sonny continued.

"I'm sure you will," Patty Jenkins said. She peered at the plot of land we were digging. "What are you building, anyways? It's not a new garden, is it?"

I wanted to ask her if there was a rule against that, too, but I was more interested in seeing her leave. "No, not a garden. It's an enclosure for a parrot." As soon as the words left my mouth, I wanted to kick myself. I waited for the barrage of questions she surely had, which probably included rules about exotic animals. To my surprise, Patty Jenkins leaned forward instead with what appeared to be genuine interest.

"A parrot? What kind exactly?"

"A macaw. He was a gift from my sister."

"Oh, I just love birds," Patty Jenkins sighed. "My parakeet Willard used to greet me every morning whistling the 'Good Morning' song. You know the song, don't you?"

I froze as Patty began to sing, even using dance moves like she was a character in *Dancing in the Rain*. This was the same woman who harassed my mother for years about the yard. Now she was singing and dancing to show tunes next to the garden.

"He sounds like a wonderful bird," I said, suddenly grateful that Avery *did not* greet me with a song every morning.

"Yes, he was quite dear to me in his short life." She looked at the framed dirt plot and then nodded her head. "Well, it appears you have everything under control, as long as the noise stays below fifty-five decibels during the day, and silent at night."

"Sure thing, Mrs. Jenkins," I said, though I had no idea how loud that was. "We won't keep you any longer; thank you for dropping by." I silently prayed she would get the cue and leave. She nodded, then looked toward the house. I couldn't miss the wistful look that crossed her face.

"If you have any questions," she said. "I mean, about raising a bird, please call me. I'm happy to help. Do you have my number?"

"Yes. Mrs. Jenkins. My mother left it on... I mean, I have it on a note pinned to my refrigerator, with all the neighbor's phone numbers."

Patty Jenkins's face relaxed again, and I saw a glimmer of sympathy in her eyes. For a moment, I was able to look past her knit brow and puckered mouth to see this different side of her.

"I'll see myself out. Oh, and dear? While you're fixing your mailbox, you may want to fix those cracks in the driveway. I'm lucky I noticed them before tripping. They're a lawsuit waiting to happen."

Aaaaand, she was back.

I shook my head at Sonny as soon as she was out of sight. "Who knew Patty Jenkins had a soft spot for birds?" I laughed. "Or Scots," I added.

"Who knew she had a soft spot for anything," he said. "And I'm not sure she understands how loud construction is. I'm totally breaking the sound ordinance once I bring out the chainsaw."

We dug for a little while longer until the autumn sun felt unbearable. I brought us both more tea, then collapsed on the deck while he continued to dig. His back muscles rippled with each shove into the earth, seeming tireless even as sweat poured off his skin. He glanced at me, then stopped working.

"I think that's enough for today," Sonny said, coming close to me. He took a swig of his tea, his belly mere inches from my face. I could smell his sweat, and it tugged at something deep inside me. He finished the tea, then put his hand on the shovel as he looked down at me. Our eyes locked, and I felt the electricity crackle between us. "Listen, I've been meaning to tell you—" He never got to finish. His phone trilled next to me on the deck. I glanced at it, my heart sinking as I saw Justine's face fill the screen. He grabbed it and answered, turning his back on me.

"Hey," he said into the phone, walking toward his truck with the shovel still in his hand. I couldn't hear the rest of the conversation, but it was enough to remind me of my place. More importantly, it reminded me who I was not.

I was not his girlfriend.

My face flushed as I realized all the ways we'd crossed the line this afternoon. Or maybe it was all in my head. Every touch, every drawn-out look, maybe I'd imagined all of it to mean so much more than it was. I studied him while he was on the phone, looking for signs of his true feelings, only to feel sick as he laughed, head tilted back, his phone still attached to his ear. A nod of his head hinted the end of their conversation, and I quickly busied myself with gathering various garden tools as he made his way back toward me.

"I can wait until tomorrow to pour the concrete, and then get the rest of it built this weekend," he said. I helped him stack the tools, and then he took a huge bundle of them toward the truck. I couldn't keep my eyes off him, even as I tried. I had to get a hold of myself. We had an event to plan, and if I kept looking at him through googly eyes, it would make me the fool.

"You got this," I reminded myself in a whisper. I blew a breath out, looking after him as he loaded the tools in the back of the truck. Buoy ambled toward me and leaned against my thigh. I rested my hand on his fur, kneading his back as he offered a friendly growl in his throat. "It's just a job," I said to Buoy, glad he couldn't talk back.

Sonny finished loading the tools and made his way back to us. I pretended I was super involved in petting Buoy, who was soaking up the extra attention. Sonny walked past me toward his shirt. I peeked back at him as he put it on, my eyes roaming over his chest and belly one more time as he slid the shirt over his head, then looking away as his face emerged.

"Here," he said, tossing me my shirt. I caught it, then pulled it over my head, tugging my hair out as I looked at him again. He was busy gathering the last of his items, not even looking in my direction. That's when I was sure I'd imagined everything.

"Is eight o'clock too early for tomorrow morning?" he asked, patting his thigh for Buoy. I shook my head.

"I'll be up. I'll have coffee ready for you," I said, hoping my smile was as casual as I was trying to sound. "Maybe we can discuss the menu for the Finnigan event while the concrete sets." He nodded before walking away, and I fought back my feelings of confusion. *It's just a job.* But then he looked over his shoulder, and his eyes rested on me for a moment longer than necessary. He shot me a half-smile, and I swear I felt it all the way in my curling toes. I couldn't keep from meeting his smile with my own loopy grin, which remained on my face even as he got in the truck. Even as he closed his door. Even as he drove down the drive, one hand waving out the window. When his truck was gone, I was still standing there, my grin plastered on my face, wondering what the hell I was going to do.

Chapter Eleven

Back in the house, Meadow took one look at me and shook her head.

"Oh girl, you got it bad," she said.

"I do not." I slid down on the couch next to her and buried my head in my hands as she laughed.

"Like you can keep anything from me."

I unburied my head and glared at her, then took a long look at her injuries.

"You're one to talk, little Miss Liar," I said.

"I don't know what you're talking about," she replied, dismissing me with a wave of her hand. "He's into you, too, you know."

My heart leaped at her words, and I realized how much I wanted them to be true. But then the memory of the phone call broadsided me. No, not just the phone call. The way he reacted. Like he couldn't be near me while he talked to her. Maybe he was into me and felt guilty. Or maybe I was just a dumb girl living in a fantasy world.

"He doesn't want me," I said. "He has Justine."

"Sure. And if she saw the way he was looking at you when your back was turned, she'd know he was into you, too."

"You were spying?" I asked it like I was offended, but her smirk let me know she was on to me. I was glad she spied. I wanted to know if she saw the same thing I thought I saw.

"You two were very entertaining. I should have made popcorn," she said. "He took off his shirt, you took off yours. He kept finding reasons to touch you. You kept finding reasons to get close to him." She raised her eyebrows a couple of times, her tilted smile widening.

"Glad we could brighten your day," I said, nudging her good arm. None of it sounded concrete enough. I wasn't convinced. "It didn't mean anything. It was hot, and we were just being friendly. Besides, if he really wanted me, he never would have chosen Wisconsin over me."

"Maybe he realized he made a mistake," she said.

"No, maybe he met a girl like Justine who was worth moving back for."

This was the truth and not all my wishful thinking. If he'd wanted to be with me, he never would have left in the first place. He'd have come back at the first sign that our long-distance relationship wasn't working. He would have tried to hold on to me. Instead, he let me go without a fight. And now that he was back, it wasn't for me, but another woman. No amount of blue margaritas, warm smiles, kind gestures, or lingering looks changed the fact that he'd replaced me.

I needed to move on. Or maybe I needed to *act* like I moved on. Maybe then my heart would catch up and be done with Sonny once and for all.

"What are you doing?" Meadow asked as I typed furiously in my phone.

"Nothing," I said, pressing send before I could overthink it.

Me: *Come over tonight. Bring your night bag.*
Blake: *So bossy. Can't. I have plans.*

"What are you doing?" Meadow repeated, her voice dripping in disbelief. I ignored her, typing furiously while my heart pounded.

Me: *Cancel them. I'll make it worth your while.*
Blake: …
Me: *Bring the tequila.*
Blake: *This is the second time in a week you've blocked Mjolnir.*

I paused for a second. Did he actually name his cock after Thor's weapon? I wanted to call him on it, but if I stalled any longer, I was going to chicken out.

Me: *Consider your battle hammer unblocked if you come over.*

"Cricket, what the hell?" Meadow peered over my shoulder at the exchange, her face a mixture of shock and amusement. "You're being ridiculous. You're not even into him."

"I don't need to be into him to screw him," I said. "Besides, it's not like we haven't before. And it's been a while, which is probably why I can't keep my mind straight around Sonny. I need to get him out of my system, and it's too short notice to figure out anything else."

"God, you make it sound like you're ordering from a menu."

"It's not like that, and you know it. Blake was always a casual thing when we were seeing each other. I'm just relieving some stress so I can keep my wits, you know?"

She studied me, her eyes narrowing as she scrutinized my expression. Inside, my heart was pounding wildly. Outside, I kept my face neutral, almost as if I wanted this.

Blake: *I'll be there in twenty.*

Meadow leaned back on the couch after reading his text over my shoulder, and she gave a loud sigh.

"Whatever," she said. "It's your life."

I was cleaning up the last of the dinner dishes by the time Blake's headlights flashed across the window. Meadow had already gone to bed, mumbling something about her injured arm preventing her from helping, and I let her have the excuse. My system was overwrought by nerves, making my stomach hurt and my skin feel cold at what I was about to do, and I welcomed the alone time.

I dried a glass slowly while watching Blake walk in a zigzag toward the house, and I shivered involuntarily. He let himself in, his eyes narrowing as he gave me a once-over. I was wearing an oversized sweater over a tank top, leggings, and slippers, but he looked at me as if I were wearing lingerie. He set the tequila bottle on the counter, then moved around me to get the shot glasses, brushing against my arm purposely. He already smelled like a bar.

"Did you start without me?"

He nodded as he poured each of us a shot. "Drink up," he said, and he held mine out to me. He slammed his before I could hold mine up for a toast. But what were we supposed to toast?

I downed the shot and he immediately filled both glasses again.

"Whoa there," I said with a laugh, still feeling the warm trail of tequila in my throat. I took a good look at him, noting his bloodshot eyes. He looked away, tossing back the shot, then nodded at mine.

"Come on, Stone, you're behind."

I sipped at mine, welcoming the way my shoulder muscles relaxed, but also taking the moment to assess the situation. Now that my nerves were starting to wane, I realized Blake was a wreck. I started to say as much, but then he moved on me, his mouth crushing down on mine before I could speak. At first, it felt like an intrusion. But the tequila worked fast, loosening my inhibitions until I finally fumbled my empty shot glass on the counter and wrapped my arms around his neck, inviting him to kiss me deeper as I pressed my body into his.

"Bedroom," he murmured, grabbing the tequila bottle. I needed no further prompting. Still, the short journey down the hall gave me a moment to question if I wanted this. My nerves were on fire, screaming yes. At the same time, my heart tugged at me, reminding me of who I *really* wanted. But Sonny wasn't here, and even if he were, he wasn't mine. So I closed the door behind me and slid my sweater off my shoulders as Blake sat on the bed and watched. He uncapped the bottle of tequila and took another swig as I kicked off my slippers. Then he unbuttoned his pants and tugged them down his legs as I stripped off my tank top.

"Jesus, Cricket," he said, staring at my breasts while I slipped out of my leggings. I wore only panties as I came closer to him, tugging at his shirt until he helped me peel it off, revealing his broad chest and sculpted body. I ran my hand over his chest and he took a quick breath in. He stroked his palm over my ass, the thin fabric of my panties the only barrier. He caught my nipple in his mouth, and it was my turn to inhale, the sensation going straight to my groin.

But something strange happened as he worked his mouth on my breast. I wanted to stop. I was turned on, but it didn't feel right. I fought my aversion as hard as I could, focusing on the way his fingers traced the hem of my panties, teasing a sensitive area on my upper thigh.

"Hold on," I whispered, leaning down to kiss him before reaching toward his feet for the tequila. I uncapped it, holding his gaze as I took a healthy swig, the liquid burning my throat. Then I chased it with his kiss, waiting for the effects to take over. My body felt light as Blake continued his worship, slipping my panties down slowly as my core ached in anticipation and nervousness. He gently pressed me back, then took off his boxers. The room wobbled, and I gripped the bed as I glanced down. He wasn't ready yet. All this, and he wasn't even hard.

"Don't worry about it," he said, and I looked up at his face. "Just kiss me a little longer and I'll get there."

So I did. I touched my tongue to his lips and traced the outline before settling at the top, flicking it lightly, just like I wanted him to lick me down below. But it wasn't him I was thinking of, it was Sonny. And the longer I kissed Blake, even as I spun under the tequila's effect, the more I realized this wasn't working for me. I pulled back at the same time he did, and both of us collapsed on the bed. Blake looked down at his flaccid cock, then back at me with a wince.

"This has never happened before," he said.

"It's probably the tequila," I said, turning on my side. It felt like my body was ahead of my mind, and the movement made the room spin. I pulled the covers over me, suddenly feeling very naked. Blake sighed, then moved to put his pants back on. He fell over in the process but continued his mission to get dressed.

"It's not the tequila," he slurred. "It's Sadie."

"Oh shit. Was that who you were seeing tonight?"

He got as far as putting his boxers on before giving up and lying back down.

"No, some other chick. I thought if I hooked up with her, I might calm down about Sadie and ask her out. But then you texted, and it sounded like a better idea."

"Wait, I'm…" I counted on my fingers. "I'm third in line?"

"No!" he said, but then he closed his eyes. "Stop yelling."

"I'm not yelling," I whispered. "But I'm confused about what's going on."

"Me too," he groaned. He didn't say anything for a moment, and I thought he'd fallen asleep. But then he turned to me. "I can't get Sadie off my mind. Every time I see her, it's like I've forgotten how to speak." He said all this in a haze, and I wasn't sure it was the way he slurred his words, or how they were filtered through the roaring in my ears. "I want to ask her out so badly, but every time I work up the nerve, my tongue gets dry and my hands get all sweaty. I thought if I slept with someone else, I'd get it out of my system so I could at least act like a human being around her. Except…" He winced again, giving me a look of weakness. And I finally understood because I was trying to do the same thing.

"Except I'm not Sadie," I said, and he nodded. "And you're not Sonny."

"Exactly," he said. Then he gave me a sharp look. "Wait, what?"

"You know *what*," I said. "I'm not over him, and you know it. I probably won't ever be over him. I'm going to die some lonely spinster in my sad little house with my sad little bird while he goes off and marries Justine and they have a million babies."

"Sounds dreadful," Blake said. "All those kids. Terrible."

I smacked his arm, then moved to grab my clothes. He did the same, but could barely grasp his shirt.

"You're not going anywhere, so you might as well get comfy," I said, tossing his shirt within his reach.

"Just don't maul me in my sleep," he said. "I'm a taken man, even if she doesn't know it yet."

"Don't worry, I won't," I said with a laugh. "And if you have to barf, be sure to make it to the toilet, all right?"

Chapter Twelve

I woke up the next morning with a foul taste in my mouth and a throbbing ache deep in my temples. I opened my eyes, squinting at the too-bright light that flooded the room, then peeked over at the clock. 7:30.

7:30! Sonny was supposed to be here at eight, and—I looked over at the lump next to me—Blake was still passed out, hidden under a mountain of covers.

"Blake, get up," I hissed, nudging him hard. He groaned but hardly moved. "Blake!"

"It's too early," he mumbled, still not moving. I crawled out of bed, my head spinning at the motion. Nausea washed over me, and I took a few deep breaths in hopes of calming my stomach. When I felt steady enough, I gripped the bottom of the blanket and pulled. Blake lay face down on the bed, mumbling into the mattress.

"What?" I asked. He turned his head, eyes still closed.

"Coffee," he moaned.

I stood there for a moment, realizing my window of opportunity to get Blake out of here was closing. Last night, I'd been so sure of the plan—sleep with Blake and get Sonny out of my system. But now, faced with the reality that Sonny was going to jump to conclusions about something that didn't happen, I....

Wait a second. Why was I worried? What exactly was Sonny going to do—tell his girlfriend on me? Besides, the plan was for him to think I had a boyfriend. Originally, this was to protect my ego. But now, it was clear my emotions were getting the better of me. If Sonny thought I was in a relationship, it would minimize the risk of either of us crossing the line. As much as I hated the fact that Sonny had moved on, I refused to be the other woman. Or at least *try* to be the other woman. The past few days, I'd flirted with that line, allowing myself to be swept up in past feelings every time Sonny was near. It was time I stood firmly on the right side of the line.

"Get in the shower and wake up," I said to Blake, this time a little more gently. "I'll go start the coffee."

I wrapped a robe around my body and left the room, Blake mumbling behind me.

"Rough night?" Meadow asked when I got downstairs. She already had a cup ready, holding it out to me as I neared. She must have known I'd have a hangover because it was missing my usual creamer and sugar—two ingredients I wasn't sure I could stomach yet.

"You're a godsend," I breathed, then sipped the bitter drink. As foul as I thought black coffee was, this was exactly what I needed.

"Seeing the shot glasses on the counter, I figured you two had quite the night. That good, huh?" She looked meaningfully at my hair, and I lifted my hand to touch it, feeling what must have looked like a wild mess. I glanced at my reflection in the microwave door, confirming the wreckage.

"Nothing happened." I peered closer at my reflection, trying to smooth my hair with my hand as my fingers snagged in the tangles. She hummed in disbelief. "Seriously," I said. I gave up, returning to my coffee. "I mean, the intention was there. But when it came down to it..." I trailed off, wordlessly urging her to read between the lines.

"Well, that sucks. But you sure look like something happened. And your breath." She wrinkled her nose, turning her head away. I breathed hard in her direction, and she laughed, jumping out of the line of fire. "Seriously, you should gargle with mouthwash, and then swallow it."

"That bad, huh?"

"It's pretty awful, even for you."

I glanced at the clock, my heart quickening at the time slipping away.

"Sonny is going to be here any moment, and I need to get dressed," I said, pouring a second cup of coffee for Blake, and topping off my own. "Can you just entertain him when he gets here? I'll get ready as fast as I can."

Meadow looked at me for a moment, not saying anything. And then, it was like a lightbulb went off. She laughed.

"You are so evil," she said. "You had this whole thing planned, didn't you? You want Sonny to catch Blake here."

"I don't know what you're talking about," I said, stealing her line as I headed out of the kitchen.

The shower was going in the hall bathroom, and I knocked on the door. "Blake? I have coffee."

"Open the door," he said. I did, and steam poured through the crack in the doorway as if escaping the clutches of hell. He slid the curtain aside, revealing that he was sitting in the tub portion, letting the hot water run over him.

"Don't take up all the hot water," I said. "I need a shower too."

"Just leave the coffee there," he said, nodding at the back of the toilet. "And don't look in the toilet."

That's when I noticed the sour smell underneath the scent of soap and steam.

"Duly noted," I said. "You have five minutes, then it's my turn."

I left him in the shower, heading to my room with the realization that I might be facing down my former boyfriend with, not only a naked man in my house, but a night after look that would scare the dead.

Behind closed doors, I looked in the mirror and tried to make sense of my unruly hair. I applied leave-in conditioner and brushed at the tangles, then scrunched my hair to bring back the curls. I left on the robe and pajamas, then touched up my lips with some tinted gloss. For my breath, I popped a few mints in my mouth, finishing them off with another swig of coffee. Counteractive, sure. But both necessary.

The doorbell rang, and I froze. I could hear Meadow opening the door and Sonny's deep voice, but nothing beyond that. The bedroom door opened, and I swung around as Blake shuffled in.

"Lover boy's here," he said, closing the door behind him. He wore nothing but a towel hung loosely around his hips, looking a whole lot better than the half-dead lump he'd been twenty minutes earlier, though still a little green around the edges.

"Are you feeling better?" I asked. "Need more coffee?"

"Maybe one for the road." He eyed the half-empty tequila bottle next to the bed. "Keep that," he said. "I'm done drinking forever."

"Forever? Really?"

He gave me a sideways look, then let loose a small grin.

"Fine, I'm done until I've recovered. Still, keep it. I can't even look at it."

I kept my back to him as he pulled the rest of his clothes on, even though nothing about his body was secret to me. I didn't turn back around until I heard him zip his pants.

"So, how do we do this?" he asked, jerking his head toward Sonny and Meadow's voices in the kitchen.

"We get you a cup of coffee, and say goodbye," I said, shrugging my shoulders like it was no big deal. He eyed me, and then a look of realization crossed his pasty face.

"Gotcha," he said, turning to the door. I followed him out, my heart racing as we headed closer to the kitchen. I wiped my sweaty hands on my robe. I peered around Blake just in time to see Sonny turn in our direction, then the dark shadow that crossed his expression. Or did I imagine it? Sonny's face relaxed into a smile.

"Hey, bro," he said, leaning forward with an extended hand. Blake shook it, giving a head nod.

"Hey. I'm on my way out. You both probably have a lot to go over, right? Cricket told me about the party you two are planning. Sounds like you have your work cut out for you."

I had to hand it to Blake for paying attention. But even more of a surprise was the lack of tension between Sonny and him. I glanced at Meadow, who just shook her head at me from behind Sonny's back.

"It's actually been effortless, with Cricket's connections and expertise." Sonny looked at me then, offering a quick wink that sent one of two messages. One, *I'm completely over you. See me playing nice with your boyfriend?* Two, *I know what you're doing, and I'm not falling for it.* Oh wait, there was a third message—*I know you're not really over me, and you swoon a little when I wink at you, so here you go.*

"Here, honey, you can use my travel mug so you don't spill in the car," I said, sliding my arm around Blake's waist. He instinctively wrapped his arm around my shoulder, looking down at me. His eyes had that same look from the party the other night, the one where I first realized Sonny was back in town, and I silently thanked him for being such a willing participant in this charade.

"My favorite one, right?" he asked as Meadow grabbed my pink one from the cabinet, the one that was covered completely in glitter.

"Uh, yeah," I said, trying to bite back my laughter. Blake took the pink mug from Meadow and poured the rest of the coffee into it.

"All right, babe," he said as his goodbye.

Side note. I have never, ever liked being called *babe*. It always seemed like one of those ownership kind of nicknames—partly because it was a shorter term for a helpless infant, and partly because it's the kind of name catcalled from the street.

"All right, babe," I echoed, turning under his arm and lifting my face to his. Blake gave me a secret smirk, then leaned down and kissed me, lingering with his lips pressed against mine, almost as if we'd spent all our passion the night before, and this was just the icing on the cake. Sonny cleared his throat, and I felt a small bit of satisfaction.

"I'm sure Cricket has already mentioned it to you, but we were talking about going to dinner on Friday at Stormy's in San Francisco. Chuck's letting me put it on the company card. You should come along."

"She hasn't," Blake said. "But—"

"We're busy." I glared at Sonny, then turned to smile at Blake. "It was supposed to be a business thing, but between Taye and the two of us, I think everything about the party is managed."

"We still have to check out Merdell Gallery," Sonny pointed out. "It's just a few miles away from Stormy's. We can go there first, sign off on the paperwork, and then head off to dinner. What do you say, *mo chridhe*? I mean, Cricket?"

His grin cut straight through me, and my eyes narrowed. Blake didn't know how I felt about being called *babe*, but Sonny did. Even more, he knew my favorite pet name he had for me—*mo chridhe*, my heart.

And that's when it occurred to me what he was doing. He may have been taken, but he was invading any space I had for moving on without him.

"You know, you're right," I said. "We should make it a double date. Blake and me, and you and Justine. It will be fun."

"Uh, Cricket, can I talk to you a second?" Blake asked. Before I could answer, he pulled me out of the kitchen and into the bird room. Avery squawked, floating down from the large branch against the wall so he could nip at Blake's shoelaces.

"We *have* to go," I said. "Just agree to it. What's the big deal?"

"The big deal is that I finally decided to take Sadie out, and have something planned for that night."

"So make it a different night," I said.

He looked up at the ceiling, resting his hand at his neck in frustration. Then he looked back down at me.

"Eventually you're going to have to tell him the truth," he said.

"Eventually Sonny and I won't be in each other's lives," I pointed out. "We're working together for just a few more weeks, and then I never have to see him again." I tugged at Blake's arm, coaxing him from the room. Avery played the other end of the tug of war, untying

Blake's shoe and pulling at the lace. "Please, Blake. Let's just go. Let's show him how serious we are."

"And why?" he asked. "What's in it for you?"

"Because…" I turned away, taking a deep breath. All the reasons I was doing this suddenly felt stupid. "You know why," I blurted out. "You started this."

"No, I think *you* started this, and now it's cutting too much into my life. I'm ready for this to be over so I can move forward with Sadie."

I let go of his arm, breathing deeply as I fought the panic inside me.

"Please, Blake." I looked back at him, hot tears brimming my eyes. "I need you, just for a few more weeks. I don't want him to think I'm a loser, or that I still want him."

"You *do* want him," Blake said. I glared at him.

"You and I have already established that," I said. "But even though he's moved on, he seems to think I can't. The last thing I need is for him to know he's wrecked me."

"*Wrecked* you? Seriously?"

"Wrecked me," I said, looking Blake straight in the eyes. And it was then that I realized it was true. I wasn't just sore about the breakup. I *loved* him, and I probably always would. With time, I could probably move on. But right now, just being around him, I kept thinking of all the ways he used to love me. Forget about the way he left me. The way he loved me was with his whole heart. He loved me the way he held me—a full-body experience. He'd engulf me with his arms, his chest, his very essence, squeezing me tight so that I could almost let go of all my body strength and he'd hold me up. This was the way he loved.

The night my parents died, Meadow and I had been in charge of all the funeral and reception details. It's strange how that happens. The most important people we'd ever known were ripped from our lives, and we were left to make sure *other* people could say goodbye. Meadow and I consoled person after person, and all the while, I felt like I was dying. I loved my parents. Everyone loves their parents, but my parents were my friends. I was especially close with my mom. I used to sit with her for hours listening to her talk because I just loved being in her presence. She had a calming sense to her, where the world could be crumbling around us, but look at the bees! Look at the blue sky! Look at the way the sunflower knows how to turn its head to follow the sun! My mom saw the world as a million little miracles, manifested in the air we breathed, the way the grass grew, and the perfection in the body segments of a worker ant.

At the end of the reception, when we'd said goodbye to the last person, all that was left were Meadow, me, and Sonny. He'd spent the whole time making sure the background stuff was taken care of. The parking had been flawless, thanks to a few buddies of his he'd recruited. The kitchen was clean, and everything was put back in its place. His phone camera held photos of the event, start to finish—something I hadn't even thought about. And once we were alone, no more guests to entertain, Sonny held on to both Meadow and me as we cried. He was our anchor, allowing us the freedom to let go and fully say goodbye when we no longer had to be strong for anyone else.

This only touched on what Sonny was to me, but it was one of the memories I clung to the hardest. I missed him. I missed *us*. And I needed to find a way to let him go.

"Please Blake," I pleaded again, and he sighed in a way that made me feel guilty and relieved at the same time. He led the way out of the bird room and back into the kitchen.

"Name the time, and we'll be there," Blake said to Sonny. I squeezed his hand twice, *thank you*. He squeezed my hand three times, *you owe me*. He pecked me on the lips before he left, and it felt almost like the kind of kiss a boyfriend would give a girlfriend. I fought the urge to see if Sonny bought it.

"Well, that was fun," Meadow said a few moments later, nudging Sonny on her way out of the room. "You kids behave yourself, all right?"

Alone with Sonny, the air in the room felt heavy. He was busy looking at his phone, almost as if I wasn't there.

"Is Finnigan really going to pay for a double date?" I asked, mostly just to break the silence. But when Sonny continued to look at this phone, the air felt like it would crush me. *Look at me*, I mentally begged, regretting the whole charade.

"Yup," Sonny said, still not acknowledging me with his eyes. He shoved his phone in his pocket, then moved past me toward the door. "Why would I lie?"

He left me standing by myself in the kitchen, his departing words echoing through my mind. I'd forgotten how cold he could be when he was upset.

I kept my distance the rest of the day. Buoy and I hung out on the porch while I curled my fingers in his long golden hair, all while Sonny slaved away on the outdoor aviary. If I had any questions about whether he remained angry with me, they were answered in the way he worked. He swung his mallet against the fence posts as if he could drive them through the earth. His jaw pulsed as he poured concrete, and he'd stir the mix with brute force. He gave laser focus to every single task, never once looking in my direction.

It was like this the rest of the week. Sonny showed up to work on the enclosure, reserving any witty banter he had for Meadow and leaving me with the cold entrails of conversation. I'd even attempted to let him off the hook, telling him I trusted his judgment on Merdell Gallery.

"*Haud yer wheesht,*" he'd muttered in response, which was his way of telling me to shut it. I didn't know whether to be offended at the insult or honored that he assumed I'd understand.

"I don't get it," I said to Meadow later that day.

"He's jealous," she answered. I wasn't so sure.

Somehow, Sonny managed to complete the aviary by midweek, and had even finished the indoor enclosure for Avery in our bird room—one that allowed for use of the living room while still giving the bird room to roam. All of it was incredible. Outside, the enclosure was like a miniature jungle, with leafy trees and misters hidden within the branches, which would keep the bird cool in the summer months. Inside, the window area of the living room was now dedicated to the bird, with large branches, a bubbling fountain, foliage, and even a birdbath for Avery to splash around.

It was obvious Sonny had put a lot of thought into both enclosures, for Avery and for me. And yet, he treated me as if I were a stranger the whole time. And when I tried to push money in his hand, he dropped it and glared at me like I'd insulted him.

"I told you I'd do it for free," he growled. "It's what friends do."

"Really? Friends?" I said, picking the dollars up off the ground before they blew away. "Because friends also talk with each other, and this is the most you've said to me all week."

He stopped putting his tools away and glared at me. But then his face softened.

"You're right," he said, running his hand over the back of his neck. "I'm sorry. I guess I just got too in my head."

"About what?" I asked, biting back the nerves it took to ask such a question. Was he in his head about me? Did he have doubts?

"I just wanted to get the enclosure right," he said. He didn't seem to notice the way my shoulders fell, or the breath I let out. "I honestly wasn't sure I'd pull it off."

"Of course you'd pull it off." I bit back my disappointment and turned toward the aviary, a dozen yards away from where Sonny was parked. Meadow stood by it, Buoy resting at her feet as she watched Avery fly from branch to branch, his squawks echoing down the driveway. Even from where we stood by his truck, I was amazed at how jungle-like the enclosure appeared. I could almost smell the tropical air. "It's perfect," I said, turning back to him. Sonny continued looking toward the enclosure, a serious look on his face.

"What happened to her?" he asked. Meadow was resting on her crutches, unmoving, appearing deep in thought as she continued watching the bird. I suspected she'd stay like that for hours if left undisturbed.

"I don't know," I said. "She won't talk."

"She's different." He looked down at me. "She's trying to be the same, but I see it. She's quieter. Almost fearful."

I'd noticed the same thing in the short time she'd been home. At first, she acted like everything was the same. But the Meadow I knew was enthusiastic about life and everything around her. She was the life of the party, stir crazy if she stayed in one spot for too long. But since being home, she'd been content to just roam the house.

"You know she didn't fall, right?" Sonny continued.

I nodded, looking at my feet. "I know something traumatic happened, but she won't tell me what it was."

I told him about the conversation I'd had with Meadow the day before Avery arrived, and then how she disappeared until the night she showed up on my doorstep.

"I have so many questions, and she shuts me off before I can ask them. She went out with some guy in Sweden and then I never heard from her again. She swears he didn't hurt her, and I think I believe her. But then, what happened?"

Meadow looked in our direction. She waved at us, and both Sonny and I waved back.

"She knows we're talking about her," I said, and Sonny murmured in agreement. "If I learn anything, I'll let you know." As soon as I said it, I felt ridiculous. Sonny wasn't in our lives anymore. At least, he wasn't supposed to be. Now that the bird enclosure was done, it was one less tie he had with me. And once the party was over, he'd be gone for good. Every day was a step closer to never seeing him again.

"Oh, I sent Taye the deposits she needed for the caterer," Sonny said, back in business mode. "Once we have the venue reserved, it's smooth sailing to the party. That reminds me..." He opened his truck door and grabbed a hardbound book off the passenger seat, then handed it to me. "Merdell Gallery," he said.

I looked at the silver embossed lettering of the venue name on a sleek black cover. Opening it, I was treated to full-page images of the art gallery on the bottom floor and the various event spaces throughout the building. I paused when I reached the two-page spread of the top floor, showing a large open space surrounded by floor-to-ceiling windows. In this image, it showed the cityscape during the day with the San Francisco Bay off in the distance. I could just imagine what it would look like at night, with the twinkling lights of the skyscrapers under a smattering of stars. I got goosebumps just looking at the photo, and already knew this venue would be the perfect location.

"I took the liberty of booking Charles' event, just so we didn't lose the space if we like it," Sonny continued when I finally looked up. "I gave them a deposit to hold the date, and they agreed to wait until this Friday for you to see it before we commit."

I hadn't forgotten about the double date, but hearing him mention it so casually sent a jolt of electricity through me as if I had. Truthfully, it was all I'd thought of. I thought of canceling. I thought of what I'd wear. I thought of what it would be like to see Justine hanging all over Sonny, or if I could keep up the charade with Blake for a whole evening. Every time I mentioned the date to Blake, he'd been less than enthusiastic. It was almost like I was dragging him to his own execution. In many ways, it was how I felt about it, too, mostly because an evening with Sonny and his girlfriend would force me to accept the fact that he'd moved on. But maybe this was exactly what I needed so I could get him out of my system for good.

"What time should we meet you there?" I asked.

"They have us down for 4 p.m. for a walkthrough, which should give us plenty of time to check it out before walking to Stormy's. Our reservations are at six, so the timing is perfect."

"Great," I said, though I felt less than great about it. "Justine seems fun. I look forward to getting to know her better," I lied.

"Same. Blake seems..." He paused, seeming to search for something to say.

"He's a good guy," I finished for him.

"I'm glad you're happy, Cricket. It's all I've ever wanted for you."

I didn't have anything to say to this. What could I say? It was a lie. If he wanted the best for me, he never would have left.

Sonny whistled for Buoy, who barreled toward us before jumping straight into the cab of the truck. "See you Friday," Sonny said, following his dog onto the seat, then shutting the door behind him.

"See you," I said, turning to go as he started the truck. The old me would have stayed put, waiting until he left to head up to the house. But now, I was halfway to the door, my back to him, as I heard the sound of his tires fade in the distance.

Chapter Thirteen

Meadow was still at the enclosure as I walked up, and I stood beside her as we both watched Avery. The bird had settled on a branch and was resting, seeming comfortable in his new outdoor home. I glanced at Meadow to see what she thought about Avery's new home, but that's when I noticed she'd been crying. She held a vibrant colored cloth, which she tucked into her pocket as soon as she caught me looking.

"Are you okay?" I asked. She nodded quickly, swiping at her nose, but staying put as she watched Avery sleep. "You've been here for almost an hour," I said. "Aren't you tired?"

"Not really," she said, offering a shaky smile.

"Come on, let's go inside. Avery is fine out here for now."

She didn't fight me, turning to hobble back toward the house. I held the door open for her and then followed her inside. We'd returned the couches to the bird room, and Meadow collapsed on one of them, resting her leg on the coffee table. By the way she grimaced, I knew she was hurting. I propped a pillow under her leg, then left to make her a cup of tea. When I returned, the cloth was back in her hand, a gold chain hanging out. She hadn't yet seen me, and I stood silently in the doorway as she slipped the chain out of the cloth, revealing an oval locket. I held my breath as she opened it, though I couldn't see the photo she was looking at. Meadow touched her finger to the image, but I must have made a noise because she snapped it shut and stuffed it back in her pocket before looking up.

"Thank you for the tea," she said, wiping at her cheek and then taking the cup. She smiled as she inhaled the scent. "Remember when Dad used to get us this blend every year for Christmas?" she asked before taking a sip.

"Kea Lani Orange Pineapple from the Sonoma Mission Inn," I said, settling in beside her with my own cup. "He has boxes of it in the pantry. I think I have enough to last a lifetime, as long as tea doesn't go bad."

We sipped in silence, and I thought about what Sonny had said about Meadow. She *was* different. All this time, she'd been playing it off that everything was fine, but there was an edge to her I'd never known before. She was more guarded. More secretive. Something was eating at her, and I wished she would let me know so I could do something; at least help her get through whatever had happened. She still hadn't been on

Instagram since that last post in Sweden, and her numbers had dropped even more. The comments were all over the map—some expressing concern, but others getting impatient with her absence. One troll wrote "I hope you died," and it took everything in me to not fire back with my own vicious comments.

Still, as we sat in the living room sipping our tea, my curiosity was getting the better of me. Over everything, but especially over Meadow's absence from social media.

"Are you quitting Wandering Meadow?" I finally asked.

Meadow shrugged. "No," she said. "I'm just taking a small break."

"How small?"

Meadow turned to me, then glanced at her arm, then her leg. "I don't want my followers to know," she said in a quiet voice.

And when she said it, I realized who she sounded like. *Me.* I was the one who stayed in the background, didn't want to bother people with my presence, was afraid of what people thought, and worried I might offend them. Meadow had always been the one who stood out, who started the party when she entered a room, and who never, ever worried about what anyone thought. The fact that she was content hiding out here all this time was strange enough. But after Sonny pointed out how withdrawn she seemed compared to her old self, I couldn't unsee it.

I wrapped my arm around her, and Meadow rested her head on my shoulder. "Tell me what happened," I said, and I felt her stiffen.

"I—"

"You fell. That's what you say. But that's not what happened. You've been moping around here for a week and a half, and it's obvious you've been through something horrible. Why can't you just tell me?"

She turned to me, the brimming tears making her blue eyes look almost neon. "It's complicated," she said, her lip trembling.

"What happened?" I whispered.

Meadow closed her eyes, taking in a shaky breath. Her hands trembled in her lap, and I reached across to touch her. She grasped my hand, her eyes opening to mine as she attempted to compose herself.

"I made a promise to someone, and this was the cost," she finally said. I opened my mouth, but she stopped me. "Please, just leave it at that. It's hard to talk about, and if I say anything else..." She paused, clamping her mouth shut. Then she looked at me, giving me a watery smile. "Just leave it alone, okay?"

"I don't understand," I said. "If someone hurt you, we should be talking to the police. We should—"

"And that's why I didn't tell you," Meadow said, pulling her hand from mine. "We can't. If we do, everything gets worse."

"What are you talking about?" I searched her face, trying to find the things she wasn't saying.

She turned away. "I shouldn't even have come here," she whispered. "I just didn't know what else to do."

"Of course you should have come here," I said. "I'm your sister. I want to take care of you."

She shook her head quickly, as if shaking the cobwebs out. Then she looked at me and smiled. She reached over and took my hand back, squeezing it.

"Thank you."

"Are you still in trouble?" I asked. "Are *we* in trouble?"

Her teary eyes widened as she shook her head no. "I'm fine," she said. "We're fine. There's nothing to worry about."

"Will you ever be able to tell me everything?" I asked. One of these days, she was going to leave. She'd go back to her regular life of traveling the world, and I wouldn't be able to protect her. I wanted to wrap her in my arms and never let go, just to keep her safe.

"I hope so," she said. "For now, can this just be enough?"

I nodded, though I was dying with questions. For one, how did the bird fit in all of this? And I still couldn't shake the feeling that August, that guy in Sweden she had mentioned, had something to do with it.

Later, when Meadow was taking a shower, I crept into her bedroom and snuck my hand in the pocket of the sweatshirt she was wearing. The cloth was there, and I pulled it out, unwrapping it until the gold locket lay in the palm of my hand. There were engravings of leaves and flowers etched in the front, and a small amethyst in the middle. I looked at the connecting bathroom door, then slipped my fingernail between the opening. It sprang ajar, and I eased it open, staring at the picture inside. It was a beautiful woman with deep mahogany skin, light hazel eyes, and long chestnut-colored hair. Her expression rested in an easy smile, warm, like she was smiling directly at the person taking the photo.

The woman was very attractive, and I would have wondered about Meadow's connection to her had it not been for the other photo in the locket. It was the same woman, but this time she was looking up, smiling at a gorgeous blue and yellow macaw on her shoulder. I peered closer to be sure, but there was no mistaking the missing patch of feathers on its chest near its wing.

I decided not to ask Meadow about the locket. It would have meant admitting I'd snooped in her belongings. That didn't stop me from wanting to know more, though. I hoped there would come a day when she felt safe enough to tell me the rest. For now, I decided to enjoy the fact that she was here and spend as much time with her as possible.

That's why, a few days later, I dedicated the evening to the first official Stone Sisters baking day. I even roped Taye into it, which was laughable because neither Meadow nor Taye ate carbs, whereas I couldn't get enough of them. So really, this was a baking day just for me.

"I don't get how you're not a gazillion pounds," Meadow said as I downed my third spoonful of cookie batter.

"Good genes," I joked. "Carbs are good for you." I licked the rest of the dough off the spoon, then took another spoonful just to prove a point. Honestly, I was starting to feel gross, but the normalcy of all of this made me want to hang on to the moment forever. The bruising on Meadow's face was almost invisible by now, and she could finally walk around the house without her crutches. She never tried the batter, but I caught Taye sneaking a few bites, making both of us laugh. Or maybe it was the Finnigan Estates brut rosé. My head buzzed with sparkling wine bliss. Judging by Taye's and Meadow's wide smiles and easy laughter, I could tell I wasn't alone.

"So, tell me about this marketing guy Cricket is working with since she won't tell me a thing." Taye was circling her finger along the rim of her glass, a wicked smile on her face as she addressed Meadow. "She claims they had a casual acquaintance a while back."

"If casual means she would have had his babies, sure," Meadow said. "But I'm not convinced Sonny and Cricket are over."

"Hello, Cricket here," I said, waving my hands. "I can hear everything you're saying."

"Did you know she's convinced him she has a boyfriend? Guess who's playing the part."

"Meadow," I warned.

"Tell me!" Taye's glass was empty, and Meadow refilled it.

"Do you remember Blake?" she asked.

"Shut up! That playboy?" Taye turned to me. "Are you still screwing him?"

"I'm going to fire you," I said.

"You can't live without me," she countered, then took a healthy sip of her wine, locking her laughing eyes with mine.

"Fine," I admitted, and probably because the wine was loosening my lips, I told her the rest of the story, starting with the moment I saw Sonny at the party.

"I knew he was that guy!" Taye slapped her hand on the counter with a laugh. Then she shot me an apologetic look. "I mean, that sucks and I'm sorry. I can't imagine what it's like to work with him."

"Torture," I admitted. I didn't admit the fireworks that went off every time I was near him. "We're supposed to go out tomorrow night," I said, to which Taye clapped her hands.

"Don't get excited," Meadow warned. "She's taking her fake boyfriend, and Sonny is bringing his impossibly hot girlfriend." I glared at Meadow's description. "Your words, not mine, Cricket," she reminded me.

"Fine. And yes, I am going to some incredible restaurant in San Francisco with my ex-boyfriend and his new girlfriend. It's going to be a blast."

"Well, at least Blake is easy to look at," Taye said.

"Yeah, but he's mad at me because he's in love with some other girl and I'm keeping him from her." I heard my own words and had to shake my head. "God, I'm like a walking soap opera."

"Things are definitely interesting," Meadow said, thoughtlessly popping a ball of cookie dough in her mouth. I widened my eyes, then laughed as she realized what she'd done. She groaned.

"Dang, that's good," she moaned. She threw a small piece of dough at me, which would have hit me if I hadn't ducked. "That's why I stay out of this stuff! I can't keep out of it if I don't!"

"You wouldn't feel that way if you just let yourself eat," I said.

"That's an interesting way to put it," Meadow said, raising an eyebrow at me.

"I'm not following. I eat what I want." I put another ball of dough in my mouth, just to prove the point.

"I don't think she's talking about food," Taye said. I narrowed my eyes as she smothered a laugh, then caught the meaningful look she cast at my sister.

"If you're talking about Sonny, it's not happening. I hardly think that would go over well with, you know, his girlfriend."

"Right," Meadow said to me, rolling her eyes. She turned back to Taye. "You should have seen them when Sonny was building the aviary. It was like strip construction. That man kept taking his shirt off, knowing exactly what it was doing to Cricket."

"That's not true!" But just the thought of it sent a shiver through me, recalling how the sweat glistened off his skin, or how his muscles rippled with each movement. Even when we weren't speaking, I couldn't keep myself from watching him, and I'd longed to know how his body felt under my hands.

"You know you want a taste of that man. Admit it." Meadow had an evil glint in her eye, and I had half a mind to throw cookie batter back at her. *A taste. Yeah right.* If Sonny so much as kissed me, I didn't think I'd know how to put the brakes on.

"Sonny and I are adults who work together," I said, ignoring the smirks Meadow and Taye were tossing at each other. "We went out, and yes, it was a lot more meaningful than I let on, Taye. But that relationship is over."

"And she still loves him," Meadow giggled. Her cheeks were flushed from the wine, and I could hear the bubbly alcohol in her laugh.

"I don't know if I'd go that far," I said. "But I miss him. And seeing him with another woman has been confusing, to say the least." To their credit, Taye and Meadow paused their giggling as I admitted the truth I'd been holding back. "He looks happier than he was before," I continued. "And I think it's because of her. If she's the reason he's happy, who am I to even pretend I have a chance?"

"Cricket, *you* made him happy," Meadow said. "That man couldn't keep his eyes off you when you were going out. He was always doing things for you, from making repairs around the house to going grocery shopping with you. Hell, he just built two whole aviaries for you. He's still doing it. Don't tell me you can't see it."

"I see a nice guy doing nice things for someone he cares about," I said. She opened her mouth, but I continued before she could speak. "He does not care about me the way he used to," I said. "But I know he cares about me as a friend because that's the kind of guy he is. To think it's anything more will do nothing but make a fool out of me. He made his choice when he left. And now, he's with someone else. I have to respect that."

"I think that's fair," Taye said. "It's too bad, but it's fair."

"Well, I think it stinks," Meadow said. Then she offered a small smile. "But I can respect your respecting. Or whatever."

We finished off two bottles of sparkling wine before Taye left, and at least a dozen cookies were gone, though I'd only eaten four—not counting the cookie dough, or the late-night Chinese food we'd ordered through DoorDash.

Later, as I wiped down the counters, I thought about what I'd said about Sonny. He *was* a good guy. As Meadow said, he'd always been generous with his time when it came to me. Like the time he spent on the birdcages. I wasn't a fool; I knew he'd spent some of his own money on the aviary to get it just right. But he'd also made it clear that he didn't want my money because that was the guy he was.

When we'd been a couple, I appreciated the things he did for me, but I realized now how much I took it for granted. I thought it was because he loved me. But now, I realized that was just Sonny, because I wasn't even his girlfriend, and he was still helping me out. Just like he was bending over backward for his boss, making sure Mr.

Finnigan had the perfect celebration event. Surely he had responsibilities in his job that went beyond anniversary parties. And yet, while building a birdcage for me and working his day job at Finnigan Estates, he'd been a reliable partner in the party planning.

Because that was the guy he was.

We had a wonderful chapter together, and I was devastated when it ended. But when I looked at where I was now, even without him in my life, I was doing okay. I missed him, but I was doing okay. And so was he. If he was happy, my only response should be happiness for him. Even if it wasn't because of me.

I mean, it was the least I could do for him.

Chapter Fourteen

I woke up the next day feeling like a honeybee in a rainstorm, and it wasn't because of the wine. All the conclusions I'd come to the night before went to the wayside as reality took its place, especially as I got ready for the dreaded double date. I was about to spend a whole evening with Sonny and his perfect girlfriend. How was I supposed to be happy for him? He'd upgraded his love life while I was just pretending I'd moved on.

This was going to be a disaster.

My phone buzzed as I applied my mascara, and I glanced at it to see the message.

Blake: *I'm sorry. Can't make it.*

I didn't even finish my other eye before I had the phone to my ear.

"Good news," Blake said, not even bothering with hello.

"Unless it's good news about getting here early, I don't want to hear it."

"Remember Sadie?" He asked this like I cared, like I wanted to know about his love life right now. "I finally worked up the nerve to ask her out after my workout this morning, and she said yes. Thing is, tonight is the only night she has free."

"No," I said. "You're busy. You're going to San Francisco with me, remember?"

"Cricket, calm down. Just hear me out."

"I don't want to hear you out!" I yelled. "I want you in some irresistibly hot suit, driving me across the Golden Gate, and making every girl wish they were going home with you but can't because you're with me!"

There was silence for a moment, then, "Jesus, Cricket. Do you even hear yourself?"

I did, and I hated it. But just the thought of facing Sonny with Justine by myself made me want to vomit. The whole thing was making me nauseous. And now, without Blake...

"Holy hell," I breathed. "You're going to make me do this alone, aren't you?"

There was more silence, though I could hear him breathing. Finally, he sighed.

"Never mind. I'll cancel on her."

Something in his voice tugged at me, and I realized the storm I was in. Even more, I realized how selfish. I was being. He was a good friend for helping me out, but now it was getting in the way of his love life. What kind of friend did I want to be?

"Don't cancel on her," I muttered as I slid to the floor, leaning my head against my dresser. "You've been wanting to ask this girl out for ages. This is a good thing, and you deserve to find real love, if this is it."

"I promised you first, though," he said.

"You didn't, though. I roped you into it, and you never promised anything."

"I didn't, did I?" he laughed. "Thank you. You know, you deserve love, too. How about telling Sonny the truth?"

"What, that I made out with you so he wouldn't think I was such a loser?"

"No, that you made a mistake when you let him go."

I pulled the phone away from my ear and glared at it as if he could see me. "I didn't make a mistake," I said, phone attached to my head again. "He made a mistake when he moved away."

"Have you ever, for a moment, thought about the lengths *you* should have gone to if you really cared about him?"

"Wow. That's kind of…"

"Honest?" he asked.

"I was going to say *low*. Maybe, *asshole-ish*."

"And honest," he said. "Look, just have fun. Don't think too hard about all of it. Who knows, you might have a good time."

"Right. Justine and I are going to be the best of friends. Maybe I can let her in on a few bedroom secrets to spice up their relationship."

"That's the spirit," Blake teased.

When we hung up, I considered my choices. I could easily cancel and just call it a night. I could take Meadow with me, but that would just reveal my fear of being alone. Or, I could woman up and just go, determined to have a good time, as Blake said.

I touched Sonny's name on my phone and waited for him to answer.

"Hello?"

"Hey," I said. "Blake can't make it tonight, so I hope you don't mind a third wheel on your date with Justine."

"Actually, it will be my date with you. Justine can't make it either."

"Seriously?" I paused, an electric jolt traveling through my body. I was somewhere between believing this was a horrible turn of events and believing the gods were smiling down on me. I closed my eyes, trying to get a hold of myself.

"Cricket?"

I realized he was still talking, and I hadn't heard anything he said.

"Sorry, what?"

"I was saying we should just go in one car. It makes no sense for us to meet there when I can just pick you up. Is that cool?"

"Yeah." I answered without thinking. But then it registered. I looked down at the robe I was wearing, then touched the frizzy waves of my hair. "Uh, what time will you be here?"

"About ten minutes," he said. "I'm already on my way."

"Drive slow," I said. He was still laughing when I hung up.

I kicked it into high gear, pulling out the outfit Meadow had helped me pick out last night. Looking at it now, I wondered if it was a mistake. Last night, when we thought I was going as Blake's date, we'd picked out this tight-fitting black dress that hid next to nothing. I squeezed it on, then turned to see how my backside fit into it.

"He's not going to know what hit him," Meadow said in the doorway.

"Which is probably why I should change. Blake isn't going, and neither is Justine." I started to pull it off, but Meadow limped across the room and stopped me.

"Why do you do this?" she asked. "Why can't you be bold and daring for once? You deserve everything you want in life. Can't you just believe that? You're worth having someone like Sonny, and more."

"But he has a girlfriend."

"He had you first!" she said. She shook her head at the look on my face. "Look, I'm not saying it's right to steal someone else's man, but if you go out there just being yourself and he falls in love with you, was he ever hers in the first place?"

"If I go as myself, I'd be wearing my strawberry gardening dress with a trowel in my hand."

"To a fancy dinner? Come on, Cricket. I've seen you dress up plenty of times, and you are a hot piece of ass, with or without a man."

"That's easy for you to say—we're identical."

"You're right," she said. "I'm saying that because I know it about myself. And the same is true for you. So will you please stop doubting who you are? It's time for you to accept that you're an incredible, strong, beautiful, and sexy woman, and any man worth his weight would count himself lucky to be around you."

I straightened the dress so that it clung to my hips, then peered at my reflection in the mirror. Once I looked past all my insecurities, I saw what Meadow saw. I realized how tired I was of living in the shadows. Maybe it was time for a change.

The bell rang, and I groaned, my hand flying to my unruly hair.

"I'll let him in, you finish getting ready. You're worth waiting for. Oh, and Cricket?"

"Yeah?"

"Don't forget to finish your eyes."

"What?" I looked in the mirror, noting the mascara on one eye, and the blonde wispy hint of lashes on the other—the curse of being a redhead. "Thanks."

As I approached the front room, I heard Meadow and Sonny deep in conversation. She was laughing at something he said, and it was almost like old times. They'd always had a sibling-like bond, which made it easy to love Sonny more. The way he'd fit in with Meadow so naturally was something I wasn't sure I'd have again. Would I ever find someone who loved my sister like I loved her?

"Hey, quit stalling and get out here," Meadow called, leaning her head over so she could see me in the hallway. Sonny did the same, and I enjoyed the way his eyes lit up when he looked at me. He stood, stepping toward me so he could take my hand. He motioned for me to turn, and I did, letting him spin me around so he could get a full view of the dress. He whistled low and slow.

"Damn, girl, you sure do clean up nice."

I felt a smile tugging at my lips, both at the compliment and at the rumbling drawl of his accent. "This old thing?" I teased, but only to hide what I really wanted to say—how delicious *he* looked. He wore a simple button-up shirt, rolled up to his elbows and showing off his tan forearms. He was due for a haircut, but I kind of liked the way his curls hung over his forehead, and how the locks skimmed the collar of his shirt. He was growing out his beard, it seemed, but it was trimmed close to his face. I wanted to run my hand against his cheek, feel his jaw pulse under my palm, feel his breath.

I breathed in at the thought, and a spark of electricity shuddered through me.

"If you're cold now, you're going to freeze later. It's at least twenty degrees cooler in the city," Sonny said, mistaking my shiver for something else. Thankfully.

"Way ahead of you." I opened the closet and grabbed a jacket Meadow had sent me ages ago that I still hadn't worn yet. A stormy grey, the jacket buttoned tight against my chest and flared at the waist, giving me a flirty hourglass shape. The look on Sonny's face let me know he approved.

"Now kids, don't be out all night. But if you are, rest assured I won't be waiting up," Meadow said, giving me a not-so-secretive wink.

I rolled my eyes, but when I glanced at Sonny, there was something in his expression that made my tummy do a slow roll.

"I'll have her home before the clock strikes twelve," he promised. Was that a flash of regret that crossed his face? Or was it my imagination? He held the door open for me, and I hesitated for a moment. I knew I should keep a wall between us, but I also liked the way this felt. I slipped through the doorway under his arm, almost as if we belonged to each other.

"Enjoy yourself," Meadow called after us, and I knew she was speaking directly to me as Sonny closed the door behind us. She was right—I *should* enjoy myself. We were both grownups, perfectly capable of being friends. We weren't doing anything wrong.

Sonny seemed to have sensed my lowered guard because he was back to being his chivalrous self by opening my car door before I slid into the seat. He didn't close the door right away as he eyed my high heels.

"Are you going to be able to walk in those?" he asked. I pulled out the flip flops I'd concealed in my purse and waved them in front of his face. "Always thinking ahead," he laughed. "That's one of the things I've always loved most about you." He closed the door while I let his use of the word *love* linger in my head, a smile tugging at my lips.

The smile faded, though, when Sonny tried to start the car. It made a whirring noise, but wouldn't turn over. He tried several times, then slammed the heel of his hand against the steering wheel.

"It's the starter," he said. "I had a feeling it was going out and thought I had more time to get it replaced. Damn!" He took the keys out and threw them across the dash.

"Stop," I said, unfastening my seatbelt and opening my door. "We'll just take my car. You can call the tow company from the road and have them take it to the shop. Hopefully it will be fixed by tomorrow. I'll even let you take my car tonight, so it's no big deal, okay?"

"Are you sure? I can give you gas money," he offered.

"I'm not taking your money," I said with a laugh. "Haven't you done enough for me? Let this be a very small token of appreciation for the beautiful bird enclosures you built for Avery. Okay?"

I ran into the house and let Meadow know what was happening so she wouldn't worry, and then we were off.

The weather lately had been unnaturally warm for early October, and I rolled the window down slightly since the air conditioner didn't work, hoping it wouldn't make my hair a frizzy mess. I also hoped Sonny would overlook the car's musty smell, which had been there since the last rainstorm. The seal on the trunk lid had failed to keep the rainwater out, and I still found patches of mildew on the fabric inside.

Sonny got off the phone with the mechanic and squeezed my knee as a thank you. I went from feeling nonchalant about it, to realizing how out of place the gesture was. He must have felt the same because he yanked his hand away. I glanced at him, and he looked embarrassed.

"Sorry, old habit," he said.

"It's fine," I said. "I mean…" I knew I should draw some kind of line, but I also didn't want to ruin our time together with a bunch of rules to our friendship. I'd already tried that, and we kept tromping all over them— crossing the line and then retreating.

And then Meadow's voice echoed in my head: *"Why can't you be bold and daring for once?"*

What if we let go of the rules? Not break the obvious ones, but not make unnecessary ones, either?

"Let's just have fun and stop worrying about how to act around each other," I said, my heart thrumming in my ears at the bold and daring thoughts I was trying to keep at bay. "Is that okay?"

Sonny belted out a deep laugh, shaking his head. "Are you saying this? Miss 'lay down the law'? Aren't there ground rules to being your friend?"

I grinned, in spite of myself. "Oh Sonny, why do you have to be so uptight?"

He laughed even harder at this.

Chapter Fifteen

The drive to San Francisco was always beautiful. Once we were past the never-ending construction in the Novato Narrows, traffic eased up and we flew past the town of San Rafael. I loved the shift of scenery along Highway 101, going from city lights to marshy horizons, to the hills of Sausalito, and then through the Robin Williams rainbow tunnel until we got our first glimpse of the ocean. Living in Petaluma had its benefits, and this was one of them—we were only a short forty-five minutes from San Francisco and the wide blue mouth of the Bay.

We reached the Golden Gate, and I was surprised to see clear blue skies. Usually, San Francisco was covered in a thick marine layer of fog, requiring a heavy jacket anytime I wanted to cross into the city. I tested the temperature through the crack in my window, pleased when met by warm and balmy air. The terra cotta towers of the bridge loomed over us, and on both sides was an endless sea covered in sailboats. It was like the whole Bay Area was taking an extended weekend, and I couldn't help imagining what life would be like to just spend the day sailing.

Sonny turned on the radio and Elvis Presley fills the car with "Blue Christmas," interrupting the picturesque setting.

"Oh, crap, I forgot," he said with a laugh. He tried to eject it, but, as both of us knew, it was going nowhere. It was June the year my parents died, and my mom had been on a holiday kick. That, or she couldn't figure out how to eject the tape, either. Now, I either drove in silence, or I succumbed to Elvis Presley's rockabilly version of all the Christmas hits.

Today, I turned it up and started singing with the King. Sonny laughed again, but soon he was joining in, his baritone voice adding the bass to my middle-range notes. I think Elvis was the only one truly on key, but it still sounded perfect to me.

"Do you remember the first year we were going out, when your mom made all of us matching knit blankets?"

"Yes! I keep mine in my room on that oversized chair," I said. "It's the perfect size to wrap all around me while I'm reading." I laughed, recalling how Mom had freaked out when I told her I was inviting Sonny to our holiday dinner since he had no family here. She hadn't even met him yet, and she still gave him the same elaborate knit blanket she'd made for Meadow and me, as if he was another member of the family. "Before

Christmas, she spent every spare moment she had knitting that blanket. She'd worked on mine and Meadow's blankets for months, but yours she hashed out in a couple of weeks. She said she'd never knit anything so fast in her life."

"I didn't understand it then," he said. "I do *now*, knowing who your mom was. But we didn't even know each other, and it was such a personal present. I would have been happy with just the meal."

"She felt bad you couldn't be with your dad," I said. "She decided then that we were your family."

A bolt of nostalgia hit me as soon as the words left my mouth, along with a stark realization. We weren't just Sonny's family, but he became mine—especially after my parents died, and then Meadow decided to travel. I would have been alone except for Sonny. But when he moved back to Wisconsin, something shut down inside me. I couldn't handle another loss.

I stuffed the realization way down, knowing if I dwelled on it too much, I'd expose my heart to Sonny.

"How is your dad?" I asked. My voice squeaked slightly, but I covered it by coughing. "Is he still managing the B&B on his own, or has he finally decided to slow down?"

Malcolm owned Skye Keeper's Cottage, a popular bed and breakfast establishment on acres of farmland that kept him busy throughout the year. I'd never met

Malcolm in person but had talked with him several times through video calls with Sonny in the past. He reminded me so much of an older version of Sonny, with his laughing blue eyes and deep baritone laugh, but he wore his white curls cut short and had a full beard that reached almost to his navel. And if I ever thought Sonny's Scottish accent was thick, it was nothing like Malcolm's. Eventually I grew used to the rolling cadence of his voice and the occasional Gaelic word that slipped into conversation, but there were many times Sonny had to translate his father's expressions.

"Da's doing well. And I don't think *slow down* is in his vocabulary. Last week he bought a drone so he could keep an eye on his cattle for miles. Can you imagine that? My seventy-two-year-old da working technology like he was born into it. He also mentioned a woman he's dating, a widow. I suppose one of these days I should fly to Scotland to see him. I never know when it will be the last time." He cleared his throat after he said it, and I could feel the discomfort that settled between us. I knew it was tied directly to the fact that I had already lost my parents and he still had his. I reached over and squeezed his hand, a gesture of peace.

"At any rate, I still have that blanket," he said, squeezing my hand back. "It's actually on my bed right now."

I was silent for a moment. Just the mention of his bed, and all I could think of were the two pillows, and who laid her head on the other one.

"Wait a second," I said, brushing away the thought. "I didn't see the blanket on your bed."

"Were you studying my bed, Stone?" He nudged my knee, and I knocked it against his hand.

"No, McIntyre, I have no interest whatsoever in your bed," I lied. "It was just on the way to the bathroom."

"Well, if you'd snooped a little further, you would have seen the blanket underneath my comforter, because it keeps me warmest that way, and Buoy won't shed his fur on it."

But I did snoop. My mind went immediately to the salt and pepper shakers. Then to Justine. Then finally to the lack of her stuff at his house.

"Can I ask you a personal question?" I asked.

"You can ask it," he said. "But I might not answer."

"Fair enough. Why doesn't Justine keep any of her stuff at your house?"

"Uh, that's a weird question," he said.

"I'm serious. I was there for over an hour, and I didn't see anything of hers. Well, I mean I saw her toothbrush."

"Her toothbrush?"

I bit my lip, realizing I'd outed my snooping. "How come she doesn't keep her other things at your house?" I asked.

"Were you looking for her stuff?"

"No," I lied again. "I just noticed. So, how come?"

"Because she has her own house." He shifted in his seat, turning the radio up as if Elvis Presley weren't loud enough. I reached over and turned it down. I was feeling bold, and I figured this was a great time to clear up some confusion.

"I had my own house when we were going out, but I also had some things at your house. You gave me my own drawer for clothes I could keep there for when I stayed over. I mean, you still had my pajama bottoms. But she has nothing like that."

"You looked in my drawers?"

"No," I said, but now kind of wishing I had. "Does she have a drawer?"

"No, she doesn't have a drawer."

"Does she stay at your house?" My hands grew clammy as I asked that, and I gripped the steering wheel, not wanting to look at him after asking that.

"That's kind of a personal question," he said.

"I warned you."

Sonny sighed. Then he took my clammy hand off the steering wheel and held it in his until I glanced at him. He had a smile on his face, and he shook his head.

"Let's not talk about our relationships. Right now, let's just be us and enjoy the day. Is that okay?"

I wanted to know more. I wanted to know everything. But at the same time, I didn't. Just knowing he was with someone else was eating me up, especially now that we were spending the day together. Especially as he held my hand, which was probably more for reassurance than anything else. Still, my hand warmed inside his, and I left it where it was, pretending, for a moment, that it meant more than a kind gesture. Maybe it was best if we didn't talk about her. Maybe I could just pretend she didn't exist.

"Okay," I said, knowing full well that this game of pretend was temporary, if not unrealistic. I moved my hand from his. A heaviness filled the car as we drove through the tollbooths and past Crissy Field. A few rollerbladers zipped down the sidewalk, passing one family flying a kite, and another throwing a frisbee for their border C=collie. It was like summertime in autumn, with people in shorts and t-shirts, grins all around, and I couldn't help feeling out of place in this overly sexy dress, next to the man I couldn't get over, and a thorny fortress guarding my tender heart.

"You okay?" he asked. I glanced over and realized he was studying my expression, which most likely matched my mood. I brushed aside my thoughts and flashed him a smile, slipping back into our game of pretend.

"I'm fine, but I'm afraid to get lost." This was the truth. I'd never been great with directions in San Francisco; the maze of streets always seemed complicated when I was behind the wheel. But Sonny had this uncanny ability of always knowing where he was, even in unfamiliar situations. San Francisco wasn't unfamiliar to him, even though I'd lived in the Bay Area much longer than he had. He knew this town like it was a second home.

"You're doing great," he said. "Just stay on this road, and when it veers to the right, go with it." Sonny directed me through traffic, up hills, and down side streets until we pulled into the Sutter-Stockton Garage, finding a spot on the fifth floor.

"Keep all your valuables hidden," he said as he looked around the car.

"Maybe I should take the stereo out and place it on top of the car so they know there's nothing worth stealing, right?"

"Good point," he said with a laugh. "Hey, hold up for a second."

I got out of the car but stayed by my door as he trotted over to my side. He hesitated for a second, then came close to me. I started to back up.

"Hold on," he said, softly this time. Then he wrapped his arms around my shoulders, drawing me in. I tensed up, my arms at my side while I waited for him to finish hugging me. But when he kept his arms around me, I realized he wasn't going to let go until I fully submitted. So I did. I rested my arms around his waist and leaned my head on his chest. I could feel the soft thrum of his heart against my ear and smell the musk of his cologne mingling with the fresh scent of soap. I inhaled, then closed my eyes and exhaled, leaning deeper into his embrace as I let go of the tension I hadn't known I was carrying. It was like every cavern in my body was overflowing with all I'd been missing. I took another deep breath at the same time he did. We held it, and then released it together, still holding on to each other. He leaned back, and his finger gently tilted my chin up so that I was looking into his blue eyes.

"Feel better, *mo chridhe*?" he murmured, and I felt breathless in his arms. Then his lips curved into a cocky grin, and I smacked his chest.

"You're a tease," I said with a laugh, pulling away. And yet, my heart was pounding, the moment on repeat in my mind.

We took the elevator down, and I tried not to touch the graffiti-covered walls as I detected the faint odor of piss. We stood next to each other in silence, the whir of the elevator the only sound. I felt the electricity between our hands, just inches apart, all while I fought the temptation to reach for his.

"It's just a few blocks away," Sonny said as the door opened to the ground level of the parking garage. He touched my back for a moment, but then lifted it. Old habits, I was sure, and I continued to feel his phantom touch long after his hand was gone.

I still couldn't get over how warm it was as we exited the shelter of the garage and stepped out into the sunshine of the city. People were in shorts and tank tops, which was a rarity even in the summer months. But here we were, inches from October, and the sun was blessing my skin.

"In case I didn't make it clear before, you look stunning," Sonny murmured, leaning in. I blushed, feeling the warmth of his words against my ear.

"I'm a tad overdressed," I said, eyeing the casual wear around us.

"No, you're a *bricht* gem. But even if you were wearing a smock, you'd still shine brighter than anyone else."

"Always the charmer, eh McIntyre?" I nudged him as we walked, even as I glowed from the compliment.

"I only speak the truth, Stone."

We reached Merdell Gallery, which was an enormous glass building bordered by a large courtyard filled with fine art. Even though Sonny had booked the appointment, I broke from him and reached the reception desk first. A woman sat at the desk, her A-line haircut with purple highlights matching the abstract art on the walls around her.

"May I help you?" she asked, her soft voice still echoing in the open room.

"We have a 4 p.m. appointment to view the terrace event space," I said.

She tapped her fingers on the desk as she scrolled through the computer. Then she looked back at me.

"Cricket Stone?" she asked, and I nodded. "And you must be Sonny McIntyre. You're a few minutes early, and Meredith Breen is wrapping up a meeting. If you'd like, you can enjoy a refreshment from the bar and look around the gallery while you wait." She waved her hand toward the corner on the other side of the room where a man in a black suit was serving wine to visitors.

"Thank you," I said, and led the way toward the table. This time, Sonny did rest his hand at my lower back, and I said nothing to discourage it. I felt light, like his hand belonged there.

The bartender handed Sonny a glass of sauvignon blanc, and he immediately passed it to me. Once his was in hand, we walked slowly through the gallery, studying the art on the walls and a few sculptures on pedestals around the room. I wanted to immerse myself in each painting, to lose myself in the swirls of acrylic and ponder the meaning of the more eclectic pieces, but all I could concentrate on was Sonny's presence, how incredible he smelled, and how normal it was to just walk side by side, looking at art. That was the best part—the normalcy. I realized how much I'd missed that. *This is a business trip, not anything else,* I reminded myself, even as I felt my soul expanding, maybe even glowing.

I did my best to distract myself by noting the features of the gallery. It wasn't just the art that was interesting; it was the room itself. Strands of tiny lights hung from the tall ceiling like stars pouring from the sky. A large fountain was in the center of the room, its soft trickle of water offering a comforting sound under the soft music that was playing from the speakers and the din of conversation that surrounded us. And this was only the gallery. As stunning as the ground floor was, I could only imagine what the terrace room looked like.

"Ms. Stone? Mr. McIntyre?"

We both turned at the soft voice. Before us was an older woman a little shorter than me, but thin as a twig. Her silver hair was gathered in a bun on the top of her head and she looked like a dancer, even though she was older than my mom would have been. That, and instead of a leotard, she wore a trouser outfit with ankle boots.

"Please, call me Cricket." I took the diminutive hand she held out to me, feeling like a giant in the process. "And this is Sonny. You must be Meredith."

"That's correct. I'm so glad you were able to come today. We don't usually have such beautiful weather."

She gestured to the wall of windows and the sunlight shining through in rays. "I don't want to keep you from the sunshine too long. Shall we?"

Meredith led us to the elevator, and I was amazed that it was made entirely of glass. I stood mesmerized as we rose to meet the hanging lights, feeling like we were in a sea of falling stars. I leaned forward to get a better look and brushed Sonny's hand by accident. When I moved out of his way, he slipped his hand in mine and tugged.

"Careful," he teased, as if I'd fall through the solid pane of glass. He didn't let go, and suddenly the lights didn't matter. The glass elevator didn't matter. Nothing mattered except my hand in his. It was hard to focus on anything else except the warmth of this touch, the contrast in rough and soft textures of his skin, the safety in his grip, and the familiarity I still felt after such a long time. I knew I should release his hand, that I should respect his relationship. But at this moment, that didn't matter either.

We moved through a solid foundation, the gallery disappearing as we reached the terrace floor. The doors opened to a large room surrounded on one side by floor-to-ceiling windows that overlooked the whole city. I'd been impressed in the glass elevator, but this was breathtaking. I finally let go of Sonny's hand and walked to the window, almost feeling vertigo at the bird's eye view of the city. Spread out in front of me were matchbox skyscrapers surrounded by a maze of streets, appearing like a model version of the real thing. I could just imagine how this would look at sunset under a fiery sky, or at night when the lights of the city twinkled around us like diamonds.

Meredith showed us the other features of the building, but the window alone was enough to know this was the right place. I glanced at Sonny, blushing as I realized he was watching me. He was probably just gauging my reaction, but I couldn't help the thoughts that flashed at me, particularly of dancing with Sonny in this room, the lights low and the city glowing all around us.

We signed the papers at the end of the tour, and Sonny cut the check for the rest of the fee. I texted the venue information to Taye so she could order and send the invitations. With only two weeks until the event, there wasn't time to spare. She texted back to let me know she was on it, then told me to have fun, especially the naughty kind.

I glanced at Sonny, my ears turning hot as if he could see what she wrote, but he was busy talking with Meredith.

Me: *There will be no naughty fun to be had.*
Taye: *Sure. Okay.*

"I'm so happy our venue will suit the needs of your event," Meredith said as she led us back toward the elevator. "Maybe someday we'll be planning an event like this for the two of you."

Sonny appeared amused at the suggestion, and I could just imagine the look of shock on my face.

"Oh, we're not together," I said. Her mouth formed a little O, then she shook her head in embarrassment.

"I'm sorry, I just assumed. You two move so naturally around each other, I thought you were married."

"We're just good friends," Sonny said. Meredith's eyes shifted from him to me, then back to him. Then she gave a slow nod, a smile on her face.

"Friendship is a beautiful thing," she said. "How lucky that you get to work with each other."

Chapter Sixteen

We were still too early for our reservations, so Sonny and I spent the next hour walking through Chinatown. Red paper lanterns swayed in the light breeze above the road. Laundry hung from balconies above restaurants, the colorful shirts and dresses adding to the carefree ambiance. Store displays beckoned at us, with tables and racks filled with vibrant clothes and tchotchkes. Sonny led me into one store with multiple levels, and we took turns showing each other our finds. The blue and white porcelain bowls. A red silk kimono. The marble figurines in "naughty" poses (take that, Taye!).

As the sun set behind the towering buildings to the west, we began making our way toward the restaurant. Stormy's was just a few blocks away, but all uphill. Once the sun disappeared, a chill settled over the city. I wrapped my coat around me as I shivered.

"You all right?" Sonny asked. His hand rested again at the small of my back, and a warm sensation traveled from his touch to the rest of my body.

"I'm good," I said, silently praying he'd keep his hand there. He did for a while. Then he removed it and took my hand. My step slowed when he did.

"Is this okay?" he asked, his hand still covering mine, but loosely.

This was the third time he'd held my hand this night. There had been an excuse for each instance, but he'd also lingered with his hand claiming mine. This time, though, there was no reason except to just hold my hand. Was this out of habit? Was it a show of friendship? Was I reading more into this than I should? The one thought I kept pushing aside was that of his girlfriend.

I grasped his hand tighter to keep it from slipping from my grasp.

"It's okay," I said.

The restaurant was crowded for a Friday night, and we had to squeeze through a sea of people just to get to the hostess. Thank goodness for reservations, because once Sonny gave her his name, she seated us right away. I ignored one guy who glared at us as we moved to a much quieter corner of the restaurant near the back. The hostess told us the specials and took our drink orders, and then it was just the two of us.

I was at a loss for words. All afternoon it had felt like old times. A comfortable ease had settled between us, and it was easy to forget the past and just be present in the moment. But now that we faced each other, I felt the stark reality of where we were and what was happening. He could spend an afternoon building a birdcage at my home, or take me out to eat tacos, or sit across from me now in a dimly lit restaurant, and it still wasn't enough to keep him from going back to *her*.

He wasn't mine anymore, and the ease of our breakup made me wonder if he ever really was.

"What are you thinking?" Sonny asked after the waiter brought our drinks. He'd ordered a Rob Roy for kicks and I had a Manhattan. The irony wasn't lost on me—two similar drinks, but mine made with rye whiskey and his with Scotch whisky. Same drink, different worlds.

"Nothing," I lied, then sipped at my drink, glancing everywhere but at him. He gave a low laugh, but I still kept my gaze averted.

"Truth or dare," he said, and I finally looked at him, raising an eyebrow.

"Really?"

"Really, Stone. Truth or dare."

"If I said dare, would you make me run naked through the restaurant or something?"

"You'll have to choose dare to find out," he said, his eyes narrowing with his wicked grin.

"That is, if I agree to play the game." I sat back in my chair, taking another sip, enjoying how the drink was already smoothing out the rough edges of my thoughts.

"Fine, you ask me first."

I knew I should resist, especially since I had no idea what he'd have in store for me when it was my turn. But the smug look on his face made me want to wipe it right off again.

"Truth or dare," I said.

"Dare."

Shit. I'd expected him to say *truth*. I looked around us, trying to think of something that was a worthy dare that wouldn't embarrass me alongside him. The options were limited. I mean, the whole point of Truth or Dare was to embarrass someone, right?

"I can hear your brain chirping, Cricket."

"This is hard!" I admitted. "If we weren't in this restaurant I'd make you do a handstand or sing your country's national anthem, or something."

"O Flower of Scotland," he began, and a chill went through me at the silkiness of his deep voice, even if slightly off-key.

"You're going to get us kicked out of here," I hissed, grabbing his hand to stop him, even as he continued. "I didn't even say that was my dare." He stopped singing.

"Is that your dare?"

I mulled it over.

"Fine," I said. "Yes. But sing quietly!"

He did, but it also happened to be when the waiter came to our table to take our order. Sonny looked at the waiter and serenaded him. To his credit, the waiter never flinched, acting as if this were a normal part of dinner service. When Sonny was done, he bowed his head.

"Are you ready to order, or do you need a few more minutes?" the waiter asked, and I smothered a laugh at the absurdity of it.

"Never mess with a Scotsman and his national anthem," Sonny said when the waiter was gone.

"At least you didn't hug him, like that waiter at Ricardo's."

"Give me another one of these," he said, raising his half-empty glass, "and I will. Now it's my turn, and I'll show you how it's done."

"Truth," I said, spitting it out before he could say anything else. I knew Sonny's wicked sense of humor. He really would have me streak through the restaurant. But the satisfied expression on his face at my choice made me realize I'd played into his hands. "Wait, I change my mind."

"You can choose dare next time," he said, leaning forward, rubbing his hands together.

"Okay, truth. But I want ground rules."

He gave me a withering stare. "You and your ground rules. Fine. What are they?"

"We can't discuss our current relationships."

He was still for a moment, then gave a small nod. "Anything else?" he asked.

"No, that's it."

Sonny studied me, and I felt my cheeks grow warm. It was as if he were undressing me, probing my mind, turning me inside out, and all he was doing was looking at me.

"Tell me your deepest, darkest fantasy," he finally said.

"Wow, just going for the kill, aren't you?"

He said nothing, a small smile playing on his lips as he waited for my answer. I beckoned him closer as I leaned in, both of us hovering over the tea light candle in the center of the table. "Brace yourself," I said, my voice husky as I lowered my head and looked up at him. He tilted his head closer. "It's dusk, the sound of frogs on the horizon, and the occasional screech from an owl hunting for its food. I'm on the front porch of a large farmhouse, no other house for miles. The lights are off and a million stars blanket the earth, including the twisting vein of the Milky Way. I'm wearing a dress, and when the hot summer wind blows, I can feel it caressing my skin. *All* my skin." I looked at him with meaning, and he exhaled slowly.

"And who's there with you?" Sonny whispered.

"You really want to know?" I played with the edge of my glass, then licked my lips. "No one. Just me." His eyes widen. "Do you want me to continue? Or are you going to keep interrupting?"

"No, go on."

"So, I'm sitting there on the porch, no one to hear me for miles. I hitch up my skirt, just a little above my knees. It's getting late, and I can feel a yearning inside me…" I pause, lick my lips again, enjoying the way his mouth is twitching, his breathing a little heavier. "…because I remember the book I have on my nightstand, and it's a really good one. So I go back inside, slip into bed, and then read until I fall asleep."

Sonny rolls his eyes as he sits back in his chair. "I should have known, you nerd."

"Hey, you wanted my deepest, darkest fantasy. That was both deep and dark. And now, I believe it's my turn, and I want truth."

"Give it your best shot."

I wanted to hit him hard because I knew he eventually would with me. And there were so many things I was wondering. What he was thinking when he left for Wisconsin. Why he didn't fight for me when I broke things off. If he still thought of me now.

And I knew if I asked anything personal, he'd follow up with something more personal.

"What is the biggest secret you ever kept from your parents?" I asked.

Sonny smiled, nodding in appreciation. "That's a good one," he admitted. "Doesn't every kid lie to their parents? How do I pick just one?"

"Try your best," I said.

He sipped his drink, appearing deep in thought. Then he set his glass down with a laugh. "I got it." He paused, giving me a serious look. "This is a pretty big one, and if you tell Da about it, I'll never forgive you."

I made the sign for Scout's Honor, then settled in for the story.

"After Mam died, I was a *gallus wean*—"

"English, Sonny."

"A troublemaker," he said. "A rotten kid. Not for any reason, except to just stir up my da. And I was usually pretty blatant about it. But there was one thing I never told him because I knew it would send him over the top."

Then he proceeded to tell me about this one night when he stole his dad's car to meet some girl a few towns over, with a mission to have it back in the garage before his father's early wake-up hour.

"This wasn't just any car," Sonny said. "This was a 1956 Jaguar XK Supersport in racing green, just like the one Steve McQueen used to drive. As you know, my da is a collector of classic cars, but this one was his jewel. Which is why I decided to drive it to meet this girl because I knew it would impress her."

"Did it work?"

"Hold your horses, Stone. You're getting ahead of the story."

I laughed, waving him to go on.

"So, I was pretty nervous about meeting this girl. I think her name was Gemma or Gillian, or something like that. Anyway, I not only stole my da's car, but I also took his crystal decanter filled with Glenturret single malt whisky. The whole decanter. The one my parents got as a wedding gift from his father."

"I don't like where this is headed," I said.

"I'm just getting started. So, there I am, sixteen years old, driving my father's car with a bottle of Glenturret under the seat. My hands are sweating all over the steering wheel, and I'm trying to think of what I'm going to say when I show up at her door."

"She didn't even know you were coming?"

Sonny chuckled, shaking his head. "I thought it would be romantic if I surprised her by throwing rocks at her window, and she looked down to see me in my studly glory with my super impressive Jaguar. Here's the thing. I wasn't cool at all. Gemma probably didn't know I existed, and as I got closer to her house, I got more and more nervous. If I'd been smart, I would have just turned around and headed back home, and no one would have known any different."

"But then you wouldn't have this cool story to tell," I said. "Please tell me you didn't start drinking then."

He tapped the side of his nose, signaling I was on the right track.

"I started in on the whisky when I was halfway there, drinking straight out of the decanter. By the time I arrived at her house, I was lit. I scraped the hubcaps on the curb, which was a pretty huge deal since they were the originals. Then I stumbled onto the lawn just as the sprinklers went on. And then I found a rock to throw at her window to get her attention. Not some cute little stones, but a rock."

"Oh, jeez." I held my breath, even as I shook with laughter.

"Yeah," he said slowly. "So her parents are still awake, and I can see them moving around in the kitchen, probably cleaning up before bed. I'm standing there on the front lawn, dripping wet, waiting for some kind of sign to let me know which room is hers. The upstairs is all dark, but I finally make out some flower decals or something on one of the windows. I remembered seeing her binder at school with flowers on it, and it made sense that it was hers. So I chucked that rock as hard as I could."

"No!" This time I laughed out loud.

"Luckily, I was so drunk, that rock didn't make it to the first floor. Unluckily, it went through the kitchen window, narrowly missing Gemma's mother."

My hand covered my mouth as he described running back to the car to drive away, but how it wouldn't start.

"I'm sitting there, minced out of my mind, when I see Gemma's da come out carrying a shotgun. The car finally starts just as he raises the gun, and I'm out of there. But not before he shoots out the back window."

"Shit!" I muttered.

"Right? That was my reaction, too. Plus, the decanter tipped over, and the whole car reeked of booze. I obviously couldn't go home. So I drove around all night long, freaking out, trying to think of what I could do. Finally, in the wee hours of the morning, it came to me. I had to lose the car." He paused for dramatic effect, and I held my breath in anticipation. "I drove it to a cliff near our home, put the car in neutral, and then pushed it until it rolled over the edge and into the ocean."

"Oh my god, Sonny," I said, laughing.

"Yeah. I was not a very bright sixteen-year-old. My da could have dealt with a blown-out window and a scotch-soaked floorboard. I'd have caught hell, but Da would still have his Jaguar." He shakes his head, offering a throaty laugh. "So now I'm stuck miles from home without a ride. The sky was getting lighter, and I knew Da would be up at any moment. Luckily, a sheep farmer picked me up and drove me a block away from my house. Da was in the shower when I finally made it home, so I opened the garage door as if it had been left open all night. I was under the covers when I heard my faither cursing loudly."

Sonny went on to describe the investigators and insurance people who summed it up to theft, and how he'd taken the blame for leaving the garage door open.

"I took a lot of heat for that, but it was worth it because my da never found out the truth."

"That is honestly not the story I was expecting," I said. "I thought you'd tell me about some childhood prank, not a high-stakes car theft."

"I told you I was an awful kid. At least, I was before then. After the car, I went straight and became Da's perfect son. And somehow the whole Jaguar thing blew over. I think my da was pretty sore about losing that car because he hasn't discussed it since."

Our food came, and we continued to share truths, letting go of the dare portion of the game. I told him about the weirdest place I'd ever had sex (a porta-potty at a park, which was also the worst thing I'd ever done). He shared about his biggest insecurity (the layer of softness that covered his abs, the same softness I'd had to refrain from touching while he built my birdcages). I shared my worst habit, but instead of using words, I lifted the saltshaker and rolled my eyes while I waved it. He nodded at my purse.

"No one's looking," he hissed.

"I can't," I said with a laugh, setting the shaker back on the table. "It's a ridiculous habit, and it needs to stop."

"Why? Who's it harming?"

"The restaurant. I'm stealing."

"They have others. Come on. I dare you."

I shot him a look, though I was fighting the impulse.

"You just took your turn, and it was Truth."

"You can win the game if you do this one thing."

I was tempted. He was giving me a reason to take them, guilt-free. The thrill was still there, thanks to being at this restaurant sitting across from Sonny, and the slight buzz from my second Manhattan.

"How about this," Sonny said. He picked up the pepper and pushed the salt toward me. "I take the pepper; you take the salt. Then we'll each have half of a matching pair."

I slid my finger over the rim of the shaker, fighting the impulse to wrap my hand around it and conceal it away.

"Would you two like to hear the dessert menu?"

I knocked the salt over, surprised by the waiter standing over us.

"I'm good," Sonny said, the pepper already missing from the table. He gave me a sly grin. "Cricket? Did you want anything?"

"No, I couldn't eat another bite." My cheeks burned, but the smile on my face was involuntary. As soon as the waiter turned, I nabbed the saltshaker and stuffed it in my purse. Then Sonny and I shared secret grins across the table until the bill was paid and we could get the hell out of there.

"Truth," Sonny said, his voice echoing through the parking garage.

"No more," I groaned.

"Just one, because if I don't ask it, I'm going to wonder about the answer for the rest of my life."

"Now you're making me nervous." And *that* was the truth. There were so many things I was keeping inside, and so far they remained there. But every question was one inch closer to revealing all my secrets, including how I wasn't over him. Judging by how smooth the whole day had been, I had a feeling I never would be.

"When you saw me that night at the Jackson Family Wines event, what was the first thought that crossed your mind?"

There were so many ways I could answer this question. The truth—that I panicked. More truth—that he looked incredible, even from across the room. Even more truth—that I grabbed Blake and made him pretend to be my boyfriend. Yeah... Not saying that.

"I was surprised," I said.

"Care to elaborate?"

"I mean, you'd moved to Wisconsin and we broke up. I didn't think I'd see you ever again. So to see you at an event I'd planned was surprising. I wasn't expecting it."

"And what about the voicemail I left you?"

The one I accidentally deleted. My mouth went dry, and I realized I couldn't get out of it.

"I deleted it."

"You…what? Did you at least listen to it?"

"No, but it's not like that. I… Where's my car?"

This was the spot where my car was supposed to be, but another car was in its space. I always took photos of where I'd parked, just to be sure I didn't lose my car. Checking the photo on my phone, this was definitely the spot, but this car was not mine.

"Shit, Cricket. Look." Sonny pointed at the ground, and I noticed the specks of glass under this car, as if a car window had been smashed.

As if *my* car window had been smashed.

"Are you kidding me? Are you fucking kidding me?" Hot tears filled my eyes as I wrapped my arms around my body. "Why the fuck would they even steal it? The car was a piece of crap. It was on its last leg. It's one of the last things I had left of theirs."

I broke open, the weight in my chest knocking the wind out of me as I cried. Sonny pulled me close and I submitted to his embrace, sobbing into his chest. It was a stupid car. I was eventually going to need to replace it.

But it would have been on my terms, not the terms of some stupid thief looking for an opportunity.

"I'm sorry," I said, pulling away so I could wipe at my face. "This is dumb. I've been needing a new car for a while. Whoever stole it probably did me a favor."

"Cricket," Sonny said, touching my arm. "It was your parents' car. It was special. It's fucked up that someone stole it, especially when it means nothing to them and everything to you. It's okay to be upset about it."

The tears kept coming, even as I tried to push them away. I kept thinking of the pieces of them I'd left in the car, and were now gone. The small crystal prism hanging from the rearview mirror that reflected rainbows throughout the car when the sun shone through it. My mom's sweater that she'd mended with patchwork material and embroidery, and that I still kept on the backseat. The birthday card in the glove compartment with a small note from both of them—my mother's neat and precise handwriting paired with the jagged edges of my dad's signature. The Elvis Presley CD.

"Oh, jeez, the Christmas album," I said, half sobbing, half laughing. "Maybe I should thank them."

"I'll get you a new one," he said, and even though I was half-joking, I appreciated that he somehow knew it meant something to me.

We filed a report with the garage attendant, who was very clear about their policy of not being responsible for theft or damage. He kept pointing at the sign that stated, "Take your keys and your valuables."

"Should I have fit the whole car in my purse?" I finally shot back.

We filled out another report with the police officer who showed up an hour later. I was exhausted by the whole ordeal and wasn't even sure how we'd find our way home. There were no more buses leaving the city, and an Uber would cost a small fortune. Just the thought of our sudden inconvenience was enough to bring on more tears. Sonny held on to me as the police officer took photos of the broken glass.

"Can I take you two somewhere?" the officer asked. It was nearing midnight at this point, and every bit of strength had left my body. I leaned on Sonny for support, and he kept his arm around my waist.

"We can manage," he said.

I didn't ask questions as the police officer drove away, or when Sonny called a friend to check on Buoy and let him out to pee. But when he hung up, he could see the curiosity in my eyes, even under my exhaustion.

"I'm tired," he said. "And you're beyond tired. I'm booking us a room and we can figure out what to do about your car in the morning."

"We can't. I—"

"It's one night between friends," he said. "If I have to sleep on the floor, I will."

And just like that, we entered the Orchard Garden Hotel, an unassuming hotel right next to Chinatown. We walked through the automatic glass doors where a bronze statue of a dancing goddess greeted us in front of a floor-to-ceiling fountain. There was marble everywhere and the bright lights made everything feel safe—a sharp contrast to the dark world outside where strangers steal your car, and no one cares. The front desk clerk, a young woman with a warm smile, heard our story with sympathetic eyes, and then set us up in the balcony suite for a discount.

"Our best room," she promised, and told us how it wasn't even available on their website, and they only booked it by special request. After the whole car nightmare, the kind gesture made me burst into tears again.

"It's been a long night," Sonny explained.

We took the elevator to the top floor, and despite my emotional state, I couldn't help noticing all the details that went into this hotel, from the varying floral bouquets to the beautiful statues and figurines. The display next to the elevator was especially impressive, sculpted to look like an ocean wave with all the details of the water droplets, and a tiny house balancing at the highest peak. It was so beautiful I was afraid to breathe.

The room was more than I could have expected. We walked in and I immediately noticed the wall of windows on one side, similar to Merdell Gallery. I passed the huge bed in the center of the room to open the sliding glass doors and step out on the balcony, just as there was a knock on the front door. Sonny went to answer it while I pulled my jacket closer and lifted my head to the stars. The city lights drowned out most of them, but I could make out a few. I suddenly felt this sense of peace wash over me, as if everything was going to be okay. The car was gone. There was nothing at this moment I could do about it. For now, we were safe, and for a short time we'd get to own a piece of San Francisco. I could hear the city below us, a chorus of car horns paired with the echoes of someone's singing reverberating off the buildings. The skyscrapers around us were lit up like jewels, and I inhaled the city air, reveling in the mixture of crisp autumn air with notes of sewer, greasy food, and car exhaust.

"The front desk sent this up for us, and I figured you could use a glass."

I turned to find Sonny standing behind me, holding two glasses of champagne. His eyes sparkled from the low lights of the city as he handed me a glass, his fingers grazing mine in the process. I shivered, but I wasn't cold. I felt a small ember burning in my core, and it seemed to grow with each bubbly sip.

Sonny sat in one of the chairs on the balcony and looked up. I took the chair next to his and leaned back, picking out a few stars in the light-polluted sky. Eventually, the evening caught up with me. I felt my exhaustion wrap around me like a weighted blanket, enhanced by the bubbles in my glass. But more than that, I was haunted by my thoughts, including the fact that Sonny was so close to me and yet so far away. The conversation we'd had earlier wormed its way into my head, the one about the voicemail, and I realized I couldn't just leave it hanging like that. It wasn't fair to him.

"I deleted your voicemail by accident," I murmured. He made a sound in his throat, then reached over and took my hand for the fourth time that night.

"It's okay. Just forget about it."

I turned to him. My hand felt warm in his. It felt right. "Can you tell me what you said that night?"

"I don't remember," he said. I shook my head.

"Lies. If you didn't remember, you wouldn't have brought it up." My heartbeat quickened, especially as I saw the discomfort on his face. Suddenly, I wanted nothing more than to know what he'd said in that message. "Just tell me."

He let go of my hand and set his glass down as he stood. A cool breeze blew through the balcony, but the space between us was colder. I stared at my knees, wishing I could disappear.

"Come on," he said. "It's late. Let's go to bed." I looked up and his hand was out. Abandoning my glass on the patio table, I accepted his hand and let him lead me to the bedroom. He pulled a pillow off the bed and laid it on the ground, then turned toward the closet for the extra blanket.

"You don't have to do that," I said. I crossed the room and picked the pillow back up. At the same time, my heart raced at what I was suggesting. Him, in bed with me. All this time apart, and I knew this would be sweet torture.

"I don't think I should sleep in that bed tonight. You have a boyfriend and—"

"You're breaking the rules," I interrupted, standing right in front of him. "We're not talking about our current relationships."

And it was then that I kicked aside my walls, including all the reasons to keep my distance. Maybe it was the champagne, or maybe it was a whole day full of mixed messages, but I needed to know where I stood with him, even if it revealed how I still felt.

I took a step closer, and then another when I saw he didn't move away. When I looked into his eyes, I read the questions I hoped were there. I was so close, I could feel his breath on my forehead as his chest moved up and down. I pressed my hands on his chest, feeling the hardness of his body, longing to feel the softness of his skin under his shirt. All this, and our eyes remained locked. The electricity seared between us. He made a small noise in his throat, and I gasped as his hands caught mine.

Don't stop this, I pleaded with my eyes, my breath feeling shallow. And then his mouth was on mine and I was breathing him in, tasting him, pulling at his shirt as his hands gripped my back.

"Cricket," he moaned as we fell on the bed, locked together. Nothing else mattered. Nothing, but getting as close to him as possible. Everything about him was both familiar and strange. I tasted a piece of home in him, mixed with all the things I'd missed over the past year.

He tugged my dress over my hips, exhaling hard when his hands reached the lace of my underwear.

"Tell me to stop," he breathed. "Please, tell me to stop."

"No," I said against his mouth. "Don't stop."

His hesitation lingered, but just for a few heartbeats. Then he was peeling my clothes off as fast as he undressed himself, until we were skin to skin. My hands explored his body, running over the hills and valleys of his back and the rippled surface of his chest and belly until I fondled the length of him. A deep groan escaped his throat. He flipped me on my back and held my hands above my head as he straddled me, staring down at me. The lights were still on, and I whimpered as I saw every part of him that I'd missed.

"Please," I begged, and he met me with a wicked grin before ducking his head, tasting my neck, then moving between my breasts as I arched my back. He took one nipple in his mouth, teasing it with his tongue before scraping it with his teeth, sending chills down my spine. "Please," I pleaded again.

"Patience, Cricket." His mouth traveled lower, leaving a trail of wet kisses in its wake.

"I don't know how much longer I can hold on. Oh!" I closed my eyes as he reached his destination. Small pulses radiated through me with each stroke of his tongue. A warm sensation started at my core and then spread through my body like lava until I was all flame, my body tingling, my mind blessedly unburdened as the orgasm shuddered through me. He released me and I moaned, needing him against me. I looked up as he ripped open the condom package, sliding on the rubber in one swift movement.

"Last chance," he whispered. "Tell me to stop."

I reached up and pulled his face to mine, locking on to his lips. He entered me, and I breathed out against his mouth, pushing against him as he filled me so deliciously. This was everywhere I was supposed to be. This was everything I'd needed. That dark empty void, that craving that couldn't be met. It was this I needed. It was him.

"Sonny," I breathed into his neck, tasting the salty sweat of his skin as he moved inside me.

This is wrong.

The thought broadsided me and I squeezed my eyes shut, willing it to go away by focusing on everything that was right. He slowed, his weight lifting slightly as he looked into my eyes.

"Are you still okay?" he whispered. He started to slide out, but I clutched at him to keep him with me.

"I'm okay." I kissed his lips lightly, then touched them with my tongue, outlining them like I was painting a picture of his face. I felt him surrender as he held on to me tighter, his movements more concentrated, more intense.

You're going to get hurt.

I closed my eyes, dug my fingers into his back, pressing against him as I felt him swell. His mouth found mine, and he groaned against me as he came, as I came, as that tension inside me released.

Reality tapped me on the shoulder, whispering its negative messages in my ear, but I turned away, lying on my side as I faced him. He was on his back, breathing hard, and then turned his head to me, smiling in between breaths. Neither of us spoke. I wasn't sure what to say anyway. All my doubts were pinpricks in my back, and anything I uttered could break the spell. And so I turned off my light, and he turned off his. Then I wrapped myself in his arms, meditating on the rise and fall of his chest, breathing in the comforting smell of our mingling scents, and listening to the beat of his heart against my ear as I drifted off to sleep.

Chapter Seventeen

We made love again the next morning, but slower. He took his time, touching my face and looking in my eyes as he rocked me gently. He'd always been an attentive lover. I hadn't forgotten, but now that he was holding me, stroking my skin, kissing the sides of my face, my lips, my neck, I remembered fully.

Back when we were in love, I used to wake up early and nestle up to him, prodding him awake until he rolled over and gave me what I wanted. Even before coffee, he managed to say more with his body than words could express.

And now here we were, wrapped up in each other in this hotel room in the city, the early morning sun shining golden rays in our room, reflecting off the mirrored skyscrapers, and Sonny's hand in my hair as he kissed me, pulling my hips closer with his other hand. He stayed inside me afterward, tracing his finger across my eyebrows and cheekbones. His eyes studied every part of me he touched. And everywhere he touched left a tingling trail, all my nerves electrified.

"You are so beautiful," he whispered, kissing my lips, then my nose, then my forehead. "But I need coffee."

"And I need a shower," I said. He got up to fiddle with the hotel room Keurig, and I took the moment to ogle his bare ass. He flexed his muscles, and I laughed.

"Go take your shower, pervy," he teased. I unwound the sheets twisted around my legs and escaped the bed, smacking his ass on the way to the bathroom.

While the shower water warmed, I turned to look at my reflection in the mirror. My hair was wild, half curls and half in crimson tangles. My lips were swollen and red, and my eyes shone a deeper blue over flushed cheeks. I looked like a woman in love, who had just been properly ravaged.

This won't end well.

"Maybe not," I whispered back to the voice of doubt. "But I'm going to enjoy it while it lasts."

I got in the shower, closing my eyes as the water poured over me from the rainfall showerhead.

"Room for one more?" Sonny asked, standing outside the glass door with two cups of coffee in his hands. I opened the door and he stepped inside, handing me one of the cups. We alternated underneath the water as we sipped the hot liquid, and I felt warm all over—not just from the water or coffee, but how much this felt like old times. Almost like we were never interrupted or were never meant to be apart. The caffeine and hot water did their part to wake us up, and conversation soon filled the space. I talked about some of the events I'd managed, and how Taye had changed everything for my business. He shared about working with Finnigan, and how hard it was for Buoy to settle back in when they moved back from Wisconsin.

"He loved going to Owen Park with me to catch some live music because there was usually food in it for him," he said. I half-listened as my mind drifted to the reason he left, which then turned into the reason he came back. And she wasn't me.

"Here, let me get your hair." Sonny took my empty cup as he kissed the tip of my nose, and I smiled, brushing aside my thoughts. I stood with my back to him as he poured shampoo onto my hair. His fingers massaged my scalp as I kept my eyes closed, and he was careful to swipe away trails of soap before they hit my eyes. I leaned against his chest, feeling the soap slipping between our skin, and I sighed at the ecstasy in this one simple act of care.

He finished washing and conditioning my hair, and then I did the same for him. I had to stand on my tiptoes as we faced each other, and he held me close so I wouldn't fall. He groaned with appreciation as I pressed my fingers into his scalp, working up a lather.

"Goddamn, that feels good. I can't believe how long it's been since you washed my hair."

"I'm not the one who moved to Wisconsin," I said. My fingers stalled, and I inwardly kicked myself for saying the words aloud when we were having such a good time. If he noticed, he didn't say anything. He just hummed in appreciation as I resumed washing his hair.

Once rinsed, he turned off the water and retrieved a towel for me before grabbing one for himself.

"Go get dressed while I, uh, let this coffee do the trick," he said, tilting his head toward the toilet.

"Ugh, gross. I'll leave the fan on." I wrapped the towel around me, then kissed him lightly on the lips before I left, closing the door behind me.

Evidence of our night lay in tangled sheets on the bed and the empty condom wrappers on the floor. I picked those up and discarded them in the trash, then studied the bed for a moment while I relived our passion. It was with a note of wistfulness, knowing our time together was ending. Or was it? What happened when we left this hotel room?

I kept the balcony door open as I dressed, enjoying the cool breeze, and counting on our room's high floor level for privacy. All I had were my clothes from the night before, so I slipped on the little black dress and flip-flops, then enjoyed a second cup of coffee on the balcony as the sun made its ascent. A pigeon lit upon the railing, checking to see if I had any food to share.

"None for you," I said. My stomach rumbled, reminding me that I hadn't had breakfast yet either. Maybe Sonny and I could eat at the restaurant downstairs before we figured out how to get home.

"Hey, do you want breakfast?" I called out, re-entering the room.

"That would be great," he called back, still in the bathroom. I wrinkled my nose, but laughed, wondering how foul the bathroom was.

My phone ringer chirped, and I saw Meadow's name on it.

"Damn," I swore, realizing I'd never told her where I was. As I reached it, Sonny's phone lit up next to mine. I glanced at his screen, and my heart plummeted at the text.

Justine: *Okay, call me when you're back.*

I let Meadow's call go to voicemail as I stood there, staring at Sonny's phone. He'd obviously talked with her while I was in the shower. I mean, why shouldn't he? But seeing her name placed a nauseous feeling in my belly, as if he'd cheated on me.

Except, he hadn't cheated on me. He'd cheated on her.

Fuck. Fuck. Fuck. Fuck.

What the fuck was I doing? What was I even thinking? He had a girlfriend, and I totally trampled all over his relationship, thinking only of my own needs.

My phone rang again just as the bathroom door opened.

"Hey," I said into the phone. Sonny came out without a towel, a flirtatious look on his face. I held a finger up, signaling for him to wait, as if he were no one, as if this were just a normal day. I tried to ignore the way his expression fell.

"Hey yourself," Meadow said. "I'm glad you're all right, and that your location services are on. So, things went well, I take it. How's the Orchard Garden Hotel?"

I moved out to the balcony, leaving Sonny alone in the room so I could talk privately.

"Things are fine, but I can't talk right now. Can we talk when I get home?"

"Take your time, sister," she said, a knowing tone to her voice.

"We're on our way out right now," I said. "See you soon."

"We are?" Sonny asked. When I turned, he passed me a glass of champagne.

"It's only eight," I pointed out.

"It's a mimosa," he countered. "But without the OJ." He sipped at his, raising an eyebrow at me. I placed my glass on the table, then moved back to the room.

"We still need to figure out how to get home," I said. "And then I have to work out my car situation since I don't have one."

"We can do that over breakfast," he said. "I thought you were hungry. Why don't we eat first, and then figure things out? Besides, I'd like to explore the city a little while we're here. I haven't been back here since I left Wisconsin."

And there it was. Another stab that he'd left. He was acting like he'd just gone on vacation instead of breaking my heart and moving on with someone else.

"We're not together, you know." I said it a little more harshly than I intended.

Sonny set his glass down and looked at me. "I think it's time we talked about this."

"There is nothing to talk about. You took a job across the country and didn't even think about how it might affect our relationship."

"I asked you to come with me."

"My whole life is here!" I shouted. I heard a window below us slam shut. "I can't leave my job," I hissed, quieter this time. "And my house."

"The house is fine," he said. "The house has always been fine. It's *you* that's not fine. You live in that house like it's some kind of monument, like it will bring them back. But it won't, Cricket."

"Shut up!" I whisper shouted. "I know it won't bring them back. But I can't just leave. It's my home."

"It's not your home, it's *their* home. There is no part of you in that house, except for the tiny bedroom you took as your own. Everything in there is your mom and dad. Where are *you*, though? What do you even want that's about you, and not everyone else?"

Angry tears flooded my eyes as his words twisted inside me. He was wrong. I chose to be there because I *wanted* to be there.

"You knew I wouldn't leave, and you still left me."

"I didn't leave *you*, Cricket. I left California. You and I were still together, and you're the one who ended things."

"You didn't fight for me!"

"Goddammit, Cricket, do you even hear yourself? You chose to stay here when I asked you to come with me. You chose to break things off with me because you weren't willing to make things work. As far as I could tell, you didn't want to be with me. What did I have to fight for? I tried, Cricket. I really tried. But you put up all these walls and made all these ground rules, and in the end, I realized I was fighting a battle I couldn't win and was losing myself in the process."

He turned away then, and I thought I saw moisture in his eyes.

"Well, it looks like you found yourself pretty quick. I'm sure Justine has been handy in that department."

"You don't even know what you're talking about," he said.

My phone rang then, and I stood while answering it, walking to the ledge so I didn't have to look at Sonny anymore.

"What?" I demanded.

"Jesus, girl. Bad night?" Blake's voice surprised me, especially since I'd expected it to be Meadow, and also because he seemed more cheerful than lately. Then I remembered the date he'd had with Sadie.

"It was fine. But I take it yours went well."

I knew Sonny was still behind me, probably listening to my every word. Justine's text flowed through my mind, along with all the things she didn't write but were apparent between the lines. The fact that she wasn't worried about him, even though he was here with me. The knowledge that we were heading back home, and I was alone while he had her. That everything that happened last night and this morning was a lie; a temporary interruption to reality.

"I miss you," I said to Blake. "I wish you could have been here. Everything would have been much better."

"Oh fuck, really," Blake groaned in my ear. "He's there, isn't he?"

I gave a sultry laugh as if he'd said something sexy. I heard Sonny's chair scoot out and his footsteps as he left the balcony.

"Yeah," I said to Blake. "I should probably go. But I want to hear all about it when I get home."

"Same, girl. I have a feeling you have a lot to tell me."

"You have no idea." I hung up the phone and turned to see the door to our bedroom closing behind Sonny, leaving me by myself. A text showed up on my phone a moment later.

Sonny: *I ordered us an Uber. It will be here in 10 minutes. See you downstairs.*

He had every reason to leave me behind, and a part of me curdled with guilt. I was being a bitch. But I couldn't let go of the text. I knew I had no right to be mad about it, but the timing was what hurt the most. I'd let my guard down, submitted to these feelings I'd been bottling up for weeks. I thought he was on the same page. Instead, he'd waited until I was out of sight to reach out to *her*.

What had I expected of him? To break things off with Justine? The thought was ridiculous, now that I was addressing it. Did I really think one night with him would make him drop everything to be with me?

And then there was everything he threw in my face. He had the audacity to tell me our breakup was my fault. *My* fault, as if I were the one who chose to leave for a brand new life.

The Uber was waiting at the curb, Sonny in the backseat, when I stepped out the hotel's glass doors onto the sidewalk. I slid beside him and put on my seatbelt, leaning my forehead against the window as the car pulled away and started the drive home. I knew the hotel room probably cost a small fortune, and that this Uber wasn't cheap, so I quietly logged into Venmo and wired Sonny $400 to cover what I hoped was my portion of the costs. I heard his phone ding with a notification, likely from the transfer, and waited for him to say something. He didn't. In fact, he remained quiet for the whole ride. I stared out the window but saw nothing as the world blurred by.

We reached my house first, and I got out, thanking the driver for the ride. I turned to Sonny, seeing only the back of his head as he looked out his window. I took a deep breath, wanting to say something that would make him turn around, begging him inwardly to just look at me. But in the end, I just shut the door and walked away, not even watching as I heard the car leave.

Avery was in the outdoor enclosure as I walked up the drive, and I stopped there and watched him for a short while. I couldn't separate Sonny from the cage, and I flashed back to the night before, his body pressed against mine and how it felt to hold him again. I never should have opened myself up to him that way, and yet, I couldn't regret it. I regretted seeing that text, the way we left the hotel, and the even larger wall that now stood between us. But I didn't regret his hands on my body, my kisses on his neck, my legs wrapped around his waist.

"I've fucked everything up," I said aloud to Avery. It didn't escape me that this was the first time I'd ever admitted any part to our breakup, but when Sonny called me on it, it stirred up a portion of the truth I'd brushed aside. I didn't fight for him. I gave up because it felt too hard, and because it meant letting go of the parts of my life that I wasn't ready to release—namely, my parents.

I'd denied it this whole time, but now in the wake of our argument, it was clearer than ever. The house *was* a shrine to my parents. The shag carpeting. The outdated decorations. The way every single thing remained in the same place. I was the one living in this house, and yet I'd taken my childhood bedroom. I thought about how much it bothered me when Meadow moved into their bedroom, as if it made her care less about them. But it didn't. It was just a bedroom. This was just a house.

My parents' car...it was just a car. And it wasn't even theirs anymore, it was mine. And yet I'd kept the crystal prism on the mirror as if I were just borrowing it for a time. I kept my mother's sweater in the backseat as if she were going to retrieve it any day now. The car wasn't even in my name, but in theirs, and I just paid the registration every year as if my mom or dad were the ones driving it.

"Uh oh, the walk of shame," Meadow teased as she joined me at Avery's cage. She looked me up and down, her eyebrows raised as she took in last night's dress.

"Someone stole the car," I said, which wiped the smug look off her face. I told her how we discovered the missing car, and how it had been late by the time we were done reporting the incident. I downplayed everything else and tried to keep out the fact that we'd slept together, but her side-eye let me know she wouldn't give up until I told her everything. So I did, including the text to Justine.

"But it could have been about anything," Meadow pointed out. I shook my head.

"It doesn't matter what it was about," I said. "The fact is, she was on his mind even after we'd hooked up. And it made me realize that he's not mine anymore, and he won't be mine because he's with her. What we did was wrong. I never should have slept with him, knowing he has a girlfriend who trusts him."

"But that's his responsibility, not yours."

"It doesn't make it right," I said, then shook my head. "I shouldn't have taken this job. I should have turned it down as soon as I knew I was going to be working with him. I had my whole life under control before Sonny showed up. Ever since we started working together, I've been a mess. I need to get my head on straight, and that starts with putting distance between Sonny and me."

Before I could talk myself out of it, I picked up the phone and touched Taye's number.

"What up, girl?"

"Sorry to call you on a Saturday, but I need to ask you a favor."

"Sure, what is it?"

I glanced at Meadow. She was watching me curiously, her good hand on her hip.

"I need you to take over all communication with Sonny McIntyre. I'm just too busy to involve myself as much as I have been, and now that we've wrapped up the venue and are in the home stretch, I don't see any reason for me to be as involved as I have been. Is that okay with you?"

"Hm."

I heard the words in her grunt—that she didn't believe me, that she knew there was more to the story, that I was being a coward.

"Sure thing, boss," she said, putting a final bow on her unspoken judgment.

"Thanks, Taye," I said, hanging up. Then I texted Sonny.

Me: *From here on out, all communication is to be conducted through my assistant, Taye Riviera. If I'm needed for any further decisions, she knows how to get in touch with me. Thank you.*

I sent it before I had time to think, knowing Meadow was reading it the whole time.

"Damn, Cricket," she said, shaking her head.

"Don't start. Sonny is a complication I don't need right now." My phone buzzed in my hand, and I looked at the screen.

Sonny: *OK.*

The one-word text infuriated me more than it should have. It took the power out of my hands and placed it in his. Just the one word and every law I was laying down gained his stamp of approval. As if he didn't care. As if I were being ridiculous.

I *was* being ridiculous.

"I need to go buy a car," I said, pulling up Uber on my phone. Meadow reached out and touched my arm. I looked at her, and she gave me a once over.

"No, you need to shower and pull yourself together. Then we can get you a car."

Freshly showered and in the back of another Uber, Meadow and I traveled to the car dealership. On the way, Meadow shared the conversation she'd shared with Zola Shoes, one of her biggest sponsors for her Instagram account, which had been dormant now for almost two weeks.

"They want to pull their sponsorship," she said. "If they do, I'll owe them a ton of money because I haven't held up my end of the bargain, and because I'm losing followers."

"How many followers have you lost so far?" I asked.

"Almost five thousand," she admitted. "It's just that I can't exactly talk about traveling when I'm sitting in my childhood home, and especially since I look like this." She indicated her face and all her injuries. She was healing every day, and the bruises were almost invisible under makeup. But she still looked weak compared to her normal state. Plus, even though her leg brace was removable, there was no hiding her cast.

"Do you have the money?" I asked, and she shook her head.

"It's not so much about the money, but the snowball effect it will have. If I lose this sponsor, I'll lose more. Which means, I need your help."

I shook my head, knowing exactly where this was headed. "No way. We've done this before, and it didn't end well."

I was referring to that day in our junior year of high school, when Meadow called in sick to her job at the ice cream shop, only to have them tell her she'd be fired if she didn't show up. It was the same day as a beach party in Bodega Bay, and she wasn't going to miss it. So she talked me into going to work for her, pretending I was her. It ended up being the hottest day of the year, and the shop was packed with people trying to cool off. During my eight-hour shift, I spilled milk water all over the floor, ripped a trash bag as I carried it to the garbage, and had to clean an overflowing grease trap. But the worst thing was having to take care of an actual human poop on the bathroom floor from someone's kid who didn't make it to the toilet. By some miracle, Meadow didn't lose her job through me. But I swore I'd never pretend to be her again.

Which was exactly what I knew she intended for me.

"It won't be the same as last time," she promised as we pulled into the parking lot of the dealership. A salesperson walked out as if they were expecting us, even though I hadn't called. I was dreading this process already, and the show of over-eagerness only solidified how painful this was going to be.

"Let's talk about this later, okay?" I was still going to say no, but I could only focus on one headache at a time.

In the end, I was glad I brought Meadow with me. Brent, the salesperson, showed me car after car, and nothing felt right until Meadow pointed out that none of them were Hondas like our parents' car.

"Did you want to look at a Honda?" Brent asked.

"No," Meadow said at the same time I said *yes*. She looked at me with an exasperated expression. "Cricket, you don't want Mom and Dad's car. You want *your* car. What have you always wanted to drive?"

"I don't know," I said, but I did. Whenever I was on the road, I constantly noticed the Subaru Crosstreks. There was something about them that screamed adventure—everything opposite of my life. I wanted that. I wanted a car that was ready for a spur-of-the-moment camping trip, or a weekend backpacking through Yosemite, or taking it on a cross-country road trip.

My gaze lingered on a light blue Crosstrek at the edge of the lot, and I could see myself behind the wheel, ready for my next adventure.

"She'd like to test drive that one," Meadow said, pointing at the car.

"Oh. No, not that one. It's too much. I just want a simple used car."

"We've already test driven a dozen of them, and none of them are for you. Why not try that one?" She asked.

"Because it's too much. How much is it?" I peered closer at the car, and my stomach dropped at the price tag.

"Don't worry about the money," Meadow said.

"Of course I'm going to worry about the money. If you haven't noticed, I'm not exactly rolling in it."

"Cricket," Meadow said, nodding her eyes at the salesperson.

"It's fine," Brent said. "We have financing plans for every budget. You might be surprised at how affordable this car actually is.

"Is that one ready to drive off the lot today?" Meadow asked.

"Are you buying this, or am I?"

"Ask then," she said.

"If I bought it, could I take it home today?" I asked. I was still trying to wrap my mind around how I was going to afford a brand-new car. But the possibility of owning it was starting to awaken my excitement.

"If you like it as is, we would just need to detail it, and you can pick it up in a few hours. Would you like to test drive it?"

An hour later, I was in the office, signing my name throughout a packet of paperwork for my brand new adventure car.

"I can't believe you talked me into this," I hissed at Meadow as we sat at the desk, waiting for Brent to come back with the final documents.

"I didn't talk you onto anything," she said with a laugh. "That car was calling to you, and you know it."

"It really was," I admitted.

Brent came back and shook my hand, letting me know I could pick it up later that afternoon once it had been detailed.

"Can our driver take you anywhere while you wait?"

"Yes," Meadow said before I could answer. She looked me over, then nodded. "This girl needs a makeover before she drives her fancy new car. I'm thinking new hair, new makeup, and a whole new outfit."

"This is a ponytail, barefaced kind of car," I said. "Not the glam look you have in mind."

"Humor me."

Chapter Eighteen

Meadow took charge once I was in the salon seat and told me she was paying for everything.

"You just bought a new car," she said. "Let me spoil your broke ass. It's the least I can do for you putting up with me these past two weeks."

"The very least," I agreed, then laughed as she smacked my arm.

We were at The Shop, an edgy salon in the center of downtown Petaluma with a collage of black and white hairstyle photos covering brick walls and modern rock blasting out of the speakers. A girl on one side of me was getting the sides of her head shaved while her blue mohawk fanned out like a peacock. On the other side, the stylist was busy shaping the mutton chops of a guy who looked too young to sport such impressive facial hair. And then there was me, sitting in a chair with my hands clenched in my lap while Meadow and the stylist discussed my new look.

"Just don't cut my hair short," I begged Meadow, and she shook her head.

"I'm not altering your image permanently," she promised. She told Madison, my stylist with arms covered in colorful tattoos, to only snip a little off the ends of my hair. Once Madison started styling, Meadow instructed her to turn me so I couldn't see my reflection. I kept my eyes closed, a little nervous about what the end result would be. That said, Meadow knew way more about style than I did, and wouldn't make me look ugly. So I settled as much as I could, closing my eyes and choosing to trust the process.

Of course, sitting there while Meadow and Madison chatted around me, I was left to my thoughts. And those thoughts kept turning back to Sonny. As hurt as I felt toward him, I couldn't help thinking of last night, along with the encore we shared this morning. The way Sonny touched me last night, the way he looked at me, how he breathed me in as he paid attention to every part of me....

"Stop smiling, you're wrinkling your eyes," Meadow hissed as Madison applied eyeshadow to my lids. I forced my mind to go blank, which was difficult now that my insides were twisting at the thought of Sonny's body pressed against mine.

"Finished," Madison said, turning my chair. "Open your eyes."

When I did, I saw Meadow. Actually, I saw me, but I looked exactly like Meadow. My flyaway messy bun was now styled in long waves framing my face. It even looked darker like hers, though Meadow promised it was the product and nothing else. My eyes were outlined with a smoky black, topped with a fading grey shadow that brought out the blue in my eyes. My freckles were lighter under tinted moisturizer, and my cheekbones more pronounced with expert contouring. Finishing it off was a dusty rose stain on my lips, my sister's signature color.

"Wow, you two really are identical," Madison said, looking from me to Meadow.

"She's older by five minutes, though," Meadow pointed out.

My sister added a few hair products to the tab before paying. Then she led me down the street to a little boutique named Ooh La Luxe. Everything in the store was cream or earth-toned, with racks of color-coordinated clothing lined up in the center of the shop. If the hair salon had seemed loud and edgy, this boutique was the exact opposite. From the chandeliers and Buddha statues to the feather plumes in vases by elegant mannequins, I couldn't help wondering how we'd afford anything in this luxurious store.

Hobbling in front of me, Meadow picked out various items and handed them to a salesgirl who had already started a room for me.

"You're getting me one outfit, not a whole wardrobe," I said.

"We'll see," she answered, then went back to shopping.

In the end, she got me three outfits, all in coordinating colors so I could mix and match. I had to admit, they were really cute. I was wearing one of them—a long duster cardigan over a t-shirt dress, paired with thigh-high heeled boots, a large-brimmed hat, and a chunky silver necklace. It was a strange combination of casual and chic that I never would have paired, and yet it worked. Even more, I liked it.

"I'm borrowing that outfit once I get this stupid cast off," Meadow said as we window shopped. "Wait, stop for a second." She pulled out her phone, and I rolled my eyes. "Come on, you look good. Let me take a few photos." I humored her, even let her direct me in a few poses. We went into a jewelry store, and she shot photos while I tried on bracelets and chatted with the owner. Then we stopped in a pet store, and she captured shots of me playing with the kittens. Finally, we stopped at Sugo Trattoria, a decadent Italian restaurant with one wall dedicated to dozens of bottles of wine and mirrors on another wall that reflected rows of dark wood tables. Meadow treated me to a late lunch that included salmon on top of salad, gorgonzola and honey bruschetta, and a glass of sparkling wine for each of us. She snapped a few photos of me across from her, then one of us together. She applied filters to each of them as we waited for the bill, and then showed them to me when she was done. My mouth fell open. It was like looking at her Instagram feed. Every photo could have been her, from shopping at an overseas boutique to sitting in an Italian cafe.

"You're really good," I said.

"I'd like to use these." Hope filled her eyes, and I sighed.

"I knew something was up." I looked over the photos again, studying them. It was really hard to tell they were me. If I had a hard time telling, then it was a sure bet no one else would. I handed the phone back to her. "Fine. But these are you, not me."

"That's the point," she said, gesturing to my whole look.

"So, this wasn't out of the goodness of your heart?"

"Partially," she said. "I mean, you look good."

"I look like you."

"Exactly. And now you can be the perfect star of Wandering Meadow, and I won't lose my sponsor."

"As long as I don't have to scoop ice cream or pick up human poop, I guess it's fine."

We spent the Uber ride back to the dealership plotting Meadow's posting calendar. Usually her posts included location tags to promote local businesses, but she insisted on keeping our hometown private.

"I don't need some rabid fan tracking me down and finding out where you live," she explained.

"Do you have stalkers?"

"Doesn't every social media influencer?" she asked. She then told me about one girl who'd hopped a plane to Peru, booking a room right next to hers while she was in the country. The girl had been harmless, but it had freaked Meadow out so much, she began only posting photos after she'd left the location. "This is a desperate situation, though," she said. She hadn't been in Sweden long enough to get any photos, and she'd already posted all her Brazil photos. So for now, she'd post as she took the photos, but keep the location private.

"I'll just say I'm in the States on a break and leave it at that, maybe act like we're on a road trip." Meadow clapped her hands, and her eyes widened. "The Subaru! We can go on a road trip with that!"

"I have to work, you know."

"You have Taye," she said. "Besides, you already laid down the law with Sonny to work through her, and you don't have any other jobs going on. You can work remotely and Taye will handle all the stuff around here."

Just the mention of Sonny's name sent a twinge of electricity through me. I brushed the thought of him aside as quickly as it came. "What about Avery?" I asked. "Who will take care of him?"

"Don't you have friends? Can Taye do it?"

I shook my head. "She's my assistant, and I already ask too much of her."

But the road trip idea piqued my curiosity. It had been a while since I'd gone anywhere, and at this moment, getting out of town felt like a welcome escape.

"Where would we go?" I asked her.

Meadow took her phone out of her purse and started scrolling through it before handing it to me. On the screen was a spiny tree, like the kind you see in a Dr. Suess book, with orange, sunlit boulders in the background.

"Joshua Tree," she said, taking the phone back from me. "A few years ago, I went to Coachella. You know, that music festival in the desert? A bunch of us camped out at Joshua Tree, but we were too busy with the festival to see much of the park. I've always wanted to go back, and now seems like the perfect opportunity."

"But it's October. Won't it be freezing?" I asked.

"Probably," she laughed. "But it's the desert. This is the perfect time to camp there. And it's only about nine or so hours away."

"Only," I laughed. It sounded safe enough, though. It wasn't like traveling to a new country or anything, and after everything that happened in San Francisco, I was ready for a change of pace. "I might know someone who'd watch Avery if we go."

Meadow grinned as if it were a done deal. Honestly, I knew it was.

I pulled out my phone as we reached the dealership. Meadow met with the salesman while I placed the phone to my ear.

"Hey, gorgeous," Blake said. "Loverboy gone?"

"You could say that. How would you like to come over for dinner tonight? Meadow and I have a proposition for you."

"Hmm… Dinner with twins. Let's see. Yeah, I think I can make that work," he teased.

"Great, see you at seven."

Hours later, headlights flashed across my brand-new Subaru in the driveway as I cleaned the kitchen. On the table was a pan-seared steak, crisp roasted potatoes, and creamed spinach, plus a bottle of Finnigan Estates sparkling wine on ice. Meadow was sitting, resting her leg and wearing the exact outfit as me—a button-up shirt dress cinched at the waist, unbuttoned three inches above our navels. Both of us wore our curly hair in messy ponytails, and feather earrings dangled from our ears.

It was a trip to see Meadow look just like me since we never dressed alike. But even more fun was seeing the expression on Blake's face when he walked in. He stopped in his tracks and did a double-take when he saw me, then gave a low whistle. I turned around as he glanced at the table, his mouth dropping open as he saw Meadow.

"Whoa, you really are twins."

It was the same thing the hairdresser said, and it still amused me.

"Blake, this is my sister Meadow. Meadow, Blake. Now, you go sit." I leaned over to take the bread rolls out of the oven. I knew the dress I was wearing had hitched up too high when I did, and I knew he was checking me out by the sound he made in his throat.

"Listen, Cricket. You two have something really awesome going on here, and normally I'd be down for this. But I think I'm a taken man, and…"

I whirled around and threw myself in his arms, hugging him tightly. "She's your girlfriend?" I squealed. He was tense for a second, but then he laughed, returning the hug. "First off, Blake, I will never involve my sister when I get it on with someone. Gross. Second, I think we established the other night that anything we had going on between the two of us is over. So get over yourself. Now, tell me everything."

Over dinner, he shared how he worked up the nerve to ask her out, and how the only night she had free was last night.

"Sorry, by the way. But I hope it worked out in your favor," he said.

"We'll get to me. It's still your turn."

Because Sadie was an astronomy major, Blake had the brilliant idea to take her to the Robert Ferguson Observatory in Sugarloaf Ridge State Park. He'd packed a thermos of hot chocolate for both of them, and they'd bundled up for a night of looking at stars and planets through the telescopes while docents taught about the night sky.

"That sounds pretty scholarly," I mused.

"I know," he said. "I even surprised myself. But she'd never been before and had always wanted to go. We talked for hours that night, holding hands in the dark. She even kissed me goodnight."

"And then?" I asked.

"And that's it."

"Wow." This was a totally different side to Blake, and judging by the faraway look on his face... "You're so smitten," I said with a laugh.

"I'm a goner," he agreed. "I have never felt this way about a girl in my life." He looked at me apologetically, but I waved him off. "She's really something. She's beautiful and smart, she laughs at all my stupid jokes. We share a lot of the same traits—"

"She's a player?" I asked.

"No, smartass," he said. "She's sarcastic like me, and when I tease her, she gives it back. She's so tiny, but I watched her inhale a double cheeseburger and fries like a pro. She likes dance music like I do. Plus, she's always smiling. She carries herself like she can handle her own, and yet she stayed by my side with her hand in mine, letting me take the lead on everything. But it wasn't this wishy-washy thing, you know? It was more like giving me free rein to manage the date. And the coolest part was how she liked everything we did. I even took her to that coffee shop you like so much."

"Brew? That one in Santa Rosa?" I felt another fleeting twinge. I pushed aside the memory of sitting at that huge table, meeting Sonny for the first time.

"Yeah, and she loved it. I told her that you introduced me to it, and she didn't even get jealous. She wants to meet you, by the way." He took another bite of food while I stared at him in shock.

"You told her about me? What did you say?"

"The truth," he said, mid-chew. "That we'd dated for a while, but it only lasted a season and wasn't meant to be anything more serious than good friends, which we are now.

"Wow. That's impressive," I said. "She doesn't care that you and I still hang out after we hooked up?"

"I think she'd care if we hooked up now," he said. "But she even told me that we both have histories and friendships that have shaped who we are, and it would be ridiculous to try to own each other's stuff." He shook his head. "I keep waiting for the bad part, like maybe she's crazy or has a jealous ex or something."

"There's still time for all that to show up," Meadow said. I shot her a dirty look. "What? It's still early, and you know how it is. We girls are good at hiding the crazy."

"Not all girls," I said, though I had to wonder if that described me. The fight I had with Sonny came to mind, and I stuffed it down as quickly as it came.

"I don't think that's her," Blake said. "At any rate, I have time to find out. We're working out together this Tuesday, and then going out again next Friday."

"Third date in a week, huh?" Meadow shot me a locker room look, and I laughed.

"He's getting them in fast," I said.

"You girls are nuts," he said. "I'm telling you, it's different. For the first time, I don't want to rush anything."

"I'm happy for you," I said, and I meant it.

"What about you?" he asked. "Were you a third wheel, or did you get Sonny all to yourself?"

"It was just the two of us," I said. I played with the button on my dress, wishing I had a better story to tell. "Let's just say I made a fool of myself and leave it at that, okay? At any rate, that's why we called you over. I have a favor to ask of you, but I'll make it worth your while."

"I'm telling you, I'm done fooling around—"

"And I told you to get over yourself."

"But you two are dressed as twins," he said.

"We *are* twins."

"I know, but I thought."

"Meadow got me a makeover today, and I ended up looking more like her than usual. So we dressed the same, just for the hell of it."

He looked at both of us, squinting his eyes to try to see the difference.

"We're identical," I assured him.

"So weird." He shook his head. "So, what's the favor, and what's my benefit?"

"The favor is staying here for a few days while Meadow and I go on a little road trip. It's kind of a work thing. We just need someone to stay with the bird, let him out every day, and make sure he has food and water."

"Okay, I can do that."

I squinted at him, not sure why that was so easy. "Don't you want to hear the benefit?"

"Sure," he said. "But it already sounds good. My roommate is driving me nuts right now, and I could use a place to chill that's quiet."

"Avery can get pretty loud," Meadow warned, and I shushed her.

"No, I'm serious. I'm cool with the bird. And if you don't mind, this will be a good place to hang out with Sadie without my roommate popping his head in every five minutes. Plus, Sadie is kind of into that whole mid-

CRISSI LANGWELL

century modern thing you all got going on here. That is if it's okay with you."

"It's just mid-century," Meadow said, wrinkling her nose. "No modern about it."

"She can come over," I said, ignoring Meadow's jab. "But if you do anything, change the sheets before I get back." It was my turn to grimace. "As far as the benefit, you know that huge UFC fight happening next week? The one with what's his face?"

"The Esposito—Rodriguez fight?" he said. Now I had this attention. He leaned forward, his eyes widening, and I grinned.

"Yeah, that one. I've already bought it. You can stream it here on the big screen with your friends as long as the bird is safe and the house remains in one piece."

"Shit, Cricket. Why didn't I know you were this cool when we were dating?"

"Blake, I wouldn't call what we were doing *dating*."

288

Chapter Nineteen

Two days later, Meadow and I were on the road and headed for the desert. Finding a site on such short notice had been next to impossible since all the campgrounds were full, but my resourceful sister always had a backup plan. She scrolled Reddit and found a guy who'd reserved a site but planned to camp out in the wilderness instead. In a matter of minutes, Meadow had secured us a campsite, and it didn't cost us a penny more than the obligatory parks pass. If it were anyone else, I'd wonder about the legitimacy of this hasty bargain. But this was Meadow—everything always worked out for her.

I eyed her leg brace as she sat in the passenger seat. Well, almost everything.

Driving the Subaru was a whole different experience than the old Honda. First, it got up to the speed of traffic in no time at all, while the Honda seemed to struggle even in school zones. Second, we were higher off the ground. The road looked different from up there. It was also incredibly easy to speed. We'd be cruising along and I'd glance at the speedometer to find we were going eighty. I had to do something about my lead foot, but the car was just too much fun to drive.

The final difference was the freedom of music choice.

"One rule," I said, and Meadow rolled her eyes.

"You and your rules," she said.

"No Elvis," I continued, ignoring her. But then I gave her a sideways look. "Do I make a lot of rules or something?" My thoughts immediately went to my last conversation with Sonny.

"It's not so much that you make rules," she said. "But you like things to be a certain way. I think you like the consistency or something, or just want to know what to expect. But the Elvis Presley rule? I can totally get behind that. Look, we can listen to the radio!"

And she switched the music on, scrolling through it until she found one playing Nirvana. Then Pearl Jam played, and I realized it was a '90s alternative station—my jams. She turned the volume up while I opened the moonroof, letting the breeze circulate inside the car. Behind me was a cooler full of food and drinks. We had our dad's huge tent in the back with a few sleeping bags and foam mats. And I'd made sure to bring plenty of those hand warmer things because I knew it was going to be freezing.

To break up the drive, we mapped out a few stops along the way. First up was a Starbucks bathroom, where we waited in the longest line ever to pee, and then in another long line to refuel. We were only an hour into driving, and the fact that we already had to pee was concerning to me.

But after that, we did great. Meadow kept the radio going, finding another station when we moved out of broadcast reach, and always something we both would like. I kept my lead foot light, though the flow of traffic seemed to move fast.

And then we reached Highway 5.

"My god, we're in the middle of nowhere," Meadow moaned. For hours, the road just went straight with nothing on it. I'd passed a rest stop about sixty miles back, and now I was regretting it because my bladder, once again, was about to burst. I finally had to pull off at a side road and squat next to the passenger side to relieve myself. For Meadow, it wasn't so easy. I held her full weight by the arms while she semi-squatted, praying I wouldn't drop her. I didn't, and she managed to pee on the ground and not on me or her leg brace. But we vowed to use the next real bathroom once we reached civilization.

We reached Twenty-Nine Palms at mid-afternoon, perking up at the sight of tiny Joshua trees scattered in otherwise barren land lining the highway. Both of us couldn't stop exclaiming as the trees grew bigger the closer we got to Joshua Tree, and we cheered as soon as we made the turn into the park. As we paid our park entrance fee at the Ranger Station, I asked the attendant if there was a place to get firewood, and she gave me a pointed look.

"First time in Joshua Tree?" she asked.

"Not mine," Meadow said, leaning across me. "But my sister hasn't been here before."

"Well," the Ranger said, raising an eyebrow at Meadow, "then you must know that firewood can only be bought outside the park." She handed me a map of the park along with my receipt. "There's a gas station on Twenty-Nine Palms that sells firewood. Good luck."

So close, and yet so far away. I made a U-turn around the Ranger Station and headed back toward the highway. Just like she said, the gas station had small bundles of wood. I stood in line behind some guy who probably drank eighteen beers before heading into the convenience market. He was flirting, or attempting to flirt, with a very bored clerk behind the counter.

"It gets cold out there," he said. "But not if you have a warm body next to you." He glanced over his shoulder at me to confirm his story. I looked away, feeling his eyes linger. I guess I was more obvious with my disinterest because he turned back to the clerk. "Not that I have anyone. But I sure wouldn't push her away."

"That's nice, Ted." The clerk looked past him and nodded at me. "Next."

I paused, not wanting to brush my warm body anywhere near Ted, who remained in my way at the desk. Finally, he moved. I let out the breath I didn't know I was holding.

"How cold does it get?" I asked in a hushed voice. I didn't want Ted to hear, who was now on the other side of the mart, talking loudly with a couple who was trying their best to ignore him.

"About forty degrees tonight," the girl said, snapping her gum as she rang up the wood bundles. "But that's without the wind, and tonight is supposed to be fairly gusty. That will be $25.87."

I swiped my card and punched in my pin, fighting a bit of regret as I did. I could handle the cold. But the wind? I'd never been one for extreme weather, and I considered wind to be the worst of it.

"Is that guy camping out in there?" I hissed, nodding my head at Ted as he exited the store.

"Him? Nah. He's my neighbor. And when he drinks, he comes here to check out the tourists. I guess today he decided to check me out instead." She winked, then looked past me at the next customer in line.

Back in the car, I flashed my parks pass at the Ranger who nodded us through, and then we were on to our site. We were staying at a place somewhat near the top of the park, but there was plenty to see on the way. The Joshua trees seemed like they were welcoming us in, waving us through as we ogled the landscape of spiny trees, thorn-filled bushes, and giant orange boulders. We reached our campground in no time at all, turning into an area that was encased in large rocks. I drove slow, craning my neck to get a better look while trying to keep my eyes on the road. Everything seemed so big, and the colors—incredible. I felt like I was in this giant sepia-toned world, bordered by an unreal blue sky.

We found our spot, and I squealed when I saw we'd be setting up camp in an alcove surrounded by climbing rocks. I wasn't a rock climber, but these rocks made me think I could be one. I imagined how it would feel to stretch my legs as I scaled the rock, especially after so much driving. But when I opened the door, the wind practically shut it again.

"Shit," I said, forcing the door open. A blast of cold air whipped against my cheeks, a sharp contrast to the sun-kissed warmth inside the car. "Wait a moment," I told Meadow as she struggled with her door. "Let me help." I buttoned my flannel, though it was too thin to make a difference, and jogged to her side of the car. "It's probably best if you stay in the car," I said. "It's too windy, and it's not like you can do much."

"I can still help," she said, rolling her eyes as she swung her legs out of the car. She'd stopped using crutches the day before, though she still brought them upon my insistence. Her gait was uneven as she grabbed a bag with her good arm and headed for our site. "Bring the tent," she called over her shoulder. "We might as well get that out of the way first."

The tent was a challenge all its own. Lucky for us, it was easy to put up on a good day. Unlucky, the wind was making everything a million times more difficult. Meadow sprawled her body across the tent as I inserted the poles. It took almost thirty minutes before the tent was upright. Even though our stuff weighed it down and the stakes weren't budging, I still put rocks in the corners of the tent to keep it from blowing away.

"Come on," Meadow said, grabbing her phone and hobbling away from the tent. "It's golden hour, and I want to get a few shots in before the sun goes down."

"Now?" I was inside the tent, ready to escape the wind and take a nap until dinner.

"Yes now! We probably only have about fifteen minutes to get in some good shots."

"Why is it golden hour if it's only a fraction of an hour," I muttered, slipping on a pair of Zola hiking boots. The wind was battering the sides of the tent, but it didn't move an inch. I dreaded going outside, missing my cozy windless bed at home.

Meadow was tugging her hair when I finally emerged from the tent, a habit she reverted to whenever she was stressed. The wind was whipping her copper locks all around her face, and I could still see the strand she kept in her hand, pulling on it as if it would stop time. I hid a smile, feeling a little less odd as she revealed one of her own quirks.

"Stop stressing. We have time," I said, pulling my own hair into a twist to keep it from knotting in the wind. "Where do you want me?"

"Let's go to that open area by the parking lot. The sun is hitting perfectly there."

We couldn't move fast due to Meadow's injuries, so the mini wasteland was going to have to do for tonight. Luckily, it was less barren than I originally thought. Meadow took pictures of me beside Joshua trees, walking among the cholla cacti, and even caught a flash of a coyote darting a few yards behind me as I did mountain pose in my hiking boots. My hair swirled around my head the whole time, and she instructed me to let it be wild.

"We are so using this shot," Meadow exclaimed, scrolling through her phone while I wiped dirt off my jeans.

"Because everyone does yoga in their hiking boots," I joked.

"Everyone *wants* to do yoga in hiking boots," she said. "At least, they will when they see these photos. People eat this stuff up. The thing that makes influencers successful isn't what they're selling, but the lifestyle that goes with it. They want the sunset in the desert, the morning yoga on a boulder, and waking up fresh in a tent. And then they want the shoes they think will give them that. Even when I'm not selling a product, I'm framing it with lifestyle shots. I'm providing a dream of inner peace that people crave, drawing them in with beautifully filtered photos, and in turn, they buy the products they believe I'm using so they can also have inner peace."

"And then, when they don't have inner peace, they just buy more products," I mused, feeling a little guilty for being a part of this. "It's just a cycle of seeking and never finding, adding to our consumer mentality."

"It's not like that, though," Meadow said. She stopped scrolling and appeared serious in the moment. "I use my platform to offer people a different look at the world, one many aren't fortunate enough to see. I don't take it for granted how lucky I am to see this view of the world, because I couldn't without my sponsors. But I can't have sponsors without people buying their products. So really, I'm in a partnership with sponsors and followers, because we all need each other to keep this dream going. My followers want the dream, and love following my adventures around the world. I need funding to give them that, and companies are willing to give me money if I share their products and people buy them. That's the cycle, and it's all wrapped around hope and dreams."

She looked back at the phone, then smiled. "Zola is going to send me a dozen shoes by the time I'm done with this."

"Ugh, count me out." I could already feel a blister forming on my heel. But they looked cute. I guess that's what mattered. I looked over Meadow's shoulder to catch a sneak peek at the photos she took. I had to admit, they were good. *Really* good. Meadow knew what she was doing, and it almost seemed like I did, too. I looked long and lean with the angles she used to take the photos, and my hair appeared to be the wind itself, swirling around my head as I held a neutral expression on my face. I bit back a smile as I actually admired the images of myself. I looked like Meadow, sure. But I also looked like a wilder version of me. I liked it. I suddenly understood what she was talking about. Looking at the photos gave me a different perspective of myself. It also revealed something about the rest of the world. I realized that everyone has a filter they run their life through, working to appear more put together than they are. In reality, though, we're all just standing in a desert, trying to keep our hair out of our faces.

The sun was cresting the horizon, sending rays of honeyed light over the desert. We paused to catch its descent behind the surrounding mountains. I was flipping cold, shaking to the bone as the last sliver of sun disappeared. But it felt good to be here with Meadow. As we limped back to camp, her with her braced leg and me with my blistered heel, I realized I didn't want to be anywhere else. I was glad I came.

By the time we reached the site, the sky was a dusty lilac with shiny sapphire stars appearing by the second, and my muscles were sore from shivering. The wind had died down some, but I couldn't stop shaking as I started the campfire. Once the first flames took hold, we huddled close, eating the sandwiches we'd packed earlier that morning with trembling fingers. Eventually we warmed and relaxed enough to lean back and take in the ethereal view. I tilted my head back and just stared, in awe at the canopy of stars that covered the earth. I couldn't remember ever seeing the sky like this, with no light pollution to dim the jeweled heavens.

Except for... I took a deep breath as my mind flooded with the memory of the weekend Sonny and I spent at the beach a few weeks after my parents died.

He'd insisted we do it, and I fought him the whole way. In the end, he won, and he packed his truck with supplies while I sulked on the front porch. Once we were there, our tent in the dunes overlooking the ocean, the waves crashing in front of us while the stars shimmered above, I realized it was everything I needed. I was finally in a place where I had no control; where the earth and the heavens were in charge and I was just a witness. Sonny knew this. He always seemed to know exactly what would get me out of my head. In this moment, when the grief over my parents was bigger than everything I knew, he showed me something bigger. He gave me a weekend to escape the demands of the world, allowing me a moment to sit in my grief and really feel it, but to also smooth the edges of my loss with the greatness of the universe.

I cried that night under those stars, the pain inside me carried on the wind and waves. He held me while I continued to grieve throughout the weekend. By the time we left, I was spent. The grief was still there. It would always be there. It was there now. But that weekend, I felt the heaviness of it lift, and could never look at the stars the same way.

Sitting here now, the endless sky of unspoiled stars shimmering down on me, I felt the same sense of awe I felt that weekend. I felt the weight lifting off my chest, the permission to be free, and the sheer holiness of just sitting and breathing, my face turned toward the sky.

I also felt Sonny. The way he touched me in our hotel bed in San Francisco. How we sipped coffee together in the shower. Even the normalcy of perusing the shelves at that boutique in Chinatown. For one day, everything felt the way it was supposed to be.

There was one thing he said that kept rolling around in my head. *What do you even want that's about you, and not everyone else?* It stung when he said it. A few days later, though, it was starting to hold some truth. What *did* I want?

I wanted my parents alive. I wanted my sister to stop traveling and stay home. I wanted everything to stay the same—safe and predictable.

"Am I boring?" I asked, turning to Meadow. She was staring at the fire, appearing deep in thought, and it occurred to me that she had heavy things weighing on her mind, as well.

"No. Why, do *you* think you're boring?"

"Maybe. Kind of. Yes." I sighed, slumping lower into my chair. "I guess I've just lived my whole life doing the same thing every day while you're out living an adventure."

"You're here now, aren't you?" she asked.

"Yeah, because you put this together. If you weren't here, I'd be at home in bed with a book, just as I am every night of the year. I'd wake up tomorrow morning and water the garden. I'd go to work and probably eat a salad for lunch. Then I'd end the day with a cup of tea and get back in bed with my book. Every day is the same, and I never thought it was a problem until now."

"What made you realize it?" she asked.

"This," I said, moving my hands to indicate all of Joshua Tree. "The fact that all of my vacations have been planned by someone else. The fact that someone would know everything about me just by spending one day with me because I live by my routine."

"I think you're exaggerating a bit," she said. "You aren't that predictable. I mean, every one of your events is different."

"Not really. I have a list of favorite vendors people happen to love, and I know the formula to planning a great event—set the mood, have good food, play good music, repeat."

Meadow rolled her eyes at me. "I've been to some of your events, Cricket, and they're amazing. You go all out on decorations, know the best chefs and caterers, and people would pay good money to see some of the bands you've booked. Not everyone has your talent."

"Yeah, but what if I've put myself in a box?" I stared back up at the sky, my eye catching a satellite right above us. I followed its trail as it coasted through the Little Dipper.

"Are you considering a career change?" Meadow asked.

"Maybe," I said. "I don't know. I think I just need a change in general."

"Come with me," she said, leaning forward. "Travel the world with me." The glow of the fire shone off her face, her expression beaming with excitement.

"I think that's going from one extreme to the other," I said, laughing. But just for a moment, I considered her offer, imagining what it would be like to bounce from place to place, country to country. Just the thought of it had my hands clenched in nervous fists.

"What do you want?" she asked.

I didn't answer right away. Of course I wanted everything to go back to the way it was before my parents died. But that wasn't possible. Even more, I realized that underneath my insistence to keep everything the same, I *craved* change. I just didn't know what that was.

"I've been trying to figure that out ever since Sonny accused me of living everyone else's life but my own."

"He said that?" She gave a low hum in her throat.

"What? You agree?"

"I don't disagree," she said. "I don't think it's as extreme as you're implying, though. You started your own business, but you've also done nothing to make Mom and Dad's house your own. When I first came home, I half expected to smell banana bread, like Mom used to bake. Besides the bird room, the whole house hasn't changed. You've put none of your personality into the house."

"What would that even look like?"

"I don't know. Flannel sheets and flowing bohemian tapestries? Plants all over the house? Bookshelves organized by color?"

"That's not half bad," I said, envisioning what she suggested.

"I'm not going to design your home for you," she said with a laugh. "But I will point out that you've put so much energy into building other people's visions, and none of that energy into your own. Maybe that's where you start. Think about what your perfect event would look like, but make that event your life. Apply it to your living space, the things you keep around you, your brand new routine, and maybe even your career."

We stayed by the fire a little while longer until the winds picked up again. The fire was already dying anyway, so we retreated to our tent. Both of us changed into leggings and sweatshirts, then huddled under three down comforters. I'd found these comforters in the back of the closet, and as I buried my face in the soft fabric, I inhaled childhood memories of snuggling in bed with my parents.

The wind whipped at the tent, and it seemed impossible to get warm. I moved closer to Meadow, who then moved closer to me, until we were holding each other's hands and shivering our way into warmth.

Eventually our body heat took over, and the bed felt comfier than I expected as our tent rattled around us.

"It's a goddamn hurricane out there," Meadow laughed as she scooted even closer. Part of me wished we hadn't come. I missed my cozy bed and controlled house temperature. But then I would have missed the adventure. There was something wild about sleeping in a windstorm, nothing but canvas separating us from the squall.

And then there was the conversation at the fire. I'd been so consumed with work, my new bird, and above all else, Sonny, that I hadn't taken a moment to think about myself. The truth was, I didn't even need all those distractions as an excuse. For as long as I could remember, I'd only gone with the flow instead of taking control of my life.

What did I want? I wasn't quite sure yet. I had a few ideas buzzing around in my brain, but nothing I was ready to admit to Meadow, or even myself. More than that, I knew what I didn't want—to be an event coordinator.

It was a scary thought. What would I do if I didn't plan events? I was good at it. It paid the bills. But it stopped being fun ages ago. I'd lost my drive for it and had reduced this career to mere science. After the first meeting, I knew which vendors would work best with certain clients. Sometimes all I had to do was look at them. I recognized it was a gift, but I wanted more. I needed variety, a bigger purpose, and maybe a sprinkle of passion. Event planning wasn't cutting it.

Meadow loosened her grip, and I felt her breathing fall into an even pattern. I thought she was asleep, but a shuddered breath interrupted the rhythm. Suddenly, all my self-focused thoughts slid away, and I recalled the look of deep thought she'd had on her face at the fire, before we'd talked about my problems.

"Is everything okay?" I asked her.

"I'm freezing," she said. She burrowed further under the covers, and I wrapped my arms around her.

"Same. But I mean, in general. Are you all right?"

She was quiet for a moment. Or maybe I just couldn't hear her above the wind. Some flap was loose on the outside and it kept whipping against the tent like staccato gunfire.

"I'm okay," she said slowly. "I have a lot on my mind, but I'm fine."

"Is it about Avery's previous owner? The one who died?" When I heard her breath hitch and felt her hands tighten in mine, I knew I'd touched on what was affecting her.

"Bruna was my friend," she finally said. "We'd been friends for years. She was one of my first followers, and we connected immediately. We only had an online friendship but chatted all the time. I went to Brazil for work, but really it was to meet her in person. It ended up being the worst decision of my life."

I was surprised when she burst into tears. I wasn't used to her vulnerable side. Even more, it upset me that she was carrying so much pain, and this was the first time I was hearing of it.

"Bruna's husband was a bad man," she said, sniffing in the darkness. "I knew something was off about him and their marriage just from some of her posts. She was always careful. She wouldn't call me on the phone and only chatted with me through Instagram. We had a video chat once, and I'd noticed a bruise on the side of her face. When I asked about it, she ended the call, and wouldn't video me again. So it was surprising when she agreed to see me when I came to Brazil. I'd asked to stay with her, but she insisted I stay at her friend's AirBnB. It was an apartment overlooking the city, with a pool and gym, which she said was much better than her house."

Meadow moved away from me and stretched out on her back. We'd brought hand warmers with us, and I placed mine against my chest to make up for the cool air between us. My sister suddenly seemed immune to the cold, as if remembering the past took the chill away.

"I realized later how amazing her house was when she brought me there a few weeks into my visit while her husband was on a business trip. She lived in a three-story home on a hill, with endless views of the ocean and forest, and enough rooms that I was afraid of getting lost. That's when I met Avery." Meadow sat up suddenly, then rummaged around in her bag for her phone. She unlocked it, then scrolled through her camera roll. "Here," she said, handing me the phone. I looked, seeing the same photo that was in Meadow's locket, but bigger. "That's Bruna with Avery, though she called him Kauan. She'd inherited the bird from her late aunt, though she didn't receive him until her *Festa de Debutantes*, her fifteenth birthday." I studied Bruna's image, her beauty even more apparent in this enlarged photo.

"What happened to her?" I asked, handing the phone back to her.

Meadow took a deep breath, looking at the photo on her phone. She touched it gently, the phone light reflecting off her tears.

"She asked me to take Avery that day. Said he'd become too much of a nuisance in the house, that her husband had grown tired of him. She asked if I knew someone who could care for him better than she could, and that's when I mentioned you. She was very strange then, telling me not to share my address with her, but to give it to her friend who would make all the arrangements. She wouldn't even let me contact her friend there, but made me wait until I'd traveled to Sweden."

Her breath caught in a sob, and I reached over and grabbed her hand, squeezing tight.

"I didn't know she was dead until the day I called you from Sweden. When I called you, I thought everything was fine. I found out later that night she was dead."

That had been the last time I'd talked to Meadow before she pulled up at my house, her body full of injuries. So many questions flooded my mind, one in particular.

"How did you find out," I asked her.

"Ivan," she said.

"Is Ivan…"

"Bruna's husband," Meadow confirmed. "He'd tracked me to Sweden somehow, probably through Bruna's phone. He said she took her life, and he accused me of causing her to do it. He said she was in love with me and wanted to leave him for me, which wasn't true. We were just friends, but he was convinced we were having an affair behind his back. He knew about the day I was at his house, knew some of what I said verbatim. I realized then that he had surveillance through his house, and I wondered if Bruna knew, too. He demanded to know where the bird was, and when I wouldn't tell him, he beat me while his men watched. He threatened to kill me, like he said I'd killed his wife. He kept trying to get me to tell him where the bird was, but I knew if I told him, it would lead him to you."

Meadow's words came out in pieces as she held her hands over her face.

"Why didn't you tell me?" I asked.

"I was a-afraid," she stuttered. "He told me not to tell anyone or he'd find out, that he knew people all over the world, and if I breathed a word of it, he'd kill everyone I knew and loved, and make me watch before killing me, too." She curled back up under the blankets and I scooted closer to her. Her body was like ice, and I wrapped my arms around her as she shuddered with sobs. "I shouldn't have come home," she said into my hair, and I shook my head in the dark.

"Of course you should have. I'm glad you did."

"I didn't know where else to go," she whispered.

"What about that guy in Sweden?" I asked. "August. Where is he in all this?"

I waited a few moments for her to answer, holding still as I felt her shaky inhales move the bedding.

"He's no one," she finally said, sniffling. "Just a friend. I probably won't see him again." She sniffed again, then gave a light laugh. "God, my good friend dies, her husband hunts me down, and all I can think of is a missed opportunity. It's so pathetic."

My mind immediately shifted to Sonny, and the mixed-up feelings I'd had about him for weeks.

"It's not that pathetic," I said. "When you know, you know. Maybe once things have died down again, you can reconnect with him. But first, we need to call the authorities."

"Were you even listening?" she asked. I felt her shift to her side so that she was facing me. "If I say anything, he'll know. All I need to do is lay low while I heal, and then go back to business as usual. All of this will eventually blow over and I won't have to worry about him."

"What makes you think he won't find you and do this again?"

"I just know, okay? I don't even think he loved Bruna, anyway. The way he spoke about her, it was an ownership thing. He'll eventually find some other woman to own and forget all about Bruna, and me."

"And you're okay with that?" I asked.

"I have to be."

Chapter Twenty

It was still dark out when I unzipped the tent. Meadow's truth burdened me from the moment I woke up. We were safe here, but what about home?

Our campsite didn't have service, so I grabbed my keys and drove to the edge of the park until my phone had one bar, then dialed Blake's number.

"Hello?" he croaked into the phone.

"Hey, just checking in," I whispered, even though there was no one around me to wake up.

"What time is it?"

I wrinkled my nose, realizing my worry had made me selfish. He was obviously fine.

"Is everything okay?" I still asked. "How's Avery?"

"He's fine, we're fine, everything is fine." Blake's voice sounded anything but fine. I heard a sleepy voice in the background asking if anything was wrong.

"Do you want coffee?" he asked in a muffled voice, and I knew he was talking to Sadie.

"Well, things sure have progressed," I teased.

"Are you done? I have more sleep to catch up on."

"Avery is an early riser," I warned him. "You may want to feed him soon if you don't want him screeching from the bird room."

He mumbled something incoherent and then hung up. But just hearing the normalcy of his voice made me feel better. I'd woken with the wind throughout the night, each time worried about things at home. What if Ivan and his cronies showed up unannounced to claim Avery? And why this bird? Don't get me wrong, I loved Avery. He was special to me. But what made him special to *them*? Was it his plucked chest? His ability to destroy a doorjamb in twenty minutes? His car alarm call in the morning? He didn't even say any words. Weren't macaws supposed to be able to speak?

At any rate, it was unlikely they even knew where the bird was, let alone Meadow. None of her followers knew I existed, and she hadn't posted anything to her Instagram since she'd left Brazil. Besides, she'd been at my house for two weeks, and no bad guys had shown their faces. I hoped they'd forgotten their obsession over my bird and moved on.

Meadow was making coffee when I returned to camp. The wind was no stronger than a light breeze, and her hair ruffled under the beanie she had slouched over her ears. She was hunched over the two-burner gas stove I'd found among our parents' camping gear, her arms crossed in front of her.

"You could have built a fire," I said.

"I was too cold," she laughed. "My fingers aren't working. It was hard enough starting the stove."

It was definitely cold, but nothing like last night's icy wind. If it stayed like this the rest of our time, I could handle it. Still, I hoped today would warm up so we could thaw out.

We'd gone through one pack of wood last night, leaving us two more for the rest of the trip. I made a vow to only use half of the bundle in my hands, arranging the smaller pieces into a teepee then dousing it with starter fluid. Soon we had a modest fire going, though it would be a while before it offered any warmth.

I joined Meadow at the stove and she handed me a cup of coffee.

"No cream," she apologized. She tilted her head as she studied me. "Are you okay?"

"I'm good," I said. "But what about you?"

"I'm okay," she said. "A bit tired, sore from sleeping on the ground, but I'm fine."

"No, that's not what I mean."

"Really, I'm fine. The thing with Ivan happened weeks ago. We haven't heard from him since, and he probably figures I don't have the bird. Besides, we have a lot to do today, and I'd rather focus on that, okay?"

"It's not just going to go away," I said.

"I know that." She huffed as she flipped the sausages in the breakfast pan. I sipped my black coffee, grimacing at the acidic taste. "Look, we can worry about this later. But for today, can we just forget it? I don't want to even think about it, all right?"

I glanced at her arm and the way she limped as she grabbed plates. He'd done this to her. If I ever got my hands on that bastard, I'd tear him apart. But when Meadow looked back at me for confirmation, I neutralized my face and smiled.

"Okay, fine," I said.

She handed me a plate of scrambled eggs, sausage, and toast, and I inhaled the savory smell. After weeks of playing hostess, this was a nice change of pace.

"I toasted the bread in the pan with the sausage grease," she explained, and I raised an eyebrow at her. "Trust me. It's delicious."

I took a small bite of the crisp bread, and my stomach gave a greedy groan as the taste hit my tongue. Holy hell, it was good. I bit into it, satisfying my sudden hunger with a huge mouthful. It was better than buttered toast.

"From now on, I'm only eating greasy toast," I promised, and she laughed.

"You should probably save that for special occasions," she said. "But yeah, it's pretty good, right?"

We inhaled breakfast and threw our paper plates in the fire. Then we watched the sunrise, and Meadow caught a few photos of it, along with some sleepy photos of me in all my camping glory.

"I look like hell," I warned her.

"You look like me, and I think you look cute. This is for my followers, so chill." She snapped a few more photos in rapid succession. I started to feel annoyed, but then I realized that all the photos really wouldn't be *me*. There was no one to judge me because everyone would think I was Meadow. I could have a double chin, stick my gut out, and make awkward poses—all normal occurrences in the life of Cricket Stone—and no one would know it was me.

"Are you pushing your neck out like that on purpose?" Meadow asked, putting her camera down. She rolled her eyes as I cracked myself up. "Don't make me give you a lesson on proper posing," she warned me.

She did anyway. As she did my makeup, she showed me ways to make my legs look longer, my neck like a giraffe's, and my cheekbones appear chiseled into my face. Then she styled my hair into an elaborate braid, an impressive feat with her limited arm mobility. It was an inside-out French braid that almost looked like a mohawk—a Viking braid, she called it. Wearing cropped cargo pants, Zola hiking boots, and a tight tank top, I looked kind of badass. I mean, as long as no one saw my goosebumps.

"Dude, it's flipping cold. I can't hike in a cardigan?"

"It's going to warm up," she said.

She was right. Again. As soon as we were ready to go, the sun's rays were warming my skin and I could tell it was going to be a beautiful day.

We kept close to camp since Meadow's movements were limited, but it didn't dampen our experience. Our campsite was full of majestic rocks and gorgeous scenery. We found a hollowed-out rock that allowed me to lie on my back and touch my boots to the rounded portion up top, my gaze settled dramatically on the horizon beyond the camera. She shot video while I climbed small boulders and jumped off, her camera clicking away as I landed. Later, we came upon a small cave that was so short, I had to crawl in. She took a picture of me at the entrance, resting on one knee, leaning my elbow on the other, my leg bent so that the boot was on display. We broke for a late lunch, then took catnaps in the sunshine, and the whole time I couldn't get it out of my head that Sonny would have loved being here with us.

It was a crazy thought. We hadn't spoken since San Francisco, and I'd done my best to keep busy so he wouldn't infiltrate my mind. But here, being busy felt a lot like being slow. There were more times of quiet than talking as both of us took in our surroundings, breathed the fresh air, and experienced the present moment so far away from any responsibilities or worries. This was exactly the kind of place Sonny loved. It made me wish

I'd been more adventurous when I was with him, and I realized how much he bent toward my comfort level, and I never tried to reach his. Besides that one camping trip, where he'd dragged me to the beach despite my resistance, he never pushed me to do anything I didn't want to. It occurred to me how much I held him back, and how his move to Wisconsin may have been his way to break through my resistance, and all I did was retreat even more.

Meadow took over the camp prep that evening. "Go take a walk or something," she said as she placed kindling in the firepit.

"You shouldn't be moving around so much," I said, noting the way she favored her leg when she retrieved the lighter from the table.

"I'm fine," she insisted. "I'm always sore in the evenings, and it's good to stretch it out a little. But I can see you have something on your mind. You've been moping for the past hour or so, and it's kind of a drag."

I rolled my eyes, but the tears that brimmed my eyes gave me away.

"Go!" she said, shooing me with her hands. "We can talk later, but go collect your thoughts. That's what this trip is about, anyway."

"I thought it was to win back your sponsor."

"That's an added benefit," she laughed. She hopped over to me and rested an arm around my shoulder. "But this is mostly for you, and what's going on between you and you-know-who."

I leaned into Meadow, then laughed when she hip-checked me away from her.

"I'm going!" I was still smiling as I brushed the tears from my eyes, then left her to tend to camp.

All around our site, other families and groups of friends were doing the same as Meadow. The sun had already left the sky, and all warmth from the day was diminishing by the minute. Even without the wind, it was cold enough to wear my heavy down jacket and still feel the chill. I wrapped it tighter around me, walking further down the road until the glowing campfires were just tiny orange dots against the shadowy rocks.

A few stars were already sprinkled across a violet canvas, and I sank to the ground, leaning against a boulder with my arms hugged around my knees as I watched the sky turn to night. A few Joshua trees loomed nearby, their shadowy branches like outstretched arms. A nearby scuttling noise alerted me to curious wood rats running through the dirt. But this time, I didn't worry about them. I was too weighed down by my guilt.

I'd ended things with Sonny. It wasn't his fault, as I'd stubbornly insisted all this time. It was mine. We could have made long-distance work. Or maybe I could have tried on Wisconsin for size.

That was a scary thought, even now in my regret, but not an impossible one. All this time in Joshua Tree, I fully expected I'd miss home. And while I missed the convenience, it wasn't the house I was missing, but the people.

One person. Sonny.

I missed who we were before he moved away, and I missed having him around when he came back to Petaluma. I missed seeing his smile, the crinkle around his eyes, and all the tiny gestures he made, almost unconsciously, that left me feeling cared for. Opening the door for me. His consuming hugs. The way he knew my thoughts before I even knew them myself. Even the past few weeks had shown me that Sonny was still the same man I'd fallen in love with way back when. It wasn't even about the generous things he did for me, but how he made me feel. Even as I fought against it, he made me feel special. Cared for. As if I were the only person in the room with him.

My definition of home had changed. I loved the coastal air, green pastures, and tall redwood trees of my hometown. But if I had a second chance with Sonny, I'd give it all up in a heartbeat. I loved him. Capital L Love. Our night in San Francisco opened the door to this truth, but now, sitting here in the cold desert under a starry sky, I was suddenly warm with the realization. He'd moved on, but I could no longer deny these feelings. Now that

I'd felt his body against mine and tasted his kisses, I never wanted to be without him again. At least, I needed to give this a fighting shot. I was done with playing it safe and living inside my cramped, orderly box. It was time. Sonny was worth fighting for.

"Good walk?" Meadow asked as I headed back into camp. The fire was blazing, and the flames glowed on her face as she ate a hot dog for dinner. "There's another hot dog on the grill for you," she said. I barely heard her. I began tidying up the things on the table, trying to consolidate it all to make packing easier.

"Yo, earth to Cricket. What are you doing?

"We've been here twenty-four hours, and the place is a mess," I said, dragging a box of clothes near the car. "I thought we could pack the car up with everything we don't need tonight so that there's even less to do tomorrow. I want to hit the road early."

"What's your rush?" she asked. "Checkout isn't until noon, and I thought we'd get a few more shots in."

I stopped what I was doing and sank into the chair next to her. Just the suggestion of staying felt like a gut punch.

"It's not that I don't love it here," I said, turning to her. "I just feel the need to go home." Her face took on a look of sympathy, and I fought the urge to give in. "There's still so much to do for the Finnigan party," I continued, hating that my voice sounded weak. "Plus, I didn't know how hard it would be to work out here. I feel bad that Taye has been handling everything while we've been prancing all over the desert."

"Aw, Cricket," she said. "When was the last time you took a vacation?"

I tilted my head, trying to remember.

"That long, huh?" She shook her head. "Taye's incredible. She could probably manage your company by herself."

"I know she can," I admitted. "Still, the party is this Friday, so I'm anxious to get back."

"And then you'll be done with Sonny, once and for all, huh?" Meadow said.

I sunk further into my chair, soaking up the heat from the fire as her words hit their mark.

"Yeah," I said. I watched the flames dancing in front of me, breaking off into embers that floated into the night.

"Uh oh, what's that?" Meadow looked closely at me, then gave a knowing nod. "Something happened here, didn't it?"

"What?"

"The desert. The quiet. Did it knock some sense into you?" She cast a smug expression at me, and I tossed one of the shirts from the box at her. "Hey," she laughed. "I'm right, aren't I?"

"Maybe. I don't know." I curled my knees up to my chest, then glanced over at her. "Yeah." She let out a whoop, then grinned at me. "But nothing's guaranteed," I continued. "Sonny and I haven't spoken since San Francisco, and things were pretty tense. Plus there's the whole fake relationship thing with Blake."

I buried my head in my knees, reality stripping away my hope. I thought about my phone call with Blake in the hotel room, how I'd laid it on pretty thick. Sonny's phone call with Justine had been tame compared to my theatrics. If I'd heard him sweet-talking her after we'd just spent the night together, it would have crushed me.

"I've made a mess of everything," I said.

"No, you haven't." Meadow took my hand. "You know I don't think Sonny's over you."

"He's moved on," I said weakly.

"Has he, though? Because he was at our house every day last week."

"Building a birdcage," I said.

"For free," she answered. "Would Blake do that for you?"

I crinkled my nose, mulling it over. "He'd want some kind of favor in exchange," I admitted. "Though he and Sadie are desecrating my bed, so probably not sexual favors."

"Thank goodness for that. He's a good guy and all, but definitely not your type. I knew that when you two first started dating."

I tilted my head at her. "You did, huh?" I said, raising an eyebrow. "You didn't even know him."

"I knew enough from everything you told me about him. I just didn't want to meddle."

I laughed at that. "Right, not you," I said, my tone dripping in sarcasm.

"That's beside the point. You're changing the subject, which is Sonny and how you're going to get him away from that hussy."

Hussy. The word felt wrong. "She's actually not a hussy," I said, sinking into my chair. "She's nice, like really nice. A little overly energetic, but sweet. And trusting. She didn't even mind when Sonny was at lunch with me, or when he and I went to San Francisco together." I took a deep breath, feeling the full weight of everything we were proposing. "I can't do this. Not to her. Not to them."

"I hate to tell you, but you already did," Meadow said. "When you and Sonny slept together, it was proof that you two aren't over each other. Besides, you had him first."

"And I let him go. Now he's with her."

"But you—"

"We messed up."

I leaned my head back, taking in the full sky, feeling smaller than ever. All the epiphanies I'd felt before were now gone. All the fight I had, gone. But the ache in my heart? That wasn't gone. That was bigger than ever.

"Do you still love him?" Meadow asked.

I considered blowing it off, chalking all of it up to a dry spell, the whiskey, a weak moment. But the truth bubbled up instead.

"With all my heart."

"Then talk with him," she said. I started to argue, but she cut me off. "I'm not telling you to make up his mind for him. But he should at least know how you feel."

Meadow's advice rolled through my mind as I packed the car that night. I even put the tent away, both of us deciding the car was much warmer than the freezing desert air. As my body settled onto the folded-out backseat, sleep washing over me, I knew she was right. This evening, I'd been so sure Sonny was worth fighting for. I still believed that. The least I could do was tell him the truth.

Whatever happened next would be his decision. All I could do was try.

Chapter Twenty-One

"Okay, when I say go, tell me about your dream job." Meadow trained her phone at me, waiting for my answer. I kept my eyes on the road, stuck on the impossibly boring and never-ending Interstate 5 on our way home. To pass the time, we were adding to Meadow's Instagram, but this one was something I could get behind.

Besides sponsored posts and filtered photos, Meadow used her platform to bring awareness to nonprofits she believed in. One of them was for "She Knows," an organization that ensured higher education and career opportunities for girls and young women. In this post, my goal was to talk about Meadow's career path beyond Instagram and share about the journey she'd taken to get there. The problem was, I didn't believe it was the path she wanted to take.

"So, I'm supposed to pretend I'm you and then talk about becoming a global marketing manager and all those classes you took before you got Instagram famous, right?"

"Right." She lifted the phone again and took aim.

"Hold on," I said. She sighed loudly. "Stop being impatient," I continued. "It's not like we don't have the time. I just want to be clear about this. Your dream job is to work at a desk, researching trends for other companies to keep them top of mind?"

"What's your point?" she asked.

"My point is that I think your dream has changed."

"I got a master's in marketing. I hate to see that go to waste."

"It's not," I said. "You're putting it to good use now. But once you're done being in the spotlight, I think we both know where you want to be."

"And where is that?" she asked.

"Behind the camera." I took my eyes off the road for a moment to shoot her a meaningful look.

"There are apps for that," she pointed out.

"And there are computer programs for that, too. What's your point? You know how to use photo tools effectively to make the image pop. I think you might have a new career path."

She looked out the window, and I could practically hear her mind going into overdrive.

"But that doesn't go with the message I'm trying to put out there. I wanted to talk about the career I had in mind while going to school."

"You can," I said. "And you can talk about the way your path changed directions and led you to a new path, and the freedom you have to choose a new course of education, like photography, to set you on a new adventure in your career."

"All right, Einstein, you go first. Tell me about your dream job."

"You mean, as you, or as Cricket?"

"As yourself. Tell me everything." Meadow raised her phone and trained it on me.

I opened my mouth to speak, but the words escaped me. It was one thing to be broadcast as Meadow. But talking about me? It was almost like I forgot my own history.

"Relax," she said, lowering her camera. "This isn't a huge deal. It's not for anyone but us. I'm just warming you up, and it's easier to talk about the things you know, right?"

"Well, I went to Sonoma State," I started.

"Wait! Let me get the camera on you." She aimed it at me. "Okay, go."

"So after high school, I was lucky enough to go to college, because that's what was expected of me."

"Hold on." Meadow put the camera down again, and I felt her stare on me. "No one told you that you had to go to college," she said. "Remember? Mom and Dad said it was our choice if we wanted to go, and we both decided to go."

"Okay, fine. They didn't say I *needed* to go, but I didn't know what else to do. I wanted a career, and college seemed like the best path."

She lifted the camera again. "And then you discovered hospitality."

"Yeah." I blew out a large breath of air. "I need to start over. This is stupid."

"Okay, new idea. No video, okay?" She lowered the phone, resting it in her lap. "Tell me about your dream job that is not event planning. If you could do something else, what would it be?"

I pondered this question for a few moments, even though the answer was there, hidden in the deepest, darkest part of me. I'd never told anyone. It felt silly, like when you ask a child what they want to be when they grew up, and they said something big like princess or astronaut. This *thing* felt the same way. It was something I wanted so bad, but it was too big to say out loud.

But then again, why not say it out loud? Plenty of people had this job. It wasn't even out of my reach—it was just far removed from what I was doing now.

I took a deep breath, gripping the steering wheel with both hands.

"I want to be a beekeeper," I blurted out. I glanced at Meadow as her mouth dropped open. Then she laughed.

"Really?"

"Really," I said. I thought I'd be devastated if she laughed at me. Instead, it was the opposite. Just saying it, I felt empowered. "I know it sounds stupid, but it means something to me. I'm not saying I would or anything, but if I did, it would almost be like continuing Mom's mission."

"Oh," she said. "So, it's more about Mom than you."

"But it's not. I mean, it started with Mom's passion for honeybees. But I grew up helping her with them, and it became my passion, too. Even now, over everything I do, the most gratification I get is when I'm in the garden, adding to the plants that keep the bees happy. I'd love to learn more about them, how to collect honey, what it takes to have a hive… Everything."

"And what would it take for you to get there?" she asked. Her phone was out again, and I realized she'd recorded everything. I didn't care though. I felt a lightness in my chest that hadn't been there in a long time.

"I guess I would start with a bee farm and see if they have an apprenticeship, and suggestions for classes I should take. I'd probably want a mentor, or to at least learn the career path of someone who's already a beekeeper. Eventually, if things go well, I'd have my own bee farm and sell honey to local grocery stores and farmer's markets."

Meadow put the phone down, then grinned at me.

"I'm using that," she said. "It's perfect."

"Wait, but you can't. That's not your dream."

"No, but it's yours. And so are all those photos in the desert. I'm posting them, but I'm posting them as you."

"But what about Ivan? Besides, no one even knows you have a twin."

When I looked at Meadow, it was clear she was serious. But there was something else. Determination. This was the Meadow I knew, the one who never lived her life according to anyone else.

"I realized I can't hide forever," she said. "We've done all this talking about truth, and I'm not living mine. I can't lie to my followers, and it's time to come clean about my absence, and why I look the way I do. I can't live in fear because of one man." She reached over and took my hand. "Besides, I want my followers to know you. How cool would it be to have sister shots on my profile? Think of how many followers you'll gain!"

"That's not my thing, and you know it," I laughed. "But it would be cool to be part of your branding now and then." I was still troubled, though. I took my hand back, placing it on the steering wheel. "Meadow, that guy hurt you really bad. You said he had connections all over the world, and that he'd know if you told anyone."

"No one has that much power," she said.

"But if you post pictures of us together, he won't need to have that much power. He'll know where you are, and he'll find both of us. We need to tell someone about him."

She stayed silent for a moment, turning to look out the window.

"This is why I didn't want to tell you," she said. I started to interject, but she stopped me. "Yes, a lot of bad stuff happened. But I'm safe now. We're safe. Just let it be, okay?"

"How can you be so sure?"

She was silent for a moment, and then let out a slow breath. "I can't call the authorities because it will make this a bigger issue than it already is, and it could put us in bigger jeopardy."

"Us?" I asked. "So he knows you're with me?"

"No," she said. Then she followed with, "Maybe."

"Shit, Meadow."

"Yes, it's possible," she admitted. "He doesn't know anything about me, but it's nothing a private investigator couldn't dig up. Besides, I'm following orders. I was advised to give you the bird to keep it hidden, and then, after Ivan released me, I was told to come here. They promised I'd be safe. So I'm choosing to trust that."

"Who, though? Who's giving you all these instructions?" I glanced over at her just as she shook her head.

"Just let it be, okay? I believe we're safe, okay? Do you trust me?"

In normal circumstances, yes. But in the moment, I realized Meadow was in way over her head. We weren't raised with secrets or elements of danger.

"We need to go into hiding," I said. "Oh god, we need to tell Taye and Blake. And Sonny! Maybe even Mr. Finnigan! Anyone I've talked with! We need to tell them to leave town, and—"

"Cricket, get a grip!" Meadow clutched my arm, shaking it. "Nothing is going to happen, okay? I'd have heard by now if we were in trouble. Save your worrying for when we have a reason to worry."

"And when will that be," I muttered. I turned to her, catching her eyeroll. "Fine, we're safe. But I can't believe you gave me a bird that could get us killed."

"Should I have ditched the bird, instead?" she asked. "Because I couldn't. I promised Bruna I'd keep him safe, and I would rather die than break a promise to her."

"You really cared for her, didn't you?" I asked. She nodded, sniffing and then letting out a shaky breath.

"Not the way Ivan thought," she said. "She was my friend, like a sister." She turned to me, shaking her head. "I mean, not like you. But kind of like you. I get..." She paused, wiping her eyes again. "I mean, I don't want to be home. I like traveling. But sometimes it gets lonely. I'm on my own, meeting up with people I just have superficial relationships with. But with Bruna, it was different. We connected on a whole new level. You would have loved her. I told her all about you, and she was supposed to meet you one day." Meadow took another shaky breath. "When she asked me to take the bird, I didn't understand why it was so important. But I knew how much that bird meant to her, so I did. And now, I will do anything to make sure Ivan never gets his hands on Avery."

"We can call him Kauan," I offered.

"No," she said. "That life is over. He's Avery now, and he's your bird." She laughed. "I see the way you care for him. You look at him the same way Bruna did. It's a perfect match."

"I have grown a little fond of that stupid bird," I admitted.

"A little?" she asked.

"I'm crazy about him," I laughed. "And he drives me crazy. But he's totally wormed his way into my heart." Just talking about him, I couldn't wait to get home and see him. I wondered if Avery suffered under Blake's care. I probably should have entrusted him in the care of someone a little more attentive.

"How about this," Meadow said. "When we get home, I'll call my contact and see if there's any news about Ivan's plans or if I should be worried."

"Has this person contacted you at all?"

"No," she said. "And I haven't contacted him. We don't want to blow his cover, so no news is good news."

"Or he's dead," I offered. I could feel her glare boring through the side of my head. "I mean, really, Meadow. No news could mean a lot of things."

"Like I said, I'll contact him when we get home. If I can't get ahold of him, then I'll involve the local authorities."

"Why wait?" I asked. "Why not call him now?"

"Because we're not in trouble."

"Meadow!"

"Cricket!" she said, using the same exasperated tone. "I don't even want to talk about this right now. You needed a vacation to get away from all your feelings about Sonny? Well, I needed a vacation from this. And right now, we're still on vacation time."

I glanced at the long road ahead and endless scenery of yellowed plains. "Fine," I said. "But as soon as we pull into the driveway, you're making that call."

"After a shower," she promised. "I stink like I've been camping all weekend. I need a hot shower before we do anything else."

She apparently also needed a nap. Meadow fell asleep a short while later, leaving me with my mind to keep me company. Leaving me with breathless thoughts over how close I came to losing my sister. Would I have even known if she'd died? Ivan had obviously done it to scare her, or he would have killed her. That's the only reason I could come up with since there was no one there to stop him. I was lucky she came home, but what if she hadn't? What if he did end up killing her? Who would have told me? There was no one to tell me she'd been in the hospital, or that she was headed home. If she'd died, would she have disappeared without a trace?

It made me realize how quickly everything could change, and how nothing in life was guaranteed. This wasn't just about Meadow's traumatic experience. This was about the life I was living now versus the life I wanted to have.

What would it be like to walk away from everything, to let go of all the *shoulds* and *expectations* in my life, and go in a completely different direction? Would it be stupid? Irresponsible? Or bold?

I didn't have the answer. All I knew was that when I talked about beekeeping with Meadow, it felt like I was uncovering a secret passageway deep within myself. The possibilities kept jumping at me. What if I did find an apprenticeship? What if I learned enough to have my own bee farm? I didn't know much about beekeeping beyond growing bee-friendly plants, but this path still made more sense than planning events.

Meadow ended up sleeping the rest of the way home. I was tired, too, but kept the window cracked so the fresh air would keep me awake. Relief flooded me as I approached our exit, and I took the offramp toward the road that led home. On the way through my neighborhood, I passed Patty Jenkins walking her dog. She had on that flowered smock she always wore. My mother swore she had a closet full of them at home, one for every day of the month.

Patty paused as my brand-new Subaru rolled by, looking at me over her skinny bifocals. I was going slow enough that I could make out the thin line of her mouth and her narrowed eyes. I wondered if she was taking mental notes about the fact that I'd purchased a new vehicle but still hadn't fixed the cracks in my driveway or straightened the tilted mailbox at the curb. Right now, she was probably plotting her letter to me from the Community Care Association about property values and tidy yards. I hoped she did. And I hoped I could handle it the same way my mother did when it came to how she kept our yard—with a healthy dose of humor and a sprinkle of sarcasm.

When I looked in my rearview mirror, Patty was still standing there, watching me drive away. I waved, and she turned away immediately. Coincidence? Probably not.

The sight of the birdcage at the top of the driveway made my heart unexpectedly leap. Now that we were home, I couldn't wait to see Avery. I missed that bird. I even missed his wake-up calls. But alongside that longing were my feelings for the man who built that birdcage. Would I think of him every time I saw that cage? Part of me hoped I would, even if I was forced to give him up.

I parked the car, then looked over at my sleeping sister. Her head was leaning against the window, her good hand resting in her lap while her casted arm rested close to her chest. Her breathing was even, and I hated to have to wake her. I was exhausted, too. But all I could think about, beyond checking on the bird, was the phone call she needed to make.

"Meadow," I murmured, touching her arm. She groaned, her eyes still closed as she curled up tighter in the chair. "Meadow," I tried again. She was out. Sighing, I decided to unpack first, and then coax her awake. She wasn't going to be much help with unpacking, anyway.

Opening the door, I inhaled the familiar scent of jasmine from the vines hanging near the driveway, along with a slightly musty smell of manure from the nearby farms. "Sonoma Aroma," the locals called it, and it was one of those things only Petalumans would understand...

…and love. Even in the stinkiest months, I loved it, as it gave me a deeper sense of home.

If I had to leave Petaluma, could I leave the smells behind? The community? Everything I'd grown up with? What if I followed through on this beekeeping venture and it took me to a new place? Even more? What if, somehow, things worked out between Sonny and me, and he asked me to move with him?

Could I leave Petaluma?

I thought about it, really mulled over the question. I thought about what it would be like to wake up in a new place, experience new smells and local customs, to meet a new community.

I was still thinking about it as I opened the back hatch and a pillow fell out. I bent to retrieve it, wondering how many other things shifted on our long journey.

I never found out. Something slammed into the back of my head, sending an electric bolt through my vision in the form of pain and sparking light. Somewhere, in the very corners of my awareness, I heard my sister's scream puncture the air, along with deep voices. I knew I should be afraid. I was aware I might die. Instead, as my body crumpled to the ground, the whole world went dark.

Chapter Twenty-Two

My head was pounding. Everything hurt, but it was my head I was most aware of. Voices all around me. Muffled. Then clear.

"There's two of her."

"They're twins, you idiot."

I opened my eyes, everything blurry. Everything spinning. A man's face in mine. I turned away, only to have him grab hold of my jaw and turn me back to him.

"Which one are you?" he asked. His breath was a mixture of spices and garlic, warm and sour in my nose. My vision stabilized and his face came into view. Coffee-colored skin. Ebony eyes. Dark facial hair. Under any other circumstance, I would have thought he was handsome. But I knew who he was.

"Ivan," I whispered. His face broke into a wide smile.

"*Você me conhece*. You know me," he purred, letting go of my face and stepping back to get a better look. "But I don't know you. *Prazer em conhecê-la*. Pleased to meet you, Cricket."

"Leave her alone," Meadow said next to me. My surroundings became clearer with each passing second. We were in the Bird Room. Ropes wound around Meadow and me, both of us in back-to-back chairs. Three men stood off to the side, glancing from us to Ivan. I took them to be Ivan's henchmen. I turned my head and saw Blake tied to a chair in the corner, his face bruised and a nasty gash on his lip. He looked at me, his eyes locking with mine.

Are you okay, I mouthed. He nodded, but I noted the scared look on his face. I felt it too. We were helpless, completely at the mercy of this unpredictable man.

"Ah, Meadow," Ivan said, stepping away to get a better look at my twin. "I made a mistake when I let you go. I thought we were coming to an understanding."

"I told you, Ivan. I don't know where your bird is."

I winced as I heard him slap her.

"Leave her alone," I cried. "She doesn't have your stupid bird."

"You see, I don't think that's true," Ivan said. He came within view again, making a show of glancing at the cage. "This is quite the enclosure, Cricket. Don't you think? Big enough for a large bird, like a macaw. Am I right?" He stepped closer to me, leaning down until his face was inches from mine. My heart thundered in my chest, my body trembling as he remained dangerously close. I fought the urge to turn away.

"*Onde está o pássaro.*" His face was so close, his features blurred together. "Tell me where the bird is."

My heartbeat pounded in my temples, and I finally looked away, only to have him force my face back to his.

"Tell me!" he screamed, spraying spit on my face with the forced words.

"I don't know," I said, shrinking as his grip tightened on my jaw. I imagined him squeezing my head until it popped, and I couldn't keep from tearing up. My eyes drifted to the enclosure, and I saw it was empty. For a moment, fear over my own safety was abated over fear for Avery. Where was the bird?

Ivan let go of my face, pushing it so that my head hit the back of Meadow's with a hard clunk. I heard her groan, and I whispered an apology even though it wasn't my fault. I watched as Ivan stalked toward Blake, a plea in my throat as his foot connected with the chair, sending Blake to the ground.

"Don't!" I screamed. Ivan's boot rested on Blake's head, and I squeezed my eyes shut, afraid to see my friend murdered in front of me.

"I told you, the bird escaped," Blake hissed. I opened my eyes, daring to look at my friend. "I'm sorry," he said to me, his voice trembling, his face pressed against the floor as Ivan's foot weighed him down. "He escaped the day you two left, and I didn't want to tell you."

"You're lying," Ivan said, removing his foot and lifting Blake again by the ropes so that he was upright. He stepped back, pulling a knife from his belt. He picked at his nail with it, but I knew this was a show of power, a way to get us to talk. He looked at me. "Tell me, Cricket. Where did you take the bird? Tell me, and your friend will walk away with all of his fingers."

"She doesn't know, Ivan. Stop being stupid," my sister snarled.

"Meadow!" I was surprised at her tone, her fearlessness, especially since she was still healing from her last encounter with him. If his warnings looked like the injuries he gave my sister, I was terrified to find out what his *final chance* looked like.

"He's insane," Meadow said. "He thinks he's entitled to anything he wants. He knows just as well as I do that Avery isn't his."

"Avery." Ivan smirked. "If you mean Kauan, you're mistaken. That bird belonged to my wife, and it's the last thing I have left of her."

"Bruna never wanted you," Meadow said forcefully. "She hated you, and the only way she could leave you was to take her own life." She choked on a sob, and I felt her body shaking next to mine. I moved my hand until I found hers and then grasped it, holding tight. "She gave Kauan to me before she died. You know this. I signed a contract. It's on the stupid surveillance camera you used to spy on her."

"That is not your bird, *vagabunda estúpida*, you stupid slut." He lunged around me, and I was jerked backward as he pulled Meadow to him. "You seduced my wife into giving you that bird because you're a money-hungry whore."

"You're the money-hungry whore," Meadow hissed. "You married her because of that bird, and the only reason you weren't the one who took her life is because you knew it would keep you from receiving any of the inheritance. Bruna was my friend and she trusted me. She gave me that bird to keep it from you, fucker."

Whatever Meadow was saying about an inheritance was news to me. But I couldn't even be curious about it. I knew this was the moment I would die. All for a bird. As much as I loved that bird, I wished it were here so that Ivan would take it and leave. Were our lives really worth less than an obnoxious macaw?

I heard the click, and I shut my eyes, fairly certain it was a gun. I thought of all my regrets, and really, there was only one. I never should have let Sonny go. I'd been so stubborn when all he'd done was bend for me. Why couldn't I bend for him? I'd never been loved by somebody so completely, and now, I never would. I was going to die, and Sonny would never know that I still loved him. Maybe he'd find happiness after I was gone.

Maybe he already had. In this moment, I hoped Justine was everything I wanted to be for him so that he would feel as loved as he'd made me feel.

"Yoohoo!"

My eyes flew open at the same time Ivan must have let go of Meadow. We slammed back to an upright position, her head hitting mine.

"Sorry," she whispered, just as unnecessarily as I had. But I ignored it. I was too grateful for the interruption that surely saved all of our lives. I also feared for whoever stepped in the door. I turned in the direction and groaned when I saw Patty Jenkins in the doorway, even more when I saw Avery on her shoulder.

"Are you missing a bird? This little fellow showed up in my backyard a few days ago. Do you know who he belongs to?"

"Mrs. Jenkins, leave!" I screamed. Ivan stepped around us, pulling a gun from the back of his pants. "Run!"

"Shit," one of the henchmen said. "Ivan, stand down."

"It's all going to be okay," Meadow hissed at me as both of Ivan's men sprang forward, one training his gun on another henchman while another knocked the gun from Ivan's hands. As Ivan fell to the ground, a stream of FBI agents swarmed the room.

"Ivan Oliveira Santos, you have the right to remain silent. Anything you say can be used against you in court…" The agent continued stating Ivan's rights as one officer knelt by us, working at the knots that kept me tied to Meadow. Another officer was doing the same for Blake.

"How are you doing?" the officer asked as he loosened the ropes. I rolled my shoulder and stretched my neck. Then I looked at Meadow. She appeared okay, despite the red handprint on her cheek. Most of all, she seemed relieved.

"I'm good now," I said.

I had so many questions, I didn't know where to start. Meadow was busy with the bird, and Blake was in the corner on the phone, probably with Sadie. The two men who I thought were bad guys were busy talking to the FBI as Ivan and his remaining underling were led from the house in handcuffs.

Patty Jenkins sidled up to me. "I knew the bird was yours the whole time," she said with a wink, eyeing Ivan on the ground. "But I also knew you were away." She nodded at Blake across the room. "I didn't think your man friend was capable of handling such a magnificent creature, so I decided to keep him for a few days until you came back. Looks like I got here just in time."

"You were almost shot," I pointed out, though I realized it really was lucky she had him. If Avery had been here, Ivan probably would have shot Blake and taken the bird. Maybe he would have waited to kill us first. Maybe he would have burned the whole house down. I shuddered at each thought, especially knowing how close we came to losing everything.

"He never would have shot anyone," Meadow said, hobbling closer to us with Avery on her shoulder. She had pieces of apple in her hand, which she gave to the bird a chunk at a time. "Detectives Andersson and Silva wouldn't have let him." She looked up at the two men who approached our circle, giving one of them a warm smile she reserved for people she cared about. I saw the look mirrored on his face, though they kept a friendly distance between them.

"Cricket, meet August and Paulo," she said. My eyes widened at the first name, and I took a better look at the man closest to my sister.

"August? From Sweden?" Now that I wasn't seeing him as some scary thug, I could see why she thought he was attractive. His blue eyes were trained on my sister, and I could sense the attraction between the two of them. "Is that the man you're dating?"

"Not dating," my sister corrected. "Just friends. But he's the friend Bruna connected me with when I signed the contract to take Kauan. I mean, Avery. We traveled to Sweden together, and he helped me get the bird to you. We thought Ivan didn't know a thing, but then we discovered he'd recorded the whole conversation. Thank goodness he had no idea August was involved."

She explained how August had been working undercover for months over an embezzlement case, and Bruna had found out. She'd been helping him until she'd taken her life.

"I'd tried to help her," Meadow said, her face breaking with emotion.

"It wasn't your fault," August reassured her, wrapping his arm around my sister. "She'd been struggling for a long time."

From what Meadow already told me, I knew Ivan kept her under close watch and control. But August filled in more about what their marriage was like. Ivan had a temper and would use it on Bruna whenever he felt she was out of line. Which was often. Bruna wore long, flowing dresses that covered her body, despite the tropical climate, because her skin was riddled with burns and bruises. The only time she got any reprieve was when he'd take off for weeks at a time, leaving her at home watched by one of his henchmen along with the cameras all over their home. She wasn't hurt during those times, but she was always watched. And she'd thought she was alone in her prison until Ivan unknowingly left August in charge.

"I'm good at my job," August said, winking at his partner. "Ivan had no idea Paulo or I were undercover when he hired us, and I'd been waiting for time alone with Bruna for months before he finally trusted me to watch her."

During those weeks, August had to work hard to gain Bruna's trust. "She thought Ivan was testing her. It wasn't until I had her talk to my chief. We showed her everything we already had on him, and she finally believed I was there to put her husband behind bars."

To gain information from Bruna, he had to get her out of the house and away from the cameras. He knew where most of them were, but Ivan was a cunning man who trusted no one, and likely had cameras hidden in places even his hired men didn't know. To gather evidence, August took Bruna on drives to the grocery store, doctors appointments, and other various errands, grilling her on the car rides about everything she knew regarding Ivan's business practices, bank accounts, friends, and anything else that seemed suspicious. Bruna shared what she knew, which wasn't everything, but enough to lead him in the right direction.

"She also told me about the inheritance that went with her bird," he said, and I looked at him sharply.

"About that," I said, glancing at Avery before looking at Meadow. "You said something about an inheritance to Ivan. The bird has an inheritance?"

"Technically, the owner of the bird has the inheritance," she said.

I had to process what she was saying. An inheritance? Money? I thought of the enclosure Sonny built. Maybe there would be enough to add more foliage or even a few toys that would interest him.

Meadow brought Avery down on her cast and stroked his long feathers. The bird's chest feathers were almost filled in, and I couldn't help wondering how much of his stress had been caused by witnessing Ivan's attacks on Bruna. Maybe the money could help me afford better food that would help with his feather growth.

Meadow explained how the bird had belonged to Bruna's great Aunt Maria, who, upon her death, left everything to her bird, Kauan. On her fifteenth birthday, Bruna received Kauan as a gift, along with a sizable monthly allowance from a trust fund set up for the bird's care.

"How sizable?" I asked.

"Let me finish the story," she said.

When Bruna was eighteen, she met Ivan and was swept away by his charm and handsome looks. He was already a wealthy man, so she didn't think he would care about Kauan or the money, but she was wrong. After they married, Ivan took control of the finances, and Bruna never saw a cent from the inheritance. She knew it was only a matter of time before he did something drastic to ensure the bird and the money were his alone.

"I was her only friend," Meadow said. "And the only one she trusted, which is why she connected me with August, who had me sign the papers." She looked at August, and then back at me with a grin. "You're going to shit your pants, Cricket, but we're rich." She pulled out her phone and touched a few icons on her screen before handing it to me. I looked at it and nearly dropped the phone.

"$50,000?"

"It just hit this morning. And that's just the first payment," she said. "Every month we get another one. And when Avery dies, if the veterinarian determines he was well cared for with no foul play contributing to his death, we get the whole amount. Basically, Aunt Maria set her bird up for life."

"Holy shit," I breathed. "How long were you going to wait until you told me?"

"I had to see if it was real first," she laughed. "It seemed too good to be true. But it hit my account this morning, and I discovered it on the way home."

I recalled the moment, just then. Meadow had given a little gasp as I was driving, and I'd swerved because I thought something had been in the road, then snapped at her when I saw her looking at her phone.

"You still need to sign the bank papers to add your name to the account," she continued, "but this money really belongs to you, since you're the one with the bird."

"No Meadow, it's too much for taking care of one bird. You should get the money, too."

It was hard not to dream about what the money meant for me, though. I looked around me, at the outdated wood paneling on the walls, the popcorn ceilings, the yellowed paint. I could pay off the house, and then I could make it more modern. I could do away with my car payment. I could...I could quit my job and start a different adventure, one that didn't have to do with money and everything to do with passion.

"What'd I miss?" Blake asked, slipping his phone in his pocket.

"Well, while you were sweet-talking your girlfriend, Meadow and I became the wealthiest bird owners we know."

Chapter Twenty-Three

Now that the excitement had died down, Meadow took the opportunity to leave with August and Paulo to catch up, though the sideways looks she'd been giving August made me believe she would have been happier if it were just the two of them. Or maybe it was just her apparent relief. Her smiles came easy now, her shoulders relaxed. Even her hobbling movement seemed quick and effortless, as if the weight lifted from her chest took away her pain, as well.

They invited me to come with them, but I'd had enough excitement for the day. Blake stayed behind with me to help clean up the damage. There wasn't much we could do for the sliding door they'd shattered to get in. I'd found large sheets of plastic in the attic, and we taped several together to cover the gaping hole.

"I'm thinking huge barn doors, like the ones you always see in the home shows." Blake stood back to study our amateur fix.

"Think bigger, Keller," I said. "Like floor to ceiling windows that open to a patio."

"That money is going to slip through your fingers fast," he mused. I shook my head.

"It's all for Avery," I pointed out. "He deserves a palace for a home."

It was dark by the time the house was put back together and Blake's things were in a duffel bag by the door. I'd been anxious to talk with Sonny today, to make things right between us and see if he felt the same way I did. But with everything we'd gone through, I just wanted to curl up in bed.

More than that, I wanted to eat.

"Are you hungry?" I asked Blake. He groaned.

"Famished. Your fridge is nothing but condiments, and I'd give anything for a burger."

"I have more than condiments," I said, walking across the kitchen to look in the refrigerator. There was a half-gallon of milk that I suspected expired, and a bag of Avery's chopped-up vegetables in the crisper drawer. Besides that, I had mustard, ketchup, mayonnaise, and a variety of salad dressings. Condiments. When I looked in the freezer, all the frozen burritos I'd stocked were gone, and all that was left was a bag of peas.

"Shit, I'm sorry," I said. "I was so in my head before we left, I didn't even think to go shopping. What did you guys eat?"

"The rest of the burritos," he said with a shrug. "But mostly we DoorDashed our meals. We didn't want to go out, anyway." I caught the sly look on his face.

"I'm happy for you," I said. "But you can hold on to the details. Should we DoorDash tonight?"

"Absolutely," he said, his phone already out. "Wait, you pay. You're rich now."

I ordered double cheeseburgers, onion rings, and milkshakes for both of us, then changed into some leggings to give my waist room to grow. After a day like today, I needed a good stress-relieving meal, and greasy burgers with dripping cheese were just the ticket.

"So, tell me how things went," I said, settling onto the couch beside him. "Not the private details, but everything else."

"Well, I initially wasn't going to invite Sadie over here," he said. "First, it was weird. And the fact that it was weird, was weird. Do you follow?"

"Not really," I said.

"If Sadie had been someone casual, I wouldn't have cared about bringing her here, even though you and I were a thing for a moment. But Sadie is anything but casual, and the thought of her being in a home where I'd been with someone else felt weird. I didn't want her to walk in and think about me being with you, so even though she knew I was staying here while you were camping, I didn't ask her to stay with me. She was the one who asked."

"Wow, that was forward of her."

"She's like that, though. She isn't afraid to have real talk. And as soon as she asked, I knew she was okay with being here and okay with our friendship."

"That's great." I smiled, realizing how different this was for Blake. It sounded like Sadie was someone he could settle down with, which was kind of a huge deal. "Maybe we could all go out and…" I dropped off, realizing that when I said *we*, I'd unintentionally meant Sonny and me.

"Yeah, she'd probably dig meeting Meadow, too," Blake said, and I nodded, pretending I'd been talking about my sister instead of my ex.

The doorbell rang, and I jumped up to get it, but Blake nudged me back on the couch, laughing as he raced from the room.

"Make sure they have napkins!" I yelled after him. I was pretty certain I'd brought the last roll of paper towels with me to Joshua Tree.

Blake came back in the room holding a box, the playfulness stripped from his demeanor.

"What's that?" I asked, reaching for the box.

"It's from Sonny," he said. I dropped the box, its contents falling to the floor. I didn't even look to see what was in it before sprinting to the door and throwing it open. My exhaustion left me as I saw his taillights rolling down the drive.

"Wait!" I yelled, skipping every other step and then running down the driveway. I tripped on one of those stupid cracks Mrs. Jenkins had been needling me about, and my feet skidded underneath me. I fell on my ass, scraping my palms on the concrete. Blake was behind me in seconds, his arms under mine as he hoisted me up. My hands stung, I was pretty sure I'd ripped my leggings, and I felt helpless as Sonny's truck turned down the road and disappeared.

"He looked like he wanted to kill me," Blake said. "It seems that's a common theme today."

I gave a halfhearted laugh, inspecting my bleeding hands. I looked up sharply as headlights filled the driveway again, but by the low profile, I realized it was probably our food.

"I'll get the food, you go wash up," Blake said. He squeezed my shoulders. "Are you okay?"

I wasn't sure if he was talking about the fall or about Sonny. I nodded, attempting a better smile, then trudged back into the house.

I washed my hands and checked my leggings, glad to see they were still intact. Once my palms were bandaged, I joined Blake in the living room. He had the food spread out on the table, and despite it being my favorite junk food, it no longer looked appetizing. I sunk to the floor and picked at a cheese-covered French fry, all while eyeing the box. An old robe of mine, one I used to wear all the time around Sonny, was halfway out of the box. I had forgotten I'd lost it, but seeing it now, the memories all came back. It was ratty and the once blue sleeves were dingy from constant wear. Plus, it was way too short— probably why it was his favorite. I reached over and pulled it out of the box, and everything that had been wrapped inside it scattered across the floor.

"Wow, he's giving you a pepper shaker?" Blake reached across the pile and picked up the shaker before I could. My heart dropped, looking at it in his hands. It was the one from San Francisco. I still had the twin in my purse, unable to let it go...unable to let go of everything I carried with it. San Francisco. His kisses. Making love. Feeling like everything I'd been looking for was finally in front of me, and then losing it all again. But along with that, the hope I had that I'd get him back. At least, the hope I'd had before this moment, right now, looking at the pepper shaker in Blake's hands, knowing that this was how Sonny was saying goodbye.

"Doesn't he know you have enough?"

"What are you talking about?" I asked, coldness creeping over me.

"Your closet. It's full of shakers."

"You looked in my closet?" I squeezed the center of my eyes to keep the tears at bay. I didn't know what bothered me more—the pepper shaker or the fact that Blake knew about my stash. Definitely the pepper shaker.

"I'm sorry, I didn't know it was off-limits. I also had no idea you loved salt and pepper shakers so much. Why so many?"

"They're just some old things my parents kept. I've been meaning to donate them for years, but haven't." I took the pepper shaker he held out to me, the cool glass feeling like ice in my hand…and in my heart. I wanted to set it down, to forget about it. Instead, I kept my fingers clasped around it, continuing to pick at my food but not really wanting to eat.

"Hey, this doesn't mean anything," Blake said, sweeping his hand over the box. "He was probably just being dramatic, trying to find a reason to see you. You could call him, you know, tell him what's going on."

I nodded but didn't move for my phone. Every time I even thought about it, my heart lurched, my body cemented to the floor.

"Goddammit, Cricket. You're making this too difficult. Just call him. Tell him what happened. Tell him how you feel."

"I can't," I whispered.

"Cricket."

"I can't!" I screamed the words this time, throwing the pepper shaker across the room. It fell with a clatter but didn't break. Avery squawked at the noise, flying to a branch to see what caused it.

I held my hands in fists at my mouth, breathing into them, and all I could think of was the day our relationship ended, how I'd called him with one intention, and hung up with our relationship in shambles.

"I didn't mean to break up with Sonny when I did," I said. I looked at Blake, my eyes filling with tears, my hands clenched in frustration. "I'd called him that day hoping to tell him how I felt without him. I missed him, but it felt impossible for us to be together. I wanted him to give me a solution, one that didn't require me to move to Eau Claire. I guess the only solution I would have accepted would have been the one where he moved back to Petaluma. But then we got into this stupid fight and I told him I didn't think this was working, that it wouldn't ever work, that I would never leave Petaluma and he could just die in Wisconsin for all I cared."

"You said that?" Blake asked.

"I didn't mean it. I don't think he thought I meant it. But then I told him it was time for me to find a real man, one who chose me first, and he just kind of lost it."

I closed my eyes, the words stabbing at me even a year later. Especially now that I had some distance from our relationship. "Fuck," I breathed. "He did everything for me. I was first in everything. When he moved back to

Wisconsin, it was the first time he did something for himself. He tried so hard to get me to come with him and I refused. Every time we talked, he asked me to at least visit him. He said I'd fall in love with the place if I just saw it, and I didn't want to because I love this home, and I love Petaluma. I was afraid if I left, I'd just forget about my parents and this place would crumble without someone taking care of it."

"You know that's not true, right?"

"I mean, yeah," I said. "Kind of. Look, I know it sounds ridiculous, but this was my parents' home, and everything they were is here. If I leave this house, I leave them."

Blake scooted over to me, slipping his arm around my shoulders. I leaned my head against him, my tears staining his shirt.

"Cricket, your parents are in here," he said, touching the center of my heart. "They don't live in this house; they live in you. That will never be taken from you, no matter where you are. Home is just a name for wherever you feel most like yourself. And Cricket, I have a feeling you haven't felt that in a while."

My shoulders shook as my tears flowed faster, his words penetrating that thing that had been festering in my soul for too long.

"Call him," Blake said. I laughed through my tears, my snot now making a mess of his sleeve.

"I am not calling him right now," I said, sitting up and gesturing to myself. "But I'll go over there tomorrow. I'll tell him everything. It's time."

Chapter Twenty-Four

My hands trembled as I drove across town. I seemed to hit every single stoplight on the way, including the lowered crossing arms as the train crept by. But I welcomed the interruptions that forced me to take my time. I needed it. I rehearsed what I was going to say over and over, and each time it came out worse.

The pepper shaker rattled in my cup holder, freely moving with each turn and stop. I looked down at it at another intersection, and the round holes positioned in a star looked back.

"You're my match," I whispered, saying it to the shaker as if it were Sonny. Someone honked behind me and I glanced at the green light before putting my foot on the gas pedal.

"We're a perfect pair, and we've spent all this time pretending we're not." I felt tears brimming my eyes, but I willed them back, not wanting to smudge my makeup before I got there. I had woken up with puffy eyes, my face red and blotchy, and it had taken some miracle work and a lot of Meadow's makeup to fix the mess. Now, jacked up on caffeine plus the adrenaline of facing Sonny in just a few minutes, I no longer felt tired. I felt energized by fear and excitement. Our lives could change in a moment. I just hoped they changed in our favor.

I went on rehearsing, trying to find the perfect way to tell him I'd lied all those weeks ago, using Blake to save myself from a bruised ego, and how I was really in love with him.

"I'm in love with you," I whispered, and I realized that of everything, this is what he needed to know most. That I loved him, that I'd never stopped loving him, and if he'd give me another chance, I'd follow him anywhere if it just meant being with him. Because when I was with him, I was home.

I pulled up to his house, pausing as I studied the soft green siding and wide porch, trying to summon more courage before I exited my car. The windows appeared dark, which wasn't all that strange since it was morning. It felt empty all the same. I searched the street for his truck and came up empty, and a sinking feeling grew in the pit of my stomach.

I opened my door and slid out, the shaker in my hand as the pavement met my feet. It didn't even feel like I was walking. My whole body felt numb with dread over a possible missed opportunity. I walked up the steps with leaden feet and the screen door whined when I eased it open. I knocked, lightly at first, and then harder. Then I listened. If Buoy were here, I'd hear his toenails on the hardwood first, then his bark. I waited, holding my breath, straining my ears for any kind of movement. I knocked again, even as my shoulders sank, disappointment flowing through me like a desert wind. I turned and sat on his porch steps, looking out at the street as I clutched the pepper shaker. Pulling out my phone, I opened my contacts until his name was in front of me. My finger hovered over his name, and I took a few deep breaths before I finally touched it.

It went straight to voicemail, which knocked the wind out of me. I listened as he gave instructions to leave a message, his deep Scottish accent rolling into my ears and through my body. And then, when it beeped, I removed the phone from my ear and hung up.

No no no no no. I needed to leave him a message. I was here, and I came with a purpose, and I was not going to let his absence keep me from telling him the truth. I picked up my phone again.

"Can I help you?"

I looked up from my phone to see an older man standing at the bottom of the steps, a clipboard in his hand.

"I'm just waiting for a friend," I said, which was kind of the truth.

"You might have the wrong house, this one's vacant."

"What?" I looked behind me, wondering if I was sitting on someone else's porch. But no, I recognized this home. It was the only sage green bungalow on the whole street. "I'm waiting for Sonny," I said.

"Do you mean Edison? He left this morning. Too bad, too. He was a good tenant. But he'd warned me this might be a short-lived situation, so he only rented month to month."

It took a few moments to register his words, and when I did, I felt my breath grow shallow.

"He left? Like, moved out?"

"Yeah, moved back to…I can't remember. Some girl's name."

"Eau Claire?"

The man's face snapped into a smile, and he pointed at me while nodding.

"That's it. Eau Claire, Wisconsin. Said his home was there."

I got up slowly, wincing as I put pressure on my scraped-up hands, one of them still holding that stupid goddamn shaker. The pain was nothing compared to the ache in my heart.

"Thank you," I murmured, and walked past the man. He said something else, but I couldn't even hear him as I opened my car door and eased into the seat.

He left me. No. He just left. There was no *me* about it. He left, and he wasn't coming back. Last night really had been a goodbye. Maybe he'd come hoping for a reason to stay. Or maybe he just came to be rid of me once and for all. I'd never know.

I drove home in a fog. No tears. No feelings. Nothing. I opened the door to the house and Meadow called out a greeting at the same time as the bird squawked its hello. I ignored both of them and dragged my feet to my room, shutting the door behind me and locking it. I set the shaker on my dresser, then I pulled back the covers on my bed, kicked off my shoes, and crawled between the sheets. I still had makeup on my face, and was wearing jeans and a sweatshirt. I kept it all on, even as my mascara felt like tear-hardened clumps and my clothes creased hard against my skin. I curled up into a fetal position, my eyes shut tight.

And then, I slept.

Chapter Twenty-Five

I heard voices outside my door, muffled behind the wood, barely reaching me under my covers. I knew they were talking about me, but I didn't care. I hadn't left the room in days except to pee or eat from a box of protein bars I'd stashed in my closet. The rest of the time, I slipped in and out of sleep.

I opened my eyes now, then squinted at the bright light streaming through my window. The plants on the sill drooped from a missed watering, and somehow their suffering made me feel less alone. I didn't care. Let them die. Let everything die. I was done.

"Cricket, I'm coming in," I heard Taye say on the other side of the door.

"It's locked, I already tried," Meadow said.

I stayed still, staring at the wall across the room as Taye wriggled the door.

"Is there a key?" she asked.

"I have no idea," Meadow said. "If there is, it's anyone's guess where it is."

Their footsteps faded down the hall, and I closed my eyes again, the heavy weight of sleep calling me to return again, to drift into nothingness, to forget. But I couldn't forget. Sonny's voice was in my ears, his face swimming in front of me, his eyes brimming with hurt and pain that I'd caused through my selfishness, my narrow thinking, and my inability to see the chance I'd let slip through my fingers. How could I have been so stupid?

Now he was gone. Again. I could feel myself drawing inward, shutting out the world and disappearing within my grief. I'd barely recovered from the last time when I saw him at the Jackson Family Wines event, and now that wound was festering. Except now it was worse because my blinders were gone. I saw my fault in this. Before, I could place the blame on his shoulders, believing I'd tried everything to keep us together. Now I saw all the ways I'd failed him, how much he gave while I just took.

"What do you even love about Eau Claire?" I'd asked him in one of our final phone calls back then. "How can it possibly be better than Petaluma?"

"It's not," he'd said. "And it is. It's just different. I love Petaluma, especially the warmer winters, but Eau Claire reminds me of home. It has the same small-town feeling as Carbost Village, where everyone knew me and my da, when our days were rotating guests at the B&B and lazy afternoons by the seas. It has the same vibrant changing seasons, the crisp winter air that stings like peppermint in the nose, and farmland for miles. Even fishing here on Dells Pond feels like fishing on Loch Harport, minus the briny air of the sea loch."

"Petaluma has a river," I'd argued.

"I know. And I went out a few times. But it wasn't the same. It never felt like home the way Eau Claire does."

"But Petaluma is *my* home," I'd said.

But it's not. At least, not in the way *Sonny* was home. Why couldn't I see it then? How long had he tried to share a part of himself with me, only to have me refuse him every time? I should have agreed to visit, to see this place that was so special to him. Maybe I would have loved Eau Claire, too, especially knowing what it meant to him. Instead, I'd stood my ground as if I was the only one who mattered. As if home was a place and not a feeling. As if this town, this house, gave me more than he ever did. But nothing compared to how it felt to be with him, to be understood by him, to be seen the way Sonny saw me. No one got me the way he did. Not even Meadow, who understood me well. But Sonny knew every part of me, and he accepted me, flaws and all. Every fear I had, every insecurity, every time I lost myself in the shadow of grief, he loved me through it all. And he helped pull me out.

Who was going to pull me out now?

"I'm coming in," Taye called, and then I jumped at the sound of her body hitting the door, my eyes flying open. "Shit, you guys have some hard doors."

"Use the hammer," Meadow said.

That's what got me out of bed. I flew to the door, unlocking it and flinging it open to see Taye with the hammer over her head, surprise on her face.

"Damn girl, I almost got you," she said, lowering the tool. Her eyes narrowed as she took me in, then she nodded, a look of understanding washing over her face as she traded glances with Meadow. "First things first, the doorknob is coming off this door."

"But—"

"No buts. I will not have you locking yourself up again. Meadow and I are here to help you, but we can't if we're unable to reach you. So the doorknob is leaving until I know you can care for yourself. Right now, you're going to get some clothes on." Her eyes swept over my body, and I looked too. I was in a tank top and underwear, my skin erupted in goosebumps from the cold air in the house. "Then you're coming to the table for breakfast."

"I'm not hungry."

Taye looked around me, eyeing the protein bar wrappers on the ground next to a pile of dirty Kleenex.

"You can't survive on protein bars," she said. "We're getting some food in you, and then we're having a talk."

I lifted my eyes to my assistant, who towered over me in her platform wedges. She studied me like she was the boss, and I nodded in agreement, seeing that any argument would be pointless. I started to close the door, but she caught it with her hand.

"I have to get dressed," I pointed out.

"You think I haven't seen a naked woman before? I don't trust you, so you'll dress with the door open."

"If I'd known you were this mean, I never would have hired you," I muttered. Taye laughed, her head tilted back.

"Glad to know you're still in there, underneath that three-day stench. Now go get dressed."

Taye removed my doorknob while I put on a pair of sweats and a sweatshirt, then threw my knotted, greasy hair into a messy bun. I looked in the mirror, and a paler version of myself stared back, my blue eyes dull over dark circles, pillow creases on my cheek. I'd had better days.

Meadow had already prepared breakfast—a bowl of oatmeal topped with a drizzle of maple honey, just like Mom used to make us on days when we needed extra comfort. I teared up at the gesture, knowing exactly what Meadow was doing.

"You just eat, and then you can talk when you're ready," she said in the same voice Mom used to use, and I laughed despite the tears that made their way down my cheeks. Then I obeyed, digging into the soft oats and bringing them to my mouth, letting the maple flavor bring me back to my youth when a mother's voice could take all my troubles away. I ate to fill that hole in my spirit, the one that started when they died, then grew when Sonny moved, and now felt bigger than my body. Each bite of oatmeal worked to mend that hole, even if it was only a little bit. It was a start.

Then, when I couldn't eat another bite, I talked as Taye and Meadow sat across from me. They never interrupted, staying silent except for a few empathetic noises. I told them everything, even the stuff they knew, because I just needed to get it out of me. I told them what I'd realized about my part in our breakup, how it felt to know Sonny was gone again, and the shame I felt in my efforts to save face, when all I had to do was be honest. I should have been honest from the start, way before we broke up. Maybe we'd still be together now. Maybe he wouldn't have moved on. Maybe I wouldn't be here now, feeling the pain of losing him all over again.

I even talked about the stupid salt and pepper shakers, the ones taking up an entire closet, each one attached to a memory. I shared about the shakers I discovered in Sonny's medicine cabinet that made me feel less alone, about the ones we stole together in San Francisco, and how it felt to see his shaker wrapped in my robe as if he couldn't stand having any ties between us.

"But he still has his shakers, right?" Meadow asked. "The little ones. He didn't give you those."

"Why would he? He doesn't even know that I discovered them. They may not have anything to do with me."

"Right. Because every man keeps a pair of salt and pepper shakers in his medicine cabinet." Meadow gave me a pointed look.

"You know what I think?" Taye asked.

"No, what." A new kind of exhaustion settled over me, one riddled with relief after sharing every secret and thought I had.

"I think you need to take a long shower while I pick out your clothes, and then get ready for the Finnigan party."

"Oh shit, that's tonight?" I winced, the exhaustion increasing at just the thought of being around people. "I really dropped the ball on that one. I'm so sorry, Taye."

She waved her hand in dismissal. "Everything was basically done. I've just been handling the RSVPs and last-minute details; nothing too big."

"I can't go," I said. A wave of panic rolled through me just thinking about it. She grabbed my hands, squeezing them until I looked at her.

"You *will* go," she said, and the firm way she said it brought me a strange sense of comfort. I didn't have to be in control. "You'll go because you put a lot of work into this, and because you're not going to let a man take that away from you."

"But—"

"No buts. I heard you speak, and from what I heard, both of you had a part in the end of your relationship. You could have done things differently. But he could have, too."

"I lied, though."

"You think you're the only person on earth who has ever lied to protect their feelings? You're not special in this, Cricket, and you're not a victim. Tonight, you're going to walk into that party and hold your head high, knowing you put together a damn good event. You can worry about Sonny and what you plan to do about this tomorrow. But today? You're Cricket Stone, owner of Bees Knees Events, the person every business owner will want to know by the end of the night."

Walking from the elevator into the top floor of Merdell Gallery was like walking into an autumn forest. I'd hired the decorators based on the work they'd done at a harvest party last year, but Taye had coordinated the final details, setting the scene for what surely would be a magical night.

Branches with vibrant fire-toned leaves covered the ceiling, ornamented with tiny fairy lights, rose gold beads, and hanging glass lanterns. In the corners of the rooms were tall branches set in large glass vases and potted Japanese Maple trees, also adorned with tiny lights. Tables were situated around the room with tea light candles, foliage centerpieces, and gourds hand-painted with intricate designs. I looked closer at the tables and swooned at the tea light candle holders made from sliced tree branches, each with a name tag to indicate seating.

The only thing more impressive than the fairyland scene inside the room was the incredible view from the wall of windows overlooking the city. I peered out the window and my breath caught at the twinkling lights of the city, like stars spread across the ground. It was just how I imagined when... I turned away. *When Sonny and I saw it first.*

I put on a brave face, my eyes sweeping over the sparkling room. It looked absolutely magical.

"Taye, you've outdone yourself," I said. My assistant watched me carefully to gauge my reaction, then she rolled her eyes with a laugh.

"You see how she takes credit for nothing?" she asked Meadow. Taye turned back to me, shaking her head. "You did this. I just helped make sure your vision came true." She looked me up and down, then hummed in appreciation. "And you sure clean up nice. It's amazing how you went from death's door to fiery vixen in one night."

"Uh, vixen? That might be a stretch." But I straightened my back, proud of how I looked tonight. Taye had pulled from her personal wardrobe when picking out my outfit for the night, choosing a sleeveless jumpsuit in black sequins with cleavage to my navel, a belted waist, and flared legs over stilettos. My red hair hung in long waves and my eyes were lined with sweeping kohl that made my blue irises seem larger.

Meadow looked every part my twin that night, her own red hair cascading down her back. She wore a coordinating dress in black sequins, long and slimming even with her leg brace. She'd covered her arm cast in a black sleeve, and it made her look more mysterious.

And then there was Taye, who couldn't help but outdo us all. Just like us, she was dressed in black, but it was a lacy corset peeking out of a suit jacket and leather pants painted on her long legs. We always chose black for our party outfits, so we'd remain in the background of the events we coordinated, but she was hard to miss. Half of her long dreads hung past her butt, the rest wrapped into a large bun on top of her head, decorated with small jewels and silver accents. A silver necklace rested between her breasts, matching her long drop earrings. She finished the look with stiletto boots that were so tall, it was almost like walking on stilts. She could pull it off, though. If it were me, I'd break my leg.

"Face it, we're all pretty hot," Meadow said. "Own it, Cricket." I started to say something, but the band chose that moment to start up, a Celtic group Sonny had booked for the night. The fiddle began and the conversation stopped in its tracks. Charles Finnigan swept onto the dance floor to the sound of applause, leading an attractive woman with long silver hair. He swung Lilith into his embrace as she laughed, and they began dancing in perfect choreography. It was obvious they knew what they were doing. The crowd stood around, clapping in time with the music as Charles spun his wife around the floor, both of them moving their feet in time with the music, appearing younger than their years. It was hard to not get swept up in the energy, and I found myself smiling as I watched them dance.

Sonny would have loved this. I couldn't help thinking it as I looked around the room, hoping to catch sight of his face. I remembered the day we toured this room, the naive visions I'd had of us dancing here together. It was funny how it only took two weeks to change everything. No, not two weeks. A year. That night in the city was an exception to the norm, and probably shouldn't have happened. I didn't regret it. I couldn't. It meant too much to me. Still, in the wake of it, standing here without him at a party he'd helped me plan, the pain was unavoidable. I scanned the crowd once last time, even though I knew it was pointless. He wasn't there, and no amount of looking would change that.

I did see Justine, however, standing next to a man with his arm around her waist. An unexpected jolt of fury shot through me. What happened to Sonny? Did they break up? Did she even care? He'd only been gone a few days, and she was smiling at this other man as if she'd never loved Sonny at all. My heartache, my hesitations with him, it had obviously been for nothing.

"I need a drink," I breathed, and Taye disappeared, re-emerging a few moments later juggling three champagne glasses. I downed mine quickly, the bubbles like tiny bursts of relief in my throat.

"Don't get drunk," she said, even as she traded my empty glass for her full one, then left to get another for herself.

The Finnigans ended their dance and bowed to the enthusiastic crowd. Charles saw me from across the room and pointed at me. Then he clapped in my direction. I brushed aside my fury about Justine and gave Charles a mock curtsy, glad to feel the effects of the champagne doing its work. At least I could pretend everything was fine. My shoulders felt less tense, my grief subdued. Right now, I was just a girl at a party that celebrated love.

Ugh, love.

"Cricket, you've outdone yourself," Mr. Finnigan said as he neared, then clasped my hands in his.

"Me? I had no idea you had those kinds of moves," I said, squeezing his hands before turning to his wife. "Hello Lilith, it's a pleasure to finally meet you."

"You, as well, Cricket. Charles speaks very highly of you. And so does a certain employee of his." She winked at me, and I bristled. Apparently I was the only one who'd been in the dark, and it made me realize even more how much I'd messed up. I felt Meadow slip her hand into mine.

"Former employee, dear." He leaned over and whispered something, and her eyes widened. She then smiled at me, but it was the kind of smile someone gives when there's so much more they want to say.

"Well, this is just a lovely party," she said, swiftly changing the subject. "I felt like I walked into a forest when we arrived. It's stunning. We'll have to hire you for our garden parties once the seasons change."

I was grateful to Charles for hiring me, and in general, I thought he was just wonderful. Lilith was, too. But as they continued their small talk, I felt like I was crawling out of my skin. The champagne was making my head feel light, especially after three days of not eating. And every time I looked across the room, I could see Justine hanging all over this guy as if Sonny never existed. I didn't know why it bothered me so much.

Wasn't it a good thing she wasn't with him anymore? I mean, it cleared the path for me to make my move. Except… If they broke up and Sonny never reached out to me, then he obviously was done with me once and for all. Or perhaps my ruse with Blake worked too well. Whatever it was, I had a sinking feeling I'd dug myself into a hole, and this time there was no way out.

The Finnigans left to mingle with other guests. I took the moment to sit at a table off to the side by the window while Taye and Meadow did a walkthrough to make sure everything was going according to plan. Taye had insisted I take it easy this night, that she would handle everything. As I watched her study the banquet table and talk with the staff, I couldn't help noticing her natural demeanor and take-charge attitude. She was so sure of herself, enough that she could probably handle this business on her own.

The last couple of days had given me some time to think. Most of it had been spent sleeping or in mourning. But there were a few moments when I'd felt a sprinkling of hope, usually after I'd eaten something and felt a small dose of energy. It was during these moments when I'd mull over my possibilities. Thanks to Avery and his bird inheritance, I could now afford to take a step back from event planning and a step forward in a new direction. Camping in Joshua Tree had opened my eyes to all the things I'd been missing out on outside my safe zone.

There were places to travel and new experiences to try. My whole life was in Petaluma, but what about the rest of the world outside our cozy town? Who said I couldn't work with bees, or sell honey at a farm stand? Who said I couldn't rent an RV and travel across the country? I was twenty-seven years old with nothing to tie me down. Okay, maybe a bird. But nothing that kept me from having adventures and discovering who I was.

It was enough to distract me from Sonny. Not all the way, but if I couldn't have him, what if I just had me? Not the me with obligations and ties that chained me to one place, but the me who stopped playing the *what if* game and started saying *what next*. There was so much I'd never experienced. Maybe it was time I let go of my fears and find out what it was like to truly live.

I kept quiet about my thoughts as Taye and Meadow joined me, but I felt the giddiness bubbling inside me. Okay, the champagne buzz helped, too. Still, I felt lighter than I should have felt, and excited about what tomorrow would bring.

"I brought you some dinner to help soak up some of that champagne," Taye said, placing a plate in front of me. My three days of fasting had helped me to fit perfectly into this pantsuit, but I was ready to sacrifice the fit over the stuffed mushrooms, roast beef sliders, and bacon-wrapped scallops on the plate. My appetite had returned full force, and I tried my best to appear ladylike as I shoved a whole mushroom in my mouth.

"You have company," Meadow said, nodding across the room. "I bet she wants to hire you."

I looked where Meadow indicated, groaning as I tried to chew quickly.

"That's Justine," I hissed when my mouth was finally free.

"*Sonny's* Justine? Then who's that with her?" Meadow hissed back.

"I don't know," I whispered, then smiled wide and stood as Justine approached. "Justine! It's so good to see you again. How are you?"

"I'm better than ever, thanks to your event. This is seriously something, Cricket." She turned to the man beside her, and I got a closer look at him. He seemed familiar, but I couldn't place who he was. "Honey, you remember Cricket? The girl I was telling you about?"

"Of course! She's hard to forget with all that red hair. I remember when Sonny first laid eyes on her. That boy couldn't stop talking about her." He flashed a grin at me, even as I felt spun trying to piece together everything he was saying. "Are you guys still together?"

"Hold on," I said, shaking my head. "We've met? Do I know you?"

"Moose," he said, extending his hand. "Lead fiddle of the Log Flume."

Everything clicked in that exact moment, and I was brought back to a memory of sitting at a large table in Brew, watching the band while this sexy Scottish stranger sat next to me.

"You're in that band Sonny used to manage!" I exclaimed. "You played fiddle!"

"That's what I said," he said, laughing.

"I'm sorry I didn't recognize you." Then I looked from him to Justine, and then their hands clasped together. My eyes widened at the giant ring on her finger. She saw what I was looking at and lifted their hands together to give me a better view of the ring.

"He just asked two weeks ago," she gushed. "It's why I couldn't join you and Sonny in the city. But I didn't want to be a third party, anyway. Secretly, I was kind of hoping you two would reconnect." She turned to Moose. "They broke up a year ago," she explained.

"Oh man, sorry. Sonny kind of keeps his personal life to himself. I never know what's going on with him. All I know is that he sweet-talked my fiancée into getting him a job at her company so he could move back to Petaluma." He looked at me for a moment, and it was like a lightbulb went off. "I think I know why."

My head was spinning with all this information, not sure what to process first. "I thought you…" I broke off, embarrassed that I'd been so wrong.

"She thought you and Sonny were an item," Meadow broke in. Justine looked at my sister, then her eyes widened as she looked at me.

"Justine, this is my sister Meadow, and my assistant Taye."

"Nice to meet you," she said, then she did another double-take between us. "Sonny told me you were a twin, but it's incredible how much you two look like each other. And ew, Sonny is like a brother to me. I've known him for years. He used to stay at my house with Moose whenever they came this way to perform."

That's when I looked at her a little closer.

"You worked at Brew!" I could see her now, a few years younger, serving beer and coffee while live music filled the place. "But you had dark hair then."

She touched her hair and smiled. "Yeah, I think I like the lighter color a little better. But looking at you two, maybe red would be a fun color."

Justine knew just as little as Moose did about Sonny's personal life, but she did know why he moved back to Petaluma. "It was you," she said. I shrunk in my chair as she shared how he'd quit the band gig to take a marketing job with Charles. They had already decided to work with me before the Jackson Family Wines event, but had attended so Sonny could show off Cricket's work. "Of course, you were already seeing someone, so I think that bummed Sonny out."

"I wasn't, though," I said. I looked at Taye and Meadow for support, and when they smirked in exchange, I glared at them. But I got it; I was on my own here. "I saw him with you," I admitted. "I thought he'd moved on, and I didn't want to look like I'd been pining over him for the past year."

"Even though you had," Meadow piped in.

"Wait, you thought he was with *me*?" Justine said, her eyes wide. "What gave you that idea?"

I thought back to that day, trying to remember what it was that made me think they were involved. "You fell," I said, piecing the day back together. "Then he caught you, and you both kind of held on to each other, smiling as if you'd known each other forever. Well, I mean, I guess you have. But it just looked more meaningful."

"I'd had quite a bit to drink that night," she admitted.

"Justine thinks she can hold her own, but she forgets how tiny she is," Moose said. "One drink and she's on the floor." He darted out of the way as she pretended to smack him.

"I probably stumbled into him, and then couldn't stand up straight." She laughed, toasting her glass in the air. "These damn wine events can be a little too much fun, if you know what I mean."

"Don't I ever," I said, nodding at my second empty glass. "What I don't understand, though, is why he said you were together. Were you in on it?"

"I don't know anything about that," she said. "Maybe it was for the same reason you did?"

I thought of his face when he saw me, the look of fury when I was in Blake's arms. It was real, wasn't it? I sank back into my chair, burying my head in my hands. "I've messed everything up, haven't I?"

Justine set her glass on the table, then knelt in front of me. "If I know Sonny, and I think that I do, you haven't messed anything up. I give him three months before he comes to win you back. Or…" She tossed a glance over her shoulder at Moose before looking back at me. "You could always go to him," she said.

It was definitely a possibility…one more to add to my sudden life of freedom, and possibly the most important one. But now that I was considering it, a small amount of fear wound its way back into my heart.

"How do you do it?" I asked Justine, then looked up at Moose. "All those months apart from each other, isn't it hard?"

"It's torture," Justine said. She stood, taking Moose's hand. "We talk every day, more than once. During the times we don't see each other, we do special things for each other. I'll bake him cookies and send them through the mail. He'll send me flowers or have dinner delivered. We have dates over video calls, dressing up as if we were on a real date. It's sweet and it sucks, all at the same time.

But then, when we can see each other, it makes it all worth it."

"And soon, we won't have to be apart," Moose said, squeezing her hand as she leaned against his shoulder.

"Are you staying here? Or…"

"Moving to Eau Claire," she said. "It's time for a change, and now is the perfect time to make it. I just told Charles last week, which only makes Sonny leaving that much worse. Charles now has to replace both of us."

She let go of Moose's hand, resting hers on my shoulder. "Long-distance relationships are hard, and you have to put a lot of work into them. But it's not impossible."

I covered her hand with mine, squeezing it. A rush of gratefulness washed over me. "I have a lot of thinking to do," I said.

"I'm sure you do," she said. She started to turn, but then whipped back around. "Oh, just in case." She rummaged through her purse until she found a scrap of paper, looking at it before handing it to me. "He gave me this before he left, but I have a feeling he'd want you to have it."

I took the paper and looked at the address in his familiar writing.

"If you ever decide to head to Eau Claire, you'll find him there. Look me up, if you do." She turned to Moose, who nodded. He took the paper and wrote his own address on the back.

"Our house is yours, anytime you decide to visit," he said. "That is, if you don't have a different place to stay." He shot me a meaningful look, and then they left us to our table.

I turned to the girls, still holding the paper. My mind was a whirlwind.

"Well, what are you going to do?" Taye asked. The same question was on Meadow's face.

"I think…" I paused, looking at the paper again. Sonny's handwriting looked back at me, seeming like a promise. I smiled, folding the paper before slipping it back into my purse. "I think I'm going to live a little."

Chapter Twenty-Six

Living a little looked a lot like giving my whole business to Taye. A few weeks after the Finnigan event, I invited my assistant over for pancakes and ended the breakfast by handing over Bees Knees Events.

"I can't. Seriously?" Taye shook her head. "No, it's too much."

I laughed at the sudden turn of the tables. Taye was usually the one who talked me off the ledge. It was quite the difference to see her looking at me with frantic eyes, plus a hint of excitement pulling at the corners of her mouth.

"You can, and you should. This is what you've been working towards, and you're more than capable now. You have a list with every single one of my contacts, and they have all worked closely with you. Plus, this company has already become well known among some big-name wine producers and in the local wedding circuit."

We'd just finished our third wedding in two weeks and I was burnt, even as I'd slowly increased the number of responsibilities on Taye's plate just to see how she handled it. At last night's wedding, I stayed in the background at the event while she ran point on every aspect of coordination. I wasn't needed once as she managed the entire event with poise and professionalism, as if she'd been doing this for years.

"You'll do fine," I continued. "With your drive and charisma, I could see you expanding it into something bigger."

"But what about you?" she asked. "What will you do?"

"I have a few things in mind," I said. "But first, I'm taking some time off for myself."

Renovation had already started on the house, beginning with the busted sliding glass door and demolition on the outdated kitchen. Next week would be my parents' old bedroom since Meadow was leaving tomorrow.

Meadow was leaving. This was hard, and I couldn't think about it without tearing up. I'd enjoyed having her with me all this time, and had grown selfish with her company. I knew she'd get back to traveling the world once she'd healed, but it was hard to imagine waking up without her here. This was why I'd done the damn thing of renting an RV for a quick West Coast road trip, this time going north. I'd even paid an extra pet deposit so that Avery could travel with me. I'd grown quite attached to this bird and was relieved when Meadow said she'd leave him with me. She was still insisting I take all the money, too, but come on. $50,000 for little old me? Besides, I liked to think of Avery as OUR bird.

And then there was Sonny. Even after everything Justine told me, I didn't try to call him, text him, or do what I really wanted to do—show up on his doorstep and profess my never-ending love for him. How fair would that be? I'd run him through the wringer this last go around, and I had a lot to atone for. Not just to him. To me, too. Before I even thought about visiting him, I needed to figure out what *living a little* truly meant for my life. I no longer wanted to be dead weight in our relationship. I wanted to meet Sonny halfway, to give just as much as he did to make our relationship grow.

There was more...and this was the scariest part of all. I wanted to get to the point where I didn't *need* him. I would always love him. This was a fact, and one I felt in every fiber of my body. But if he refused me, if he decided he was done and there was nothing I could do to change his mind, I wanted the strength to be able to wish him well in life and walk away.

Taye left that evening with all of my files, plus a huge retainer to help get her on her feet. She already let me know that her first order of business was to hire an intern. I wished her luck because I'd already hired the best.

That night, Meadow and I resumed packing all her clothes into three suitcases.

"First off, I thought you only came here with one suitcase," Huffing, I pushed my weight on one bag as I struggled with the zipper. "Second, how do you plan to navigate three suitcases as one person?"

"I'll have some help," she admitted, and I stopped what I was doing. She had a soft smile on her face, a secret one. I recognized that look.

"August, right?" I asked, and she bit back a grin.

"He flies into San Francisco tomorrow, and then we're headed to Costa Rica for a few weeks. I plan to make him take all my photos and earn his keep."

"So, just a friend?"

"Nah, security detail. You can never be too safe." She winked at me, and I could just imagine what kind of surveillance would be happening between the two of them.

"I demand details every chance you get," I ordered, and she laughed as she held her pinky to mine.

"I promise," she said. "And when you're done finding yourself, I expect to be invited to your and Sonny's wedding."

"Nothing is guaranteed," I said. "Especially when you jinx it like that."

"I'm not jinxing it," she countered. "I'm putting it out to the Universe. Cricket Stone and Sonny McIntyre, together forever with their furry and feathered children, Buoy and Avery."

"That's how I'll sign our Christmas cards," I laughed.

She bounced up, and then landed full weight on the suitcase so I could finish zipping it. Then we did the same for the others. We ended the night eating Chinese takeout from the cartons, splitting the last bottle of Finnigan Estates sparkling wine, and laughing over old family photos in the endless albums my mom had created through the years.

"Why did she dress us the same?" Meadow moaned, pointing at the handmade gingham dresses we wore as kids. Even then, Meadow looked pretty and delicate, her red hair neat in braids. I, on the other hand, had skinned knees and long socks with scuffed white shoes. My hair must have been in braids at one point, but only one of them had stuck. The other was a lopsided pigtail.

"If I had twins, I'd probably dress them the same, too," I admitted. "You know, to celebrate the fact that they're a pair. After all, there's something special and unique about twins."

Meadow reached over and grabbed my hand, squeezing it as she blinked back the moisture in her eyes. "I'm going to miss you so much," she said. I put my container down and wrapped my arms around her. Now that she was completely healed, she was so much easier to hug.

"I'm going to miss you, too."

She pulled back and looked at me. "You know, you can always come with me. We can travel the world, make it a full-time twins thing. My audience will go nuts, and my sponsors will probably give us two of everything."

"Right, starting with your mini-vacation to Costa Rica. I wonder how much August will appreciate it."

Meadow got a sly look on her face. "He'll love it."

I swatted her in mock disgust. "I'm not going with you," I said. "Traveling the world is your thing. I'm still breaking in my training wheels. Besides, I think I need a stationary place to call home."

"Or a person?" Meadow looked at me, her face beaming with hope.

"Or a person," I agreed.

She was gone by the time I woke up the next morning. We'd said our goodbyes before bed, full of tears and promises of daily calls. I'd snuck a pair of salt and pepper shakers in her bag when she wasn't looking, and I knew she'd get a kick out of them. They were the first ones I'd ever taken. My date had ditched me at homecoming, and the impulsive act made me feel wild. I had no idea what I'd started with those first shakers.

Now, I had a tender feeling for my younger self. I embraced that meek, insecure girl from the past, loving her as if she were my child standing in front of me. I wished I really could pull my younger self aside and tell her how special she was, how many gifts she had, and how worthy she was of being loved.

By giving Meadow those first shakers, it was a tender way to say goodbye to the girl I once was and move forward into the woman I was meant to be.

The rest of the shakers were in a box, ready to donate. Well, not all of them. I was human, after all. I still had the shakers I stole from Brew on the day I met Sonny, the ones from my parents' funeral, and the ones from San Francisco, including Sonny's pepper shaker. I also kept the ones Sonny stole for me from The Bird House, but only because they were now Avery's toys. If I lingered too long by the box, I was tempted to keep others, as well, especially the ones tied to wonderful memories. This included the ones from the first time I saw Sonny again at the Jackson Family Wines event. But all of those memories existed inside me. I didn't need a physical object to remember.

The house now empty, I puttered around my outdated kitchen for the last time. The plan was for the house to be finished by the time I returned, and I was both excited and nervous about the whole thing. But most of all, I saw this as a strong step forward. This was no longer my parents' home; it was mine. It was time to make it my own.

It was weird to say goodbye to a house, but that's what I did for the rest of my day. I caressed the arms of my father's chair as if it were his arms instead, thanking it for supporting my hard-working dad at the end of each day. I laid back on each couch and thanked them for being so comfortable for afternoon naps, emergency cry sessions, or just a place to sit while I read my favorite book. I touched the wood paneling and apologized for always thinking it was ugly, assuring it that someone must have liked it enough to put it there in the first place.

Then there was my parents' bedroom. The bed was staying, but everything else would be donated or tossed. I ran my hands over the yellowed curtains, trying to remember when they were white, and thanked them for shielding the room from sunlight all these years. I shuffled my feet on the matted-down shag carpet that had once been gold but was now a dingy shade of brown, and I thanked it for being so comforting on my bare feet all these years. I thanked the walls for housing my parents and the ceiling for keeping them dry, and the mirrored closet for still holding all their clothes which were now in boxes ready to donate beside the saltshakers and every other box of items I no longer needed.

They were all just things. My parents didn't exist in them. I carried them in my heart.

That night, as I lay in my bed, the cool November breeze moving my curtains like spirits, I allowed my memories in this home to wrap around me and keep me warm. The Christmas mornings when Meadow and I would race to see what Santa brought us. The secret stories we shared after our parents thought we were asleep. The teenage escapades that had us sneaking in and out of our bedroom window. The rainy days when I sat on the floor heater and lost myself in a book. And warm summer nights listening to owls hoot in the nearby fields, or the frogs singing in the creek. The frogs and owls would be back in the spring, still belting out the songs they sang every night. They'd be back, but would I?

I still wasn't sure.

Avery and I left the next morning before the sun came up. The RV was packed, and the donation boxes were left on the porch ready for pickup. I must have glanced at them a dozen times, wondering if there was maybe something I'd regret giving away. In the end, I left them where they sat in the early morning moonlight, driving away before I could change my mind again.

We took our time over the next few days, stretching a two-day drive north into seven by stopping at every interesting roadside attraction. Avery could have cared less, though I discovered he loved the feel of the moving vehicle. I'd bought a special cage for him that the RV company installed themselves, and he would rock his head from time to time, making happy noises in his throat. Whenever I stopped, I'd strap on his bird harness and take him for a walk around whatever town we were in, enjoying the stares of people mesmerized by my gorgeous macaw. I felt every part the bird parent— proud of my sweet bird, and happy to have him as company. It brought me back to my trip with Meadow, except Avery was a better listener. When he wasn't squawking, that is.

We only traveled to Mendocino the first day, content to park at a spot near the ocean so I could peruse the quaint oceanside town the first day, and then listen to crashing waves at night. The next day we crossed the Oregon border and stayed in Bishop Creek where I ordered take-out from the Foggy Bottom Bar & Grill and watched the Chetco River flow into the ocean from the Beachfront RV Park. Then it was on to Port Orford, then Coos Bay, then Astoria before we headed into Washington.

I aimed to stay present the whole time, using Avery as my sounding board on what I wanted to do with my life, how I'd held myself back all these years, and what I would have given to turn the clocks back and do everything differently. Avery was silent most of the time, save for a few squawks.

I traveled all the way to the Canadian border, but I didn't try to cross. I had my passport, but Avery didn't have his, and I didn't want to have any trouble. Instead, I drove back down to Seattle where I stayed for a few days, showing Avery the fish market (he loved that), the gum wall (he was not impressed), and the way the ocean looked from the piers (he was more interested in the seagulls). I stayed long enough to watch people walking by. I read stories from their faces and wondered what they read in mine. I also stayed long enough to think about where I was going after this, and what I wanted.

When I left, I still didn't know.

Actually, that's a lie. I wanted Sonny. I was just afraid he'd outgrown me, or that, even after all this soul searching, I still wouldn't be enough for him. Avery told me I was overthinking things, and that if I was meant to be with Sonny, he'd accept me as I was.

I told Avery that human emotions were much more complicated than the emotions of birds. That was in Chehalis, Washington. He didn't speak to me again until Portland, Oregon when I bribed him with a birdseed cone.

The whole trip took two weeks, and we arrived home in the dead of night. The contractor and I had been on numerous video calls throughout the journey, so I'd already received several sneak peeks at various new features. But mostly, the house was a surprise.

I opened the brand-new oak door and turned on the lights, and my breath caught in my throat. The soft glow from the canned lights revealed gorgeous stone floors laid out in slate tiles, a step-down living room that wrapped around the birdcage Sonny built, and beautiful new couches against freshly painted walls the color of sand. The kitchen almost looked bigger, despite being the same footprint. The clean look of white cabinets over grey quartz countertops made the room look like it belonged in a magazine. Fresh flowers were on my new farmhouse wood table under a modern square light fixture. I picked up the card and smiled when I saw they were from Blake and Sadie, welcoming me into my new home.

Across the way was the family room, a large window making up the entire wall. Despite the late hour, I opened the sliding door and stepped out into the cool night. Even though it was fall, I heard a solitary frog croak from the nearby creek, reminding me that even though it looked different, this was still the place I grew up. I hugged my arms around my shoulders and looked up at the stars. They smiled down at me, the same way they did in Joshua Tree, the same as when I was a child, and the same way they would from anywhere in the world.

Home was a feeling, not a place, and I was beginning to understand what that meant.

I pulled out my phone and looked at the time. It was one in the morning here, which meant it was late morning in Sweden, where Meadow had been since a few days ago.

"Hey," I said when she answered. "How was Costa Rica?"

"We can talk about that later. How's the house?"

"It's so beautiful," I said. "Why didn't I do this sooner?"

"I don't know. Take me on a tour."

I switched the phone to video and walked her through all the parts I'd already been, plus let her say *goodnight* to a sleeping Avery.

"How about Mom and Dad's room? How does that look?" she asked.

"You mean, my room?"

Cricket's grin filled the screen. "Whoa. Big steps there, sis. Have you seen it yet?"

"Not yet," I said. "I wanted you there with me."

The hallway toward the bedrooms had always been the darkest part of the house. Now when I flipped the switch, the soft light bathed the passageway. I walked the hallway without speaking, my hands feeling clammy as I reached the door to my parent's room. No. *My* room.

"Are you ready?" I asked Meadow.

"I was going to ask you the same thing. Are *you* ready?"

"I think so." I put my hand on the doorknob and took a deep breath before opening it.

"Oh, wow," Meadow said from the phone. I wasn't sure how I felt. My first reaction was sadness. The bed was still there, but everything else about my parents was gone. I took a few more breaths, and then I saw the wide sliding doors and the elegance in the long white curtains. My leafy green plants now hung by the windows, sure to catch some of the best sunlight in the house during daytime hours. Just like the rest of the house, the shag carpet was gone, replaced by gorgeous stone-grey hardwood. I stepped into the bathroom and marveled at the soaking tub and separate shower, and the sleekness of the smooth gray countertops, identical to the ones in the kitchen. A flip of the switch and the slate floors began to heat under my feet.

"Oh yeah," I said to Meadow. "This is so my bedroom."

That night as I drifted off, I thought about all the things I loved. The stars in the sky and my garden in spring. The sound of frogs in the creek and kids playing at the park. Big colorful macaws that listened to my stories, and a certain blonde retriever that loved to lay his head in my lap.

And I loved Sonny. Even with the guilt on my shoulders, I loved that he sacrificed his comfort to ensure

I had mine, and that he gave up his home so he could be with me. I loved that he tried to bring me to his, then came back for me, even though I failed him both times. And I loved that he finally put himself first because I hadn't yet.

I finally drifted off to sleep, Sonny's face swimming in and out of my dreams. And when I woke up in the morning, my bare legs sliding across the silky sheets, the down comforter hugging me in its warmth, Sonny was my very first thought.

And I knew what I needed to do.

Chapter Twenty-Seven

Wandering Meadow

The adventurist John Muir once said, "The world's big and I want to have a good look at it before it gets dark." Friends, I have traveled the world with these words as my mantra, exploring different locations to see the beauty outside my homeland, to learn new cultures, to make new friends, and to share everything I see with all of you. I wanted a good look at the world before it got dark. And then, when it did get dark, I looked up at the stars and saw worlds larger than ours.

The past few years have offered me an adventure beyond anything I could ever have imagined. I've truly enjoyed wandering this world, and I couldn't have experienced this journey without you. Now, I'm embarking on a new journey: LOVE. Friends, meet August, the man who stole the heart of this world wanderer. I've traveled far and wide looking for adventure. I didn't expect my adventures to lead me home.

This is not my last post here on Wandering Meadow, but it is my farewell to roaming the world as my profession. I'll still explore from time to time. After all, once you've been bitten by the travel bug, you're infected for life. However, my adventure in love includes settling down in my new country of Sweden. Stick around if you'd like to be part of our journey.

The photo on my sister's Instagram showed her looking into August's eyes, his hands tangled in her hair as they smiled at each other. It had been six months since they started dating, but they'd waited until now to make the announcement. The comments were mostly filled with those that wished them well, including a few who claimed to have known something was different about Meadow. They had no idea. In a few more months she'd be unable to hide her growing belly, a pregnancy that caught all of us off guard. It was a happy surprise, though, and all the more reason for Meadow to practice staying in one place.

I wondered how long that would last. I had a feeling my niece or nephew would become a world traveler from a very young age.

I put my phone away and climbed out of bed, shivering from the cool spring air. My slippers were positioned next to my bed, and I slid my feet into them to avoid touching the frigid floors, then padded across the room to grab my first cup of coffee. Thank goodness for automatic timers! The pot was full, and I planned to drink half of it before starting my day.

For now, I was content to stand at my kitchen window, look out at the Wisconsin fog that had settled on the darkened pasture, and marvel at this crazy life of mine.

The past six months had been a whirlwind, from dodging death to gaining an inheritance, and then finally learning that to live a little, I needed to get rid of the boxes I'd placed myself in.

The first to go was the house.

Okay, so I didn't get rid of it completely, but my attachment to it changed once I had it remodeled. It became a new home, with modern features and beautiful designs. It was the kind of home I'd be happy to live in. But it also made me realize that a home like this could be anywhere, and the memories of living in this home would always be with me, no matter where I was. I began to wonder what it would be like to live in a new home, and eventually that wonder morphed into a full-blown obsession.

Maybe this is how it started for Meadow, that she thought about traveling enough that it soon became the air she breathed, and something she had to experience for herself.

For me, it started with job searching. I'd first thought of beekeeping when Meadow and I camped in Joshua Tree. Back then, it had been a passing thought, a musing. I didn't take it any more seriously than one of those *what if* questions. But now that money wasn't a concern and I had nothing but time, those *what if* questions really did

CRISSI LANGWELL

turn into *what's next*, starting with my research on different bee farms in the area. On a whim, I also looked at ones in Eau Claire, Wisconsin. *What if* Eau Claire could be my home?

By surprise, I learned that Wisconsin was one of the top ten honey-producing states. It was on the list with California, and I saw that as a sign. The sign became bigger when I found a job posting for a beekeeping internship at Chippewa Bee Farm—no experience necessary. The pay was shit, but it wasn't like I needed money. Besides, it was a live-in position, which was more than I was looking for. Not only was the job perfect, but at the end of the interview, I learned they had a solarium they used as an aviary.

It was settled, Avery and I were moving to Eau Claire. Even better, Blake and Sadie, who had been house hunting together for the past month, agreed to become my tenants at the Stone family house. As of now, they were raising parakeets in the indoor aviary, and the outdoor one was now their chicken coop where they gathered fresh eggs every morning. The last time I talked with Blake, he said the chickens seemed to love their tropical environment.

And me? I was awake before the sun in a tiny shack in Eau Claire, sipping my coffee, and ready to welcome another day in my new life.

One would think that with all these love connections happening around me, plus my new home, I'd also be lucky in love. I was, in a sense. I loved my life. I loved the path I was on. I loved that I felt more like myself than I ever had before. I felt in charge of my adventure but kept my options open so I wouldn't miss any opportunities coming my way.

But as far as Sonny was concerned? I still hadn't contacted him. The address Justine gave me was in my top dresser drawer, the ink partially rubbed off from how many times I handled it, wondering if I should just go there. I'd searched for it on Google Maps and found it was only a few miles from where I lived. I drove by it once, long enough to take in the yellow siding and large front yard, plus Sonny's truck in the driveway, before I took off. I wanted to see him, but not yet. I needed more time.

Besides, I loved Eau Claire. At least, I loved what I knew of it so far. I'd only been here a month, but I made use of every spare moment I had to play tourist in my new town. I'd already enjoyed a kayak ride in Dells Pond, breathing in the murky air as I searched for hints of Sonny's Scotland. I'd listened to live music at the Oxbow Hotel, happily invisible in the crowd. I even hiked to the waterfalls at Big Falls County Park. Basically, I'd done more in Eau Claire in one month than I had most of my life in Petaluma.

And today was another first—heading to the farmer's market to sell honey. Each week, Troy, my boss, chose three interns to join him at the farmer's market, and it was considered an honor to be picked. I hadn't gone yet since I was still so new, and I didn't expect it when he asked if I wanted to.

"Of course!" I said. This meant waking up at four in the morning, like I did, packing up the truck, and heading across town—all before the sun came up.

"So, first-timer, huh?" Eric said from across the back of the pickup. I nervously held on to the side as we went over another bump, my other arm draped over a box of honey jars. Apparently, this was legal as long as it had to do with farm work, but it still felt unsafe.

"Yeah, anything I should know?"

"Just the initiation," he said. "It's always the new person's job to unload the truck. I hope you lift heavy because some of these crates are packed."

I'd been around Eric long enough to know half of what he said was bullshit, but I kept my face blank.

"Don't listen to him," Ingrid whispered next to me when he started joking with the other guys. "When we park, go talk to Troy first and don't come back until someone picks up the first box. Eric is always trying to get out of unloading the truck, and this trick hasn't worked yet."

"Good to know," I said with a laugh, then gasped as we went over another bump.

"You get used to it after a while," Ingrid assured me.

"Also good to know."

We reached the parking lot, the sky just starting to turn pink, and Troy pulled into our spot. I jumped out of the truck first and made a beeline for my boss. When I looked over my shoulder at Eric, he grinned, wagging a finger at me before picking up a crate. The other thing I knew about Eric was that he was a good sport.

"Did you need anything?" Troy asked as he stepped out of the cab.

"Nah," I said. I didn't want him to think I was incompetent on my first day or stalling to help out. "I just wanted to thank you again for including me today." I jogged off before he could answer, immediately setting to work to help get our booth together. I grabbed a crate, my frozen hands straining not to drop it. I wished I'd worn gloves, or at least something heavier than the black and white flannel I'd thrown on over my thermal this morning. But the flannel had been a gift from Sonny, and I liked to keep him close, even if I was still too chicken to let him know I was in town.

The morning passed faster than I thought it would, and soon I was so hot I kept the flannel tied around my waist. I hadn't realized how popular Chippewa Honey was, though Troy's other products may have had something to do with it. He produced a really tasty Honey Whiskey that was sold out before nine o'clock. I knew it was tasty because he gave me a bottle as soon as I got the job, and I'd celebrated a little hard with it that night. I couldn't keep it out of my head that Sonny would love it. Not the way he loved Scotch, but he would have loved it just the same.

Whenever I was in public, my first impulse was to check my surroundings for his familiar face. Today was no exception. Every time there was a lull in customers, I took a moment to scan the crowd. All I saw was a sea of strangers, as usual.

"Hey, take the register for a moment while I go to the bathroom," Ingrid said. She left just as a man came up with questions about honey production. I knew some answers, but not all, and shrank as he asked me about the shelf life of honey.

"Uh, it's uh," I stalled, trying to remember if this was something Troy told me before.

"If kept properly, honey will never spoil," Troy said, coming next to me. I stepped back as he took over the sale, feeling like a failure.

"No one knows everything right away," he said once the man bought his honey and left. "You're doing fine."

I nodded, though I had to work hard to stop feeling down on myself. I'd spent my whole life trying to meet expectations, especially my own. It was difficult to not continue the cycle.

Another man approached our booth, and I stepped up to serve him, but then recognized him as the flower vendor from across the way. He pointed down the row of booths.

"I think someone lost their dog. It's not yours, is it?"

I turned to see a blonde bushy tail disappear into the crowd. I didn't think anything of it when I put my fingers to my mouth and whistled. It was only when I dropped my hand that I realized what I'd done and who I was calling.

A golden retriever emerged from the crowd, a wide grin on his face as he searched for the source of the whistle. I stepped into the middle of the row and his tail thumped as soon as he saw me. He took off running, and even though my heart pounded at what this meant, I knelt on the ground and took the full weight of him as he threw himself at me. He was all wags and licks as he jumped around me, and I laughed as I wrapped my arms around him, scruffing his fur and scrunching his ears.

"Buoy!"

My heart leaped as I heard Sonny yell, and then whistle the same way I had. Buoy made to run, but I held on to him for a moment.

"Hold on, boy," I said as he sat obediently, even as he whined. I untied my flannel from my waist and then wrapped it around his neck, my heart beating wildly as I did. As soon as it was knotted, I let go and Buoy shot into the crowd.

Then I stood there, holding my breath. I wasn't ready to face him. Or was I? Would I ever be? And the shirt thing, it was stupid. It was also safe. If he didn't want me, I wouldn't have to see it in his face. He'd reject the shirt, not me. He'd—

"Cricket!"

I heard his call somewhere in the crowd, and I straightened up. My hands were shaking as I saw people move to the sides. And then he was there, his wild eyes searching until they found me. My shirt was crumpled in his hands, and Buoy grinned at his side. Sonny took a few steps forward, and I tried to read the intensity in his face. His mouth was tight, his jaw pulsing, his eyes never leaving mine. I couldn't move, and when he reached me, I let out the breath I didn't know I was holding.

"Sonny, I—"

And then, he was kissing me. I felt my flannel brush my hand as it fell to the ground, and then his fingers were tangled in my hair, his mouth searching mine. I pressed against him, lifting my shaky arms around him until his body kept me from sinking. The relief was real. The want. The need. I tasted his tears before I felt my own. He then pressed his forehead against mine, both of us breathing the same air.

"I don't care if you're with someone else," he said, his voice cracking. "Because I'm yours, and you're mine, and I can't spend another day without you."

"I'm not with anyone." I clung to Sonny as he pulled back and looked at me closely. "I never was," I continued. "It was all a stupid lie to protect my pride. I thought you'd moved on, and I didn't want you to know I still loved you."

"I never moved on," he said.

I had so many questions, so many blanks to fill in. But I couldn't stop the tears streaming down my face as I studied his face. Now that he was here, his arms around me, I regretted not reaching out to him sooner. We'd lost so much time, and I couldn't wait to start making it up to him. But first…

"Hold on," I said to Sonny before trotting over to Troy. My boss was beaming at me, but it didn't do much to assuage my guilt.

"I can tell something more important than this honey stand is happening between you and that young man," Troy said when I approached him.

"Troy, I—"

"Go," he said, nodding toward Sonny again. "The honey will be here next weekend, and I expect you on my crew. But today, you're fired."

"What?"

"Just for today," he laughed. "Go do what needs to happen, and I'll see you back at the farm when you're ready."

I wrapped my arms around him in a bear hug while he chuckled in my embrace.

"Slacker!" Eric called out behind me, and I turned to see him grinning. Beside him, Ingrid gave me a secret thumbs-up. I shrugged, but I couldn't bite back the smile plastered on my face.

Sonny drove us to a nearby coffee shop so we could catch up. It didn't serve beer like Brew, but the acoustic band in the corner had a fiddle. I felt like the Universe was smiling at us.

Over lattes and pastries, we rehashed everything that had happened over the last several months, beginning with the part I played in the whole Justine fiasco.

"You were so convinced I was with her, I decided it was safer to just play along," he said.

"What do you mean, safer?"

"I mean, you had a boyfriend, or at least I thought you did. If you thought I had a girlfriend, maybe it would keep me from jumping your bones," he said. "I figured I'd play it cool, make you fall back in love with me, and then I could tell you the truth. But then San Francisco happened, and well…" He trailed off, wrinkling his nose as he peered at me.

"Obviously, lies have gotten us nowhere," I laughed. "But wait, what about the toothbrushes?"

"What toothbrushes?"

"The toothbrushes! You had two of them? Who was the other for?"

He rolled his eyes, but he looked a little embarrassed. "Don't laugh, okay?" he said. "This is going to sound so stupid."

"I doubt it," I said. "Hello, I'm the one who had the fake relationship? I think you're fine."

"My toothbrush was lonely," he blurted out. I widened my eyes at first, but then bit back a giggle.

"I think you need to unpack that," I said. He sighed, running his hand through his hair.

"Okay, so after I moved back to Eau Claire the first time, one of the things I missed the most was seeing your toothbrush in there next to mine," he said. "My toothbrush looked the way I felt, and I didn't think both of us needed to suffer. So I bought another one to keep it company."

"You bought your toothbrush a friend?" I squeaked.

"See, I told you it was stupid."

"No, it's sweet," I said. "Did you name it?"

"Now you're just making fun of me." He paused. "It was Cricket."

"You named your toothbrush after me?"

"No, you dope. I pretended it was *your* toothbrush. It made it seem like you were close enough to spend the night, even though you were thousands of miles away. Then, after you broke up with me, I couldn't just throw it away. So I kept it. And when I moved back to Petaluma, I brought it with me." He ducked his head. "I guess I kind of hoped you'd use it."

"Oh wow. Sonny." I'd stopped laughing, my hand covering my heart.

"Stop gushing," he said. "Enough about the stupid toothbrush. I want to hear about you. What did I miss?"

I wanted to ask him about the salt and pepper shakers I'd also discovered in the medicine cabinet, but he looked like he was done being mushy. Besides, now that I knew about the toothbrushes, I had a feeling I knew why he had shakers in there, too.

"Well, things definitely weren't boring," I said, and told him about camping in Joshua Tree with Meadow, and then coming home to Ivan and his henchmen.

"Wait, what?" His hand clenched around his coffee, and I imagined he was pretending it was Ivan's head.

"I'm fine," I assured him. "It's done with. He's behind bars, and they had enough evidence about this and his other crimes to lock him away for the rest of his life. What's done is done. And now, thanks to Avery, Meadow and I are set for life." I told him about the inheritance, but the angry expression never left his face.

"I shouldn't have left you," he said.

For a moment, I was stuck between two meanings. I knew he was talking about that evening when he dropped off my things, and then the next day when he moved back to Eau Claire. But in a way, it almost seemed like a nod to the past, when he moved away the first time. What if he hadn't left? Would we be together still? More importantly, who would I be?

"I'm glad you left," I said. The glower left his expression, replaced by a look of surprise. "I missed you every day," I continued. "And I thought of you constantly. But I needed that time to grow. Our whole relationship, I leaned on you for strength. And you came through for me time and again. But I really needed to learn how to depend on myself. I learned a lot since you've been gone."

I told him about the solo road trip I took with Avery, and then how I gave my business to Taye. "I'm a beekeeper now," I said. "I mean, I'm just an apprentice, but I'm learning about beekeeping and making honey."

"You live here? In Eau Claire?"

"I do. I moved here last month. I live in a portable home that's about a third the size of my bedroom in Petaluma, but it's really cute and totally mine. And I'm happy."

"You are, huh?"

He was teasing, but I saw the question in his eyes. I reached over and placed my hand on his. He turned his hand, lacing his fingers through mine.

"I could be happier," I said, never breaking eye contact. I felt a rush of emotion flow through me as his grip tightened on mine. "I just needed to be a whole person. For you, and for me." I looked down at our hands, at how his fingers perfectly curved over mine, forming a protective bond. "I did a lot of soul-searching the past few months," I continued. "For a long time, I placed the end of our relationship on your shoulders, believing it was your fault we weren't together. But in San Francisco, you pointed out how I was the one not fighting for us. At the time, I was furious with you, sure that you were wrong. But over time, I realized all the ways you bent to meet my needs, and how I wasn't even trying to meet yours."

"You met my needs, Cricket. I wouldn't have fallen in love with you if you hadn't."

"I'm talking about this," I said, gesturing widely. "Eau Claire. You love it here, and now I understand why."

Sonny kissed the top of my head, and then he took my hand in his, weaving his fingers through mine. "Cricket, don't you know *you* are my home? Eau Claire is just a place. My home is with you."

I looked up at him, fighting back the tears, trying to stay cool. "Are you sure? Eau Claire is pretty great. I've been to Dells Pond. Some say if you close your eyes, you may even smell Scotland."

"Someone told you that?" he said, poking me in the ribs. "I don't ever remember saying that, but it's the truth."

"You told me a long time ago, back when you tried to convince me how wonderful this place is. I just wasn't listening. But I'm listening now, Sonny."

He was quiet for a moment. His hand stayed on mine, and he rubbed his thumb over my fingers, filling the silence with his touch.

"I understand what you mean about needing to be whole," he said. "But I've always seen you as a whole person. You're a lot stronger than you give yourself credit for. I mean, look at you now. You're here in a town that's completely new to you, and where you know no one."

"I know you," I said. He started to argue, but I cut him off. "I know, I didn't show up on your doorstep or anything. But I knew you were here. I felt you here. Everything I did was with you in mind. It's more than that, though. I never would have made this kind of move before. I think I needed to lose you to finally find myself."

"Uh, you're welcome?" he laughed. "Are you done finding yourself?"

I nodded, smiling. "I'm afraid you're stuck with me, McIntyre. Wherever you go, I go. Even if you move back to Scotland, I don't care. I don't ever want to lose you again."

"Scotland?" He tilted his head as if pondering the move.

"Anywhere," I promised.

"Careful, Cricket," he said, his eyes darkening, a half-smile softening his face. "I may just take you up on that." He winked, but I could still see his wheels turning. "I just have one last question for you."

"Yeah?"

"Can you find yourself in my bed?"

I tried to bite back a smile, to be coy and mysterious. But the grin broke through as I loosened my hand from his.

"I thought you'd never ask," I said, grabbing my purse off the back of my chair. "Oh, before we go, I think I have something that belongs to you." I reached into my purse, fumbling until I felt the familiar shape. I grasped its slender glass neck, pulling it out and then placing it in the palm of his hand. He stared at it for a moment, then a smile crept onto his face.

"I'll add it to my collection," he said.

"Your collection?" I asked. "As in, you have more than one?"

"Quiet, you. *Haud yer wheesht!*" he teased. He wrinkled his nose at me. "They remind me of you, all right?"

"As in, they remind you of that weird girl who steals salt and pepper shakers?" I put my hand on my hips and waited for his answer. He reached over and took my hand, then pulled me close to him.

"No, they remind me that life is bland without you," he said, taking a finger to move a piece of hair out of my face. He smiled down at me, then pecked the tip of my nose. "But now that you're back, I don't think I need them anymore."

Then he claimed my mouth, right there in front of the whole café. I didn't care who saw. I wrapped my arms around his neck and deepened our kiss. I kissed him like a hurricane, the winds of my emotions funneling from my mouth to his. He kissed me like the ocean, consuming me like a tsunami.

When his mouth broke from mine, it was with reluctance. He took my hand, tilting his head toward the door. "We have unfinished business, Stone," he murmured, his deep voice vibrating through every fiber of my being.

"Lead the way, McIntyre," I said, then kept hold of his hand as we left for much better ways to get reacquainted.

And the salt and pepper shakers? As far as I know, they're still sitting on a table in the middle of a café located in Eau Claire, Wisconsin.

Thank you for reading *For the Birds*!
Are you curious about what Sonny was thinking
when he first saw Cricket after so long apart?
Read *Flipping the Bird*, a free novella at
bit.ly/FTB-freeshortstory
(this is case sensitive)

If you enjoyed *For the Birds*, please take a
moment to leave a review wherever you share
your book reviews. Book reviews are a
wonderful way to give back to the authors you
love, and to help other readers discover their
books.

Thank you!

Acknowledgments

With every book I read, I always look forward to reading the acknowledgments page. I'm probably one of the few, but I appreciate how the author reveals the people and moments that helped make their book a reality.

So, for those of you who read the acknowledgments, here's a really long one.

It all started with a song.

In 2020, I went through a bit of a writing slump. When I say a bit, what I really mean was that I was ready to throw in the towel because the book I was working on was bringing me zero joy, and I felt like I was out of ideas.

To be fair, there was this whole pandemic thing going on, and it was hard to concentrate on anything creative when we were all supposed to isolate from everyone and change our lives, all in favor of staying alive. However, my writing slump started before the pandemic, and 2020 just made it worse.

And then, inspiration hit me out of left field in the form of a quarantine album, specifically one of the songs on the album.

If you've followed me for a while, you already know I am a huge Bon Iver fan. I have every single album of theirs, plus a lot of their side projects, and have been known to listen to nothing else but Bon Iver for months at a time. You guys, I have a Bon Iver pillow. It's serious.

So when Taylor Swift released her very first indie album featuring Bon Iver on one of her songs, I practically threw my wallet at her.

Side note.

Can we take a moment to bow down to the queen? Taylor Swift not only released *one* whole album during quarantine, a time when most of us were stripped of all creative energy, but she released *TWO* albums (plus a re-do album to get back what was rightfully hers. Now if only she could get back that red scarf…).

With *Folklore* and *Evermore*, Taylor Swift stepped outside her usual genre, gathering folk indie greats like Aaron Dessner of The National, Justin Vernon of my beloved Bon Iver, and Jack Antonoff of Fun. to help her create an album that reached so much further than what she was already capable of.

Can this just be a lesson to all of us? We can accomplish great things by seeking the talents and wisdom of those around us. *Folklore* and *Evermore* were the music darlings of 2020, and I will fight anyone who says different.

Which brings me to the inspiration behind *For the Birds*.

I was already listening to Taylor Swift's surprise *Folklore* album on repeat, especially the song "Exile" since Justin Vernon's deep voice was like honey to my soul.

And then...the story flowed through me.

I was at work that day, and as soon as my lunch break came, I headed to my favorite writing spot near the Petaluma River and began writing everything I knew about this story as it swept through my soul. And it was all based on "Exile."

The song is about ex-lovers who see each other from across the room, one of them already moved on. The song goes on with a feeling of regret about the love they lost, but also a lot of hurt feelings over the reason they broke up.

Home was a huge theme in "Exile," and home is a huge theme in *For the Birds*. This song breaks my heart every single time I listen to it, and as I planned *For the Birds*, my heart kept chipping at the love story that was supposed to be but ended too soon.

So, my first thank you goes to Taylor Swift and Justin Vernon for singing the song that sparked Cricket and Sonny's story.

Next, my parents, Gary and Nancy, and my sisters, Melissa and Heather. So much of Cricket and Meadow's lives were inspired by my own childhood and the relationships I shared with my family. I was lucky to have had a wonderful childhood that included an outdated house (wood paneling, really???), my parents' tree bed (yes, it exists!), my mother's gorgeous yard garden, frogs singing into the night, and sisterly friendships that have only gotten stronger with the years.

This book would have never happened if it hadn't been for my beloved writing critique group, the Novelistas—Ana Manwaring, Jan Flynn, and Heather Chavez. These three ladies cheered me on and helped me polish this book in ways I never could have done alone. They are also all incredible authors, and names you need to know.

My kids, Summer, Lucas, and Andrew, who inspire me in all the ways they've grown into incredible adults. I'm so proud of you, it's ridiculous. Summer was also one of my first readers, helping me retain that twenty-something voice I sometimes forget now that I'm in my forties. Look for her upcoming debut novel, *A Drop of Faerie's Blood*, coming soon.

Can we thank anyone here? I'd like to thank my cat, Cleo, for just being adorable, and the star of my Instagram posts. Also, to the whole entire town of Petaluma, for being the kind of place I love to write about and call home.

And a very special thank you to my husband Shawn, for being humorous and fun, chivalrous and thoughtful, and for supporting every one of my dreams, even when I don't believe in myself. You are the kind of man women want to read about, which is why you may recognize some of Sonny's ways as your own. Thank you for being my very favorite book boyfriend.

Finally, a huge and full of gratitude thank you to YOU, the reader. Thank you for trusting me with your time as you read my stories, for every review, and for continuing with me on this crazy book journey. Reading is life, and I'm glad to be one of the authors you enjoy reading.

Turn the page for a sneak peek at
Crissi Langwell's upcoming novel

Forever Your Baby

book 1 of the Sunset Bay series

Forever Your Baby

A sneak peek at book 1 of the Sunset Bay series

I opened my eyes and saw my own reflection in his green iris, surrounded by a kaleidoscope of life. Toes dipped in the ocean. A sky full of dramatic clouds. The smell of a mossy forest. Warm kisses in the rain.

They say it starts with the eyes. That feeling. That jolt of electricity. That moment when you just know your path is about to take a serious turn. Now I believed it.

"Are you okay?" he asked.

Let me back this story up. I'd just graduated high school that afternoon, top honors with a partial scholarship to UCSD, and while everyone else had family cheering them on, I had no one. I'd told my mom beforehand about my graduation. I'd stuck the invitation on the refrigerator and reminded her every few days, and still she didn't show up. Not that I expected it. I hadn't seen my mom in days, probably staying at some nameless loser's house. I drove myself to graduation, bracing myself for silence when I walked across the stage. Instead, I heard my best friend Maren's amplified voice in the back.

"You fucking rock, Claire!"

How do I describe my friendship with Maren? She was the dark to my light, the yang to my yin. It was like we were two halves of one whole, with nothing similar in the other. I studied hard and finished high school strong. Maren dropped out at the beginning of the year and had been MIA the past few months. In fact, her presence at my graduation was completely unexpected.

"Where have you been?" I demanded when I finally found her in the crowd after the ceremony. She responded by flinging herself at me, engulfing me in a bone crushing hug.

"Around," she said once she released me. With Maren, this was the only answer I knew I'd get. "Hey, there's a rager across town tonight. Come with me."

"Who's throwing it?"

"Some theater guy I met a few days ago. Brad, I think. Or Brian. I don't know. All I know is that it's supposed to be huge."

I had tickets for Grad Night already, the traditional all-night sober party in the high school gym. It had sounded fun at the time, but so did sitting in bed with a book in an empty house. Now that Maren was here, though, this third option sounded intriguing. Especially after she told me the theme.

"Masquerade?" I squeaked.

"Yeah, weird, right?"

"Maren, how are we supposed to pull together masquerade costumes?" I said this even as I did a mental recollect of what I had in my closet. A few years of homecoming dresses. Some odds and ends in the Halloween costume box. Random material from my mom's short-lived experiment with being Suzy Homemaker.

Back at my house, we pulled all these items out. By the time we were dressed, my room was trashed but we looked incredible. Maren wore a dress I hadn't worn since junior high, which fit her wiry frame like opaque plastic wrap. The deep blue matched her eyes perfectly, though they were hidden behind a strip of black lace. With the form fitting gown and her sleek black hair, she was somewhere between dancer and dominatrix. I, on the other hand, went full princess. I had on my mother's old prom dress, an ice blue strapless ball gown with a navy cloak to keep me warm. It was so 1980s, but I didn't care. My amber eyes shone through the eye holes on my black mask, which appeared almost gold with the heavy shading and black mascara Maren had helped me apply. Finishing it off was a silver tiara with clear glass jewels, set on top of my piled blonde curls.

"Cinderella, I believe we're ready for the ball." Maren grinned at me through rust-colored lips, and I felt a flurry of butterflies over a night that I was sure would be full of surprises.

That was an understatement. Maren had taken off within the first hour, and I'd spent the rest of the night sipping a drink that tasted something like gasoline and orange juice as I pretended to have fun. The house was this tiny shack on the outskirts of Sunset Bay, and full of people in wide interpretations of what masquerade meant, including some guy in a full body dinosaur costume with a tail that cleared the path behind him.

I sat on the edge of a dirty couch, trying not to touch the couple making out next to me as I mulled over abandoning Maren for that book waiting for me in bed.

"Fuck this," I muttered, standing quickly. Unfortunately, the heel of my shoe was caught in the tulle under my dress, and I pitched forward, flinging the contents of my red Solo cup.

That was the last thing I remembered before opening my eyes and looking into his. His mask covered the top half of his face, but his jade eyes pierced the pounding in my head, tempting me to wherever he might ask me to go.

"Are you okay?" he yelled, his voice competing with the techno music.

"I think," I started, lifting a hand to the back of my head. There was a tender knot on my scalp, and I winced as my fingers brushed over it. My crown was tangled in my hair, and I noted the syrupy wetness within the strands. Alarmed, I sat straight up, knocking my head into his chin. He grunted at the same time I did, releasing me as he rubbed his chin.

"Sorry," I groaned, rubbing the new wound on my forehead as I inspected my sticky hand. No blood, just that godawful orange drink. I looked down at my dress, noting the dark stains spreading on the material. I moved to get up, but he stopped me with a hand on my arm.

"Easy there, Sparky. You've had a little much to drink."

"I'm not drunk," I snapped, pulling my arm from his grasp. I tried getting up again, but my shoe was still caught in my dress. Frustrated, I tore off my heels, ripping the tulle in the process. "Fuck!" Even in my anger, I realized it didn't matter. The dress was ruined and my mom probably wouldn't miss it. She wouldn't even know it was missing if I threw it away, just like she didn't notice me. And Maren was no better. "I'll be so glad to get out of this fucking hell hole," I muttered.

"Hey, a place with free booze isn't that bad," the guy said, offering his hand again. This time I took it, flashing him a weary smile once I was back on my feet.

"Not the house," I said. "I'm talking about this town. These people. Everything. I feel like my whole life has been on hold, and I'll be so glad to get the fuck out of Sunset Bay and leave it all behind."

I brushed past him, but my bare foot slid through that stupid drink, and I flailed my arms to keep my footing.

"Drunk or not, let me help you," he said, his hand gripping my arm before I could land on my ass. I sighed, letting him guide me to the front door even though I knew I could do it on my own. I took one last glance at the party behind me, and decided Maren was a big girl and could handle her own. After all, she abandoned me first.

"Are you sure you're all right?" he asked once we were outside. I shivered in the breeze, pulling my cloak closer to me. But the fresh air felt good in my lungs. I breathed in deep, and even under the stench of my putrid drink-covered dress, I detected his soft scent. A hint of wind mixed with a healthy dose of sunshine and gusty dreams. At least, that's what came to mind as I inhaled, and what I mentally batted away as I nodded in reply to his answer.

"I'm fine," I said, looking down the street for my car. Then I groaned. Maren had been the one to drive, even though her car looked like she'd been living in it. I had no way of getting home without her. As soon as I realized this, I sat down heavily on the step, weighing my options. I could call a cab, except I had no money. I'd call my mom, but I was still mad at her for standing me up at graduation. Besides, if she didn't answer my earlier reminder texts, what made me think she'd answer me now?

"You don't look fine," he said, sitting beside me. I scooted over to make room for him, but didn't look up. I could already feel the tears welling up in my eyes, and I didn't want him to see me cry. "Are you okay to drive?" he asked.

"For the millionth time, I'm not drunk. As you can see, I'm wearing my drink." I figured if I could stay angry enough, I'd avoid crying in front of him. Wrong. I immediately burst into tears. "I don't have a ride," I finally blurted out. "I have no idea where I am, my friend ditched me, and I don't know anyone. On top of everything, I graduated today and my mom…" I wiped my face, even as the tears kept coming. "Never mind. None of this matters. In a few months, I'll be out of here and won't have to worry about any of this."

He stood without speaking as I tried my hardest to pull myself together. I heard the door open, the sounds of the party invading the silence before he closed the door again, leaving me alone.

"That's just great, Claire," I muttered. "The only decent person at this party, and you scare him off." I stood on shaky legs, my head throbbing from the lump. I wondered how long it would take me to walk before I recognized my surroundings. The door opened again, and the guy was back, this time holding another red plastic cup.

"It's water," he assured me, extending it toward me. I took it, my fingers brushing his, sending a current of warmth through my hand and up my arm before I exhaled it with my breath.

"Thank you." I lifted the cup to my lips, cooling myself with icy relief.

"I'll take you home, if you want," he said.

I started to say no, but then I thought about my other options, of which there were none.

"I don't even know your name," I said.

"I'm—"

"Wait, don't tell me," I said, laughing into my cup. "If you tell me, I'll have something to remember from this day and honestly, I just want to forget everything."

"Fair enough," he said. He touched his mask. "I guess it kind of matches the whole masquerade thing, though I think we're part of a small group that understands what masquerade really is. Did you see the dinosaur?"

"Ugh, don't remind me."

His car was thankfully cleaner than Maren's. It also smelled like him, a scent I found more intoxicating by the minute. I tried to ignore it, but I couldn't escape the heady feeling it gave me as he navigated the turns of the neighborhood, eventually landing on a street I recognized. From there, I gave him directions to my house. But as we approached, I saw my mom's car in the driveway, and a strange car next to that. We passed the house and I said nothing to slow him down, letting the ball of dread grow in my belly. We reached the end of the street, and he idled at the stop sign.

"Right, or left?"

"I, uh, right," I stammered. He turned right, and I realized my error immediately at the dead end. "I mean left."

He pulled to the side of the road and put the car in park. "You do have a house, right?" he asked. I fiddled with my dress, then brushed at the drink stain as if it would make a difference.

"We passed my house," I admitted. He started to put the car in gear again, but I placed my hand on his arm. His skin was warm, and there was a tattoo of a palm with an eye in the center on the inside of his forearm. I was tempted to grip his arm like he gripped mine earlier. The magnetic pull between us was unlike anything I'd ever known, and I wondered if I was the only one experiencing it. He looked down at my hand, and I removed it. "I don't want to go home yet," I said. I noticed the question in his eyes, but I was afraid to let him ask it. "Can we just hang out for a while?"

He paused, seeming to mull over what I was requesting. I shook my head, offering a small laugh.

"Sorry. I'm assuming you have nothing to do. You probably want to get back to the party."

"I don't want to be anywhere but here with you," he said. This time, there was no question.

I took a moment to assess the situation. I was in a car with some guy I didn't know. And yet, I was affected by him in a way I could only describe as otherworldly. There was this transcendental pull between us that made it hard to breathe, and I couldn't stop imagining what his hands would be like underneath this awful dress.

I didn't even know his name.

He leaned in slightly, pausing as if he was extending an invitation. I closed the space and his lips met mine. My hands fumbled with the seatbelt until it unclipped, and I scooted into his arms as he kissed me. He tasted like honey and mint, his tongue rolling across mine like a tumbleweed in a windstorm.

He lifted his lips from mine, and then looked at me, his eyes shining through his mask from the streetlight overhead.

"How much did you drink?" he asked.

This time I wasn't offended. I recognized the question underneath the question.

I'd never done it before. Not with my first real boyfriend in my sophomore year. Not with the guy who pressured me for three months in my junior year before dumping me for someone who would. And not for Jed

Thomas who took me to senior prom and thought my cherry was his reward for the night. He stopped speaking to me after that night.

I wasn't saving myself for marriage or anything. But I was saving it for someone who was worth it. And in that moment, sitting in a car with a nameless man, I couldn't help feeling like it was a good night to throw caution to the wind. The whole day had gone to pot. He was the only saving grace. And even though I didn't know his name, and I'd probably never know him after that night, I wanted something just for me.

"I'm sober enough to know I want this," I said. "And I drank enough to want more."

Forever Your Baby is the first book in the Sunset Bay series, coming soon! Join my VIP Readers Club to keep up with release news and sneak peeks at upcoming novels.

bit.ly/CrissiVIP

Books by Crissi Langwell

ROMANCE

For the Birds

Numbered

Come Here, Cupcake

WOMEN'S FICTION

The Road to Hope

Hope at the Crossroads

Hope for the Broken Girl

A Symphony of Cicadas

YOUNG ADULT

Loving the Wind

Forever Thirteen

www.crissilangwell.com

About Crissi Langwell

Crissi Langwell writes stories that come from the heart, from romantic love stories to magical fairytales that happen worlds away. She pulls her inspiration from the ocean and breathes freely among redwoods. She lives in Northern California with her husband and their blended family of three young adult kids, and a spoiled and sassy cat. Find her at crissilangwell.com.